COOL HAND HANK
BY
KATHLEEN EAGLE

AND

A COWBOY'S
REDEMPTION
BY
JEANNIE WATT

MILLS &
BOON

Dear Reader,

A warm welcome back to the Double D Wild Horse Sanctuary!

When I started writing *One Cowboy, One Christmas* I had no idea that Sally Drexler was going to be such a strong character that she would demand her own book. But what a strong woman she turned out to be. Nothing will stop Sally from living her life to the fullest. She has a wonderful sense of humour, is completely committed to the wild horses that have taken over the Double D Ranch, and she loves fiercely. She has learned to live in the moment because she can't be sure how she'll feel tomorrow. She's thrilled that her sister has found a love to last a lifetime, but she has no thought of discovering that kind of joy for herself.

Enter Hank Night Horse. Hank is a private man, one who has suffered losses of his own. He's a horseman, a healer, a man who gives without expecting — without even *wanting* much in return. Hank is my kind of hero. He's strong, complex, protective (particularly of his own heart), and oh so cool.

If you're a horse lover like me, check out the Black Hills Wild Horse Sanctuary on line. Douglas O. Hyde founded the program in 1988, and it is the inspiration for the Double D Wild Horse Sanctuary.

Now, come with me to a place where wildness reigns and love conquers all.

All my best, always,

Kathleen

COOL HAND HANK

BY
KATHLEEN EAGLE

First published in Great Britain 2011
Harlequin Mills & Boon Limited,
Eton House, 18-24 Paradise Road, Richmond, Surrey TW9 1SR

COOL HAND HANK © Kathleen Eagle 2010

ISBN: 978 0 263 88864 5

23-0211

Harlequin Mills & Boon policy is to use papers that are natural, renewable and recyclable products and made from wood grown in sustainable forests. The logging and manufacturing processes conform to the legal environmental regulations of the country of origin.

Printed and bound in Spain
by Litografia Rosés S.A., Barcelona

Kathleen Eagle published her first book, a Romance Writers of America Golden Heart Award winner, in 1984. Since then she has published more than forty books, including historical and contemporary, series and single-title, earning her nearly every award in the industry. Her books have consistently appeared on regional and national bestseller lists, including the *USA TODAY* list and the *New York Times* extended bestseller list.

Kathleen lives in Minnesota with her husband, who is Lakota Sioux. They have three grown children and three lively grandchildren.

For my nieces and nephews
and to honor the memory
of Phyllis Eagle McKee

Chapter One

Hank Night Horse believed in minding his own business except when something better crossed his path. A naked woman was something better.

Technically, Hank was crossing her path. He was about to step out of the trees onto the lakeshore, and she was rising out of the lake onto the far end of the dock, but the breathtaking sight of her made her his business. She was as bold and beautiful as all outdoors, and she was making herself at home. Maybe she hadn't noticed the moonrise, couldn't tell how its white light made her skin gleam like a beacon on the water.

At his side, Phoebe saw her, too, but she knew better than to give their position away without a signal.

With all that skin showing, the woman looked edible. Phoebe was trying to decide whether to point or pounce. Hank knew his dog. He couldn't help smiling as the woman turned to reach for a towel hanging over a piling. She was slender but womanly, with a long, sleek back and a sweet little ass. If he moved, if he made the slightest sound, he would kill a perfect moment. It would be a shame to see her…

…stumble, flail, go down on one knee. From graceful to gawky in the blink of an eye, the woman plunged headlong into the lake without a sound issuing from her throat. Hank was stunned.

Phoebe took off like a shot, and their cover was blown.

Fall back, regroup, find new cover.

She had the water, and he had the dog. *Excuse my dog. She has no manners.* And the woman…

…should have surfaced by now. *Maybe the water had her.*

Phoebe was paddling to beat hell. Hank skittered sideways down the pine-needle-strewn path until his boots hit the dock, reminding him that whatever he was about to do, the boots had to go.

And then what? He was a man of many talents, but swimming wasn't one of them. If the adoption people had told him Phoebe lived for the water, he would have walked right past her and taken the Chihuahua in the next cage. Instead, he'd saddled himself with a big yellow bitch who thought she was a seal. Or a dolphin. Dolphins could rescue swimmers, couldn't they?

Dive, baby, dive.

Swish! The woman's head broke the water's surface like a popped cork. Phoebe paddled in a circle around her, yapping exuberantly as though she'd scared up some game.

The woman spat a water-filled "Damn!" toward the open lake as Phoebe circled in front of her. "Hey! Where'd you come from?"

"She's with me." The water sprite whirled in Hank's direction. "You okay?"

"Fine. Where did *you* come from?"

Hank jerked his chin toward his shoulder and the pine woods behind his back. "My dog—*Phoebe, get over here*—my dog thought I shot you."

The woman laughed. A quick, unexpected burst of pure glee, which Phoebe echoed, adding gruff bass to bright brass.

"Are you coming in, too?"

He hadn't thought it through. Hadn't even realized he was sitting at the end of the dock with one boot half off. "Not if I don't have to. It looked like you fell."

"I did." Eyeing him merrily, she pushed herself closer with one smooth breast stroke. Her pale body glimmered beneath the rippling water. "I have fins for arms and two left feet that want to be part of a tail." She looked over at the dog paddling alongside her. "I'm not dead in the water. Sorry, Phoebe."

"She thought you were flapping your wings. If you really had fins, she wouldn't've bothered."

"But you would have?"

He pulled his boot back on. "The way you went down, I thought you'd had a heart attack or something."

"Klutz attack." She bobbed in place now, her arms stirring the water just beneath the surface. She made not going under look deceptively easy. "The water's fine once you get used to it. Now that I'm back in I wouldn't mind company."

"You've got some." He glanced straight down. Booted feet dangled over dark water. *Damn.* He felt like he was the one caught with his pants down. Had to get up now. He'd recover his dignity once he had something solid underfoot. Needed something to hang on to, and words were all he had. *Keep talking.* "That dog won't hunt, but she sure loves to swim."

"And you?"

He scooted toward the piling. "I'm not givin' up the best seat in the house." *Until I can grab that post.*

"So you're one of those guys who'd rather look than leap."

"I'm one of those guys who'd rather watch than drown."

There was that laugh again, warm and husky, like

an instrument played well and often. "And you were going to save me exactly how?"

"By throwin' you a life boot." He smiled, more for his hand striking the post than his wit striking her funny.

"No need to." Her voice echoed in the night. "My feet are touching bottom."

"You serious?"

"If I stood up, the water would only be up to my waist."

"From what I saw, that would make it about two feet deep."

"Come try it out." She dared him with a wicked, deep-throated chuckle. "Bring your depth finder."

What a sight. The strange woman and the dog he fed every damn day were treading in tandem, two against one. Phoebe should have known better.

"I've got a measuring stick." Hank grinned. "But it retracts in the cold."

"Speaking of cold…" She hooked her arm over Phoebe's shoulders. "If you're not going to join us, I'd like to take another stab at getting out."

Post in hand, he stood. "My feet are touching bottom."

"Not mine."

"Yours is wet." He laid his hand on the towel she'd left hanging over the post. "Bring it up here and I'll dry it for you."

"One free look is all you get, cowboy. A second will cost you."

"How much?"

With the pounding of her fist she sent a waterspout into his face. He staggered back as Phoebe bounded onto the lakeshore.

"Damn! You must have ice water in your veins, woman."

"Warm hands, cold heart. Go back where you came from, please." She assumed a witchy pitch. "And your little dog, too."

If he could've, he would've. Back to the little house in the North Dakota hills where he'd grown up, where his brother lived with his wife and kids, and where the only water anybody had to worry about was spring runoff. Even though he liked the Black Hills—what red-blooded Lakota didn't?—he wasn't big on weddings or wild women. But Hank Night Horse was a man who kept his word.

He touched the brim of his hat. "Nice meeting you."

So this was what a *real* wedding was all about.

Hank scanned the schedule he'd been handed at the Hilltop Lodge reception desk along with the key to a room with "a great view of the lake." He'd told Scott—the host, according to the badge on the blue jacket—he'd already had a great view at the lake. Scott had promised him an even better one at sunrise, and Hank said he wouldn't miss it. But a wedding was something else. He'd witnessed a few horseback weddings sandwiched between rodeo events, and he'd stood up for one of his cousins in front of a judge, but he'd never actually watched a guy jump through so many hoops just to trade promises.

Damn. A three-day schedule? His friend had claimed to be done with weekend-event schedules now that he'd hung up his spurs, but you'd never know it by the list Hank was looking at now. Social hour, wedding rehearsal, rehearsal dinner. He had to laugh at the thought of a rodeo cowboy publicly practicing his walk down the aisle. The sound of Western-boot heels crossing the wood floor brought the picture to life.

"What's so funny, Horse?" Zach Beaudry clapped a hand on Hank's shoulder. "You laughin' at me? You wait till it's your turn."

"For this?" Grinning, Hank turned, brandishing the flower-flocked paper beneath his friend's nose. "If you don't draw a number, you don't take a turn."

"My advice?" Zach snatched the schedule and traded it for a handshake. "Take a number. You don't wanna miss the ride of a lifetime."

"Here's two, just for you. Number one, I patch you cowboys up for a living. I know all about that *ride of a lifetime.* And number two…" Hank gave his starry-eyed friend a loose-fisted tap in the chest. No man wore his heart on his sleeve quite like a lovesick cowboy. "Nobody's askin' you for advice this weekend, Beaudry.

It's like asking the guy holding the trophy how he feels about winning."

"Damn, you're a smart-ass. Be careful you don't outsmart yourself. Come meet my family."

Hank followed Zach through a lobby full of rustic pine furniture, leather upholstery, and glass-eyed trophy heads. Rough-hewn beams supported the towering ceiling, and a fieldstone fireplace dominated one wall. They passed through a timber-framed archway into a huge dining room—bar at one end, dance floor at the other, rectangular tables scattered in between—flanked by enormous windows overlooking the lake. Hank wondered whether the shoreline was visible from the terrace beyond the massive glass doors. According to the plaque in the front entry, the lodge and the lakefront were products of a Depression-era Federal construction project, and everything about them was rough-hewn, but grand.

"This is my bride," Zach was saying, and Hank turned from the windows to the woman linking arms with her man. "Annie, Hank Night Horse."

She was small and pretty, and her smile seemed a little too familiar. But the way it danced in her blue eyes didn't connect, didn't feel like it had anything to do with him. And her curly golden ponytail looked bone dry. Hank held his breath and offered a handshake.

"Our wedding singer," the bride said in a soft, shy voice. "Thank you for coming, Hank."

"Sure." And relieved. He was sure he'd never heard the voice before, so he looked his buddy in the eye and smiled. "You did well, Beaudry."

"I did, didn't I?" Zach put his arm around his intended. "She's got a sister."

"You don't say." Hank lifted one shoulder. "I'm willing to sing for a piece of your wedding cake, but that's as far as I go."

"I'm just sayin', you got a great solo voice, man, but that solo livin' gets old."

"I'll bet it does. I know I don't like to go anywhere without Phoebe."

"She's here? Phoebe's here?" Zach's face lit up like a kid who smelled puppy. "Annie, if we can't get married on horseback, how 'bout we put Phoebe in the wedding party? She could carry the rings. She's like the physician's assistant's assistant. Hank's pretty good with his hands, but Phoebe's got heart. He's stitchin' a guy up, she's lovin' him up like only man's best friend knows how to do. Helps you cowboy up so you can climb back on another bull."

"He can't," Ann assured Hank. "We wrote it into the contract."

"That's good, 'cause I'm tired of sewing him up and watching him rip out my stitches in the next go-round."

"Where's Phoebe?" Zach demanded. "I'll bet she's not tired of me."

"She's outside. Caused me some trouble, so she's in the doghouse."

"No way. You tell Phoebe she can—" Zach glanced past Hank and gave a high sign. "Sally! Over here! I want you to meet somebody."

"Can he swim?"

That was the voice. "Sounds like I'm out of my depth again." Hank turned and hit her feet first with a gaze that traveled slowly upward, from the red toenails she'd claimed to be touching bottom to the blue neckline that dipped between pale breasts. He paused, smiled, connected with her eyes—blue, but more vibrant than her sister's—and paid homage again with the touch of his finger to the brim of his hat. Her short blond hair looked freshly fixed. "I like your dress."

"What's that? You like me dressed?"

"That, too. But clothes don't make the woman." He'd already seen what did.

"So true. I didn't catch your name."

"Hank Night Horse."

Ann looked up at Zach. "I have a feeling we missed something."

"I have a feeling this is the sister," Hank said as he offered his hand. Hers was slight and much colder than advertised. He gave it a few extra seconds to take on a little heat. He had plenty to spare.

"And this is the music man." Sounding as cool as her hand felt, Sally looked him straight in the eye. For someone who'd been laughing it up less than an hour ago, she sure wasn't giving him much quarter.

"Hank, Sally Drexler, soon to be my sister-in-law. Have you two already…"

"I took Phoebe for a walk right after we pulled in. She tried to retrieve Sally from the lake."

"Aw, you gotta love Phoebe," Zach said cheerfully. "Hank's part of the medical team working the rodeo circuit, and Phoebe's his bedside manner."

Sally's eyes brightened. "I've spent a lot of time around the rodeo circuit. I used to be a stock contractor. Zach delivered the thrills and I furnished the spills. But that was probably before your time."

"I just hand out the pills."

"He does a lot more than that," Zach said. "Pops joints back in place, sets bones, makes the prettiest stitches you ever saw. Plus, he shoes horses on the side."

Sally challenged Hank's credentials with a high-headed smile. "All that and a wedding singer, too?"

"First time." Hank gave Ann an indulgent smile. "I hear brides can be hard to please, and I'm a what-you-hear-is-what-you-get kind of a guy. I don't mind being the funeral singer. You get no complaints from the star of the show."

"You're listed on the program without the name of the song, which I really wanted…" Ann glanced at Zach. They were already developing their own code.

Good start, Hank thought. He and his former wife had never gotten that far.

"But we agreed to leave it up to you," Zach filled in.

"It's my gift. I want it to be a surprise."

Ann shrugged. "I promise not to complain."

"I promise not to sing 'Streets of Laredo.'" Hank glanced across the room. A handful of people were gathered at the bar. Two women were setting bowls of flowers on the white-draped table. He turned to Sally. "What's your wedding assignment?"

"Maid of honor, of course. It's a plum role. By the way," she reported to her sister, "more gifts were delivered here today. I had the desk clerk store them under lock and key. There's actually one from Dan Tutan."

Tutan. Hank frowned. He hadn't heard the name since he was a kid, when he'd heard it whispered respectfully, sometimes uneasily, eventually contemptuously around the Night Horse home.

"Or his wife," Ann was saying. "She takes neighborliness seriously."

"Dan Tutan's your neighbor?" Hank asked.

Sally sighed. "A few miles down the road. Not close enough so we have to see him every day. But before I say *fortunately,* is he a friend of yours?"

"Nope."

"Well, he'd like to turn our wild-horse sanctuary into a dog-food factory."

"Why's that?"

"The horses like to mess with him," Zach said. "They know he's extremely messable."

"Tutan's had a pretty sweet deal on grazing leases around here for so long he's forgotten what a lease is," Sally said. "We're bidding on some leases and some grazing permits that he's held for years, and we've got a good chance at them because of the sanctuary. We're a retirement home for unadoptable wild horses. We give them grassland instead of a Bureau of Land Management feedlot. So Tutan doesn't like us much these days. How do you know him?"

"My father knew him." Hank glanced away. "Tutan wouldn't know me from an Indian-head penny."

"He'd know the penny," Sally said. "Damn Tootin' never walks away from any kind of money."

Zach clapped a hand on Hank's shoulder. "Don't tell him which one we picked up for a song."

"Damn Tootin'." Hank chuckled. He didn't think he'd heard that one.

"Were they friends?" Sally asked. "Your father and my neighbor?"

"My dad worked for Tutan for a while. Long time ago. No, they weren't friends."

"Good. I'm not good at watching what I say about people I hate." Sally linked arms with her sister. "I'd get the bomb squad to check out his gift if I were you. And then put it in the regifting pile."

"Tell us how you really feel, Sally," Zach teased. He winked at Hank. "I'm glad you're giving us live music. That's something she can't regift."

"I'm recording everything," Sally said. "Hell, if your singer's any good, I'll burn a few CDs for Christmas presents. The frugal rancher's three R's: regift, repurpose, recycle." She poked Zach in the chest as though she were testing for doneness. "But we can't regift your brother's trip, so you're going to use that one."

"We'll get to it. There's no rush."

"No rush to go on your honeymoon?" Sally flashed Hank a smile. "What's this guy's problem, Doc?"

"Can't say."

"You're ducking behind that confidentiality screen, aren't you?" She turned back to Zach. "Your extremely wealthy brother hands you the extreme honeymoon, the wedding trip of your dreams, the one you mapped out with your bride, and you're saying *we'll get to it?* Like *anytime* is honeymoon time?"

"Well, isn't it?" Zach held up a cautionary hand. "Hold on, now, I haven't said *I do* yet. I gotta go work on those vows some more, make sure we both say *I do it anytime. All the time. Rain or shine.*"

The bride blushed.

The maid of honor laughed. "Say what you want, cowboy. I figure a nice long, romantic honeymoon will guarantee me a niece or nephew nine months later. If you don't get away from the Double D, what you'll do is exactly what you've been doing, which is working your fool britches off."

"*Britches off* is step one, Sally," Zach said. "It's not much work, and it's no guarantee, but it's a start. Right, Hank?"

Hank answered his friend with a look. The conversation had veered into no-comment land.

"I can handle the Double D." Sally glanced back and forth between Zach and Ann. "I'm *fine*."

"We're here for a wedding," Ann said, "which is a one-time thing, and we're doing it up right. Right here. Right now. We're going to rehearse." Ann offered a hand for the taking. "Hank?"

"You want me to practice walkin' and talkin', fine." Hank took the bride's hand with a smile. "But I don't rehearse my songs in public. It's bad luck."

"Let's walk and talk, then. Help me make a list of reasons why Zach should ride horses instead of bulls."

Sally hung back, watching her sister walk away with two attractive men. Two cowboys. Lucky Annie. As far as Sally was concerned, there were only two kinds of men out West: cowboys and culls. She didn't know any men from back East.

Sally had been around a lot of cowboys, and most of them were pretty easy to figure. All you had to do was take a look at the shirt. A cowboy wore his heart on his sleeve and a number on his back. He lived day to day and traveled rodeo to rodeo, accumulating cash and consequences. He was addicted to adrenaline, and he'd paid dearly for his sky-highs with rock-bottom lows. By the time he'd filled his PRCA permit with enough wins to earn the right to call himself a Professional Rodeo Cowboy, he'd paid in some combination of torn flesh, spilled blood and broken bone.

Such was the story of Zach Beaudry. He'd been the up-and-coming bull rider to beat until he'd met up with the unbecoming end of a bull's horn. Like the rest of his kind, he knew how to tough it out. Hunker down and cowboy up. Put the pieces back together and get back on the road. Which had led him to Annie's doorstep.

Hank Night Horse had the look of a cowboy. He was lean and rangy, built to fork a horse and cut to the chase. But a full place setting required a spoon. Sally smiled to herself as she pictured his possibilities. He looked great going away. She could paste herself against that long, tapered back and snug her thighs under his, tuck his tight butt into her warm bowl and be fortified. She could back up to him and invite him to curl his strong body around her brittle one and make her over. It could happen. In her dreams, anyway.

Hank turned to say something to Annie, who turned to say something to Zach and then back to Hank again. Conspiring. Setting Sally up. She knew what they were up to, and she didn't mind as long as this crazy body of hers was working properly. The fall from the dock hadn't been a good sign, but she was back in control now. And Hank Night Horse was turning back, giving her another one of those rousing once-overs. *You and me, woman.* He was coming for her, and, ah! she saw how fine he looked coming and knew how readily and happily she would come and come and come if the table were set with a man like Hank Night Horse. It wouldn't matter how much time he had to spare as long as it was—what was the expression? *Quality time.* Remission from illness was like a blue space between clouds. Either make the most of it, or stay in your box.

"Care to join me in the back row?" he asked.

"Am I your assignment?" She threw her voice into her sister's key. "If you're not going to rehearse your song, could you keep an eye on Sally?"

"I didn't quite catch what they said," he claimed with a twinkle in his eye. "Something about *drink.* I'm supposed to buy you one or keep you from falling in. Either way, I could be in for some trouble. Are you a troublemaker, Sally?"

"I do my best. And I know you're lying, because I'm not allowed to drink."

"Anything?"

"Anything with alcohol in it."

"Who said anything about alcohol?" He gave her a challenging look, his eyes growing darker and hooded, his full lips twitching slightly, unwilling to smile. "And who makes the rules?"

"Sensible Sally." She gave the smile he denied her. "That was her alter ego down at the lake. Shameless Sally."

"She's got the right idea. Shame shouldn't be allowed, either." He tucked his thumbs into the front pockets of his jeans. "So, what'll it be?"

She looked at her watch. "Rehearsal in five. Can't hardly whip up a good batch of trouble in five minutes. Sensible Sally drinks green tea on the rocks with a twist."

Hank decided to "make that two," and they left the dining room, glasses in hand, no hurry in their feet. Sally felt a growing reluctance to catch up with the little wedding party in the lodge library. The lakeside setting for the ceremony would be set up tomorrow, so tonight's indoor rehearsal was literally a dry run. Sally knew her part. She'd seen it played out a hundred ways in movies, read the scene in dozens of books. Sensible Sally stayed in the house a lot. Shameless Sally couldn't go out to play until the unreliable body caught up with the willing spirit, and now that the two were working in tandem, she would go where the spirit moved her.

"Look!" She pointed to a window, grabbed Hank's arm and towed him out the front door on to the huge covered porch. A procession of trail riders passed under the yard lights on their way to the pasture below the lodge. "How was the ride?" Sally called out.

"Beautiful!" said one of the helmeted riders. "Made it to the top of Harney Peak."

"Let's go up there tomorrow," Sally said to Hank. "You ride, don't you? We should…" She turned to the riders. "Where did you get the horses?"

"We brought our own. We're a club."

"But there's a hack stable close by," said the last rider as she passed under the light. "Ask at the desk."

Sally looked up at Hank. "We could go really early." She turned, cupped her hand around her cheek and shouted at the last rider's back. "How long did it take?"

"All day!"

Sally scowled. "I'll bet I could take a marker to the programs and change the time. The lake is beautiful this time of day. *Night.*" She pointed to the white moon hovering above the ponderosa pines. "It'll be full tomorrow. Imagine Annie in her white gown, and Zach…well, he's wearing black, but can't you just see it? Moonlight on the lake?"

"I did, yeah. Beautiful."

"They don't need us. They wouldn't even notice. Look." She took his hand and led him to the end of the porch, pointed to the tall, bright corner windows that showcased the rehearsal getting under way in the library.

Sally could see Zach's niece and nephew perusing the bookshelves that flanked the stone fireplace. Zach was having a chat with his brother, Sam. Annie and the minister were poking through a sheaf of papers. "My baby sister's getting married tomorrow," she whispered. Hard to believe. The window might have been a movie screen, except that she knew these people—some better than others—and what they were doing was exactly what they'd been talking about for months. It was happening. Sally's little sister was getting married. "They won't notice anyone but each other tomorrow." She squeezed Hank's hand. "Let's do it."

"Do it?"

"Tomorrow. Let's ride to the top of Harney Peak."

"Zach's a good man. They don't come much better."

"Oh, I know that." She drew a deep breath and laughed. "But I love the smell of horse in the morning."

He laughed with her, and that felt good. Even better when he took control of the hand-holding and led her back into the lodge as though they were in this together, a two-part unit joining a group of two-and-more-part units. She could come to like this man much more than Sensible Sally would normally permit.

The first person they ran into when they entered the library was the wizened cowboy who would be giving

Annie away. Hoolie was draped over a pair of crutches near the door, prompting Sally to ask gently whether his ankle was bothering him again, whether he was coming or going.

"Thinkin' about getting outta the way until they decide what they want me to do. One of them kids tripped and near busted my cast."

"It was an accident," the sandy-haired boy called out over the top of the book he'd been reading.

"Man, they can hear good when they want to, can't they?" the wiry cowboy muttered, glancing at Hank. Then he turned to the boy. "I know you're sorry, Jim. No hard feelings. I can still hobble."

"Hank, this is Henry Hoolihan, our foreman."

"Hoolie." He offered Hank his hand. "Nobody's called me Henry since I was Jim's age. Who dug that up?"

"I don't know, but it's on the program," Sally said. "Jim and Star are Zach's brother's kids. Say hello to Hank Night Horse, Zach's doctor."

The children sang out as instructed, but Hoolie said, "Doctor?"

Hank glanced at Hoolie's cast. "I work the rodeo circuit as a physician's assistant. Zach's been a pretty steady customer the last few seasons." As one, the three turned their attention to the couple attending to wedding business on the far side of the room. "He's a good hand."

"Was," Sally said. "He says he's retiring."

"The body can only take so much," Hank said. "Some guys don't know when to quit. I'm glad Zach's not one of those guys." He looked at Sally. "He's still a good hand."

"We love Zach," Sally said with a smile. "Don't we, Hoolie? I'm being summoned. Let's get this over with so we can eat. And then on to the fun stuff." She touched Hank's sleeve. "Keep your program handy. We had one dull moment scheduled in, but then you came along and buffed it up, thank you very much."

"The pleasure was mine." He eyed her hand and then raised his dark gaze to her eyes as he leaned close to her ear. "Seein' as how the buff was yours."

Sally's neck tingled. An icy-hot shiver blew apart and streaked gloriously throughout her body. She stood still, waiting for the feel of another warm, magic breath.

"Sally, we need you!"

She let her hand slide to the edge of Hank's cuff where she could feel his working-man's skin. "Hold that thought," she said.

At dinner, Sally did her maid-of-honor duty by making the rounds among family and friends. Sally and Ann had lived on the Drexler ranch in South Dakota all their lives. But the family had been reduced to the two of them, along with Hoolie, who had come to work for their father before they were born, outlived him, and earned the privilege of giving the bride away.

And now they had Zach, who brought his mother, Hilda, and brother, Sam, to the Drexler fold—hardly big enough to fold—along with Sam's new wife, Maggie, and their two children. But the Beaudrys made their home in Montana, and Zach had become a rolling stone until he'd rolled to a stop at the Double D. The wedding was Zach's reunion with the Beaudrys as well as his formal initiation into the Drexler clan. The Beaudrys couldn't contain their joy, and why try?

Duty done in the middle of the circle, Sally moved to the edge, where Hank had laid claim to the observer's station, a post she had come to know all too well in recent years. She had made her peace with it, while Hank seemed quite comfortable there. Maybe he could teach her something. He'd moved from the table where they'd shared dinner with Hoolie and Hilda to a corner conversation area near the bar. When he saw her coming, he moved again, from a big leather chair to a love seat. She was invited.

"They're all going on a moonlight hayride," she reported as she sat down. "I'm supposed to fetch you."

He smiled. "Good luck."

"Ready for another dull moment?"

"Looking forward to it." He lifted his arm over her head and laid it along the back of the love seat. "You?"

"I don't feel like changing clothes. When I take these off, that'll be it for the night."

"Big day tomorrow."

"Big day." She laid her head back and let it rest against his arm. "They're good people, aren't they? Why would Zach stay away from home so long?"

"Wouldn't know."

"But you know him well enough to vouch for his character."

"Yep." He shifted a little closer. "Tell me more about your mustang sanctuary. How do you support it?"

"We get some support from federal programs. Before my dad died, the Double D was one of the biggest cattle ranches in the state, and we still have a small cow-calf operation. We're also permitted to sell some of the colts off the wild mares."

"Is there much of a market these days?"

"They sell pretty well if they're at least green broke. Even better if they're broke to ride. But the market fluctuates with the rest of the economy, and right now it's tough. I have a plan, but I put it on hold for the wedding."

"Is that why they're holding off on the honeymoon?"

"Oh, no." She turned her head to give him a warning glance. "They don't know I have a new plan in the works. They're trying to put the honeymoon on hold because they don't want to leave me—" she raised her brow and gave a suggestive little smile "—to my own devices."

"Sounds like you have a reputation."

"I did, but I haven't been keeping up. A reputation

is something you have to tend, just like a garden." She made growing, blooming, stepping-out gestures. "You want it to get big enough to precede you."

"Except when you get caught with your pants down."

"Depends on your perspective." She turned up the tease in her smile. "I can't speak for yours, but from mine, sooner or later you'll get my attention. It's better if you're not a *sooner*. Laters are generally slower and longer."

He shook his head, rewarding her with a slow smile. "You're a little smart-ass."

"Ah, but I grow on you."

"We'll see." But he crossed his near leg over the far one before she had a chance. "You can't hire somebody to help out while they're honeymooning?"

"Are you looking for a job?"

"I have two jobs," he reminded her. "I'm a farrier and a physician's assistant. My services are in high demand on the rodeo circuit."

"They'd be pretty handy around the Double D, too. If we had someone like you on staff, Zach and Annie would leave tomorrow. The day after at the latest."

"How big…how *many* on your staff?"

"Four, counting Hoolie. We get volunteers to work with some of the horses, but a lot of them are kids. Mostly from the reservation. Annie teaches at the high school."

"How long did they plan to be gone?"

"About three weeks. But then Hoolie got tangled up in some barbed wire and broke his ankle." She sat up and took new interest. "You wouldn't have to stay around the whole time. Seriously. You could be on call."

"That's why I'm not on any kind of staff. Been there, done that, found out I don't much like being on call. You work a rodeo, you're there for the weekend. The pay's good, and you get to have a life."

"Doing what? You have a family?" She hadn't missed something, had she?

"I used to be married. Had a son. He died."

"Oh. I'm so sorry."

"Yeah, me, too. But I got my life back, and I'm not short on things to do."

"Neither am I. It's time that's the kicker, isn't it?"

"I probably don't think of time the same way you do."

No kidding. "Not very many people do."

"A day is a day. You fill it with how you feel."

"That's interesting. I couldn't've said it better. Right now, tonight…" She stretched her arms straight and strong, crooning a saucy, "I feeeel good." She slid him a glance. "Hey, you're smiling."

"You're growin' on me."

Chapter Two

"Oh, Annie."

Sally's sister turned from the mirror, eyes shining like stars. Her golden hair was swept up from the sides and anchored by a pearl-encrusted comb and a cascading veil. The off-the-shoulder neckline and body-skimming lines of her elegant ivory dress were simple and stunning and perfectly suited to the woman who stood there, eclipsing all the dreams the two sisters had conjured over the years.

The photographer quietly snapped pictures, allowing the moment to unfold. Sally was dumbfounded. How many times had they gotten dressed together, given each other a last-minute review? Sally had helped Annie choose each piece of her wedding ensemble, had overseen the fittings and giggled with her over their memories of dresses and dates, new measurements and old tastes, the never-ending Double D "chest jest"—a size Annie had at one time nearly reached—and the ever-after girlish dreams. And now all the pieces had come together, adding up to a vision that came as no real surprise to Sally even as it brought rare tears to her eyes. This was it. Annie was the fairy-tale bride.

Blinking furiously, Sally handed over the bouquet of white calla lilies, drew a deep breath and blew a wobbly whistle. "Whoa. Wow. Okay, Hoolie thinks he can get by without crutches, but I know what it's like to fall on your face in front of an audience, so I think we should put my cane in his hand right when the music starts."

"It's not a long walk. A few steps. I'm almost there, Sally." Annie grabbed Sally's hand, and the camera hummed. "Why am I shaking like this?"

"They're big steps." Baby sister was taking big steps, and Sally was the only Drexler left to hold her hand.

She wanted to hug her, hold her a little longer, but she made do with squeezing her hand rather than making smudges or wrinkles or tears. Annie wasn't leaving, but life would be different after today.

"I wonder if *he's* nervous. Do you think he's shaking like this?" Annie laughed and shook her head. "Probably not. He's a cowboy. He rides…*used to* ride bulls for a living. What's a little—" she turned for another glance in the mirror, complete with bouquet, and smiled "—wedding?"

"There's no such thing as a *little* wedding," Sally said, speaking from her all-too-frequent experience as a captive TV watcher. "By the numbers, this one is little. But it's big by my calculations."

"I know. It's all Sam's fault."

"I'm not calculating in dollars. Zach's brother's money definitely falls into the easy-come-easy-go category, and since there's so much of it, why not enjoy the frills? I'm talking about *big,* as in big as life. This is your wedding, and it means the world to me."

Sally touched the simple strand of pearls around her sister's neck. They had belonged to their mother, whom Sally saw so unmistakably in Annie's big, soft eyes and bow-shaped mouth and dainty chin. Sally looked more like their father, but she was the one who clearly remembered Mom. Sally was the keeper of Drexler memories.

"I'll be kinda glad when it's all…" Annie gave her head a quick toss. "No, I'm glad now. I'm ready. I feel beautiful. And you look beautiful, Sally." Annie turned her sister so that the mirror made a framed portrait unlike any they'd taken together before. They'd been big and lively, little and sweet. One primary, one pastel. One ready to go first, the other pleased to follow.

"I love you so much," Annie whispered, and Sally had no doubt. But Annie was the one once meant to wait while Sally went ahead. And it wasn't that Sally was resentful of the reversal—she really did look good in her chic, fluid blue waterfall of a dress, Annie's gift of opals around her neck and studding her ears, fragrant gardenias in her hair—but she was unsure of her footing. Annie was taking a big step.

Where did that leave Sally?

"Me, too, you," she said as she squeezed that ever-dependable hand again. "Lest we spoil the makeup, consider yourself kissed."

"You know you're not losing a sister, don't you? You're gaining a brother. And we're not going anywhere. We're partners, and we're family, and we're going to—"

"—be late for your wedding. Listen. I am fine." She enunciated each word forcefully, willing her sister to make sense of three simple words and move on. "Look at me. No cane, no pain." *Enjoy this with me while it lasts*. She needlessly fluffed Annie's veil. "This is your day, honey. Take a deep breath. Your man is out there waiting and, yes, probably feeling just the way you are. When you take each other's hands…" Sally smiled, blinking furiously because she *would not cry*. "Tell me what it's like, okay? That moment."

Annie nodded as she pulled her hand free, placed

a finger lightly at the outside corner of Sally's eye, caught a single tear and touched it to her lips.

Granite spires bound the crystalline-blue lake on the far side, the perfect backdrop for a hand-woven red willow arch decked out with a profusion of flowers. Guests were seated in white folding chairs. Zach's niece led the way, tossing handfuls of white rose petals on a path of fresh green pine needles. Sally followed, taking measured steps in time with the string quartet's elegant processional. Looking as handsome and relaxed in his black tux as he did in well-worn jeans, Zach waited for his bride. His brother, Sam—a little taller, a little darker, a little less at ease—stood like a sentry overseeing his charges. Daughter, son, wife, mother, brother—Sam's eyes attended to each one. He was clearly the Beaudry caretaker. *Funny,* Sally thought. *That's Annie, not me.*

Before she'd been diagnosed with multiple sclerosis, Sally had been the seeker, the doer, the risk taker. She'd cared passionately, but she'd never *taken care.* That was Annie's role. Careful, care-giving, selfless Annie.

Sally paused before the minister and looked the groom in the eye. *Be good to her, Zach. Be the man she deserves.* She pivoted and took her place, knowing she'd made her point. She felt Annie step up to fill the space she and Zach had left for her, but she couldn't quite turn to watch Hoolie place her sister's hand in Zach's. It was enough to see the movement from the corner of her eye, where Annie had touched her for a tear.

It was happening. Annie was interlacing her life with someone new, becoming someone else's next of kin. Sally clutched two handfuls of flowers and listened to identical promises exchanged in voices that complemented each other in a way she hadn't heard before. It was a pure sound and a simple truth. Annie and Zach belonged together.

And they stood together, hand in hand, while Hank played an acoustic guitar and sang "Cowboy, Take Her Away" in a deep, resonant voice that was made for a love song. He'd said his gift was his song, and he sang to the couple as though no one else was there and every note, every word had been written just for them. Sally was enchanted. Her beautiful sister, her new brother, the music and the man who made it—she wanted to suck it all in and keep it alive within her in a way that the video camera could never do.

At the end of the song, Hank said, "Kiss her, Zach." And he did, cheered on by friends and family, who showered them with white rose petals as they retreated down the path. The guests followed, and the violinists made merry music at the back of the line as it wended its way up a gentle slope between stands of tall pines. When they reached the lodge's gravel driveway, Zach swept his bride up in his arms and carried her across the path and up the steps to the front porch, where he set her down and kissed her again. Women sighed. Men whooped. Cowboy hats sailed skyward.

Annie and Zach were hitched.

"You're a lucky man." Sally raised her glass of sparkling water in toast.

"Yeah, I know." Sam put his arm around his new wife, Maggie. "I hit the jackpot."

Maggie looked up at him. "*You* did?"

"Trusted you and got myself a whole family."

"I think Sally's talking about winning the lottery," Maggie said. "It's crazy. Real people don't win the lottery."

"Well, it was complicated," Sam said. "It was Star's mother's ticket—our daughter, Star—but she died before she could claim it. In fact, we thought the damn thing was lost in a car accident, but it turned up, kinda like…" He waved his hand as though words failed.

"Miraculously," Maggie supplied.

"To put it mildly," Sam said. "It's been a year, but it still doesn't seem real. We're trying to manage it sensibly. You don't want to go crazy. You want to put some of it to good use now, give some away, make sure there's plenty left for the kids. I've never known any rich people, never thought I'd like them much."

"He won't give up his job," Maggie said.

Sam laughed. "She won't, either."

"I'm part-time now, but our little clinic needs nurses, and I'm a good one. We just moved into a house we built on Sam's land. It's a gorgeous spot." Maggie made a sweeping gesture. "Kind of like this, but the lake is smaller and the mountains are bigger. You have to come for a visit."

"Where's Hank?" Sam asked, searching over the heads of the guests. "Man, that guy can sing. He about killed my brother with that song." He grinned at Zach. "He didn't leave yet, did he?"

Did he?

Sally hugged her new brother-in-law. "Where's Hank?"

"I'll tell you a little secret about ol' Hank. He don't like compliments. He does his thing, and then he disappears for a while. He sang at a funeral once—bull rider, wrecked his pickup. Hank tore everybody up singin' over that kid. And then he disappeared. I found him playin' fetch with Phoebe." Zach glanced over the balcony railing. "He's around."

"Hey, cowboy." Annie joined the group, entwining her arm with her new husband's and beaming up at him as though he'd just hung the moon. "Take me away."

A skyward glance assured Sally that the moon wasn't up yet. The sun had slipped behind the trees, but there was still plenty of light for searching the

grounds. She didn't have to go far. She found Phoebe
first. The dog greeted her with a friendly bark, and the
man followed, emerging from a stand of pines near a
picnic table. He carried his jacket slung over his shoulder, white shirtsleeves rolled halfway up his forearms,
black hat tipped low on his forehead.

Sally scratched Phoebe behind the ears and caught
a little drool in the process. Hank tapped his thigh, and
the dog heeled. With a hand signal, he had her sitting.

"Impressive," Sally said.

"She's willing to humor me because you're not as
appealing as you were last night. If you were splashing around in the lake she'd be all over you."

"And you?"

"The only part that didn't appeal to me last night
was the water."

"You were wonderful," she said, and he questioned
her with a look. "Today. Your music. You play beautifully, and you sing like—"

"Thanks." He swung his jacket down from his
shoulder. "It's a good song."

"It's a *lovely* song. Perfect. I don't think I've heard
it before."

"Aw, c'mon. You gotta love those Dixie Chicks. I
had to change a couple of words to make it work."

"You made it yours. *Theirs.* Annie's and Zach's.
That'll be their song now." Feeling a sudden chill, she
hugged herself and rubbed her bare upper arms.

"What a gift, Hank. That's something they'll take with them throughout their journey together. *Their song.*"

"You're layin' it on a little thick, there, Sally," he teased as he laid his jacket over her shoulders.

"Never. I'm no gusher. If anything, that was an understatement. My little sister just got married, Hank. If I could sing, I'd be…" She adjusted the jacket and began to sway. "You know what? I can dance." She did a tiny two-step, added a slow twirl, and then a more enthusiastic two-step and a spin. "I can dance. *I can…*"

She lost the twinkle in her toes, stumbled, and landed in a hoop made of two strong arms.

"Oops. I tend to be a little clumsy when I get excited. All I need is a strong partner." She copped a feel of his working-man's biceps as she steadied herself and eased up on him, catching a knowing look beneath the brim of his hat. He thought it a pratfall.

She smiled. "How about it?"

He took his time about tilting her upright, the corner of his mouth twitching. "How about I do the singin' and you do the dancin'?"

"They didn't set this up very well. The best man is married. What fun is that for a maid of honor?"

He bent to retrieve his jacket from the grass. "What kind of fun are you looking for?"

"The loosen-your-tie-and-kick-your-shoes-off kind. How about you?"

"If I start taking more clothes off, the party's over."

He draped his jacket over her shoulders again. "I'll settle for a good meal and a little music."

"Ah, the quiet type. A challenge is always fun." She linked arms with him and made a sweeping gesture toward the lodge. "Shall we? Dinner's coming up soon. Right now the bar is open and the drinks are free."

"Free drinks would take away any challenge if I didn't have this booze-sniffin' bitch with me." The dog whined and perked her ears. "See? Phoebe don't miss a trick. No way am I goin' near any open bar, so just save me a seat at the dinner table."

"I've already arranged the place cards. You're next to me on the wagon." She had him walking now. Ambling. She was in no hurry. "Have you thought about my suggestion?"

"What suggestion?"

"Think of it as sort of a working vacation. Not hard labor, mind you. More like backup. Hang out with Hoolie and me. We can be quite entertaining. And according to Zach, you're unattached and somewhat flexible in your schedule." She looked up and gave a perfunctory smile. "I asked."

"Why would you do that?"

"Filling out your résumé. I didn't tell him you were thinking about applying for the job. So far, this is just between you and me."

"You're serious."

"Of course I'm serious. I want my sister's wedding to be perfect, and the perfect wedding includes a fabulous honeymoon." She gave his arm what she hoped felt like a winning squeeze. "I don't know what your somewhat flexible schedule looks like for the next few weeks, but you wouldn't have to miss any rodeos. Come and go as you please, but stow your gear with us for a while. That way there's another man around, and the honeymooners have nothing to worry about."

"What about the man? Should I be worried?"

"You don't strike me as a worrier."

"Long as I'm not hangin' with troublemakers, I got nothin' to worry about."

"No worries, then." She laughed. "I really don't make trouble. I fall into it sometimes, but who doesn't?" She looked up. "You?"

"Not lately."

"Maybe you need a little adventure in your life, Hank. Get out there, you know? Try new things. New people. I like to get while the gettin's good, but I'm always careful. You gotta be careful with the good stuff, right? Good people, good ideas, good times— there's a certain balance. A little daring goes a long way with a lot of careful." She wagged an instructive finger. "If we had an emergency, we'd call you."

"There's nobody crazier than Zach Beaudry when it comes to risking his neck, and you can tell him I said so."

"And he'll say he's changed." She stopped, turned, blocked his progress. "Will you think about it? What's three weeks?"

"How much time do I have to think about it?"

"About three hours." She pulled his jacket in tighter. "Do you have horses? I could pay you in horses. You know, the Indian way."

"Yeah, I know the Indian way. But you're talkin' Sally's way, and I'm goin' Hank's way. Nice try, though." He smiled. "I do like the way you swim."

"Dance with me tonight, and I'll swim with you later."

"For me, that's a whole lotta daring and not much careful." He slipped his arm around her shoulders. "Be damned if I'm not tempted to jump in."

Hank generally steered clear of big parties, but the Beaudry wedding was turning out to be a pretty good time. With beef for dinner and the prospect of Sally for dessert, he was happy to loosen his belt now and put his boots under her bed later. She hadn't been kidding about arranging the place cards. She'd given up her seat at the bride's table, supposedly so the best man could sit with his wife. She'd grabbed Hilda Beaudry and nodded toward Hoolie and Hank, who'd claimed a table on the sidelines and started in on the bread basket. It was a good setup. Hank wouldn't presume to guess where Hoolie pictured parking his boots tonight, but he secretly wished the old man whatever he could score. Hilda was definitely enjoying the company.

"It's too bad you can't dance tonight, Hoolie," Hilda said, genuinely grieved.

Hoolie checked all his pockets. "Too many hidey-holes in this monkey suit. I don't know where my pocket knife went to. You got one on you, Hank? I'm gonna cut this damn thing off."

"No nudity here, Hoolie." Sally winked at Hank. "Wait till we're back in camp."

"Is that where you're hiding all the Double D's?" Hank scanned the room. "'Cause I ain't seein' any in this crowd."

"I'm talkin' about this mummy's boot I got on my foot," Hoolie grumbled.

"How long you had it on?" Hank asked.

"About a month."

"About a week," Sally said.

"Sorry, Hoolie. You got a ways to go."

"I broke a wing before. Twice." Hoolie flapped his folded arm. "But never a leg. Sure cramps a guy's style."

"I'll request the Funky Chicken," Hilda promised. "When the mother of the groom and the father of the bride are both unattached, they get one of those spot-light dances. Right, Sally?"

"Absolutely. We make our own rules. Don't we, Hoolie? I think I might have found us a sitter." She flashed Hank a smile. "Hank's almost convinced."

"What kind of a sitter?" Hoolie scowled.

"The kind who looks like he can keep the mice at bay while the cats go play. Hank's perfect, so help me put him over the edge." She laid her hand on Hank's shoulder and crooned, "Come on out to the big Double D, where the horses run wild and the cowboys live free."

Hank chuckled. "Yeah, that's gonna do it."

"Hell, yeah, we want those kids to have their honeymoon." Hoolie leaned closer to Hank. "You like horses?"

"He's a farrier," Sally said.

"Thought you was an MA or a PD or some kind of code for junior doctor."

"PA," Hank said. "Physician's assistant."

"For people, right? And you can shoe horses besides?" Hoolie grinned. "Yeah, you need to come see our place. You got some time? Say about—"

"Three weeks? They don't trust you to mind the store either, Hoolie?" Hank asked.

"They would if I hadn't gone and—"

Sally whapped Hoolie in the chest and nodded toward a paunchy silhouette in an oversized straw hat looming in the doorway to the dining room. "What's he doing here?"

Hoolie peered, squinted. "Don't ask me."

"Annie thought about inviting the Tutans. Double D diplomacy, she said, but after the last stunt he pulled—I know damn well it was him—I said it was him or me." Sally's hand found Hank's forearm again, but like Hoolie, he was zeroed in on the uninvited guest. "He cut our fence," she was saying. "We keep the old horses in a separate pasture, and Tutan cut the fence. He said he didn't, but it was definitely cut, and that's how Hoolie broke his ankle."

"That was my own damn fault."

"We have special fencing separating the young horses from the retirees and the convalescents. Those horses don't get through a four-strand fence without help." Sally slid her chair back. "I'm sure it was a trap. I don't know if it was set for the horses or for you, but I know he did it to cause us trouble. And he's about to get his."

"Hold on, girl." Hoolie's chair legs scraped the floor. "Not now."

"I don't want him anywhere near Annie's wedding."

"C'mon." Hank was the first one to his feet. "This is my kind of fun. Don't worry, Hoolie. We'll keep it civil." He smiled as he helped Sally with her chair. "But there's nothing wrong with showin' a little claw."

Tutan. The name ping-ponged within the walls of Hank's head as he took in the face for the first time. He kept pace with Sally, who had a point to make with every deliberate step. *No hurry. I'm in charge here.* His admiration for the woman's style grew with every moment he spent with her. And now, here was Dan Tutan. Her lease challenger. His father's leash holder. *Mr.* Tutan.

"We're on our way to Rapid City, thought we'd stop in and offer our best wishes. Did you get our gift?"

"We did. Thanks, but you really shouldn't have."

No *hello,* no *go to hell.* The way Sally was bristling and the man was posturing, Hank expected a little snarling. He was disappointed.

"We've been neighbors a long time, Sally." The man with the round, red face adjusted his hat, hitched up his pants, and finally folded his arms over his barrel chest. "We figured our invitation got lost in the mail."

"Annie wanted to keep it small. Family and close friends."

He eyed Hank. "Close friends?"

"Hank Night Horse." No handshake. A nod and a name were more than enough. "I've known Zach a long time."

"Night Horse." Tutan went snake eyed. "I had a guy by that name working for me years ago. Any relation to you?"

Keep looking, Mr. Tutan. "Where was he from?"

"I don't think he was from around here. Coulda been Montana. Isn't that where Beaudry's from?"

"Yeah, it is."

"I like that Crow Indian country up there. Real pretty. Is that where you're from?"

"Nope." *Crow country is Crow country.* "But Night Horse is a common name. Kinda like Drexler and Tutan."

"That guy that worked for me…there's something…" He kept staring, the rude bastard. But he shook his head. "No, if I remember right, he was shaped more like me." He patted his belly and laughed. "And he was a good hand. Except when he got to drinking. Fell off the wagon and got himself killed somehow. Hard to tell by the time his body was found, but they thought he might've been out hunting. That's one sport you don't want to mix with too much Everclear." He shook his head. "Tragic."

"Sounds like it." Hank stared dispassionately, kept his tone tame and his fists tucked into his elbows.

"Maybe that wasn't his name. Pretty sure it was some kinda Horse." Tutan turned to Sally. "You're looking fit. Some new kind of—"

"I'm doing well, thanks. *Very* well."

"Good. Good to hear." He tried to peer past Sally, but it was Hoolie who limped into view. "Good man, Hoolihan," Tutan enthused. "There's sure no keeping you down. Where's the bride? I just want to give her my best. I've known these girls most of their lives, and I want little Annie to know that the Tutans wish her well."

"She's on a tight schedule," Hank said. "We'll tell her you stopped in."

"This time tomorrow I guess the happy couple will be off on a nice honeymoon."

"That's the main reason I'm here." Hank drew a deep breath, steadying himself. "Zach and Annie won't have a thing to worry about. I'll be keepin' these two in line."

"You're gonna have your hands full, son." Tutan threaded his thumbs under his belly roll and over his belt as he moved in on Sally. "Tell your sister I wish her well. She and Beaudry would do well to get out of this crazy horse thing you've got going and live their lives. You and your wild ideas. You're just trying to keep your sister from leaving you without—"

Hank caught Sally in time to save Tutan from what undoubtedly would have been a nice right hook if she'd followed through.

Backpedaling, Tutan wagged his finger. "Your father's rolling over in his grave over what you've done to the Double D, Sally."

"This is a private party, Tutan," Hoolie said.

Tutan's angry gaze didn't waver. "Hell, girl, I'm sorry for all your troubles, but I ain't rollin' over. I've got a *real* ranch to run."

"Let me go," Sally grumbled as Tutan turned on his heel and stomped across the lobby.

Hank eased up, but he wasn't letting go until Tutan was out the door. "Marriage and murder are too much for one day."

She drew herself up and challenged him with a look. "You're the one who suggested showing some claw."

"A *little.*"

"Night Horse," she said quietly. "He said the man worked for him."

"And you heard my answer."

"What I heard was…" She took his warning from his eyes. "Did you mean it? About helping out?"

"Actually, I was just sayin' it to help out, but then he went and called me *son.*" He gave a curt nod. "Yeah, if it'll make a difference, I'll stay."

"Let's go tell the bride and groom." She grabbed his hand. "You're just full of great gifts. They'll be calling you Santa Claus."

"You might be callin' me Scrooge. You kids won't be having any parties with me in charge."

"Actually…" She leaned in close, and he had half a mind to take that flower out of her hair so he could smell only Sally. She was giving him those eyes again, full of fireworks and mischief. "I'm looking forward to that part about the party being over."

He laughed. "You're the damnedest woman I ever met."

"Only when I'm at my best."

"Sally!" Glistening with bride shine, Annie burst on the scene, brushing Hank's arm as she reached for her sister. "Are you okay? Somebody said…"

"Everything's okay. Look. Not a scratch on me, and Tutan got off easy. Come with me to the bathroom." Sally put her unscratched arm around her sister's shoulders and wheeled her in the opposite direction. "I gotta go talk her down," she told Hank in parting. "Keep the big surprise under your hat."

For how long? Hank wondered as he watched the Drexlers head for the women's sanctuary. He'd be walking around with a bombshell under his hat until somebody took the detonator out of his mouth by whispering Thanks, Hank, but you won't be needed after all.

"It was nothing." Sally snatched a tissue from the box beside the sink and used it to dab a lipstick smudge from her sister's cheek. "Tutan said he was on his way to Rapid City and just stopped in to make sure you got his gift. Don't open it. It's probably some kind of curse on your firstborn."

"Did you put any scratches on him?"

"I came so close. If Hank hadn't interfered…"

"Then what?" Annie prompted. But before Sally's very eyes, the question of *what* took a mental backseat to the *who*. Annie smiled. "*Hank.* Zach was right. He said you two would hit it off."

"I'd like to see more of him." At least as much as he'd seen of her. Feeling good, looking fine—she glanced at herself in the mirror, just to make sure, yes—for now and however much longer, she would do her best to see and know, give and take with a man, *this* man.

She raised a cautionary finger. "Remember, Annie, I tell *who* I want, *when* and *if* I want. And for right now, I'm as healthy as you are. You haven't said anything, have you?"

"I hardly know the man."

Sally nodded. "I would have hit him."

"Hank?"

"No, Tutan. It would have felt *so good*. But Hank held me back." She smiled. "And that felt even better."

Annie gave her that what-are-you-up-to? look. She always recognized the signs. "You didn't sign us up for one of those reality shows, did you?"

"You mean like 'My Big Fat Redneck Wedding'?" Sally snapped her fingers. "Hey, we could have gotten some publicity for the sanctuary. I wish I'd thought of that." She laughed. "Just kidding."

"Seriously, you're having a good time?"

"I'm gonna dance my shoes off tonight, little sister." Sally fussed with Annie's golden curls. "You're so beautiful."

"You're giving me that look. What else have you got up your sleeve?"

"Are you kidding? I can barely hide my boobs in this dress." Sally winked. She could barely contain herself. "It's no wonder you're a teacher—you read me like a book. I do have a little surprise for you. I think. I hope. Like you said, we hardly know the man."

"Another song?"

"You want another song?" Sally leaned closer to the mirror and adjusted her décolleté. "I'll see what I can do."

Hank sang "Can I Have This Dance?" for Zach and Ann Beaudry, who waltzed alone in the spot-light, surrounded by family and friends smiling in the dark. Beautiful people. Sally's throat tingled. Her eyes smarted with happy tears. Her heart was fuller than she could have imagined in the days before the wedding, when her only sister was still a bride-to-be and Hank Night Horse was simply a name on a list. She wanted to catch the moment and slip it into a magic bottle, preserve it in all its sensory glory for a time when her senses would not serve and she would turn to memory.

Hank left the cheers and applause to the bride and groom and the music for the wedding party dance to the DJ. Sally smiled as the best man reported for duty, but by the time she was able to get a good look past Sam's nicely tailored shoulder, her private man of the hour had disappeared. She added his modesty to the growing list of his irresistible qualities and committed herself to leaving him alone for a few minutes.

But when she escaped to the terrace, her commitment fell by the wayside at the sight of the guitar leaning against the balcony along with the man seated on the top rail. A sinking feeling in her legs urged her to pull him down before he fell backward, but she fought her foolishness with a slow, deep breath. Strong sensation was good, even the silly, sinking kind. Anything was better than numbness, which would be slinking back sooner or later along with whatever other anomalies the erratic disease lurking in her body had in store. She threw back her shoulders and walked the planks, taking care not to turn an ankle over the kitten heels that had been her compromise to the killer spikes she'd longed to wear just this once and the safe flats Annie had tried to talk her into.

He watched her. He didn't smile much, this man with the breathtaking voice, but as the bright lights and music fell away from the starry night, he summoned her with his steady gaze.

"What took you so long?" he asked quietly.

"I've danced with Sam and his boy, Jimmy. I've danced with Zach. I've even danced with their mother. But I have not danced with you. Do you always sing and run?"

"Yep."

"If I didn't know better, I might have gone looking for you at the bar."

"But you do know better."

"I do." She stood close enough to touch him, but she laid her hand on the railing and reveled in the feel of the wood and the wanting. "You've been with Phoebe?"

"Took her for a walk. Had to keep her on a tight leash when some guy came along with something that looked like a giant poodle. Phoebe was ready to tear into that thing."

"Blessed are the peacemakers."

"You're right." He came down from the railing like a cat, languidly stretching one long leg at a time, pulled her to him with one arm, took her free hand and tucked it against his chest. "We should dance."

"Mmm-hmm. This is nice." She swayed in his arms, brushing against him just enough to incite sweet shivers. "Peaceful, but not still."

"If I didn't know better, I'd say we'd met before."

"In another life?"

"How many do you have?"

"Three at least, maybe more. But I'm sure this is the only one I've met you in."

He laughed. He thought she was joking.

"So far," she said, and he drew her closer. She rested her head on his shoulder and inhaled his zesty scent, wondering what he tasted like and how soon she would find out. "But I know what you mean. It feels like we needed no introduction."

"It was a jaw-dropping introduction. Maybe it wasn't necessary, but I sure wouldn't trade it for a handshake."

"You barged in on the life behind door number one. Good choice."

"Phoebe has good instincts."

If anyone but her sister had interrupted, Sally would have hissed mightily.

"Is this a private party?" Annie ventured.

Sally peeked around Hank's shoulder and smiled.

"Not if we can wangle a private audience with the bride and groom." She gave Hank's hand a quick squeeze. "We have a proposition for you."

Zach laughed. "I told you somebody was getting propositioned."

"Tell them, Hank." Sally flashed him a smile, but he wouldn't buy in that far. She turned the smile on her sister. "You two are going on that honeymoon."

"Maybe this fall," Ann said. "Or this winter, or—"

"Maybe *this week*. I ran a little contest, and Hank won himself an all-expenses-paid vacation at the Double D Dude Ranch."

"Wait a minute," Hank said. Sally held her breath. "I thought you ran a little want ad, and I got *hired*."

Sally exhaled a laugh, inhaled relief. "You didn't qualify for the job, but all applicants were automatically entered into the drawing for a vacation, and you're our winner."

"What'd I tell you, Horse?" Zach clapped his hand on his friend's shoulder. "You come to my wedding, you're bound to get lucky."

"Sally, you didn't." Ann's eyes sparkled. She was on top of the world, but she would gladly make room for her sister.

"Didn't what? Award the grand prize already? He's not *that* lucky." Sally glanced askance, giving Hank a coy smile. "But the winner of the vacation may become eligible for—"

"No, no, no," Ann said. "It's the second-sweetest offer I've heard all day, but we can't go halfway around the world and leave Hank to take care of things at the Double D. It's way too much to ask. He has places to go and things to do."

"Which is why I'll be the one taking care of things at the Double D. All Hank has to take care of is your peace of mind. And he's happy to do that." Sally linked arms with Hank. He wasn't going anywhere anytime soon. "Right, Hank?"

"Absolutely. You two lovebirds enjoy yourselves. I'll stand guard over the nest while you're gone."

"Oh, Hank, we really appreciate the offer, but with—"

"But nothing," Sally said. "It's perfect."

"I have a couple of commitments to work around, but Sally's been telling me about the program you're running, and I'm interested. I can use a little—" Hank slid Sally a conspiratorial glance. "—diversion."

"Can we trust these two?" Ann asked her new husband.

"I can vouch for Hank. Salt of the earth. Even if we had eggs in the nest, I'd trust him."

"Nobody's vouched for *you* yet," the bride reminded her sister. She looked up at Zach. "Is it safe to leave the salt of the earth with a shaker that doesn't always have her head screwed on straight?"

"I do like to shake things up," Sally said. She

glanced up at Hank. "I used to be a mover, too, but that's a lot of work."

"I don't shake easy," he told her.

"Hank's the right man for the job," Zach said. "I'd even trust him with Zelda."

"You hear that?" Sally asked Ann. "If Zach's willing to leave the keys to his precious pickup in Hank's hands, you know your sister is safe."

"Can we still do it? I mean, we canceled the reservations, but we still have the tickets." Ann turned to Hank. "I don't travel that much, and I would've been happy with an extra night right here in the Hills, but Sam gave us this trip to Australia. *Australia.* I've always wanted to…"

"You go, Mrs. Beaudry," Hank said. "Live the dream."

"I owe you, man."

"Damn straight, cowboy." Hank waved a cautionary finger at the groom, but his warning was for the bride. "I don't ever wanna see this guy on my exam table again."

"That makes two of us. But Sally—"

"Best behavior," Sally promised. "Pinky swear."

Chapter Three

Hank had never considered himself to be a cowboy, but he was a horseman. He owned two mares, pastured them at what was now really his brother Greg's place up north, just across the state line. Hank also owned some of the land, but Greg's cattle used it. All Hank asked in return was a room, a mailing address and a place to keep a few horses. He didn't take up much space.

Hank was no breeder or fancier, wasn't out to acquire pedigrees or trophies. He'd rescued the two mares from a farm foreclosure. They'd been bony and riddled with parasites, about as sad eyed and desperate as the old man who was losing all he had and looking for somebody, *any*body with a heart to take in the last of his stock. Hank had even offered to adopt the farmer, but his niece had shown up for that end of the rescue. Wormed, fed up, trimmed up and turned out on Dakota grass, the two mares had turned out to be pretty nice. Not the best of his rescues—he'd taken in a sweet-tempered colt that had gone to a couple looking for a friend for their autistic child—but they would make good saddle horses if he ever found the time to work with them.

Three hundred miles northeast of the Hilltop Lodge, Hank checked in at home and took care of his personal business. The next day he drove nearly the same distance due south to the Double D. Not that he was in a killing hurry to start his "vacation"—a vacation for Hank would have meant stringing together a few nights in what he loosely termed his own bed—but he had promises to keep and curiosity to satisfy. He cared a lot about his friend, Zach Beaudry. He'd heard a lot about the Double D. He'd thought a lot about Sally Drexler. He had a bad feeling about her neighbor. It all added up to a sense of purpose, and Hank Night Horse was a man of purpose.

He called ahead to make sure he knew where he was going once he ran out of map markings. The two-story farmhouse was off the state highway at the end of about three miles of sparsely graveled road. He found Sally waiting for him on the sprawling covered porch. She came down the steps to greet him.

"Hey, Phoebe."

Okay, so she greeted his dog first. Unlike Hank, Phoebe was not above making a slobbering fool of herself.

"You just missed the honeymooners," Sally told him, her eyes unmistakably alight for him.

"You got time for TV?" He wasn't above grinning.

"I've always got time for a comedian." She took a hands-on-hips stance and gave his pickup with its custom long-box cap an appreciative once-over. The sleek, slide-in cargo box was outfitted for his business and his gypsy lifestyle. "You must have done just about what the newlyweds did. Grabbed your gear and run. Of course, they had a plane to catch. Are you hungry? Tired? Ready to rock 'n' roll?"

"I'll do anything that doesn't involve sitting."

She raised her brow. "Interested in reclining?"

"If I do that, I'm liable to be out for a while."

"Then let's walk and talk before we eat, drink and be merry." She gave a come-on gesture. "I'll show you around."

Her walk wasn't quite as smooth as her talk. He'd noticed it before, but it was so subtle, he'd dismissed it as another of her quirks. Sally wasn't your standard model female in any way, shape or form. She was special. Easy to follow, hard to figure, no doubt heavy on the upkeep.

Hardly the best fit for Hank Night Horse. He was an

ordinary man who talked with a straight tongue and tried to walk a straight line. He understood most people—once you figured out what they wanted, for better or worse they were generally predictable—but Sally was like a horse he'd ridden for an elderly neighbor when he was a kid. Four out of five days the beautiful Arabian was smart, spirited, smooth-gaited, a dream to ride. But on the fifth day she'd likely take off with him and run like a hellcat until they hit some kind of a wall. She was four-fifths dream and one-fifth damned, but she was special. And four days out of five, she sure was fun to play with.

He wasn't sure about the hitch in Sally's gait. It was slight and oddly sporadic. An old injury wouldn't seem to explain it, and maybe there was no explanation. Maybe it was just Sally.

They entered the machine shed through a side door, which was propped open for ventilation. Hoolie looked up from a workbench and then slid off the stool before he remembered he wasn't going anywhere without his crutch.

He grinned anyway and reached for Hank's handshake. "Did you bring all the tools of your trades? My saddle horse could use corrective shoes, and I'll pay you to take this damn mummy boot off my hoof."

"Like I told you before, you take that off too soon, you'll pay dearly. Your horse is a different story. My pickup is a blacksmith shop on wheels. Phoebe!" The dog was headed for the door.

"Does she get along with other dogs?" Sally asked.

"Sure does. She's around dogs all the time."

A warning growl sounded outside the door.

"Well, that makes one of them," Hoolie said ominously as a black-and-white shepherd slunk across the threshold, teeth bared.

"Baby!"

Sally bolted for the door, but she fell flat on her face before she got there. Tripped over her own feet like one of the TV comedians she'd claimed she always had time for. She was doing a shaky push-up on the concrete by the time Hank got to her. She tried to wave him off, her attention fixed on the dogs.

Hoolie came on strong once he had his crutch in place. "Here, you dogs, you want a piece o' me?"

The clamor settled into a war of whines, both bitches determined to get in the last whimper as Hoolie and his crutch prevailed.

Hank found himself down on one knee beside a woman who was on her way up. "You okay?"

"Yes! Yes, of course." She laughed as she braced her hand on his shoulder. "Totally wasn't ready for that. Scared me."

"They're okay," Hoolie called out. "Phoebe wants to play. Baby wants to lay down a few rules first."

"I'll give 'em some rules," Hank grumbled, discomfited by the loss of his dignity and his own confusion as to where it had gone.

Sally laughed again. "What are you, the Dog Whisperer?"

"I'm the alpha." He signaled Phoebe to stay put while the shepherd took a fallback position. "You got any other dogs around here?" he asked Sally.

"Baby's an only dog."

"That's her problem. We'll fix it, though. We'll teach her some manners. Won't we, Phoeb?" Hank patted the dog's silky head. "Scared you, huh?"

"It sure startled me." Sally twisted her arm for a look at her skinned elbow. "I didn't want to lose you over a dogfight. You've probably noticed I can be kind of a klutz sometimes. Two left feet." She gave a perfunctory smile. "Except when I dance."

"You stick to dancing and leave us to referee the dogs."

"Only if you'll dance with me, Henry." She was giving him that too cute look. "Do you know that song? You're supposed to say, *Okay, Baby.*"

Hank shook his head. "Nobody calls me Henry."

"That's your real name, isn't it?" She flashed a smile at Hoolie. "Henry's a fine name."

"*No*body calls me Henry."

"Ah, the soft underbelly. Our guardian is ticklish, Hoolie."

"I know the feeling," Hoolie said.

"I can handle a dogfight, but that name is a deal breaker."

"Duly noted." Sally slid a glance at Hoolie, who chuckled.

"Okay, now aren't you supposed to have some wild horses around here somewhere?"

"That's the rumor. But first, the tour." She gave an after-you gesture. "Please follow the silk thread."

Hank raised his brow and responded in kind. He knew her game. She was like his patients on the rodeo circuit—too stubborn to say they were hurt, so you didn't ask. You watched how they moved. *If* they'd let you.

"No go?" She grabbed his arm and coaxed him by her side. "All right, then, when you're ready to put your road-weary butt in a saddle, I'll show you horses, Henry. *Hank.*"

"You're askin' for it, woman."

"For what?" She met his loaded look with a coy smile. "Oh, no. I'm just hackin' on you. Make no mistake, when it comes to serious matters, I don't fool around." She glanced away. "Well, I do, but I don't ask. Do you?"

What he didn't do was answer foolish questions.

By the time he'd seen the outbuildings—shop, machine shed, barn, loafing shed, grain bins, bunk house—the suggestion of food held considerable appeal. He was impressed with what he'd seen so far. It was a nice layout, but the cattle operation was a shadow of what it had been in its heyday, two genera-tions ago. According to Hank's tour guide, the Double D ran a small herd of cattle, partly to satisfy state requirements to claim agricultural status and partly for income. But the ranch's main enterprise was the wild-horse sanctuary, and it was decidedly nonprofit. An unusual concept for a third-generation rancher, but Sally Drexler was an unusual rancher. Hank looked forward to seeing the horses.

After his stomach stopped growling.

He hit the front steps heavily to cover the noise as he headed for the door behind Sally, but the twinkle in her eyes let him know she wasn't deaf. Embarrassing. He didn't like to give anything away unintentionally. Not even the fact that he hadn't taken time to eat anything before he left home.

Beset by the aroma of juicy beef, his stomach spoke up again as he followed her in the house while Phoebe protested having the door shut in her face.

"She can come in, as long as she's okay around cats," Sally said. "Sounds like she's hungry. We usually don't eat supper around here until pretty late, but we never keep the critters waiting."

"Something smells good." He stood like a maypole while Sally circled around him. "Enough to eat." He watched her let Phoebe in. "Right now."

She turned one of her bright-eyed smiles on him. "Right now?"

"Be glad to help you get it on."

"Would you?"

"On the table."

"I've always wanted to try that," she told him over her shoulder as she led the way through foodless territory. "But let's eat first."

Willing as he was, he didn't have to help much. He was a straight shooter, and she was a woman who loved to tease. She'd had supper simmering in a Crock-Pot, ready to dish up anytime. She put him to slicing bread and filling water glasses while she washed salad greens. Hoolie came in the back door all slicked down and washed up precisely at five-fifteen.

Pretty late, my ass.

Pretty tasty. Pretty entertaining. Pretty woman. Maybe he could get used to a little teasing.

"How much of the Double D can you reach on wheels?" Hank asked as he sipped his coffee. "You use ATVs?"

"Hell, no," Hoolie said. "Too damn noisy. This is a ranch, not a playground."

"I'm with you on that score." And he'd told his brother as much last night when Greg had shown off a picture of the one he wanted. A kid's toy, Hank had said.

"We can cover a lot of ground in a pickup, but there's places we don't go except on horseback."

"We have some totally pristine grassland here," Sally said. "Some of it is pretty remote."

"I'll stow my gear in the bunkhouse, and then maybe we could all take a little pickup ride," Hank suggested. "Give me a feel for what's out there while it's still light."

"We can do that." Sally sounded hesitant. "But we have a room for you here in the house."

"I'm fine with the bunkhouse."

"We get kids out here sometimes helpin' out. Volunteers come and go. You'll be better off in the house." Hoolie shrugged. "I snore."

"We're hoping to add on to the bunkhouse to give Hoolie more privacy." Sally and Hoolie exchanged looks. "Definitely on the to-do list."

"Definitely," Hoolie said. "Sally's used to having Annie around. And Zach, too, since he come along. We don't want Sally rattlin' around here alone at night."

"She could get into trouble?" Hank set his cup down. "Hell, whatever works. I just figured..."

"It's a big house," Hoolie said. "And you're a guest more than anything. I'm the hired man."

Hank looked at Sally. He had something she wanted, and she'd decided it was hers for the taking. She'd try to tease it out of him, would she? He gave a suggestive smile. *Game on, woman. Your house, my play.*

"Do *you* snore?" he asked her.

"I've never had any complaints."

Hoolie took Sally's unspoken hint and begged off the after-supper tour. "I'll let you take my pickup." He offered Hank two keys and a metal Road Runner trinket on a key ring.

Ignoring the handoff, Hank nodded at Sally. "She's giving the tour."

"This thing he offers is a great honor," Sally quipped, B-movie style. "To refuse would be an insult."

"She's a 1968 C10," Hoolie boasted. "She's a great little go-fer pickup. Short box with a six-pony engine. Overhauled her myself."

"Classic," Hank said appreciatively. "My dad had one when I was a kid. Got her used, ran her into the ground. He was on the road a lot."

"Don't know how many times the odometer's turned over on this one, but she runs like a top. You gotta try 'er out."

"My pleasure."

Watching Hank handle the big steering wheel and palm the knob on the gearshift was Sally's pleasure. She'd stopped driving altogether after proving she really could hit the broad side of the barn. It was the first time she'd lost all feeling in her right leg, the one that gave her the most trouble. She'd been backing up to the barn with a load of mineral blocks when suddenly the leg was gone. Might as well have been lopped off at the hip. By the time she'd moved the dead weight by hand, her tailgate had smashed through the tack-room wall.

The damage to the barn had been easy to repair. Her

pickup, like her pride, had become an early victim of her unpredictable body. But her independence had begun to erode that day, and with it went bits of confidence. Dealing with the disease wasn't as difficult as plugging up holes in her spirit. During bad times she'd start springing holes right and left, and she could feel herself draining away. She'd learned to take advantage of the very thing that made MS so cruel—its capricious nature. When the symptoms ebbed, she dammed up all her leaks and charged ahead, full speed, total Sally. She took pleasure in the little things, like the way it felt to get up and walk whenever the spirit moved her, the feel of water lapping against bare skin, the smell of a summer night and the look of a man's hands taking charge.

Phoebe was sitting pretty in the pickup box behind the back window, her blond ears flapping in the breeze. They plied the fence line at a leisurely pace, following tire tracks worn in the sod. Sally pointed out the "geriatric bachelor band" grazing in a shallow draw. They were too old for the adoption program, and some of them had spent years in holding facilities—essentially feedlot conditions—before finding a home at the Double D. Heads bobbed, ears perked at the sound of the engine, and they moved as one, like a school of fish.

"They have no use for us, especially this time of year," she said with a smile. "Which means we're doing something right." She nodded for a swing to the west, punched the glove-compartment button and felt around for the binoculars. "From the top of that hill we might get a look at some of the two-year-olds. There are some beauties in that bunch. Do you like Spanish Mustangs?"

He swung the big steering wheel. "I don't see too many."

"They don't come shoe shopping?"

"I work mostly rodeos, so I see a lot of quarter horses." The engine growled as he downshifted for the hill. "I did shoe a couple of mustangs at an endurance ride last fall. They had real pretty feet."

"We need to interest more people in adopting these horses. The BLM had an auction out in Wyoming last month and sold less than half the number they projected. If they don't find any more takers and we can't make room for them, some of them will end up..." She glimpsed movement below the hill and to the right, but she had to turn her head to see what it was. Her right eye was going out on her again. *Damn.* "Look!" She pushed the binoculars against his arm. "Stop! Hurry, before they get away."

"Look, stop, hurry?" He complied, chuckling. "How about hurry, stop, look? Or—"

"Shh!" She tapped him with the binoculars again, and he took them and focused. "How many? Can you tell?"

"Eight. Nine."

"See any you like?"

"Nice red roan. Three buckskins. Aw, man, would you look at that bay."

He offered her a turn with the binoculars, but she shook them off. "I can't use those things. But I know which one you mean. He looks just like his daddy. Fabulous Spanish Sulphur Mustang stallion we call Don Quixote." She nodded as he put the binoculars up to his face again. *Stop, take a look, really see.* "Give that boy another year, and you'd have yourself an endurance racer, a cutting horse, whatever your pleasure."

"You won't have any trouble finding him a good home." He glanced at her. "If you're having trouble with numbers, show me what's left after the next auction."

"We can usually place a few more with special programs. Police units, military, youth programs, even prisons."

"After all's said and done, show me what's left. Never met a horse I didn't like." He handed her the binoculars. "I'd sure like to see that bay up close."

"You will. They're getting cut this week."

"All of them?"

"Only the ones with balls. If you like the bay when you see him up close, he could be spared." She smiled at him as she snapped the glove compartment shut. "Which puts his balls in your court."

"Damn." He chuckled as he lifted his hand to the key in the ignition.

"He'd make a wonderful stud." She stayed his hand

with hers and slid to the middle of the bench seat. "This is my favorite time of day. Between sunset and dusk. Late meadowlarks, early crickets."

He said nothing. The enigmatic look in his eyes wasn't what she expected. Maybe she'd misread his signals. Maybe her receptors were on the blink. Life's ultimate joke. Just when she was getting the *go* light on all major systems except her troublesome right eye, which wasn't a major system at the moment.

She would not take this lying down.

Who was she kidding? She'd take him any way she could get him, but in a small pickup, lying down wasn't gonna happen.

Alternatives?

"Did you ever go parking in your father's C10?" she asked.

"He was dead and the pickup was gone by the time I started meetin' up with girls after sunset."

"Where did you meet them?"

"Down by the river. You're fifteen and you get a chance to be with a girl, you're not lookin' to take the high ground."

"Fifteen?"

"Late bloomer." He moved the seat back as far as it would go and put his arm around her. "I like this time of day, too, Sally."

He leaned over her slowly, fingers in her hair, thumb grazing her cheek, lips moistened and parted just enough to make hers quiver on the cusp of his kiss. He made her feel dear and delicate, and she was having none of it. She slipped her arm around his neck and answered his sweet approach with her spicy reception. She was no weak-kneed quiverer. She could match him slam for bam and thank you, man. She didn't need coddling, and she told him as much with a heat-seeking kiss.

The catch in his breath pleased her. The new-found need in his kiss thrilled her. She answered in kind, kissing him like there was no time like the present. Because there wasn't. Deep, caring kisses like his were rare. She drew a breath full of the salty taste and sexy scent of him and grazed his chest with her breasts. They drew taut within her clothing. She pushed her fingers through his hair, curled them and rubbed it against the center of her palm. She would fill her senses with him while she could, because she could. She slipped her free hand between them, found his belly, hard and flat as his belt buckle. She took the measure of both.

He nuzzled the side of her neck and groaned. "I'm not fifteen anymore," he whispered. "I can wait."

"Why would you? I'm not a girl."

He raised his head and smiled at her. "In this light you could be. Young and scared. A little confused, maybe."

She frowned. "But since I'm none of those things…"

"I don't know that." He caressed her face with the backs of his fingers. "Who said you could call all the shots?"

"Is there something wrong with me?" She swallowed hard. "I mean, something you don't like?"

"Uh-uh. Everything looks just right."

"Looks can deceive." She dragged her fingers from his belt to his zipper. "But this feels right."

"You don't wanna believe that guy." He moved his hips just enough to let her know that there was nothing wrong with him, either. "No matter what the question, he's only got one answer."

"He's honest," she whispered. "Stands up for what he believes in."

He kissed her again, so fully and thoroughly that the taste of his lips and the darting of his tongue, the strength of his arms and the sharp intake of his breath satisfied all her wishes. She had feeling in every part of her body. She didn't want it to go away, not one tingle, not one spark, and she reached around him and held him the way he held her. Maybe more so. Maybe harder and stronger and more desirous of him than he could possibly be of her, but she was honest. Her embrace was true to what she felt, and feeling was everything.

"Easy," he whispered, and she realized she had sounded some sort of alarm, made some desperate little noise. "You okay?"

She nodded. Laughed a little. God, she was such a *woman.* She was the one who was scaring him.

"Look at Phoebe," he said, and she turned toward the back window and laughed with him even though she couldn't really see anything. Her right eye had gone dark and her left was looking at the top of the seat. "I'm not hurtin' her, Phoeb. I swear."

The dog barked.

"Tell her," he whispered.

"I'm okay, Phoebe."

The dog jumped out of the box and up on the passenger's side door.

"Don't—"

Too late. Sally had already opened the door, and the dog was in her lap.

"Cut it out, Phoeb. I didn't break her. Down!"

Phoebe sat on the floor and laid her head on Sally's thigh.

Sally stroked her silky head. "The physician's assistant's assistant. We girls look after each other, don't we, Phoebe?"

"You can tell she's never been parking."

"It can be almost as much fun as skinny-dipping." Sally smiled into the big, round eyes looking up at her from her lap.

"And almost as risky," Hank said. But he still had his arm around her shoulders, and she loved the way it felt.

"I won't hurt him either, Phoebe. I swear."

* * *

Hoolie came out of the bunkhouse to meet them as soon as they parked his truck.

"You had a call from your favorite neighbor," he told Sally. "Claims a loose horse caused him to run into the ditch. I drove all the way up to his place and back, didn't see nothin'. No horse, no fence down, nothin'. Did you see anything?"

"We saw horses." Hank tossed Hoolie his keys. "Nice ride."

"They're right where they're supposed to be," Sally said.

"Except the high one Damn Tootin' rode in on. He said he reported *the incident* to the sheriff. You know what he's tryin' to do, don't you?"

"Drive me to commit murder?"

"Build some kind of a case. You know how he loves to sue people."

"Good. We'll kick his ass in court. That might be more fun than murder."

"Maybe he's trying to wear you down." Hoolie planted his hands on his indeterminate hips. "Keep you dancin' till you drop."

Sally sighed. "The trouble is he's got friends in high places."

"So do you," Hoolie said. "Maybe not so much around here, but there's high places all over the country, and they're full of horse lovers."

"Good point." Sally glanced at Hank. "The trouble is, sometimes those high places are too far off. All politics is local."

"A politician is your friend until he gets a better offer."

"*The trouble is* we don't have any more to offer."

"I didn't say *more*. I said better." Hoolie folded his arms. "Don't dance for him. You can put your energy to better use. Not to mention your considerable imagination."

"Another good point." She smiled. "Thank you for persisting in making it."

"No trouble." He stepped back. "I'll say good night, then."

Hank took his keys from his pocket, clicked the remote and whistled for Phoebe.

"Where are you going?" Instantly, Sally wished she could call back the question, or at least the anxious tone.

"Nowhere. Putting Phoebe to bed and getting my stuff."

"You're making her sleep in the pickup? Phoebe!" The dog perked her ears, but she stood her master's ground. "Oh, Hank, she can come in the house with you."

"You keep your dog in the house?" He sounded surprised. "We go by house rules."

"Baby has her own corner in the bunkhouse. We

have a cat in the house, but she doesn't believe in dogs. She barely acknowledges people. I'll bet Phoebe's used to sleeping with you."

"The Lakota don't sleep with their dogs," he said. "Phoebe sleeps wherever I put her bed. Where do you want her?"

"I didn't mean to insult you. I just didn't want you to think you had to—"

He challenged her with a hard look and a harder stance. "What's the big damn deal about my sleeping arrangements?"

"It's no big damn deal. You do what you want. I just want Phoebe to be comfortable."

"Comfortable? Okay, she likes to sleep on the east side of the house near an outside door and an open window on a feather bed."

"That can be arranged." She spun away and tripped.

He caught her. "What's wrong, Sally?"

"Defensive clumsiness. When I get rattled, I spaz out sometimes. Great way to ruin a dramatic gesture." She glowered. "What's your excuse?"

"Defensive gruffness."

"That's against house rules, but we'll call it even since it sounded like good ol'-fashioned sarcasm to me. I can hardly fault anybody for that." She signaled, "No penalty."

"You sure you want me to bring her bed in the house?"

"I'm sure this dog gets every vaccination and pre-
ventive treatment on any vet's list. So I want you to
put her bed where the sun don't shine—" she smiled
"—in the afternoon."

He hauled his duffel bag and Phoebe's denim
pillow into the house and settled the dog down. He
wasn't kidding about the outside door. Then he
followed Sally through the living room, around the
stairs, and down the hall, where they crossed paths
with a calico cat, which scampered up the stairs.

"This is my room," Sally said of the first door in the
hall. "It's also my office. Next is the main bath. I'll
work around your shower schedule." She pushed the
last door open and flipped the light on. "I'm putting
you in this room because Zach and Annie have the
upstairs. This used to be Grandma's room, which is
why everything's purple. But now it's a guest room. I
think you'll be comfortable. The trees shade the
windows and keep it cool. There's a half bath through
there. Say the word if you need anything. Help yourself in the kitchen anytime, anything you want. There's
a TV in the den, just off the living room. And, um…"
She looked up at him. "Thank you for doing this for
us."

"No trouble."

"That I can't guarantee. Sleep well."

"You, too. I enjoyed the tour."

She gave a little nod, a wistful smile. She didn't

quite know what to make of him, and he hadn't quite decided what to do with her.

It was going to be an interesting three weeks.

Chapter Four

"Kevin's back," Hoolie announced as he came thumping in the back door. "Add one for supper. Any coffee left?"

"It's cold, but you can nuke it. I'm brewing iced tea."

Sally laid aside the ice pack she'd been using on her right eye and filled the teakettle. Hoolie was still banging around in the mudroom, and she was only getting about half of what he was saying, but she'd catch up on the rerun. He had a habit of repeating himself, especially if one of the teens court-ordered to work at the sanctuary was giving him trouble.

"So I've got him ridin' fence along the highway," was the upshot as he clomped into the kitchen. "You know damn well there was no horse on the road, but that don't mean Tutan didn't put another hole in the fence to back up his story. We got some volunteers set to help cut hay this weekend. So Hank and me, we're gonna…" He noticed the ice pack. "You feelin' okay, big sister?"

"I'm not okay with that question." Cold packs were her standard first-line remedy, and they were helping. Loss of vision in one eye wasn't unusual with multiple sclerosis, but neither was remission. She'd had this problem before and regained a good measure of sight back. She'd do it again without losing ground anywhere else. Not for a good long while.

She closed the microwave door on his cold coffee and pressed the button. "My health is my business. I want nothing but positive health vibes. That wheelchair is staying in the basement. There's only one person around here who needs a cane."

"Crutch."

"This reprieve could last for months. Years, maybe."

"Trouble with your eye again?"

"A little, but I'm loading up on vitamins." She believed in vitamins. Exercise, meditation, hydrotherapy—she believed in believing. She popped the microwave open and handed Hoolie his coffee. "You and Hank are going to what?"

"Move the cows."

"You can't ride with that ankle."

"I'm not okay with that order." He pulled two chairs away from the kitchen table, sat in one and propped his foot with its dirtier-by-the-day cast on the other. "I'm taking this damn thing off. My foot itches. That means the mummy boot has been on long enough."

"What does Hank say?"

Hoolie questioned her with a look.

"He's a professional."

"You ask him about your eye, and I'll ask him about my ankle."

"No deal." She snatched the whistling kettle off the stove. "I know more about MS than most doctors. These symptoms come and go. Eventually, some of them come and stay, but I'm not on any fast track to eventually." She pointed to his ankle. "*That* is going to heal. Give it time, and it'll go the way of all your other previously broken bones."

"My health is my business," he echoed in an irritating falsetto.

"Not when all your stories end with *I got the scars to prove it.*"

"I tell it like I remember it. The truth is always in there somewhere." He sipped his coffee. "I said I'd look after you."

"Look all you want. Just don't talk about it." She laid a hand on his bony shoulder. "I'll ride with Hank. We'll move the cows, and then we'll ride out to Coyote Creek and see if we can get a look at the Don."

"If something happens, you tell him why. You wouldn't fall so much if you'd keep a cane handy when you get tired or—"

"Three weeks." She squeezed his shoulder. "That's all I'm asking."

Hank was finishing up the hooves on the saddle horses when Sally came looking for him in the barn. From the first, he'd had her figured for a night person. Seemed he was right. Their ships would be passing mid to late morning, which was fine by him. Hoolie had filled him up with a hearty breakfast while they planned a few things out. He met one of the helpers he kept hearing about—Indian kid named Kevin Thunder Shield, who showed up ready to ride. Hoolie hooked the kid up with a horse and gave him an assignment, but Hank couldn't let the gelding go without a hoof trimming. And he wasn't herding any cattle until the rest of the saddle horses got the same treatment.

"That looks great," Sally said of the third set of hooves he'd filed. "You are *good*."

"The trim's the important part. Right, girl?" He patted the black mare's rump. She'd behaved well. Hard to believe she'd ever been wild. "The shoes are icing on the cake. It's getting the right trim that makes the difference for most horses."

"We go easy on the icing around here."

"And that's fine. These horses don't have to hang out in stalls and watch their toenails grow. Except that one." He pointed to a big gray gelding. "Without shoeing that crack will keep growing."

Sally ran her hand down the horse's leg toward the hoof. "I didn't see that."

"I'll take care of it when we get back. Hoolie and me, we're gonna do some cowboyin'."

She straightened and faced him with folded arms. "You were going to let Hoolie ride with that cast on his foot?"

"I was gonna ride with Hoolie. Figured he could do what he wanted with his foot."

"Any objection to riding with me?"

He shrugged. "I'm here to help out."

"Weak," she warned.

"Let me try again. Objection? Hell, no. My pleasure."

"That's the spirit." She gave a tight smile. "I'm an excellent cowboy."

"I don't doubt it."

She sighed and put her arms around the big gray gelding's neck, nuzzling his thick black mane. "But I was hoping to ride Tank."

"Tank?" Hank chortled. "I'll have Tank retreaded for you by tomorrow." He started loading his files and nippers into his shoe box. "I thought I'd try a Double D mustang. Maybe Zach has some started. I'm a pretty good finisher."

"Me, too."

"Once they're green broke, I can put a nice handle on 'em."

"I'll bet." She raked her fingers through the gelding's mane. "Tank was my first adoption. When I picked him out ten years ago, he was as wild as they come. I was a stock contractor back then, but Tank really opened my eyes."

Hank eyed the horse. "He's no Spanish Mustang."

"Of course not. Like so many wild horses, he's got a lot of draft blood in him. You know, a lot of them just sort of walked off into the sunset back in the days when farmers started going horseless. And during the Depression, when they were going homeless. Tank's forebears were equine hobos." She unhooked one of the horse's crossties. "Can't you just see them running across a herd of mustangs in the Badlands? Freeee at last!" she whinnied, and Tank's ears snapped to attention.

Hank couldn't help smiling. "Until they got their farm-boy asses kicked."

"This big steel-drivin' man's gonna fix your hoof, Tank, so let's let that remark pass." She hooked a lead rope to the halter, scratched the horse's neck, and he lowered his head. "If he calls you farm boy, he's Henry," she said in the horse's ear.

"Nothin' wrong with Henry."

"I didn't say there was. Some of my best friends are named Henry."

"Hoolie?" he asked. She nodded. "Like I said, it's a good backup name. What's yours? Bet your mama didn't name you Sally."

"Ain't tellin'. It's a good name, but it doesn't fit me, so I don't use it." She pointed to a small buckskin gelding. "I'm riding him. He fits me well. We call him Little Henry."

Hank cracked up.

They rode side by side, soaking in sights and sounds and smells of summer in South Dakota without talking much. It was enough to point out the circling hawk, the coyote on the hill, the hidden gopher hole and to keep riding, keep looking and listening to the birds in the air, the insects in the grass, the thump-swish-thump of their mounts. It all felt right to Hank, as though he, too, had found a fit. Be damned if he'd try to work up some discomfort over feeling comfortable, not while it was working for him. This feeling was sacred.

He'd gotten away from the traditional practices his parents' generation had struggled to take back from obscurity—ceremonies nobody wanted to explain and a language hardly anybody used—but he'd soaked up the stories. The People had emerged from the Black Hills. *Paha Sapa.* White Buffalo Calf Woman had given them the pipe, and the horse—*Sunka Wakan,* or sacred dog—had given them a leg up in a land only the Lakota truly understood and appreciated in its natural state. It was grassland. Pull the grass up by the roots, and the earth would fly away. Tell the river how to run, and you would pay a price that had less to do with money than with home. And home, for the Lakota, had less to do with a place to live than with a place to walk.

Preferably a dry one.

Hank loved the stories and honored the wisdom even if he'd taken up a different kind of medicine. Even if he'd let his family fall apart—the traditional Lakota's worst nightmare—he believed that all people were relatives. All things? Being equal—not in this lifetime. But being relative? Sure. Relative to family life, being alone sucked.

Relative to reservation life, the old ways were healthy and holy. Relative to urban life, the reservation wasn't half bad.

But relative to anyplace he'd ever been—and he'd been all over—the vicinity of the Black Hills felt right.

The Double D was southeast of the Hills, but Hank could see their silhouette looming at the edge of the grasslands like a hazy purple mirage, a distant village of ghost tipis. The sight was beyond beautiful. Its power worked his soul's compass like polar magnetism. His whole body knew what it was about. It had been years since he'd pushed cattle on horseback, and while the method hadn't changed, he realized the madness was gone. He was no longer the angry young man who resented the cattlemen who leased the Indian land its owners couldn't afford to use. It didn't matter that none of the animals belonged to him or that the land they were crossing was claimed by someone else. He was one with the horse, and the woman who rode abreast of him functioned easily as his partner. Cows moved willingly as long as their calves bleated regularly to check in. They must have known the grass was greener wherever they were headed. Maybe they trusted Sally not to let them down. They belonged to her, after all. They must have known something.

You've never had much luck with women, Night Horse. Maybe you should take it from her animals. Just go along with her. Nothing to worry about.

Either that or just take it. Take as much as she offers. Hell, the first few weeks are always the best.

Hank drew in a whole chestful of clean Black Hills air. He had a bad habit of thinking too deep and breathing too shallow. He was attracted to this woman, pure and simple. Thinking only complicated the matter.

Stop thinking, Night Horse. Enjoy the pure and simple. She's pure. You're simple.

Sally loved the way her world looked from the top of a horse. The way Little Henry's gait made her hips move, the way he smelled, the way he snorted and strutted and swished his tail and made her sit up a little straighter, feel just slightly bigger than life—she loved every heady detail. But put the joy of sitting her horse together with the pleasure of watching Hank sit his, and Sally was all sweet spot. Watching him swing down from the saddle and open a wire gate gave her goose bumps. Pushing the cattle through the gate gave a taste of success, and making it happen together rubbed her utterly the right way.

She watched him muscle the wire loop over the top of the gate post, admired his easy mount, lit up inside when he looked her way as if to say, *What can I do for you now?*

"Follow me," she called out. "Let's take a ride to the wild side."

Little Henry pricked his ears, and Sally shifted her weight and gave him his head. She bid her hat good riddance as the wind rushed through her hair. Hank could have flown past her if he wanted to—his mare was faster than her little gelding—but he gave his horse cues according to her pace. When they reached the creek, Little Henry splashed right in. The crossing required a few yards of swimming this time of year, but nothing major.

For Sally.

She *whooped* and the water *swooshed* as Little Henry bounded up on dry land. Wet to the hip, she was loving every drop of water, every ray of sunshine, every bit of breeze. She circled her mount and saw Hank eyeing the water warily from the opposite bank.

"Don't worry," she called out. "She's a good swimmer."

"I'm not."

"You don't have to be. I promise."

He looked up at her. He'd held on to his hat, but clearly he wasn't so sure about the value of her promise.

"I can go back and lead you across."

"Hell, no." He continued to stare at the water. "What's my horse's name?"

"Ribsy."

"What kind of a name is that for a horse?"

"It's from a book. My sister named her." What difference did it make? What the heck was in a horse's name? He wasn't moving. Wasn't looking at anything but the water. Needed a moment, maybe. "My sister, the teacher. It's a kid's book." No connection. "Ribsy's Henry's best friend." Still no movement. "Ribsy's a dog."

He looked up. "This horse is named after a dog?"

"*Henry and Ribsy.* Ribsy's a dog."

"*Hoka Hey!*" Hank called out as he nudged the mare with his boot heels.

She took the plunge. Hank kept his seat, and the big black easily ferried him across the water. He looked a little sallow, but his dignity was still intact.

"What did you call me?" Sally asked, grinning like a proud instructor. "Hooker something?"

"I said, *Hoka Hey!* It's a good day to die." He leaned forward and patted the mare's neck. "*Sunka Wakan.*"

"That's right," she enthused. "It means *holy dog,* doesn't it? Well, there you go. Ribsy, Phoebe and me, we're your destiny. Stick with us, and your hydrophobia will be cured."

"What's that?" He glanced back at the murky water. "A monster with a bunch of arms?"

"I think that's a hydra."

"Yep. They're all down there." He looked up at her and smiled sheepishly as he joined her on the high ground. "Kind of embarrassing. I had a bad experience when I was a kid."

"Maybe you should try a different war cry."

They covered a lot of ground and saw a couple of eagles, a few deer and a few dozen mustangs before they found Don Quixote, a stout bay who'd surrounded himself with the prettiest mares on the Double D. There were roans and paints, mouse-brown grullos, buckskins and "blondies." After what had turned out to be a more tiring ride than she'd expected, Sally was energized simply by the sight of them, mainly courtesy of her left eye. But the vision of blue sky, green grass, striated hills and a motley band of mustangs was glorious. She didn't have to see Hank's excitement. She could feel it. His rapt interest was palpable.

"Let's get down for a while," he said quietly, as though speaking might disturb something.

She nodded. He must have sensed her weariness

because he swung to the ground and came to her, and she dismounted with far less grace than she would have wished. He noticed. He didn't say anything, but he took her full weight in his arms, drew her up to him and recharged her with a deep, delicious kiss.

It wasn't until he took his lips from hers that she realized she couldn't feel her right leg. She had to hang on to him—not that she didn't want to, but not for this reason.

"You made the earth move under my feet," she said. "Either Night Horse or Charley horse, I'm not sure— ah!" The sound of sharp pain was an innocent lie, if there was such a thing. Everybody understood pain, at least to some extent. Numbness was harder to explain.

"Damn cousin Charley's beatin' my time." He supported her against his right side. "Can't let him get away with it." He brought the horses along on the left and found a little grass for everybody on the shady side of a clump of chokecherry bushes.

"Better already." Her butt welcomed contact with good old terra firma, but she felt obliged to protest. "I'm okay now."

"Not so fast. I know how to—"

"Seriously, it's coming back."

"That's Charley for you. Right calf?" He massaged with practiced hands. She didn't feel much at first, but her nerves responded steadily to his gentle kneading. "This can be a sign of calcium deficiency."

"I'll load up on it tomorrow."

"I'm a big believer in truth and supplements for all."

"Good to know."

"Better?"

"Infinitely. Like your talents." Smiling, she grabbed his hand. "Wait. I think he's moving into my feet."

"Sorry, Charley," he quipped as he slid his hands down to her boot.

She stilled them with hers. "I'll take a rain check."

"Sounds good." He went to his saddle and brought back the canvas pack he'd tied behind the cantle. Squatting on his heels, he took out a bottle of water and cracked open the plastic cap. "It might be warm, but it's wet."

"You think of everything." She took a long drink.

"Second nature when you spend your life on the road."

"I'll bet you're starving. I do have supper waiting in the refrigerator. I almost brought something along, but then I thought, no, we'll be sweaty and dirty, and we'll appreciate it more after we get back, and it's nice and fresh and…" She handed him the bottle. "Annie would have packed a nice picnic. She's like you. She thinks of everything."

He took a drink from the bottle and laughed. "It's just water."

"I'm easy." She smiled. "Simple pleasures. I don't do this often enough. I used to ride out here all the time, but it's become…" She gazed at the bluffs in the distance. "I've become lazy. It's easier to hop in the pickup. And now that Zach's come on board…"

"You don't get out here in a pickup. It's too rough."

"And we don't want this area disturbed by anything motorized." She pointed west. "There's some public land beyond those hills. Very isolated. And there's tribal land adjoining that." She swung her hand in a northerly arc. "If…*when* we get those new leases, we'll almost double our carrying capacity. The Tribal Council has been very supportive of our program, but Dan Tutan's been leasing it forever, and he pays practically nothing for grazing permits on the public land. He has his own support from Pierre all the way to Washington."

"You're running publicly protected wild horses for the Bureau of Land Management, aren't you? You should get preference. Plus, if you've got the Tribal Council…"

"We have the majority. We're…pretty sure we do."

"You can never be too sure about those Indians."

"I'm not too sure about *you*." She smiled. "But I know what *assume* makes out of me." She lifted one shoulder. "And Tutan's been taking us all for granted for far too long. He knows how to work the system. Like anything involving property, it's all about location."

"Tell us about it." He glanced at the barren draw below. "I've got some beachfront reservation land for sale. Complete with a big bridge."

"I'll take it," she enthused. "Where do I sign?"

"I'll have my people draw up the treaty." He adjusted his hat by the brim, leaned back on his elbows and eyed her for a moment. "You've got a good thing goin' here. Why push it?"

"Because we can." She leaned closer. "Because the push needs to be made. More needs to be done, and we can do it. All we have to do is show that our program is viable, that we can handle more land, more stock, and we're in the catbird's seat. Tutan's free rein over the range will soon be over. For a considerable piece of these grasslands, it's back to nature."

"This part doesn't look like it's ever been away."

"My father never got much use out of this part of the ranch. He would have sold it, but back then there weren't any takers. But the takers are…" The look in his eyes set her back on her heels. *The takers are what? The takers are who?* "I don't want to take any more land. I want to set some aside, and I'm willing to pay for the privilege of standing aside." She smiled. "Pay with what? you may ask. My sister asks every other day. I have to get creative about getting more public support."

"I seem to recall some mention of a plan."

"Plan? What plan?" Mock innocence was one of her favorite shticks.

"It was on hold for the wedding. Then you had to get the honeymoon back on track. You are one smooth operator, Sally." He plucked a droopy-headed grass stem and stuck it in the corner of his mouth. "So, what's the plan, and how many days before you have it in place? You've got what? Twenty-one?"

"Give or take." She smiled. "Sam told the newly-weds to stay as long as they wanted."

"And Zach told me if I had any problems, he could be back in twenty-four hours."

"No worries, mate."

"If I were a worrier, the words *creative* and *plan* might give me pause."

"I'm glad you're not." Arms around her legs, she drew her knees up for a chin rest. "Because if I had a plan, I'd really want to tell you about it. I would *really* value your thoughts. You strike me as a practical man. And I'm a creative woman." She gave a slow, sensual smile. "Yin and yang."

"Hmm. If I were a thinking man, my first thought would be…" He winked. "Somebody's yin-yangin' my chain."

She groaned. "Is that what passes for humor where you come from?"

"Well, there's Indian humor, and there's eduma-cated Indian humor."

"Edumacated?"

"Half-assed educated, which is a dangerous thing."

"Zach says you're the best doc he knows."

"If they ain't broke, I can fix 'em up good enough for the next round. You can't take the cowboy out of the rodeo unless he's out cold. Then he can't argue." He tossed his chewed grass. "'Course, I'm not a doctor. Started out to be, got myself edumacated."

"Meaning?"

"Got married, had a kid, dropped out of school."

"Happens to a lot of us. Even without the marriage and kid part." She thought twice, but it wasn't enough to stop her. "What happened to your son?"

"He got hit by a car. He was in a coma for six months. By the time he died…" He drew a long, deep breath and sighed. "By the time we let him go, we had nothin' left." He lifted one shoulder as he scanned the hills. "Bottom line, I thought she was watchin' him, she thought I was watchin' him." He shook his head, gave a mirthless chuckle. "It's not the bottom line that kills you. It's all the garbage you have to wade through before you find it. And when you do, hell, there's no way to forgive if you can't even look at each other anymore."

Sally could not speak. Her throat burned, and she knew it would be a mistake to open her mouth. She knew hospitals. Technicians with their tests, nurses with their needles, doctors with no answers—she knew them all. She imagined them easily. She knew what it felt like to be poked and prodded and eye-balled. It could be painful. It was often scary. When it became part of life's routine, it was miserable, maddening, frustrating, and it hurt. Physically, when it was your own body, it hurt. Sometimes you thought, *if this kills me, that'll be it. Over and out.* She could imagine that part. Easily. What she could not imagine was sitting beside the bed rather than lying in it, watching over your child, losing your child piece by piece until finally the terrible word had to be said.

She reached for his hand. He flinched, but she caught him before he could draw away and kissed him, there on the backs of his healing fingers, rough knuckles, tough skin. She met his wary gaze. Her eyesight was a little hazy, but her heart was not. Whatever she was feeling, it wasn't pity. Wouldn't give it, couldn't take it.

He smiled, just enough to let her know he understood.

"So." He glanced away, withdrew his hand, gave a brief nod. "Back to the plan."

Hank thought it over on the ride back. She was pretty quiet—must've talked herself out—and he had time to watch the evening sky begin to change colors while he thought about the land, the horses, Sally and her big plan. She wanted to publicize the merits of the sanctuary and the appeal of owning a once-wild horse. She'd done some Internet research and pitched the idea of a documentary, but only a couple of documentary producers had responded, and they'd said the story had been done. She needed a new angle.

"I have a killer idea that I haven't told anybody about except Hoolie. And now you." Her secret Henrys, she'd called them, but he couldn't see her keeping any secrets the way this one had tumbled out of her. She wanted to hold a competition for horse trainers. They would choose a horse from the best of the three- and four-year-olds, and they would commit to conditioning, gentling and training the horse to perform. She would bring in experienced judges, award *big, huge* cash prizes and auction off the horses. "It's got everything," she'd claimed. "History, romance, suspense, sports, gorgeous animals in trouble, beautiful people who care, and lots and lots of money."

Hank had enjoyed the sound of her enthusiasm so much, he hadn't asked whether the beautiful people cared about the animals or the money. He hadn't asked where the money would come from. Maybe Zach's brother, Sam, would sponsor the whole thing. He'd hit the jackpot, and he seemed like a good guy.

Covering the last mile between a job well done and supper, Hank knew one thing about the woman riding at his side: she lived for wild horses. She was the real Mustang Sally. She was serious about her dream, and no matter how big the undertaking, she would do what she had to do to make it come true. He was sure she had him figured into her doings somehow. It would be fascinating to watch the woman roll out the rest of her strategy. She'd already shown him she could get something out of him he never, *ever* gave.

Now it was his turn. She was keeping something close to the chest, some heavy weight that bore down on her. He'd seen it knock her over. He'd watched her get right back up. He wouldn't press her—she had enough pressure—but she was going to have to strip off more than her clothes. Whatever she was figuring him for, trust would be the price for Night Horse insurance.

They crossed paths with Hoolie on his way out the back door. The way he said *hope you two had a nice time* made it sound like he was mad about something—supper, maybe, although he said he and Kevin hadn't waited—and Hank questioned Sally with a look. She smiled, shrugged it off, said *we did* to the slamming door. "Grumpy old men," she stage-whispered.

"I got twenty-twenty hearing, big sister."

"I love you, too, ya big grump." She lowered her voice. "The older he gets, the more he sounds like a mother hen."

"Thirty-thirty," was the rejoinder from the yard.

"Shoot me, then," Sally called back, eyes sparkling. "Chicken sandwich anyone?" she whispered.

She wasn't kidding about the chicken. Hank was used to cold suppers, but not like this. Sally piled on the fruits and vegetables, fresh-picked garden greens, potato salad and whole-grain bread. At first glance, it struck him as a woman's kind of meal. At first bite, a man found himself taking his time. No rush to fill up when there was taste and talk on the table.

"I think your plan for a horse-training contest could work." He could tell he had her at *work,* but he added, "I'd compete."

"I was hoping you'd help me run it."

"That wouldn't play to my strong suit. I'm not much of a runner." He leaned back in his chair and eyed her thoughtfully. "Especially behind a friend's back. What do the newlyweds think about running a contest?"

"They're on their honeymoon, for which I thank you very much." Sally popped a green grape into her mouth. "Annie thinks we've already bitten off more than we can chew. She's very careful, very conservative."

"And she married a cowboy?"

"You toss *careful* and *conservative* out the door when you fall in love. At least, that's what I've heard." She went for another grape. "I don't have time for *conservative.* Or patience. I know it's a virtue, but time doesn't stand still while we take small bites and chew thoroughly. This land and these horses look tough, but they're vulnerable. They're right for each other— they *need* each other. We've come a long way getting them back together, and we can't backtrack. Every acre we add to our program is home for another horse." She lifted one shoulder. "Okay, a tenth of a horse, which is why we need more acres. They need space. Wide-open space. You can't have wild horses without wild places."

"I'm down with you on wildness, but I'm no organizer."

"I just need an able-bodied ally. Somebody who knows horses." She leaned toward him. "You wouldn't have to stick around. Just help me get started. Back me up."

"I'm not from this reservation," he reminded her. "I can back you up, but you're always gonna have holdouts on the council."

"I know, but you're cousins, right?"

"We're all related."

"I'm not saying you all look alike to me. The Oglala and the Hunkpapa are like cousins, aren't they? And you're Hunkpapa."

"A woman who knows her Indians." He gave half a smile.

"Not *my* Indians. And I know cousins compete with each other, just like sisters do."

"When we say *all my relatives,* we mean you, too."

"But you don't include *Damn Tootin'.* He's all about Tutan, and nobody else."

"We won't let him in the circle or the contest," Hank assured her. "I'm here for you, Sally. For three weeks. What do you want me to do?"

"I've already written a proposal, and the BLM is

sending someone out to look me over. Basically make sure I can do what I said I could do, which is set the thing up and make it happen."

"And your sister doesn't know about any of this?"

"I want to see if it's even feasible first. I need to pass muster with the bureaucrats so they'll let us use the horses this way. If the BLM approves, I know Annie and Zach will be thrilled. And won't that be some wedding present?" She reached across the table and laid her hand on his arm. "Just help me look good, okay? Me and the horses."

"You look fine, Sally. You and the horses."

"Thanks." She drew a deep breath. "My only other worry is Tutan and his little shenanigans. Not to mention his connections."

"You know…" He turned his arm beneath her hand and drew it back until their palms slid together. "I don't like Tutan."

"He doesn't know his Indians." She smiled and pressed her hand around his. "Why didn't you tell him the Night Horse who worked for him was your father?"

"I'm not tellin' him anything." He lifted one shoulder. "He's probably checked me out, probably knows by now."

"What happened?" she asked gently.

"My father had some problems, but he wasn't afraid to work." He looked into her eyes, saw no prejudgment, no preemptive pity. Nothing but willingness to listen. "Jobs are hard to find on the reservation, so he'd go wherever the work was and do whatever he was asked to do. He used to hire on for Tutan, and he'd be gone for weeks at a time.

"Come deer season, Tutan liked to have weekend hunting parties for his friends—probably some of those important connections you're talking about—and he'd take one of his hired hands along to bird-dog for him. You know, beat the brush, flush out the game. Half those guys didn't know the butt from the barrel, but they knew how to party."

"Which resulted in the so-called hunting accident."

"Out there alone, got drunk, fell on his gun." He shook his head. "Tragic."

"How old were you?"

"Old enough to know that dog wouldn't hunt. Not unless he was on somebody's payroll." He shook his head. "He wouldn't take my brother and me hunting. Said he'd had enough of it when he was a kid. He didn't hunt for sport. He called and said he wasn't coming home that weekend because Mr. Tutan's friends wanted to do some hunting, and Dad was gonna make some extra cash.

"He'd been dead for weeks when they found him. Tutan had about as much to say as he did the other night. He thought John Night Horse had gone home after he'd drawn his last wages for the season. Tutan didn't post his land, so, sure, hunters came around all the time, but nobody had stopped in that weekend, friends or otherwise."

"So it could have been an accident."

"I didn't think so, but who listens to a twelve-year-old kid?"

"What about your mother?"

"People believe what they want to believe, she said. Indian blood is cheap. Accidents, suicide, murder—what's the difference? Dead is dead. And she proved that by dying when I was fifteen."

"What do you believe?" she asked softly.

"I believe life is life." He gave her hand a gentle squeeze. "From first breath to last, it's up to you to live it in a good way."

"I'll drink to that." She took up her water with her free hand, paused mid-toast and took a closer look at her glass. "What about blood? Are some kinds dearer than others?"

"You're lookin' at one Indian whose blood ain't cheap." He waited for her eyes to actually meet his. "O positive. Universal donor." He smiled. "Priceless."

Chapter Five

Sally was up early.

She'd checked her e-mail—the honeymooners had landed safely and a group of church campers wanted to schedule a day trip to the sanctuary—and paid some bills online before leaving the room that had served variously as the "front" bedroom, the den, the office and now all three rolled up into Sally's lair. She refused to consider it her confines, but there were times when parts of her body wouldn't do much. For Annie's sake she came out for meals, but otherwise she worked long hours in the office. She profiled every animal on the place, recorded every piece of machinery, kept the books, researched everything from parasites to nonprofits and hatched plans. Her motto was: When the Moving Gets Tough, the Tough Get Moving. One of these days she was going to stitch up the words into a little plaque.

Just as soon as she learned to stitch, which wasn't happening anytime soon. Not as long as the good times were walkin' instead of rollin'.

She helped herself to coffee, popped an English muffin in the toaster and glanced out the back window.

Here came Grumpy.

She couldn't get it through Hoolie's head that as long as she could get up and go, she was going. He knew as well as she did that her physical condition was predictably unpredictable. Most people didn't believe they could get seriously sick or hurt anytime. They *knew* it, but they didn't *believe* it. Sally remembered what that carefree, wasted-on-the-healthy frame of mind was like. She'd been there, BMS—before multiple sclerosis. MS had made a believer of her. Her body could turn on her anytime. Just a matter of time.

She'd had to admit that her eye had been bothering her. She was in the knowing-but-not-really-believing stage—was that the same as denial?—but Hoolie couldn't be denied. He was old and dear, and he knew better. Annie was young and dear, and she could be put off. So, yes, she'd been waking up some mornings—just *some*—feeling like she had something in her right eye. And sometimes—like the other night in the pickup with Hank—it would totally blur up as though she were crying Vaseline. Weird. These things often hit her when she was feeling stressed, which was hardly what she'd been feeling that night.

Hoolie mounted the back steps, crutch thumping, black shepherd in tow. He told the dog to stay outside, but she took off as soon as the door closed, presumably in search of somebody else to herd.

"Have you guys *edumacated* Phoebe and Baby yet?" The word was Hank's. She felt giddy about knowing it and saying it, like a girl with a crush. She laughed at the funny look Hoolie gave her. "Hank's teaching me to talk Indian. He got himself *edumacated.* I guess it's learning the hard way."

"Seems like a real smart fella. Zach says he's halfway to bein' a doctor and twice as good as most of them he knows. Guess he's met a few." He glanced down at his cast. "So, if I have any more trouble with this, I can probably…you know…"

"Ask him to take a look. I doubt if he'd charge you much." She pulled a chair out from the table and spun it around. "You know, you're supposed to use two crutches."

He ignored the comment, but he accepted the chair.

"I didn't mean to get testy last night. You were gone a long time, and it's been a while since you've been on a horse."

"It was wonderful." She positioned a second chair

for his footstool. "It was just what the halfway doctor would have ordered. *If* orders were in order."

"What's he chargin' for fixing up Tank's hooves? He's out there now gettin' set to work on him. You might wanna go watch and learn."

"Like I've never seen horseshoeing done before." She headed for the coffeepot.

"Not like this. Hank's firing up for a hot shoeing. Got his portable forge out. Took his shirt off. Got a nice set of tools all laid out." He nodded his thanks for the coffee she handed him. "Sometimes they charge extra for hot shoeing, but they say it's worth it."

She laughed. "If I didn't know you better, I'd say you were playing a game that has everything to do with firing up, nothing to do with horseshoes."

"Game? What game? I'm just sayin'…"

"I have a couple of volunteers coming in today, and I thought we'd get them started on—"

"Mowing the ditches along the right-of-way and putting up the new snow fence. I'm already on it." He raised one unruly eyebrow. "In case you wanted to take Hank something cold and wet, there's pop in the fridge."

"I don't want to give him the wrong idea. I'll just take him some ice water." *In a tall, sweaty glass.*

The smell of burning charcoal drifted through the barn's side door, where Sally was greeted by wagging tails and canine smiles. Phoebe and Baby were buds. The Dog Whisperer had spoken.

Her ear followed the soft metallic *tap tap tap* to the bright side of the barn where the big door stood open, the big gray gelding was cross-tied and the big bronze man wielded hammer over nail. Wearing a short leather apron over his jeans, Hank bent to the task supporting the horse's front leg on his knee, lining hoof up with shoe and chewing on a nail. His shoulders glistened, forearms flexed, hair curtained his face, sweat rolled down the side of his face. He looked magnificent.

He plucked the horseshoe nail from his mouth, lined it up, and spoke without sparing her a glance. "I had to score and burn the hoof a little bit above the crack. That's the key to keeping a quarter crack like this from reaching the corona. You keep shoes on him until the hoof grows out, he'll be fine. You say he's never been shod?" *Tap tap tap.*

"I didn't see that crack. I should've noticed."

"I'm not faulting you." He lowered the gelding's leg and straightened slowly. Maybe his back was stiff. More likely, he wanted to prolong the unfolding of his smooth, strapping, sweaty, dirt-streaked torso. He smiled. "I'm impressed with how cooperative he is."

"He's a good boy." She watched Hank out of the corner of her good eye as she patted the horse's flank. "Aren't you, Tanksy? You're still my boy. Henry isn't half as smooth as you are, so don't worry about being replaced."

"You have no idea." His hammer clanked into the wooden toolbox.

"I was talking about *Little* Henry. You thought I meant you? You've asked me not to call you that, so don't worry."

"Are you worried, Tank?" He scratched the horse's face. "Me, neither."

"I do love a smooth ride."

He nodded at her glass of water. "Is that for me?"

"You're welcome to it."

"Did you bring it for me?"

"Hoolie said you were out here in the hot, um…" She laughed and handed it to him. "I did. Hoolie suggested pop, but I thought water would be—"

"Thanks." In three long gulps he drained half the big tumbler.

Then he tipped his head back and let the water overflow the corners of his mouth, slide down his neck and over the hills and valleys of his chest. She watched his Adam's apple bobble once before he lifted the glass from his lips and dribbled the rest of the water over his face. A thin rivulet coursed quickly down the middle of his sleek torso and disappeared behind his belt buckle. She imagined it puddling in his belly button. Thank God she had perfectly clear vision in one eye.

Her gaze retraced its route slowly. She knew what she'd find when her train of thought reached the station. Dark-eyed male satisfaction. They loved it when a woman took the time to look, didn't mind letting it show that she liked what she saw.

"I could get you some more."

He gave a slow smile as he handed her the glass. "That hit the spot."

Touched off by his smile, her popgun laugh tickled her throat on its way out. Oh, she did like the way this man made her feel. She turned carefully—this was no time for an uneven keel—and froze halfway through her next step. And it was all his doing. His hand on her arm.

Instantly carefree, she reversed her turn and lifted her face for the kiss she felt coming. She hooked her arm over his shoulder and pressed the cool glass against his back. She felt the shock of it—or of her—shimmy through him, felt his damp heat against her breasts, smelled the fire from his portable forge and horse sweat and barn dust and the heady scent of Hank at work. She pressed close and kissed back and gave a sound of raw need and deep delight.

"Pardon my sweat," he whispered.

"It hit the spot." She giggled. A mortifying sound, but there it was, like a bee in a jar—a bright, girlish buzz in her throat. "Different strokes for different spots."

"Mmm." He let go of her arm as he stepped back, glancing at the smudge he'd left. "I stroked you a new one."

"Put your mark on me, did you?" She checked her arm, nodded, felt deliciously, dementedly silly. "I didn't mean to interrupt."

"Yeah, you did."

"I did. My boy needed a break." She glanced at the horse. "Tanks!" The animal raised his head. "You're quite welcome."

Hank chuckled. "I love me some comic relief. Have a seat, Sally. The show gets better."

"I believe it. I don't think I've ever been kissed by a man wearing an apron." Or one who hauled an anvil around. She took in the array of long handles extending from his toolbox—tongs and nippers, hammers and rasps. A bucket of water stood near the small, conical forge. "Why are you hot shoeing him? Because of the crack?"

"I pulled a side clip out of the shoe for support behind the crack. You want the hoof to grow out right, you make the right shoe." He lifted another steel masterpiece at the end of his tongs for closer inspection. "And if the shoe fits…"

"Mustangs rarely have hoof problems."

"Not if they have room to run on ground that isn't plowed or paved over."

"Or chopped up into small pastures and overgrazed." Disagreement over Western land management had raged around her all her life, but she'd taken up the opposite side of the land-use argument since her days as a rodeo stock contractor. Wildlife, including horses, needed protection. "I don't know what my father would think of what we've done with his ranch. He was a cattleman."

"You don't worry about what your neighbor says, do you?"

"Tutan? No. I worry about what he does, or what he could do. He acts like we're the ones who don't belong here, like the horses are intruding on his God-given grazing rights. Where does he get off, thinking he's entitled to use a piece of land any way he wants just because it's there?"

"Where I come from, we ask that question a lot." He poked through the nails in the tray on top of the toolbox.

She grimaced. "Serious case of the pot calling the kettle black, huh?"

"Maybe." He came up smiling. "After that kiss, I gotta wonder what else you've got cookin'."

She laughed. "I'm an acquired taste. At least that's what I'm told."

"Sounds complicated."

"And you're a meat-and-potatoes man?"

"Some people like to cover it all up with sauce, but I prefer to know what's in the pot." He ducked under the cross-tie and took up the next hoof on the far side of the horse. "Tell you what, Tank, if the kiss was any indication, she's not as complicated as she thinks she is."

She took the hint and walked away laughing.

* * *

Right.

And Hank wasn't champing at the bit to haul her back in his arms and ram his tongue down her throat.

Sally was a woman, the creature conceived for the sole purpose of complicating a man's life. She was what she thought she was and then some. Her kiss was complex, compounding his interest, confounding his brain. What did she want from him? Besides sex. That he could do, *would* do in his own good time and to their mutual satisfaction. She'd piqued his interest in more ways than one. But beyond a man's two or three straight-forward ways lay the mystifying maze of women's ways, where men could sure lose their way in a hurry.

Hank didn't care about the color of a pot so much as what it was made of and whether he could grab it by the handle without getting burned. Pretty damn hard to earn a living with blistered hands. He couldn't help wondering about that little hitch in her step as he watched her walk away.

Sashay away. Was that it? She was either flirting or hurting.

Or both. He couldn't help wondering.

He finished shoeing Tank, and then he trimmed Ribsy's hooves. He liked this work. He'd picked it up after Deborah left him. It was either fill his hands with tools or a bottle. He wouldn't want to do it full time—horseshoeing could be hard on the back—but what had started out as a therapeutic hobby had become a rewarding sideline, and working with his hands gave him time to clear his head.

Sally's interruption was like a paddle plunked in a pool. She'd stirred him up a little, but everything had cleared up when she went away.

Only she hadn't gone far. After he turned the horses out, he ran into her a few yards from the kitchen door. She was playing in real water, aiming a garden hose at a tiered planter with one hand, waving him down with the other.

"Come see the house that Zach built!"

"What house?" It looked like a huge green wedding cake with three metal scarecrows stuck into it.

"This strawberry planter. Sort of like a house."

Damn, that water looked good.

"The boys made this for us. They made these wonderful sculptures for us for Christmas. See, that's Zach with a bull." She pointed to a metal figure with a twist of sheet metal for a hat and contorted hay-rake tines serving as bowed legs and handlebar horns. "And Hoolie. And Kevin."

He studied the pieces of implement parts and scrap metal welded together, recognizing a head here, a couple of arms there, maybe a dog or a horse, another…

"And Hank!"

She blasted his ass with the hose.

If she was hoping for noise, she wasn't getting any. He turned and walked into the onslaught without hesitation, letting the water cool his chest, drench the front of his jeans, turn the dust on his boots to mud. It felt fine. Even better when he tossed his hat toward the house, took the hose from her hand, leaned over and turned the water on the back of his head. He raked it through his hair and then slurped a drink while he zeroed in on his next move. With his free hand he spun her around and shoved the end of the hose into the back of her pants.

"Eeeyiiiii!"

She snatched at the hose, grabbed, yanked and failed. "I'm caught!"

"Just barely dropped my line." He reached for the hose. "Here, stand—"

But she went down as though he'd pulled a rug out from under her, landed flat on her face in the mud.

"You okay? What happened?"

"Nothing! I tripped."

"I'm sorry. Here, let me—" her arm was tucked behind her back like a chicken wing, grappling with the hose, which she was about to dislodge "—turn it off."

"No! Leave it on. Leave it!"

"You'll slip." He stopped in his tracks. She wanted to play? He jumped over the spray she shot at him, wrested the hose away and offered her a hand. "I'm not goin' down with you if that's what you're thinkin'."

"I can do it." She waved his hand off. "I'm fine. I

can do it myself." Like a child with something to prove, she scrabbled to her feet. "See? Now…" She spread her arms wide. "Fire away. C'mon! With the hose."

"I just knocked you over with the hose."

"Bet you can't do it again." Hands on her hips, she stood firm. "Come on, hose me off."

A quick, cold shot bought Hank another round of music to his inner boy's ear. Her shrieks dissolved into laughter, at once sucking him in and drawing him out. She looked and sounded as fine as she claimed to be, and he had to laugh with her. She would have it no other way. The dogs got in on the act, and all four of them were soaked by the time Hank assumed the role of killjoy and turned off the water.

"Ah, that felt good," he admitted as they planted wet bottoms on the sun-warmed cement steps. "Now what? We go in and track up the floor, or we sit out here looking like two dogs left in the rain?"

"Speak for yourself." Sally puffed out her chest. Her wet white shirt had become a translucent third skin, her bra a silky second, and a hint of nipples the ultimate attraction. "I look like a cool cat."

"Am I your mirror?" He mussed her hair, and she countered with claw and yowl. "You do look cute."

She returned the hair mussing. "You do, too."

He nodded. "When are you gonna tell me what's goin' on with you?"

Her smile faded, and the light in her eyes dimmed.

He felt as though he'd hit her. It wasn't like him to pry, but he'd seen too many missteps, and he had a gut feeling.

He glanced away. He wouldn't ask again.

"Zach made that, huh?" He braced his elbows on his knees, laced his fingers together and stared at the planter. "When do I get some strawberries?"

"You like strawberries?" To his relief, she had perked up. "Would you rather have them for dessert tonight or breakfast tomorrow?"

"I'll take them whenever they're ready. I don't think I've ever had homegrown strawberries."

"How about homemade ice cream?" She smiled. "I've got you now, haven't I? My sister's the cook in the family, but we've got this great little machine that makes the best ice cream. That's my summertime specialty. Do you like watermelon?"

He grimaced.

"How about sweet corn? We planted tons of it. Annie's the gardener around here, too, but I really took an interest this year. The weather's been great. It feels good to dig around in the dirt. Good therapy."

"For what?"

"Anything. You name it, Doc."

"You're an interesting case. Mind if I look for a few more clues?"

"Knock yourself out."

"I've tried that, and think I'll pass." He gave a humorless chuckle. "Actually, I've done that, too. Down and out. From what I was told, it ain't pretty."

"When you're as clumsy as I am, you learn how to catch yourself."

"That's not what I see. You've learned how to *protect* yourself."

"Same thing."

"Uh-uh. I'm not a doctor, Sally, but I've done some doctoring."

"And I've done some knocking my head against the wall. Nothing a little session with Mother Earth can't cure. Down and dirty." She gave him her saucy Sally look, the one that made him itch in places it wasn't polite to scratch. "Down *in,* not out. Down deep and inside and underneath." She laid her hand on his thigh. "And you, my flawlessly fit friend with the healing hands, even you've stumbled."

"A time or two, yeah."

"And what did you do? You picked yourself up, hosed yourself off, got back in the game. Right? The more time you spend thinking about it, talking about it, picking it apart, the harder it is to get back up and get moving again." She gave him a merciless little pat before she took her hand away. "A time or two? Is that all? You're quite a paragon, Mr. Night Horse."

"Yep."

"You dry?"

"I've been dry for a while." Seven years. Lucky

seven. "I'll flip you for the shower." He pulled a quarter from his jeans. "What do you want?"

"Heads we go separate, tails we go in together."

Damn. "What do you want?"

"Ask me no questions, I'll tell you no lies." She had a half-scared look in her eyes that didn't match up with her smart mouth. "Figure it out."

She was pushing too hard, questioning herself, lying to herself, and he wasn't going there with her. He grabbed her shoulders and held her at forearm's length, willing her to give it up. Not her body. Her act. *Cut the crap, Sally.*

The look in her eyes was killing him. He covered her mouth with his and gave the kiss she had coming, the one that said *This is me, baby. Give me the real you.*

Her eyes were closed when he lifted his head. She opened them slowly, and for an instant she was his. But she promptly covered.

"That's a start," she tossed out, smiling too quickly. "There's nothing wrong with me that a little physical therapy can't put right."

"You're the damnedest woman I've ever met."

"That's what they all say."

"That won't work, either." He drew himself away. "I know people, Sally. I know when someone's been around the block a few times, and you haven't. We both have hurts, and yours didn't come from knocking yourself out. They're not of your own making." He flipped, slapped the coin on the back of his hand, and challenged her. "You either come clean with me or we ain't comin', Sally. At least not together. Heads or tails?"

"Be my guest."

Sally escaped directly to the laundry room. Three weeks. Was it too much to ask? Three weeks of remission, three weeks with a man, *this* man, *the same damn three weeks*. Couldn't she have her wish, her way for three, just *three* short weeks? She pulled a load of fluffy towels from the dryer, satisfied her nose with the fresh scent, and folded each one carefully, telling herself to straighten up, put her house in order, stop acting like a female in heat. He was willing to kiss her. He was a good kisser. It was something. She needed *something*.

Her armload of towels was something he needed, and when she heard the water running she told herself she would just slip them inside the bathroom door if the one from her room was open. The towel stand was within no-peek reach. The tub-shower combination was on the adjoining wall. The door hinges were quiet. There would be no disturbance.

As long as the curtain was closed, which it wasn't. As long as she didn't look in the mirror on the opposite wall, which she did. She would have backed away if she could have. She would have been able to if his astonishing body had presented itself to her right eye instead of her left, her good eye. But the stars were aligned for full disclosure, and her good eye was thrilled. His head was tipped back, his eyes closed, his chest taking on water, one hand braced on the wall and the other pleasuring himself.

Damn him. Why wasn't he letting her do that?

Any man who preferred his hand to a woman's body was just plain...

...not interested in the woman. For whatever reason.

Maybe it was just him.

More likely it was her. Her imperfect body.

Hell, nobody was perfect. Surely he knew that. *No body was perfect.*

Except maybe his. Damn, he looked delicious, all warm and wet and hard as rock candy. Her heart pounded, her mouth watered, and her throat went dry.

Was this what he called *coming clean?*

She called it a terrible thing to waste. She called it the worst travesty of justice she'd yet to confront, and she'd confronted some doozies. What god had she offended? Which goddess had abandoned her?

What in hell was she doing wrong?

Well, for one thing, she was staring. She unloaded the towels, stepped back, pulled the door almost shut, and then she committed the losing error. She lifted her gaze from his hand to his eyes. They were open, of course, and they had her dead to rights.

* * *

He came into the kitchen carrying his duffel bag.

She was sitting on a tall kitchen stool concentrating on keeping her hands from shaking while she shelled peas into a glass bowl. "Are you leaving?" she asked softly.

"No. I gave my word. I'll be back after I find a place to stay."

"Hank, I'm..." She sighed. She couldn't say it. She was feeling a riot of emotion, but sorry simply wasn't part of it. "You're the damnedest man I've ever met."

"Then I'd say you've met a lot of boys who only looked like men."

"You had your free look. Now I've had mine."

"Fair enough." He took a step closer, offering her no quarter. "The next one's gonna cost us both. We drop the play-acting and get real. No protection except a scrap of rubber."

"Get real? Haven't you had enough reality?"

"I don't know if I've had any."

"But that's what you're looking for?"

"If I'm looking for something, that would be it. I like your ass, Sally. Hell, I like your sass. What I don't like is the chip on your shoulder. I could knock it off, easy." He shook his head, lowered his voice. "But that wouldn't get us anywhere, would it?"

"Stay here, Hank." She pushed the bowl aside. "I really want you to stay here."

"What for?"

"For the sake of…" She lowered one leg, and her bare foot touched the floor, a cold shock. "For my sake. This chip is getting pretty heavy."

"Like I said…"

"I know, but it draws your attention, doesn't it?"

"A chip is a chip, honey. I've seen a lot of them. I know what they're about." The look in his eyes went from cold to kind. "Fear and pain."

"I'm not—"

"*I'm* not. I'm not your antidote." He waved his free hand as though sweeping cobwebs. "Let's clear the air, Sally."

She bristled. "Why? I like it steamy."

"I don't like feeling crowded. One minute we're getting to know each other, having a little fun, the next you're…" He scowled. "What do you want from me?"

"How does friendship with benefits strike you?"

"Like something out of a TV show." He gave half a smile, but the light went out of his eyes. "I can fly you to paradise on my benefits, but not for free. I'll babysit for free. You want peep shows? You want slap and tickle? That's extra."

"Wow." She clapped her hands. "Congratulations, cowboy. Way to slap my chip into next week."

"That's all it takes? You disappoint me."

"Sorry, but it's just not fair to talk about paradise

when you're throwing me under the straight-talk express."

He glowered at her. She glared right back.

One corner of his mouth twitched.

She smiled, straight up.

"Okay." He wagged his head, gave a reluctant chuckle. "Look, Sally, I've had friendship with benefits. Sooner or later one messes up the other."

"Is three weeks your idea of sooner? Or later?"

He laughed. "It's my idea of eternity if we're gonna keep this up."

"We're not. We're even." Her voice dropped to a notch above a whisper. "You took my chip, I take your point."

"I don't think so, but we'll see. Go take your shower." He tossed the duffel bag, and it slid across the floor until it hit the wall. "One of the benefits of my friendship: I'm one hell of a cook."

Chapter Six

When the call came from BLM Wild Horse Specialist Max Becker, Sally was filling out forms on the computer. Bureau forms begat Bureau calls, and Sally was not a fan of either. But Max was one of the good guys.

"So far, so good." His tone was heavy on *so far*. "Everybody I talk to likes your proposal for a trainers' competition. It falls right in line with some of our other incentive programs, and I know you'd do it up right. I'm a big Mustang Sally fan. But I just got another letter from somebody who isn't."

"Dan Tutan."

"Let's see. Yep. That would be him. Says you're letting the horses run wild." Max laughed. "Guess he's

a comedian on the side. Anyway, he copied your con-
gressional delegation and some lawyer, along with the
Cattlemen's League and the governor of South Dakota."

"Threatening what? To sue me and the horse I
rode in on?"

"To strike his magic match and hold some big feet
to the flame until he gets me fired." He chuckled. "The
horse I rode in on gets roasted over my coals."

"Are you scared?"

"Are you? This guy lives right down the road from
you. Sounds like he's the kind who rams push into
shove and takes credit for casualties."

"He's a dinosaur. They weren't green, were they?
Tutan's not green. Kill, baby, kill. That's his motto."

"Well, I gotta tell you, Sally, there's a lotta people
in the Bureau right now he can get to back his play.
The district manager's going deaf from the miners
and drillers screaming in one ear and the hunters and
ranchers barking in the other. The rangeland management specialist rolls out his tri-colored, multiple-use
spreadsheet, and before I know it, all those little
boxes are filled up with test drills and grazing
permits. He's got a few deer and antelope playing
around in the margins, but there's no place to put my
horses. They say we have to gather up another five
hundred by the end of the summer. And I say…" He
sighed wearily. "I say, give Sally Drexler's proposal

a shot. And they say, *Shot? Euth injection, or is she talking guns?*"

"Are you serious?"

"You know I'm serious, and you know where I stand, but the squeeze gets tighter every day. All options are on the table, and that includes the one no horse lover wants to hear."

"They're protected," she insisted, but she knew the Wild Free-Roaming Horses and Burros Act had been challenged continually since 1971. With so many horses confined to holding facilities, the *free-roaming* part was becoming a joke. Some in Congress were saying that *protection* was just another word for nothing left to waste money on. A welfare program for wild horses they called it, and the horse was not an endangered species. "Where's *your* spreadsheet, Max?"

"Under my pillow."

Sally groaned. "Who's the comedian now?"

"That's all I've got going for me at one of those damn meetings. Guess I'm gonna have to break down and call the Video Professor about one of those free computer-training programs."

"I'll send you one. What else do I have to do to get the go-ahead on this project?"

"It would help if your neighbor would back off."

"What else?"

"I'm willing to work with you, Sally. I can appraise trainer applications with you, and I can set up the adoption after the competition is over. I'll be down in your area in a couple of weeks. You need sponsors."

"I have them." *Almost.* Zach's brother was going to contribute to the sanctuary. She hadn't asked him to sponsor the contest yet.

"Do you have enough help out there? I hear Little Horsin' Annie got hitched to that rodeo cowboy you had working for you. That's one way to reduce the payroll."

"And Zach brought a friend onboard. A farrier." Hank wasn't there at the moment. He'd left early yesterday for a rodeo not far from the Wyoming office Max was calling from, but he'd be back today. "A *volunteer* farrier."

"Now if we can just marry you off to a veterinarian," Max teased. "Your sanctuary is a little piece of horse heaven, Sally. I'm in your corner."

She felt so much better. Max Becker was in her corner. Damn Tootin' was calling in favors from his hunting buddies. And Hank Night Horse was on board with her for three weeks. Minus three days, and he was surely counting.

Maybe she could reason with Tutan. Compromise somehow. *Come on, Dan, let's share. Let's join forces and save the world.*

Not likely. Threatening him was more his speed. But with what? Letters, litigation, lawmakers. *It's who you know that counts.*

Sally was surrounded by people who counted. She was committed to a way of life, a legacy, a whole population of animals that counted. She was needed. *She* counted. Marrying her off to a veterinarian, doctor, lawyer or Indian chief would not make a difference in how much Sally Drexler contributed to the sanctuary.

She had work to do. Some of the horses would be tamed so that some could remain wild. *Wild.* Not kept alive in a holding pen. The sanctuary wasn't wilderness, and public land wasn't exactly open range, but it was a fair imitation of freedom. Sally had learned from the mustangs—you take your bliss where you find it, and you run with it when you can.

Tutan needed some tutoring on that particular point, but maybe Sally hadn't chosen the best way to go about it during their last meeting. She'd known the man all her life, and she'd never liked him. She'd been friends with his daughter, Mary, who had declared her freedom from her overbearing father by joining the army. She hadn't seen much of his shy, ever-cloistered wife since her friend left. Maybe Mary's mother could be recruited to her cause. Audrey Tutan was a gentle soul, and Sally knew she could gain her sympathy, which might count for something. Possibly a moratorium on complaints to the BLM. Maybe a purloining of letters.

Otherwise she would move to Plan B. She would

build a threat bomb. The components were yet to be determined.

Hoolie had all volunteer hands on deck for haying, which made it a good time for Sally to pay a visit to the Tutan ranch, especially since Dan was probably out in the field, too. Fresh off the call from the BLM, Sally was itching to try her hand at woman-to-woman diplomacy.

Trying her hand at driving was another matter. It had been a couple of years since she'd driven, but she was feeling good today. Good and irritated. She was powered up, and her mission wouldn't take long. She scanned the array of keys hanging on hooks in the mudroom. She decided she could handle Hoolie's little go-fer pickup. She'd be back before anyone knew she was gone.

Sally hadn't missed driving as much as she'd thought she would. She'd never told anyone, but there had been times when she'd scared herself when she was behind the wheel, even before her nervous system had started going haywire. She took it slow, kept the dust wake to a minimum, and reached the highway without incident. And why shouldn't she? Her vision in her left eye was better than what a lot of people could claim in both eyes put together. Five slow and easy miles up the road she drove through Tutan's fancy wooden gate.

Audrey Tutan answered her front door tentatively,

as though the sunlight was too strong or the air outside was too thick. She had always reminded Sally of a caged bird. Her hair had been white ever since Sally could remember, and she had always been fair in the face and thin everywhere—lips, hips, hands, voice. She looked confused as she peered from the shadows. "Dan isn't here right now."

Sally tipped her head to one side and smiled. *Remember me, Mrs. Tutan?* "I really came to see you."

"You did?" Audrey brightened as she drew the door back. "Well, that's very nice. Please come in, Sally. You're looking well. Dan said as much after he saw you at the wedding. I mean, when he stopped by the, um… He said Hoolie was the only one using a cane." Audrey caught herself. "I hope Hoolie's all right."

"He broke his ankle, but he'll be fine."

"Was it nice?" She closed the door. "Annie's wedding, I mean. Come sit with me. I'm all by myself today."

"It was lovely." Sally followed the tiny woman into the living room with its massive pine furniture and heavily draped windows. "Very small. Family, mostly."

"When you girls were all in school, we were like family." Audrey turned, took Sally's hand and drew her down beside her on the spruce-and-pinecone sofa. "I miss those days."

"I do, too. I miss Mary. Have you heard from her

recently? We were e-mailing regularly, but so much has been happening…"

"She must be okay." Audrey glanced away. "I would've heard otherwise."

"Time gets away from us, doesn't it?" Sally gave the bony, loose-skinned hand a slight squeeze. "Audrey, I don't understand why Dan is so completely opposed to what we've done with the Double D."

"He says it's hard enough to make a living raising cattle these days without competing with animal rights fanat—" she pressed her lips tight "—folks. You know how he is."

"You know me better than that, Audrey. I'm no fanatic, but I've always loved horses. So does Mary. She used to come over all the time, and we'd ride fence and check cows. The sanctuary is a dream come true for me."

"Dan says there's plenty of horses in the world."

"How do you feel about it?"

"I'm staying out of it. He's getting older. The kids are gone. I've never been much help as far as the cattle operation goes." She shook her head slowly, a helpless gesture. "If Dan says the horses are a nuisance…"

"He's been complaining about us to the BLM. We're trying to expand the program, and he's been calling the district office in Wyoming and complaining about the people coming in and out, the horses, the fence, the way we manage just about everything."

Audrey withdrew her hand, twisted her head to the side and spoke into her shoulder. "He says you're moving in on his grass."

"It's not his grass," Sally said gently. "We're taking unadoptable horses out of crowded pens. We're giving older animals a place to live out their lives the way nature intended. Audrey, they used to slaughter them by the thousands."

"I remember."

"It could happen again." She lowered her voice. "There's talk of allowing them to be rounded up and sold for slaughter."

"I don't like to see animals suffer, but I don't know how I can help you, Sally. Dan doesn't talk to me about these things."

"I was hoping you might talk to him."

"It wouldn't matter what I said. Ranching is his life. He knows his business." Her eyes were empty. "The older we get, the less we talk."

Sally couldn't keep pressing. It was too much like throwing a stick for an old dog. For Audrey's sake, she was glad she had come, and she asked, *hoped* she would return the favor. But she knew it wouldn't happen.

Now she was eager to get home. Barreling down Tutan's gravel approach toward the highway, Sally thought about options for getting Damn Tootin' off her back. Call the law. Call Congress. Call the media.

Call…what time would Hank be home? *Back.* What time would he be…

She was homing in on the gatepost on the left side, favoring the left side, her good side. She missed the movement on the right, the pickup turning onto the approach from the far lane, her fuzzy lane. There it was, left. Wheel hard right. Clutch, brake—leg? Leg! *Crunch.* Engine, killed. Gatepost? *Bull's-eye.*

Alive? *Check.* Conscious? *Must be.* Hurt? *Stay tuned.*

"What the hell are you trying to do?"

Tutan.

Rewind. Over and out.

"Are you all right?"

The last thing Sally wanted to see was that fat red face, but she carefully turned her head to the left anyway. Sure enough.

"I think so." She felt around the inside of the door for the handle.

"You better be sure. You wrecked your truck."

"Hoolie's truck."

"Did you break anything?"

"Hoolie's truck."

"I'd better call for help."

"Just let me…" She couldn't see much, but a roaring engine, screeching brakes and flying gravel were distinctive sounds. Had the two-lane highway become the scene of a demolition derby?

So was the voice calling for "Hoolie?"

Hank!

"It's not Hoolie," Tutan shouted. "I don't think she's hurt."

"Don't touch her. Sally?"

"This seat belt is a piece of crap." She hoped she sounded disgusted. She wasn't ready to look up and let him see the face of a rattled klutz.

"Take it easy. Do you hurt anywhere?" He reached through the side window and touched the side of her neck. "Your head?"

She closed her eyes and let relief wash over her. "I can't feel…anything…"

"Nothing? How about—"

"She's not even supposed to drive, for God's sake. Look what she's done." Red face, red voice. *Red filled her head.* "With her medical problems? I don't know what you people think you're doing, letting this girl get behind the wheel."

"Stay out of the way, Tutan." Hank opened the driver's side door. "Sit, Phoebe."

"Phoebe?" Sally whined. The dog answered in kind.

"She's okay, Phoeb. Tell her, Sally."

"I'm okay, Phoeb. Nothing hurts. I mean, I don't think I'm—"

"Is she bleeding? Anything broken? That's all you need on top of your MS, Sally. You almost hit me."

"*I will hit you* if you don't back off." Hank slid his

arms under her legs and behind her back. "See if it hurts to put your arms around my neck. Slow and easy, okay? You tell me if you feel the slightest…"

"You were outta control, Sally. I don't know what you're doing over here, but you coulda just called. Your father was my friend." The red voice followed, but Sally kept her face tucked against Hank's shoulder. "How long is that thing gonna be sittin' here?" the red voice demanded from a faraway place.

"I'm taking care of her first," Hank said. "If that *thing* ain't here when I come back for it, I'll be looking for you."

"Look what she did to my gate!"

"Which way should we go?" Hank looked up and down the highway, but he was running a checklist in his mind. No blood, bruises, bumps, breaks. He was pretty sure she hadn't been injured, but *pretty* was the operative word.

"You know the way home," she said quietly.

"I don't know the way to your doctor. Did you hit your head? That's the main thing."

"I lost my head. I do that sometimes." She paused. "Sometimes I need a good thumping."

"Well, you got one." He laid two fingertips on the signal-light switch. He was feeling impatient. "If you're not gonna tell me where to find your doctor, I'll go with my best guess."

"Which one do you want? My GP? My neurologist? My—"

"North or south?" he clipped. "Let's start there."

"South," she said. She reached into the backseat, where she got a hand-licking from an ally. "Take me home. I think I'm okay, but if not, I trust you."

He stepped on the brake and turned to her, scowling. "I don't know whether you're lyin' to both of us or just me, but trust me on this. I'm not taking you anyplace that doesn't have an X-ray lab."

"North."

He pulled into the highway and stared straight ahead. Yes, he'd heard. Yes, he knew what MS was. Basically. Questions? Comments? Not without an invitation from Sally.

But for Sally, there was nothing more to say. She'd blown her chance at three weeks of let's pretend by acting stupidly for one day. She glanced at the dashboard clock. *One hour* out of one day. He probably would have guessed before her time was up, but it was too soon. If she hadn't pushed, she could have been normal for a while longer. She could have deluded herself almost completely during this remission. Maybe it was over. Maybe her body had beaten the disease or at least found a way to hold it in check. Maybe she would actually live the scene she'd imagined so many times—the one where she was surrounded by cheerful people wearing white, proclaiming miracles. People, not angels. *It could happen.*

No. What could have happened—up until an hour ago—was a lovely three-week affair with a man who didn't look at her and hear a voice in the back of his head saying, *Don't forget, she's incurable.*

Hank waited in a chair outside one of the small, rural clinic's three exam rooms. Phoebe lay at his feet.

MS. So that was it. He should have known. *Would have* known if he'd been halfway objective. *Damn Tootin'.* Damn Tutan for telling him. He'd wanted Sally to tell him. Trust him. *Come clean,* he'd said, as if whatever she was keeping from him was something dirty. *Dirty secrets.* What other kind would a person want to keep?

From the beginning, objectivity hadn't been an option with Sally. He'd stayed out of the water, but that didn't mean he hadn't gone under. He knew the signs. He'd been there before. The trick was not to fight it. If you let go, you were supposed to be able to float. So he'd heard. Now that they were on par with each other in the personal-history department, maybe they could explore the options she'd laid out on the table. She wanted a friend. She needed certain benefits.

He was her man.

When the door opened, he almost jumped to attention.

"Dr. Bergen says I'm fine."

"That isn't exactly what I said." The doctor adjusted her wire-framed glasses. "I don't see any injuries except a bump on the head and probably some back strain, although Sally says it's nothing. She tells me you're a PA. You'll be around for a while?"

"I'm helping out at the ranch."

"The sanctuary," Sally said. "Hank's taking a working vacation. He's sort of an experiment. If he gives us a good review, I'm going to offer that as a volunteer option on our Web site." She glanced at Hank. "I'm working on a Web site."

The gray-haired woman gave an appreciative nod. "I could go for something like that. I've always wanted to volunteer for Doctors Without Borders, but this place can't spare me for more than a few days at a time."

"Rural clinics are hurting for staff," Hank said.

"Hank just got back from a rodeo. He patches up cowboys for a living, so he can still—"

"Did you take any X-rays?" he asked.

"None indicated." Dr. Bergen eyed Sally as though she might have missed something. "You're not experiencing any numbness now, right? Other than the vision in your right eye, which you were having problems with before the accident." Back to Hank. "Any sign of concussion, bring her back right away. How long have you been a rodeo medic?"

"Seven years."

"Well, then, you've probably had almost as much

experience with injuries like this as I have. Of course, multiple sclerosis complicates things a bit."

"I don't suppose you've run into too many cowboys with MS." Sally gave him her Sally-go-round-the-roses look.

"You're my first."

"Good." She smiled at the doctor. "We never forget our first."

"Make an appointment to see your neurologist as soon as you can get in. You're good to go." Dr. Bergen waved a business card she'd been palming all along. "This is where I'll find the Web site?"

"As soon as we launch it. If you know any veterinarians, we're always looking for volunteers."

Sally's limp was more noticeable as the three of them headed for the pickup, sitting there with the front tire kissing the curb and the back end a good three feet away. *Somebody* had sure been in a hurry.

"I like your style, Sally." He opened the door for her and offered her a hand, thinking his style wasn't too shabby, either. She questioned him with a look—like maybe she could read his mind about the way she walked—and she grabbed the door handle and hauled herself up onto the running board. "The business card, the volunteer comment. Opportunity comes knockin', you're not afraid to jump."

"Opportunity must be jumped while the jumping's good."

He laughed as he let Phoebe in back. He buckled himself in while Sally picked up where she'd left off.

"In my case, while the jumpers are in good jumping order."

"Ah, Sally." He shook his head, chuckling. "You are the damnedest… Did you think it would matter to me that you have MS?"

"Hmm, how should I answer this question? I hope it matters. Or…" She drew herself up and turned to him with a perfunctory smile. "I *knew* it would matter. It matters to everybody. When I'm using a cane, sometimes a wheelchair, that's the first thing people see." She raised an instructive finger. "Maybe it throws them off, maybe it doesn't, but that's who I become. And it's less than I am, and I get tired of waiting for them to catch up to me. When I'm having myself a nice little remission, why should I tell people? Especially people who won't be around that long."

Good question.

"Maybe because some people don't know what to make of all this jumping." He plugged the key into the ignition, shrugged, gave her a look that was probably more sheepish than he intended. "Some of us are scared spitless when it comes to jumping."

"Not you." Her eyes softened. "You were ready to jump when you thought I'd fallen in the lake."

"I wasn't thinking."

"But you've been thinking ever since. Thinking,

there's something wrong with this woman. Can't quite figure out what it is, but..."

"Not wrong. Risky. I like to know what I'm getting into. The ol' look-before-you-leap routine."

"You already looked!"

"Yeah, I did. And I was goin' for it." He gave a mid-forehead salute. "I had the image fixed in my mind."

"You saw yourself swimming?"

"Hell, no." He smiled. *Honey, cut me some slack.* "I saw myself giving you mouth-to-mouth."

"Now you tell me. I would have thrashed around and swallowed some water for you. Right, Phoebe? I've never had a water rescue." She returned his smile. "Your Damn Tootin' rescue was beautifully executed. Nice entry. Perfect timing. Thank you for that."

"It would've been sweet to put my fist through his face."

"I know." She dropped her head back on the headrest and stared at the ceiling. "How much damage did I do to Hoolie's pickup? I wish I could get it fixed before he sees it." She smacked her forehead with the heel of her hand. "Stupid."

"Don't beat yourself up." He reached for her smacking hand. "You can't help being a woman driver."

She raised her brow and smiled sweetly. "I guess not. If you like, I can teach you how to parallel park."

Chapter Seven

Hank had been the perfect gentleman. He had seen her to her bedroom door, asked about a heating pad, brought her cold packs and Sleepytime tea, and gone to the front door to answer Hoolie's "Where the hell's my pickup?" On his way out, he'd suggested a warm bath, even offered to fill the tub. She'd thanked him, said she'd take it from there knowing full well she was doing no such thing. She was letting him answer for her, and she was shamefully content to do so.

But she indulged herself with bath salts and a few bubbles. Why not? It was what she did best. Overextend, underperform. She wasn't hurting much—she'd never claimed she was—but water was always wonderful. *Feel while the feelin's good.* She laid her head back, closed her eyes and soaked it up.

Sally didn't need sight or sound—the door made no noise—when she was hooked into feeling. When the feeling was good, she felt change. New electricity, energy, presence. Manpower. She opened her eyes and smiled.

He wore black jeans. Nothing more. She hoped.

She drew a deep breath and sat up. Foam cascaded over her breasts, tickling her imagination. *Don't look now, but we are hot.* "I'm sorry you didn't catch me doing something more interesting."

"I'm not here to watch."

But he was. Something interesting was happening in the tub, and he was fascinated. He closed the door behind him without looking anywhere else.

"You came to play?"

"Brought you a bath toy." He plunged his hand in his pocket and pulled out a foil packet. "Rubber duck."

"Is that your bath toy of choice?"

"It's the one that's gonna float your boat."

She shrieked with delight as he stepped into the tub, jeans and all. Water sloshed onto the floor, bubble islands rocked back and forth. She drew her knees up to make room, but he took hold of her ankles, straightened her legs and wrapped them around his waist.

"I don't see how." She wiggled her bottom—a hen

getting comfortable in a flooded nest—and stroked his beautiful, brawny shoulders.

"You'll figure something out." His smiling eyes plumbed the depths of hers, tempting a little, teasing a lot. "You wanna get into my jeans, woman, you're gonna work for it."

"While you—"

"—find out what you taste like." He ducked as he slipped his hands around her, thumbs tucked into her armpits, lifting her until her nipple touched his lips. He brushed her so slightly, made her wind up so tightly that she almost interfered. But she held on, and he made it worthwhile with his nibbling lips and the barest tip of his flickering tongue and the warm whisper of his breath. "Sweet cakes with foam." He smiled against her nipple. "Which has a bite to it." He suckled, and then chuckled as he teased with his nose. "Not the kind I was hoping for."

"Sorry," she whispered.

"I don't mind swallowing."

"My kind of man." She buried her fingers in his hair. "You'll come out…smelling like a rose."

He grew and stirred beneath her. "Only for you."

She used his hair to ease his head back until his lips were within reach of hers, and then she kissed him. His thumbs toyed with her breasts, and their tongues played tag. He trailed fingers down her side, over her belly, between her legs and teased her most sensitive flesh until she thought she would die for want of him inside her. But he permitted only the edge of madness and not the full measure. It was at once excruciating and exhilarating, too bright to keep and too fine to let go. She closed her eyes, sheltered them against his neck, and gave herself over.

"Not fair," she whispered when the shuddering subsided.

He turned his mouth to hers and kissed her kindly. He was big and hard beneath her, fit to bust his zipper. She tightened her seat and rolled her hips slowly, raising wants and making waves. His kiss turned hungry, and he tasted every part of her mouth, but he couldn't seem to get his fill. He groaned. "Not fair."

She reached for the soap bottle, pumped a dollop into her palm, rubbed her hands together and lathered him—shoulders, arms, chest. She laughed when her turnabout with his nipples had him sucking air through his teeth. She took the measure of his rib cage, his flat belly, belly button, jeans button. Beneath the bath water it came undone easily. She hoped he would not.

He stilled her hand, poised on the zipper tab. "If I get caught in the teeth, it's all over."

She slipped her hand into his pants, becoming his protection. The tip of his penis pushed against the heel of her soapy hand. She smiled. *This puppy wants out.* She inched the zipper down. "Lift up."

"We're at T minus ten, honey. Any more *up* and it's *liftoff*."

"Hips, silly."

He braced his arms on the sides of the tub and lifted. And when she had his jeans down, she lowered her face into the water and took advantage of his precarious position, just for a moment. Just for a bit of pleasure he would not soon forget. The limited-time offer ended when the breath she could no longer hold became bubbles. He gave a pained laugh as she rose over him like Nessie, pushed her hair back and settled on his lap with an added bonus. It was hard to tell who was torturing whom as he opened the condom and she put it on him, but the pleasure that followed was mutual.

They stepped out of the tub into almost as much water as they left behind. They dried each other with thick bath sheets and traded more kisses and dove into her bed for more exploration and discovery. Every nerve in Sally's body was on high alert. None slept. None missed the smallest trick.

And, oh, from head to toe, she felt wonderful.

"Tell me how you feel." He braced up on his arm and rested his head on his hand. Moonlight streamed through the window with cool night air and cricket calls. He smoothed her hair back from her forehead, his fingertips barely brushing the bump above her eyebrow. Marble sized. Not a shooter, but not a pee-wee either. Big and hard enough to give him concern.

"Happy." Her eyes were closed. Her mouth formed a soft crescent. "Drained and dreamy."

"How 'bout a massage?"

"Mmm...later." She turned toward him, tucked her whole body into him. "How about a snuggle?"

"I'm not letting you go to sleep yet."

"Why not?"

"I'm not ready."

She looked up, eyes wide with mock shock. "What kind of a man are you?"

"You have to ask?"

"Oh, that's right." Her eyes drifted closed, and that sweet, satisfied smile returned. "The doctoring kind."

"I'm not a doctor."

"And it's a good thing. I really don't like doctors." She laid her hand on his chest. "Play doctors, yes. Real doctors, no."

"How's your head?"

"I told you. Drained and dreamy."

"If you fall asleep, I'll just have to wake you up." His thumb grazed the knot on her head. "Still the same size."

"I have other bumps you can play with." She claimed his hand, drew it down and held it against her breast. "When you touch them you make them feel much bigger."

He chuckled. "You're the damnedest woman I've ever met."

"I think so, too, sometimes. I get all tucked up inside, and I—"

"*Tucked* up?"

"That's what I said, Henry. Tucked up." Clutching his hand in both of hers, she turned to her back and scooted up against him, like a small creature seeking shelter from the wind or shade from the high-plains sun. "I sort of suck myself inward. I become a prune, and I imagine myself screaming, 'Come on, you demons, try to take a piece of me now.' But I don't. I stay quiet and still, and I focus on getting through the next breath. I think that's what it's like to be damned."

"Me, too. It's not burning. It's drowning."

"And it's not painful. You know you're damned when you don't feel anything."

"I don't know about that. I've seen—"

"I do," she insisted. And then softly, "I do know. When you can't feel, you'd take anything. A hot poker. A wrecking ball." She drew a deep breath, and then let it go quickly. "Oh, I shouldn't say *I know*. Only part of me doesn't feel sometimes, and it comes back. It always comes back. I don't claim to know what it's like not to feel anything at all." She pressed his hand tight to her breastbone, and he uncurled his fingers and felt her heartbeat in the hollow of his palm. "I'm not a drama queen. I promise."

"I promise to stop calling you the damnedest woman, and we'll leave it there."

"No, no, then I'd be just another damned woman. One of your many damned women. If I'm the damnedest one you know, I'm queen of something. Queen of the damned, that's me." She stretched, full body, like a cat. "I'm not giving up the damnedest title without a fight. The next damned woman comes along, you can't call her *damnedest* unless she can take the crown from my cold, dead hands."

He laughed. "God, you're beautiful."

"I love your hands. They feel cool."

"They do? Maybe that's why you feel so nice and warm."

"I always do. It's part of the package." She looked up at him. "So now—I've avoided it as long as I can—the dreaded question."

"What's that?"

"Did you have to tow Hoolie's pickup? What did he say when he saw it? Was he—I'm such a coward—did he think it could be fixed?"

"That's three dreaded questions." One mental sigh of relief after another. "Starting with number two—because this really says it all—he wanted to know about you. Where were you, how bad were you hurt, had you seen a doctor, and all like that. As for question number one, the pickup started right up, and we took off before the devil knew we were there. We got back, he wanted to know what you were doin' over there. I said, damned if I know. I was just goin' down the road and saw his C10. Damn good thing you stopped, he said, and I said amen to that."

"You sound just like him."

"Is that a bad thing?"

"There's only one Hoolie," she said firmly, as though he thought otherwise. "What about question number three?"

"I know it can be fixed, but if it'll keep you awake for a while, you can keep worrying."

She smiled big. "One Hoolie, one Hank. One Little Henry, one medium-size Henry, one big beautiful Henry. I'm blessed."

"So much for queen of the damned."

"Damned crown's giving me a headache, anyway."

"As long as it's not me." He kissed the bump on her forehead. "Got that? I don't wanna be anybody's headache."

"I don't either. Let's make a pact." She lifted her chin. "Let's kiss on it."

Sally turned Hank down for breakfast. All she wanted to do was sleep. He decided to give her a couple of hours before checking up on her one more time, and then he'd get after Tutan's damn gate. He'd have it fixed good as new, maybe better, and then he'd welcome the criticism, the complaints, hell, the law-

suit. Bring it on. Sooner or later he'd give Damn
Tootin' the tuning up he deserved. He hadn't figured
out just what form it would take, but there would be
a suitable settlement. But for now, Tutan's property
would be repaired.

Hank found Hoolie and Kevin in the machine shop,
their heads under the hood of the C10, which they'd
driven back from the scene of the accident without
incident. Hank stationed himself on the third side of
the male-bonding altar. A pickup engine was as good
as a campfire.

Maybe better.

"Yep," Hoolie said, "she's gonna be good as new,
soon as her replacement parts come." He patted the
dented fender tenderly. "I've already found the headlamp
housing and this whole quarter panel on the Internet."

Hank acknowledged the find with a raised brow.

"You search the Internet much? Any tool you can
think of for shoeing horses, you just put the words in
the box…." Two bony index fingers proudly demon-
strated on the air keyboard. "You want the good stuff,
put the word *vintage* in there somewhere. Press Enter,
and here they come. Like cake, like pie. You ever play
Scavenger Hunt?"

"Nope." Hank glanced across the man-bonding pit
at Kevin. "You?"

Kevin shrugged. "Sounds like what I got arrested
for last year."

"You gotta learn the rules of the game, boy. The tricks of the trade. You should see all my bookmarks. You scavenge around on the Internet, you can buy and sell, you can trade, you can—"

"Snag yourself a rich widow," said Kevin. "Come on, Hoolie, I've seen you friending the women on Facebook."

Hoolie folded his arms. "No harm in exchanging e-mails with females."

"You want the good stuff, you leave out the word *vintage*," Hank said.

"The best e-pal is a gal with a little age on her," Hoolie advised. "If she asks for pictures before the third message, one of us is swingin' on the wrong porch."

"How's Sally?" Kevin asked Hank.

"I kept her up all night, so she's sleeping in this morning. She hit her head. She's got a goose egg the size of your *pahsu*."

"His what?"

"Nose," Kevin said. "And mine ain't that big, so it's no excuse to keep her from getting her rest."

"I see a lotta concussions. You let her go to sleep too soon, she might not wake up."

"Hank's halfways a doctor," Hoolie told Kevin. "Physician's practitioner, they call it."

"Physician's assistant," Hank amended.

"What was she doing over at Tutan's?" Hoolie asked. "Did she say?"

"We didn't get into it." Hank leaned his forearms on the fender and admired the old six-banger engine. "She feels real bad about the damage on this baby."

"She, uh…she's a terrible driver."

"I know she has MS." He said it quietly, without looking up. "Tutan was turning into the approach, and they nearly collided. She couldn't work the pedals. 'Course he pitied her for having MS and ripped into her for driving." He glanced across the engine at Hoolie. "She coulda told me herself."

"We don't talk about it unless she…you know. It's for her to decide. Lately she's been…you'd never know unless…"

"Unless somebody told you." Hank nodded. Pride. He knew what that was like. "The leases she's trying to get, the horse-training challenge, she's pretty determined."

"That's Sally for you."

For *him?*

Hell, it had nothing to do with him. Sally was determined to be Sally. She'd honed the edge on her defensive game long before he came along. Which was understandable. Nothing personal, which was good. Under the circumstances, friends with benefits probably made perfect sense, especially since he wouldn't be around long.

"What's it gonna take?" Hank straightened his back, braced his hands on the pickup fender. "More people, money, connections, what?"

"Yeah, all that and maybe a guardian angel. I don't think she oughta be takin' so much on. Zach and Annie don't know the half of it." Hoolie smiled. "Sally's the one who got the sanctuary started. I didn't think much of the idea at first. Now I can't imagine a better one."

"She's supposed to make an appointment with her neurologist. I'd like to be the one to take her."

"I'd offer you my pickup, but…"

"We'll take mine. I'll take the topper off and leave it in the shop if it won't be in the way. About everything I own is in it."

"No problem," Hoolie said.

"We might be gone overnight. You never know. Can you handle—"

"'Course we can." Hoolie eyed Hank anxiously. "She's okay, isn't she? She's just getting double-checked, right?"

"Yep. When you're special, you see a specialist." Hank rapped his knuckles on the fender. "Right now, I've got some repairs to make on Tutan's front gate."

"I'll go with you," Kevin said eagerly.

"I need you here." Hoolie had cold water for Kevin, heated advice for Hank. "Don't let him push you around. Sally had a good reason for goin' over there. Whatever it was."

"You think he'll try to push me?" He could only hope.

"No. He ain't that stupid."

"Unfortunately." Kevin was greatly disappointed.

* * *

Hank tried the Tutans' doorbell, but there was no sound. He knocked on the door. Either way, it was a formality. If there was anyone home, they'd seen him coming a mile away. He gave a full minute before turning to leave. The door whined softly, a tentative opening, slight shape in the shadows.

"I'm looking for Dan Tutan. The name's Hank Night Horse. I'm helping out over at the Double D."

"Night Horse?" It was a woman's voice.

"I'm a friend of Zach Beaudry's. I came to fix the front gate."

"Oh." The door opened, and a small, mostly gray lady emerged. She wore a blue shirt and tan pants, but everything else about her seemed gray. "Dan's out cutting hay. How's Sally? Is she home?" She hung on to the doorknob with one hand and the door frame with the other, but she seemed hesitant, like she was trying to decide whether she should try to block an end run or step aside and let him score. "I was going to call, but I didn't want to cause any upset."

"I took her to the clinic. No injury to speak of."

"Tell her I hope she's…" She dropped her gaze along with her left hand. She looked defeated. "Tell her I'm sorry."

"Sorry for…"

"Upsetting her. I know stress causes those spells sometimes, where she loses control over her legs or something. All she wanted me to do was talk to him."

"Talk to your husband?"

"He's got his side, too. Who's to say?" The thought of two sides seemed to buck her up some. "Tell you the truth, I wish he'd cut back on the cattle. We don't need a big operation anymore. He's got nobody to take over for him. Kids are gone. They've got their own lives. But…" She gave an open-handed gesture, a sigh. "Sally was my daughter Mary's best friend."

"Sally stopped by to visit with *you,* then."

"Hardly ever see her anymore. She's like me—doesn't get out much, especially in the winter."

"She's completely dedicated to the horses. She wants to get along. She was just hoping you'd put a good word in your husband's ear."

"It wouldn't make any difference. He doesn't want to give up those grazing permits, plus the Indian land. He has some influence with…important friends, I guess you could say."

"It doesn't hurt to have important friends."

"Or *any* friends. We all need friends." She frowned. "Dan didn't say anything about you coming to fix the gate."

"He said a little something *to me* about the gate. You can tell him I came by with materials and offered to fix it like it was."

"Are you…?" She gave him a quizzical look. "Did you know John Night Horse? He used to work for us." He stood uncomfortably for her scrutiny. It surprised and almost disappointed him when she shook her head. "No, that was a long time ago. You would have been a child."

"I would have been twelve."

"He was related to you, then." She gave him a moment to make his claim, and when he offered none, she looked relieved. "He was a good man. I don't think they ever really found out what happened. But he was a good man."

Hank nodded. Like some TV prosecutor, he almost said, *no more questions.* Mrs. Tutan probably took most people for good, even though she was mostly a sad woman. Pumping her for information was like kicking a wounded animal. She clearly lived her life on a need-to-know basis. She didn't know what had happened to John Night Horse, didn't want to know. She hadn't told Tutan why Sally had come over, and wouldn't tell Tutan about Hank's call unless she was asked for some reason. She wouldn't want to cause an upset.

Hank had missed lunch. Sally was trying hard not to miss him, telling herself that last night he'd given her something she'd never had before, and that was all she wanted to think about now. Not the whys or the wherefores or whether it would happen again.

Replay the experience, Sally. Everything he said and did, everything you felt and felt and felt. Keep it alive inside, where nothing can take it away and you can have it over and over again, no matter what.

But she couldn't help watching the road while she watered the garden, listening for his pickup when she turned off the faucet. He'd gone to the neighbors' on a peace-making mission, which—given he had no real duty to any part of the Double D—was so far above the call it was almost saintly.

Whys and wherefores be damned, she waited. She watched and listened, and when she saw the flash of white on the highway, heard the rumble of the engine and felt the promise of having him back, she was content with whatever he was up to, as long as she was part of it. And she knew she was.

There was no we're-a-couple-now kiss when he met her in the yard. She could have offered, but she was tuning in to his cues, which went against all her instincts. She wanted to jump his bones and plant one on him. She made do with returning his glad-to-see-you smile and telling him she'd saved him some lunch.

He closed the back door behind them, grabbed her arm, turned her and drew her to him. His kiss brought last night forward. It was still with him, too. She clung to him and celebrated, trading kiss for kiss with equal satisfaction.

"How's your head?" He pulled back so he could get a look.

"All better."

He smiled wistfully as he measured the lump on her

forehead with his thumb. "Not quite, but you're still alive and kissing."

"You fixed Tutan's gate?"

"Not yet. He wasn't around, and his wife wouldn't give me the go-ahead. We tried, huh?"

She slipped her arm around his waist and walked him into the kitchen. "I have an appointment in Rapid City tomorrow. Hoolie says you're taking me."

"Makes sense, doesn't it?"

"Not if you're doing it because you're, you know…"

He laughed. "A halfways doctor?"

"Hoolie's a kick, isn't he?" She slid away, went to the refrigerator and took out the sandwiches she'd made for him. "I know that's the real reason Zach talked you into staying." She took a plate from the cupboard. "I didn't care then—I just wanted them to go on a honeymoon, for heaven's sake—but I wasn't planning to con you into being my personal halfway doctor. I don't want you to…" She turned to him, her hands, braced on the counter, bracketing her hips. "You don't need to be involved in my medical issues."

"Okay."

"That's not one of the benefits."

"Is there a list somewhere? I know our arrangement was pretty vague, but you start talkin' benefits, seems like there should be some negotiation."

"I'm serious, Hank. You were absolutely right— you're not the cure for what ails me. And I'm not your patient." She gave a shy smile. "I want to be something you don't already have."

"That covers a lot of territory." He lifted one shoulder. "I have friends. One or two, anyway."

"Women?"

"I know some women." His smile was slow and lazy. "None like you."

"That's nice. I like that. And I appreciate your offer to drive me to Rapid city. I just don't want you to feel like you have to—" she drew a deep breath and sighed "—take care of me."

"I don't feel like I have to do anything. What time is your appointment?"

"Nine." She perked up some. "And there's something I want to show you afterward. It's a little bit out of the way, but I really think it's important for you to see it."

"Out of the way in what direction?"

"North and east."

"Perfect. You show me yours, and I'll show you mine." He loaned her an actual smile. "I've got a few things to take care of at home."

"Cool! We'll take the high road to the day horses and the low road to the Night Horses."

"What's the quickest way for me to get to that food behind you?"

She returned his smile with interest. "The toll road."

Chapter Eight

"Mr. Night Horse?" The crisp voice jerked Hank out of his waiting-room-aquarium reverie. He blinked up at the red-haired, flourpaste-faced woman standing over him. "This way, please."

He followed the crepe-soled shoes and ample ass down a bright, narrow hallway. If she was taking him to a different part of the clinic, it probably wasn't a good sign. He imagined Sally "resting comfortably," tried to imagine what might have come up, what he could say or do to add to her comfort. Back to the friendship part of the bargain. He'd lied. He had more than one or two friends.

He'd told the truth. There was none like her.

The nurse rapped on the door before ushering him into a plush exam room. Specialists had it made.

This one was losing his dark hair a patch at a time, but he was letting the sides grow to compensate. He wore a crisp shirt and tie with his white coat, and he stood to gladhand Hank. "Sally's all set, doing just fine. She was telling me you're a rodeo medic. I have a friend who works with the Justin Sportsmedicine Team. Rod Benoit from Billings. Wondered if you've run into him."

"Dr. Benoit. Sure." Hank held a flat hand five feet above the floor. "Little guy with big hair. Crazy mustache."

"That's Rod. If he hadn't gone into medicine, he would've been a cowboy. He loves rodeo. Been pushing helmets and safety vests on bull riders for years."

"He's made a lot of headway." Hank chuckled. "So to speak."

"It's a good program. I see a lot of sports injuries. I know cowboys don't like to take off their hats except to eat or pray, but I'm a big supporter of helmets."

"Yeah, me, too."

"I just wanted to meet you. When Sally said she had a rodeo medic sitting out there in the waiting room, I told my nurse, I said, bring him on back."

Hank only had eyes for Sally, who was sitting in the corner, curiously quiet.

"Oh, she's fine," the doctor said. "Far as I can tell, none of her marbles fell out."

"So there's nothing…"

"She looks a lot better than the last time she was in. Well, except for her vision in that right eye, but that—"

"That's why I'm not driving." Sally sprang from the chair as though her name had been called.

"No, that's not why. That's not what caused the accident. We all have our limitations, and you know yours. You can't deny the disease, Sally." The doctor turned to Hank. "Tell Benoit Tony Schmidt said hello." He snapped his fingers. "Almost forgot." Schmidt took a folded check from his pocket, snapped it open with his thumb and handed it to Sally. "On my account."

With the door closed behind them, Hank turned to Sally. "*He* pays *you?*"

"He supports the sanctuary. I told him about the Wild Horse Challenge, and he wrote out a check." She gestured eagerly toward an exit sign at the end of the hallway. "We can go out this way."

"That nurse came to get me, I didn't know what was goin' on."

"He just wanted to meet you."

"And how did that come about?"

"He wanted to know how I got here. So I told him all about you." She turned to him as she leaned on the push bar of a side door. "What did you *think* was going on?"

"Hell, I thought something was wrong." He reached past her to lend his hand to their escape. "The way the nurse said, 'This way, please.' And then Dr. Tony's quizzing me like he's checkin' out my credentials."

"He thinks what you do is pretty cool. He says it's become a highly specialized field since I was involved as a stock contractor. There aren't that many of you, and I'm monopolizing an important team member."

"He said that?"

"*I* said that." She was on the march to his pickup, and he noticed her limp was more pronounced. "He said the part about you being such a rarity, and I just said…" He clicked the remote to unlock the door while she stood with her back to him. "I didn't say anything. Do they think I'm a child? A helpless, hopeless…" She jerked on the door handle. "I hate being talked around."

Hank knew what she meant. Talked down to, talked around, ignored. It was no way to treat people. He laid his hand on her shoulder. "You're not the kind to put up with it, either."

She turned her head, scowling. "What's that supposed to mean?"

"It means we're both rarities. Some people don't know how to act around us." He reached for the door handle, but she hung on. "Let me show you how a cowboy treats a lady." She hung on still. "An *Indian* cowboy. Rare as hen's teeth."

Her scowl melted. Her hand gave way to his claim

to the privilege of opening the door. He wanted to kiss her right out there in public, but he figured the way she was looking at him, the way he felt looking at her said it all without letting anyone else in.

"Hank," she said, just when he was ready to roll. "I also think what you do is pretty cool. It's way more important than repairing busted gates and driving me around."

"I just came back from an event in Wyoming. I call my own shots. I think you know that." He stopped at the street corner. *Yield, shift gears, move on.* "So, I'm calling on you to call our next turn. We're headed east on thirty-four? How far?"

Forty miles east of town, she showed him her second-worst nightmare. She asked him not to stop the pickup, but to slow down and take a good look at the two hundred "unadoptable" horses ware-housed on a few acres of land owned by a private contractor. They had been rounded up by helicopter and removed from public land where they were supposed to be left to roam freely. One by one the unattractive, unhealthy, uncooperative and other-wise unlucky creatures that had passed their sell-by date turned sad eyes toward the road. These were some of the horses an expanded Double D sanctu-ary would accommodate.

"If all goes well," Sally said, more to the faces in the field than the man who had her back.

The edgy growl of the pickup's big engine echoed Hank's feeling. He'd heard about the holding facilities, but he hadn't seen one. "Why can't we stop?" This crawling along the shoulder of the road was not how he rolled. "Are we being watched? Through a rifle scope, maybe?"

"You have to admit, I add considerable excitement to your life."

"Hell, you're a walk in the park."

"Didn't you notice that sign back there?"

"Which one?" He was looking for a gate.

She turned to him, all cocky, giving him that *what-of-it?* look. "I'm practically blind in one eye, but I'm pretty sure it said Stay in Your Car."

"Oh, *that* sign." And *that* Sally. The unsinkable one. "That was just the top line. The practically blind line. The twenty-twenty line said, Entering Sioux Indian Country."

"It did not."

"The next one will. Watch your picnic basket. If they smell food, you're in real trouble."

She smiled for him, her eyes gleaming, defying deficiency. "You keep the engine running while I open the gate."

He laughed. "I was thinkin' the same way."

"Which is why we can't stop." She turned to the window. "Hang in there," she told the watchers. "We'll be back." And to Hank, "Won't we?"

How had he missed it? It was always the eyes that got to him—somebody looking to him to toss her a bone or toss him in the air, to take away her trouble or take away his pain. The eyes had it, said it, got to him and stayed with him long after his were closed for the night. More each day he was finding himself lost in Sally's eyes, but somehow he'd missed her loss. It was physical, and he was all about *physical.* As long as he didn't see any medical problems, she didn't have any. Right? He was the doctor. *Halfway.*

But he could have sworn she saw him clearly. Whether she accepted what she saw as what she got was another matter, *her* matter.

So, what the hell was the matter with him? If this was a classic case of the blind leading the blind…

He put his foot down. The pickup leaped onto the blacktop, engine roaring on the front end, tires kicking gravel out the back.

"It's only one eye, you know," she said.

"What?"

"My right eye's been sucky lately, but I have X-ray vision on the driver's side. I can see the wheels turning in your head. What are we doing?"

"Damn if I know." Getting away from a gate he couldn't open, pain he couldn't touch, eyes he wouldn't forget. "Tutan has friends in high places. I've got relations in all kinds of places. You're gonna meet my sister-in law."

* * *

Sally had been sleeping. She hadn't meant to, but Hank had gone silent on her, and she'd dozed off. Her mouth had probably exposed still more of her less-than-appealing side by falling open. When she opened her eyes, she saw tall grass in myriad shades of green and tan carpeting mile after mile of rolling plains. Buffalo grass it was called, but it fed horses just as well. Cattle, too, but they were relative newcomers. Before the cattle and the cattlemen, all of it had been Indian Country. Hank pointed out a sign that did, indeed, declare that they were entering the small portion that was left. South Dakota buttes and badlands softened into hills and bluffs as they traveled north.

The Night Horse place was tucked into the hills. In a suburb it would have been called a tract house. Here it was a "scattered site"—a modest home without neighbors. Cattle and a few horses grazed the hillsides. A few cottonwood trees, a small swing set, a couple of cars and a vegetable garden filled the yard.

A slightly shorter, somewhat heavier version of Hank without the cowboy hat emerged from the front door as Hank and Sally closed the pickup doors.

"Back so soon, brother?"

"I smelled frybread."

Sally inhaled deeply. Hot lard, sage smoke and tomato plants.

"Where's Phoebe?"

"She's hangin' with friends." Hank turned, winked at Sally as she approached. Either that or he was squinting into the sun. She chose the wink. "Sally, my little brother, Greg."

"Is this that Sally you were talking about?" Greg's eyes had a quicker sparkle than his brother's. Quick and sweet, as opposed to slow and killer. "Look at her smile. Yeah, he's been talking you up."

"You told your doctor about me, I told my big-mouth brother about you," Hank confessed. "I guess that means something, huh?"

"It means you're a fast worker when you put your mind to it." Greg punched his brother's shoulder. "We've got fresh frybread and *wojapi*. Come and eat."

Kay Night Horse welcomed Sally to her kitchen with a glass of wild mint tea and a chair next to the counter. Golden-brown squares of bread were piled high in a cardboard box next to a huge iron skillet on the stove. Steeped mint and steamy fruit scents mingled with deep-fat frying and yeast.

Sally nodded toward the oil-stained box. "I can tell that's the fresh frybread, but Greg mentioned canned something, and it smells like berries."

"Juneberries," Kay said. "Dried from last year. We're a couple of weeks away from fresh. Don't you pick juneberries?"

"I wouldn't know a juneberry from a june bug. My sister offers wild-plum jam to any of her students who'll bring her the plums. Annie's a wonderful cook."

"Sally's sister teaches at Winter Count Day School," Hank said. The men had taken chairs at the table. "Isn't that where you went to school, Kay?"

"For a year, but then I went to Pierre. How long has your sister been there?"

"Five years. She's younger."

"Sally and her sister turned their ranch into a home on the range for wild horses." Hank nodded as Kay set a glass of tea on the table in front of him. "Since there's already a Home on the Range for Boys, they call it the Double D Ranch."

Sally caught Greg looking doubtfully at her chest. "My father's name was Don Drexler. My *grand*father's name was Don Drexler." She laughed. "We do get some strange calls when we advertise for volunteers."

"What did this guy say?" Greg wanted to know. Hank whacked the back of his brother's head, and everyone laughed.

More animated than she'd yet seen him, Hank described the wild-horse sanctuary and the need to expand it. He had the air of a man on his home turf, but he kept Sally center stage. She was Mustang Sally, Snow White and St. Francis rolled up into one. And he was just the man to hook her up.

"Does the name Tutan ring a bell, little brother?"

Greg gave the name a moment's pause. "Was that the

guy who owned the ranch where the old man was killed?"

Hank nodded. "He's Sally's neighbor. He's also her main opposition. There's some remote country west of Sally's place that should be part of that sanctuary. It's prime for mustangs. Nobody would ever bother them. Some of it's tribal land." He raised his voice toward the kitchen. "Do you still have relatives on the council down there, Kay?"

"I've got one who generally looks out for the landowners, two who side with the Indian ranchers, and one who'll butt heads with anybody." Kay refilled Sally's glass. "Your neighbor leases Indian land?"

"Some." Sally held up her hand and whispered *thanks.* "If I can get those leases, I can get the grazing permits on the adjoining public land. We could accommodate twice as many mustangs."

Greg grinned. "What's in it for us?"

"Horses."

He laughed. "Looks like you've finally found a soul mate, brother. Did you show her your latest rescues? My brother's a soft touch when it comes to horses."

"They become part of who you are," Sally said. "They can lift a person off the ground—body, mind and spirit. They've been such wonderful partners for us for so long that we forget they were once wild. Like dogs and cats, domestic horses should have wild relatives. We must make sure of it. Some roots must be preserved, some seeds, some…"

She glanced at the brown faces, the brown eyes turned her way, and she could feel herself turning red. She lowered her gaze, studied the glass of pale tea. Wild mint. The scent of wild berries filled her nose. "We bring some of the horses in for people to adopt, to keep and use so that some can be left alone."

"Do you think they know?" Hank asked. "The one who doesn't get away, does he say to himself, I'll stand in a corral the rest of my life so my relations can run free?"

"I think so," Sally said hopefully. "I really do. And that's what we get out of the deal. We get to be with the ones who sacrifice. Maybe they can teach us something."

"Sure. If we can figure out how to learn."

"People adopt horses for their own use, but they go to all kinds of programs as well." Sally leaned into the discussion. "They're amazing, these horses. They're incredibly sensitive, and lend that sensitivity to us, in our lives…" She lifted one shoulder. "They've helped me."

"One of my cousins got in on a horse-training program in the prison in Nevada. It changed his life." Kay brought a plate of frybread and a bowl of hot fruit pudding to the table. "See if you like this, Sally. The missionaries taught us to make frybread, but the *wojapi* is what makes it really good, and that's ours."

Sally savored the food. It was almost as good as Annie's blueberry pie, which was to die for. As was the generous and gentle man who shared his family with her. He believed in her cause, and this was proof.

"I have to go pick up the girls from basketball camp," Kay told the group after taking a phone call. "They missed the bus again."

Sally started gathering dishes off the table. "May I ride along with you?" She glanced at Hank, who nodded and smiled.

Once the dusty, white Chevy was rolling on smooth blacktop, Sally turned from her polite questions about Hank's athletic nieces—questions eliciting little more than a word or two in response—to her real concern. "I don't mean to put you on the spot with your relatives on the Tribal Council. I don't usually ask for favors five minutes after I meet someone."

Kay didn't miss a beat. "How much time did Hank get?"

"Funny you should ask. Within the first five minutes, I think I did him a favor." She chuckled. "Of course, I could be flattering myself."

"First he's singing for some cowboy's wedding—he tried that song out for us, and *jeez* that was pretty."

"It was wonderful."

"And then he's helping this cowboy out for a few weeks, and then it's all Mustang Sally and Kay, can you help us out? I don't know what you did for him, but I hope it lasted more than five minutes."

Sally stared. She gave it at least five seconds. And then she burst out laughing. She had met her no-bull match in Kay Night Horse. When she caught her breath, she told Kay the skinny-dipping story, and they shared a good laugh.

"I'll do what I can for your sanctuary because Hank wants me to," Kay said. "If he says it's a good thing, then it is. What you said about the wild horses goes for Hank, too. He's helped a lot of people. The kind who won't let just anyone get too close."

"I know."

"That's the kind he wants to be. Tries to be. Lift a person off the ground, brush him off and send him on his way. You do that day after day, you keep your guard up, you should be fine."

"My, um…this friend who's a doctor, he was eager to meet Hank. He says—"

"He took care of Greg after their mother died. Hank was fifteen. They stayed with relatives, but Hank looked after his little brother. When Hank got into the Indians in Medicine program at the university, Greg stayed with him. Stayed with him for a while after Hank got married."

"Was he there when Hank's son was killed?"

"Greg was with me by then." Kay glanced at her as she slowed for a turn at a T in the road. "Deborah— Hank's wife—she was pretty and everything, maybe not as smart as she thought she was, but smart enough. It turned out she couldn't do real life. When that little boy died and that woman left, Hank's world caved in on him. But he's a survivor. He's the kind who picks himself up and goes at it again, only twice as hard as he was before. He'll turn himself inside out for you if that's what you want."

It wasn't. And he wouldn't. Kay had it all wrong. "We haven't known each other very long."

"Like I said, the way you talked about the horses, you could have been talking about Hank."

"Amazing," Sally whispered, thought about it, turned to Kay and smiled. "Did I use the word *amazing?*"

"Amazing he let you get close to him so quick."

"Don't worry. His guard is secure. And I'm harmless."

The look Kay gave said *we'll see.* But she smiled. "At least you come with some horses."

Nothing had been said about how long they would be staying or where they would be sleeping, but Hank and Sally sat outside on kitchen chairs as dusk fell and traded stories with Greg and Kay. Stars appeared and so did the guitars. In the old days, Hank said as he strummed, he and his little brother had often sung together for their supper. But those days were gone, Greg crooned as he tightened his E string. Now dessert would do nicely.

Sally was charmed by the music, mesmerized by the stars glittering against the black-velvet sky. When she saw flashes of color, she thought her bad eye was playing a good trick on her. Her senses were, after all, weirdly wired. Maybe she was hearing in color. She closed one eye at a time, and the stars danced for her, but the colors vanished.

Kay touched her arm and pointed. There it was again, a bit brighter, a little braver. Hank looked up, strummed a final chord, and grabbed Sally's hand. "Grand finale," he said as he pulled her out of the chair. "You guys comin'?"

"Can't." Greg hit a low note. "Kids."

Hank's pickup roared to the top of the steep hill behind the house. He cut the engine, and all seemed suddenly quiet. Cut the lights, and all was dark. He grabbed a couple of blankets out of the back, spread one over the crisp grass, and with a sweeping gesture offered Sally the best seat in the universe. A soft breeze rustled the grass, a few crickets held a powwow in the draw below, and a brigade of ghostly rainbows jostled in the northern sky.

"Northern lights," Sally whispered. "I haven't seen them since I was a girl."

"You're still a girl." He stretched out on his back and tucked his arms beneath his head.

"Oh, no, I'm not." She lay down beside him. "You need a woman."

"We used to come up here at night when we were boys. No girls. But you're right. We thought about women. Each of us got to pick one to bring up here. If we couldn't get that one, we'd be out of luck."

"Who did you pick?"

"Natalie Wood. I'd've had her for sure if she wasn't dead. Greg was gonna get Madonna. He wanted to see what was under those cones. I told him a woman who shows that much skin in public can't be trusted." He chuckled. "We were boys."

"Natalie Wood," she mused. She wondered what Deborah looked like. She wouldn't ask. *Natalie Wood* she could say aloud, but not *Deborah*. Deborah was not harmless.

He sat up. She woke up from her musing, looked up and followed his lead. One by one the lights were turning on—a battalion of vertical rainbows bobbing shoulder to shoulder to shoulder across the night sky. The colors were vivid, the palette complete. So vast was the sky, so enormous the display that it was impossible to be separate from it. Sally's vision cleared. Her body melted. She became blue-green. She ebbed and flowed with the swells of refracted light. She was beautiful.

She was flawless.

She touched Hank's arm, just to be sure he was still there. He put his hand on her thigh. So cool. She could feel it right through her jeans. Deliciously bracing, like springwater. Wherever the lights took them, they were going there together.

"Lie back," he told her when the lights began to recede. He unbuttoned her jeans, unzipped, unleashed his mouth and all its unsettling skills on her belly. He lowered her clothing, nibbled and tickled and tongued until all the colors of the rainbow rushed ahead of his painstaking advance on her sentient core. She could neither keep still nor silent. "Keep your eyes on the skies," he whispered. "Still there?"

"Yes." It was all she could manage. A single word for infinity fading too fast.

"Don't close your eyes yet." He kissed her high inside her thigh and low between her thighs. "Still?"

"Yes, but…"

"Close your eyes and open your legs for me," he whispered, his breath soft and stimulating. She could hardly move, and so he helped her. The lights were still there, and his tongue charged them up, more brilliant than before. Brighter than icy morning, more dazzling than sun through rain.

He caught her colorful thrills and delicate spills on his lips and delivered them to hers, let her taste her essence, which only made her crave his. They peeled each other bare and touched, tasted, breathed each other in until they blended so perfectly that her leading him to her and his going inside was inevitable.

They made their own rainbow.

Chapter Nine

The brown-and-white sedan with the word *Sheriff* emblazoned on the sides was the second most unwelcome traveler on the three-mile stretch of gravel between the highway and the Drexler house. Not that Sally had anything against Cal Jenner—she'd voted for him three times—but the news he brought almost always had something to do with the owner of the *most* unwelcome vehicle.

"You've got horses on the road again, Sally," Cal announced as he closed the door with the letters *S-h-e* behind him and hitched up his brown pants. "I don't see a gate open, don't see any fence down, but they're getting out somewhere."

"Kevin!" Hank beckoned with a gesture. The boy took the rubber ball from Phoebe's mouth, tossed it up and hit a pop fly into the shelter belt, sending both dogs on a tear before he dropped the bat and headed for home. "How far south?" Hank asked the lawman.

"They're actually about four miles north of here."

"I've been gone for a couple of days, just drove down that road not thirty minutes ago," Sally protested. "Somebody's messing with our fences."

"Probably some of your volunteers. Have you taken on any new recruits lately?"

"No, but even if we had they wouldn't be cutting our fences."

"I didn't see any sign of anything like that goin' on," Cal said. "You got any better ideas?"

"Well, let me think." Sally tapped her chin and rolled her eyes skyward.

Cal shook his head. "Dan hasn't complained to me in—I don't know—couple weeks at least. Now, I have heard from the BLM out there in Wyoming. They want to know how you're doing. I say, *how they're doing what?* And they say, how you're doing with the community. Which is a loaded question, and I'm trained to duck and cover."

Sally wasn't amused. "Are you getting reports on us from anyone else?"

"Nope."

"Then why are you ducking?"

"I admire what you're doing, Sally. You know that. I want to see the Sheriff's Posse go completely Spanish Mustang." Cal turned to Hank. "We've got braggin' rights to six adopted mustangs on the drill team now. I'll take them over any other horse in the bunch. The spirit of the old West lives in those horses. I'm all for—"

"You don't get any other complaints," Hank affirmed.

"An anonymous call once in a while. Horses on the highway. Usually there's nothing to it, but I always check it out."

"You mention that to the BLM?"

"If they ask."

Hank laid his hand on Kevin's shoulder. "There's some horses out on the right of way, a few miles north. Saddle up and run 'em across the road and through the west gate. Make sure that side's secure."

"In with the cattle?" Kevin asked.

"For now." Hank turned to Sally. "I'll have a look on the east side."

She nodded. "We keep our fence in good repair. You know that, Cal."

"Yours is better than most."

"Riding fence is everybody's favorite assignment around here." She glanced at Kevin, who was beating a path back to the barn, eager to carry out Hank's order.

"On the other hand," Cal added, "if horses are the spirit, cattle are the lifeblood of this part of the country."

"We have cattle, too. The Drexlers have been here longer than the Tutans. We've changed our focus." Sally divided her smile between the two men. "It used to be disappointing not to make any money ranching. These days we're *purposely* not making a profit."

"Somebody has to make enough profit to pay some taxes, or the county's got no way to gas up my squad car." Turning to Hank, Cal adjusted his tan Stetson by the brim. "If you see any new breaks in the fence or something doesn't look right, you give me a call."

Two days later Hank found an opening in a cross-fence between the Drexlers' land and Tutan's. No breaks. No cuts. This time, the fence had been taken down from the posts. It could easily be put back up, and no one would be the wiser. Was that the plan?

He swung down from Ribsy's saddle for a closer look when a distant rifle shot nearly caused him a long walk back to the house.

"Easy, girl."

He'd nearly calmed her down before another shot was fired and he opted for an awkward running remount over losing the reins. He loped the mustang in a tight circle to distract her from taking off across the flat, which was what her one-track mind was set on. He started to head back the way he had come— no way would the mare go along with any human-brained investigation—when he noticed a small carcass. Prairie dog. *Dogs*. He counted five. He'd ridden into their little town and found carnage.

Another distant gunshot.

"Easy, Ribs."

Who in hell would be shooting prairie dogs in a wildlife sanctuary?

Damn Tootin'. Who the hell else? Hank wondered how many hands he hired to keep his ranch going while he ran around playing games.

He had a pretty good idea where the shots were coming from. He'd taken a ride out this way, noticed a couple of dog towns and thought he'd come back sometime with a pair of binoculars and watch the big birds make meat. He could watch hawks and eagles all day long. But little men with big shotguns? Not so much.

Hank headed for high ground, following the fence line. The scrub brush on the bluffs hid him from the rider of an ATV pushing through the draw below with a discordant whine that set Hank's teeth on edge. Then he saw the rider's game. He was running horses. He was terrorizing a band of four mares, three foals and a stud. And the stud was Don Quixote. A shot rang out, and the horses flew past. Hank looked down and saw the rifle barrel and a green baseball cap at least a hundred yards below.

With a little backtracking he was able to circle behind the shooter without being seen or heard.

Leaving Ribsy ground-tied a few yards behind enemy lines, Hank was able to get close enough to count coup or cause a coronary. With luck, both.

"Going hunting, Mr. Tutan?"

Hank gave himself a moment to enjoy the look of a man who'd just heard a ghost. His brother favored their father in looks and build, but Hank had the voice. Not that John Night Horse had been much of a talker, but whenever he showed up in church, he always sang his heart out. Tutan's eyes bulged in a ruddy face gone pasty as he looked right and left, searching for the voice's owner.

"What's in season this time of year?" Hank stepped out from behind a scraggly clutch of chokecherry bushes.

"It's you." Tutan clapped his hand over his eyes. The color drained from his lips, and Hank had to wonder whose luck was in play. If the man keeled over, Hank might have to find a new profession. "Damn, you scared me," Tutan gasped.

"Did you take me for someone else, Mr. Tutan?" He said the name the way he'd heard it long ago, with his father's distinctive inflection.

"Night Horse," Tutan said carefully. "What was he to you?"

"I'll tell you what he wasn't." Hank raised his chin. "He wasn't a hunter. Had no patience for it. Didn't own a gun. Said he'd eaten enough deer meat growing up to last him a lifetime."

Tutan's eyes narrowed. "You don't look much like him."

"What happened to him?"

"Sounds like you know more about him than I do."

"Maybe." Hank nodded toward the draw. "That's quite a horse, isn't it?"

"Which one?"

"The one you're gunnin' for."

"They're protected. They're good for nothin' but making trouble, but the law says you gotta leave 'em alone. Even when they run right through your fence." Tutan hefted his rifle as though he'd just remembered he had it with him. He wore a loaded hunter's vest over his white T-shirt. "What's not protected is those damn prairie dogs. It's open season on those sonsabitches."

"You're running those horses."

"I don't know who that is on the four-wheeler. Figured it must be one of Sally's people. Or Annie's. Or yours, maybe." He turned his head and spat. "I'm shooting prairie dogs."

"You're on the wrong side of the fence."

"They're the ones on the wrong side of the fence." He shouldered his rifle and pointed it toward the foot of the hill. "Look down there. See? I hit one, two, three. Oops. Still twitching." He aimed and fired. "That's four. They're pests. They destroy good pasture. A cow, a horse, she steps in one of those holes and *snap* goes the leg. She's all done." He turned and squinted up at Hank. "Fence is down again. Bet you've got horses scattered from here to Texas." He nodded toward the low ground. "Those prairie dogs don't give a rat's ass whose side of the fence they dig up. Horses don't care about fences. Why should I?"

"Because you're claiming to be the injured party."

"*That's* an injured party." Tutan waved his rifle at the dead prairie dogs and laughed. "Tell the Drexler girls they don't have to thank me. It's something I like to do in my spare time."

"Anything happens to that horse, I'm comin' after you."

Tutan tucked the butt of his rifle into his armpit, pointing the barrel at the ground. He gave a cold smile. "I'll leave the light on for you."

Nothing riled Hank more than a mean-spirited smile.

Sally stared at her stick. She hadn't used it in two and a half months—*months*—but she could've used it today. After getting her fingers tied up in tack and caught once in a drawer, once in a cupboard door, she'd pronounced herself "all thumbs" and turned the job of straightening out the tack room over to a volunteer. She'd tripped over her own feet on the way back to the house, and she'd cursed the words and the placement of a rail fence four feet out of reach.

All thumbs. Numb thumbs would have been more accurate. But who would get it besides somebody like her? *Tripped over her own feet.* Normal people did that all the time. But normal people had no trouble getting back up.

A few more days. Was that too much to ask? Couldn't she be an ordinary, active, fully functional woman for just a few more days? A few more days living in a whole woman's body with the whole, healthy man whose boots were bringing him to her right now, across the wood floor in the foyer, into the hallway. She knew the measure of his stride, the sound of his boot heels, the feel of his presence in the house.

She hadn't wasted any time using her senses while the disease was sleeping. Maybe they'd given her more of him than she would want to be left with in his absence, but she wasn't about to back down. She turned, saw him standing there in her doorway, and willed herself—for the hundredth time since she'd last picked herself up when no one was looking, which meant it didn't count—to hold out just *a few more days.*

"Guess what." Springing from her desk chair like an eager school girl was a private test. Publicly passing, she smiled accordingly. "I just had a call from a guy named Logan Wolf Track. He's on the Tribal Council, and he's related to Kay Night Horse." She put her arms around him and gave a full-press squeeze, another personal best. "She already put in a good word for us."

"'Course she did. What did he say?"

"They'll be voting at their next meeting. He says

he's looked at our application, and he's quite familiar with the sanctuary. He's been up on the back roads, and he says he really likes the stallion, and that's a nice band of mares he's got running with him and all like that. So, I know he's on the horses' side, which is good. And I don't think he likes Tutan."

"Why not?"

"He didn't say it in so many words. It was kind of an oh-yeah-*that*-guy response. Maybe it was just a tone, but I got the distinct impression he's on our side." She laid her fingertip on his square chin. "So, thank you."

"Thank my sister-in-law."

"I did. I will again. And I won't pop any corks until after the vote is taken, but I'm feeling good about it."

"Yeah. That's…" Hands on her shoulders, he drew himself from her arms. She dropped them quickly to her sides and started her own withdrawal, but he caught her hand before it was complete. "The honey-mooners should be back soon, huh?"

"In another week. But that doesn't mean…" She squeezed his hand despite her inclination to pull away. "You're free to go anytime you need to. Or want to."

"We still have to separate out those horses Kevin ran in off the road. We'll take care of that this morn-ing." He rubbed his thumb over the back of her hand. He was trying to tell her something, but he was *all thumbs*. "But Kevin got them in without any help."

"Kevin's come a long way."

He met her gaze. "I just had a run-in with Tutan."

"The fence was down?"

"Yeah, but that's not the half of it. He was shooting prairie dogs."

"No law against that."

"On your property."

"Double D property?"

"Your side of the fence, where all those dog towns are."

"They've gotten out of control in that area on both sides of the fence. I haven't decided what to do about it."

"Is letting Tutan have at 'em one of the options?"

"Well, no, but I don't want you to—"

"Because whatever he's up to, it's about horses, not prairie dogs. Some young guy was runnin' your Spanish stud and his band up and down that draw, and Tutan's all gun happy. Then I come along, and he starts shootin' off his mouth."

"Oh, Hank. You two are fuse meets powder keg."

"No, we're not. He's nothing. No fire, no fire-power, *nothing*. But I'm not goin' anywhere until Zach gets back."

"Are you supposed to be somewhere else?"

"Doesn't matter."

"Are you scheduled for a rodeo this weekend?"

"I'm not goin' anywhere, and I'm not callin' anybody. I don't want you to, either. Let them take all the time they want. I'm just checking."

"They haven't changed their plans," she said quietly. "One more week. We'll call the sheriff, Hank. We'll be fine. You do what you need to do."

"I need to stay. I made Zach a promise. Hell, I made Tutan a promise. I need to be here until Zach comes back."

The weekend passed without incident. Not that there weren't happenings. Feel-good happenings— the kind Sally craved above all else—and concerning happenings, which she covered pretty well, she thought, keeping her concerns to herself. She would not bring the cane out until Hank left. He knew about it, but not firsthand. If she played her cards just right, she could preserve her dignity.

The feel-goods—or the good feels—were happening with delightful regularity. She pitted Little Henry against big Ribsy in a cutting contest, separating wild horses from a herd of watchful bovine mothers. Little Henry lost only because Sally lost her stirrups— actually lost her feet for a little while there, but the two of them were the only ones who knew. Under the circumstances, not losing her seat was a major, if private, victory. Cutting was a tricky feat for any rider, with her horse changing direction at the drop of a hat, stopping on a dime. Both mustangs had improved their cutting skills under Zach's hand in testament to Sally's claim that mustangs could be trained for almost anything.

Her aching butt was a glorious feeling. She hadn't put a horse through any real paces in a long time. Better to have ached and lost than never to have ached at all. But it was the moaning and groaning every time she sat down that brought her the best reward. Hank took her to his room, stripped her down, buttered her up with lotion, kneaded her muscles into putty, and made slow, sumptuous love to her until every nerve in her body grabbed a part in her physical version of the *Hallelujah Chorus*.

"I'm going to miss this," she told him as she lay in his arms, languidly stroking his hard, lean hip.

"That's not the part you'll miss. Come on."

"It's not the only part, but it's *part* of the part. They're bolted together." She stroked him, back to front. "Without the bolt, you'd lose your screw."

"Naughty girl." He grabbed hold of her bottom and pressed her against him. "Without the bolt, *you'd* lose *your* screw."

"And I would definitely miss that." She looked up at him in the dark. "I'm going to miss all of you. Especially your hands." She kissed his shoulder. "I love the way they feel on me. Anywhere, anytime. Your hands touching me makes me feel special."

"You are."

"A cool connection. A warm kinship."

He kissed her hair, the bump on her forehead, her nearly blind eye. Her heart fell. He had her deficiencies all mapped out. Except the hair. She had good hair. Knowing Hank, the hair kiss was a diversionary tactic. He knew her legs were about to start giving her real trouble again. Not so special. Very undignified.

"I hope we hear from the BLM about the training contest this week."

"I hope you do, too. I hope it works out."

"Thank you." That wasn't what she wanted to hear. "You don't have to…You know, you could just enter the contest. If you had the time." He tossed off a chuckle. "But I know you have places to go and people to see."

"I don't have a place to be, or people to see. What I have is a job. I have things to do. That's something you never run out of—never runs out on you. There's always something to do."

"Of course. I know exactly what you mean."

"If you need any help with your mustangs… You probably don't need much shoeing, but maybe with the contest…"

"If they approve."

"If they approve."

"Max Becker probably thinks I have a screw loose, just proposing such a thing."

"Your screws are none of Max Becker's goddamn

business." He braced up on one elbow and cupped her face in his other hand. "Not as long as I'm here."

Hoolie and Sally met the newlyweds at the Rapid City Airport. They came off the plane holding hands, still looking like they weren't about to come down from the clouds anytime soon.

"Getting from Sydney to New York was the easy part," Zach said. He looked tired, but at least part of the bleariness was clearly deliriousness. It was contagious. Sally felt a little dizzy herself.

"New York to South Dakota is the real stretch," Zach was saying. "But I could get used to that first-class treatment. They just keep pourin' on the bubbly."

"*That* explains it." Sally laughed. "And I thought you were still—"

"Except the Denver to Rapid City leg. That twenty-passenger egg crate, that's your reality check."

"The reality is, you're still married."

"Oh, yeah. It's official." Zach threw an arm around Hoolie's shoulders as they headed for baggage. "How's ol' Hank been makin' out?"

Hoolie nearly choked on his cherry Slurpee.

"You'll have to ask him," Sally said. "After I look up the directions for turning myself into a fly on the wall."

Zach gave his wife the high brow. "I'm thinkin' things went well."

"I'm thinking you don't know my sister."

On the way home, the women sat in the backseat of Zach's beloved pickup, Zelda Blue, and the men sat in the front, South Dakota style. Zach fondled Zelda's steering wheel, and Annie teased him about his separation anxiety every time they'd ridden in a foreign vehicle. Hoolie wanted to know if they'd seen any Australian "Brombies" like the horses in *The Man From Snowy River,* and Zach turned up the country music and sang along with Willie and Waylon and the boys.

Annie took pointed notice of her sister's cane. "How are you feeling?" she asked quietly.

It was the wrong question. Sally was neither ready nor willing to make up an answer.

Hank hated goodbyes. If he had anything to say about it, it wouldn't be the forever kind—he was planning on seeing Sally again, one way or another—but he didn't want to say goodbye to the time they'd shared. Even with the same woman, a guy never knew who he might be saying hello to the next time around.

He decided to be gone when the family got back. Let them tell their stories back and forth, show pictures, give out souvenirs. He'd give Sally a call tonight and explain. He just didn't want his last three weeks getting thrown into the mix with somebody else's honeymoon.

Before he headed for the Denver Stock Show, he

had one stop to make. He wanted to make an indelible impression on Tutan, make sure the man knew exactly who he was dealing with and that it wasn't time for counting because the dealing wasn't done.

Tutan was just toolin' into his yard on a familiar-looking ATV. Hank purposely parked in the man's road to let him know he was there for a powwow and got out of the pickup. A man with decent manners would have done the same, met in the middle and given his visitor a courteous ear. Not Damn Tootin'.

"Zach and Annie are coming home today," Hank shouted over the infernal small-engine racket.

"So?"

He nodded toward the yard light. "I saw your light on."

"It's always on," Tutan bellowed. "What's on your mind?"

"Shut this thing off and I'll tell you!"

Tutan complied, folded his arms across his barrel chest, and kept his seat.

"You got the news about the tribal leases?"

"I did. You can be damn sure it's not the final word. I've had those leases since—"

"It's the final word, Mr. Tutan. Indians love horses. There's no gettin' around that fact."

"So, you went to the tribe and said something about John Night Horse. Am I right? But he wasn't from this reservation, and neither are you. You got no right coming down here and making trouble over something that happened years ago."

Hank's blood ran cold, which kept him cool while he stared steely eyed through a red haze and spoke carefully measured words. "What *exactly* happened?"

"Nobody knows." Tutan gave an insolent shrug. "He'd been dead for who knows how long by the time they found him. Been drinking. Looked like he might've been hunting. Might've fallen on his gun. Might've…" He stared straight at Hank's face. "Who the hell knows?"

"And no one was with him."

"Might've been. Nobody ever came forward, so there's no way to find out, is there? It happened a long time ago." Tutan's eyes narrowed. "What was he to you?"

"He was my father."

"I figured as much. You should've told me right away. I know it's a little late, but you have my condolences."

Unable to look at the man any longer, Hank stared across Tutan's alfalfa field at the hills bolstering the blue horizon. He had what he wanted for now. Back to nature for Lakota land, open spaces for a few more wild horses.

"You still hold some Indian lease land," Hank reminded Tutan.

"That's right. And the way I heard it, I still have some support on the Council."

"You could lose the rest of your leases," Hank warned. "I'm not from this reservation, but we're all related. You mess with those mustangs, you'll regret it."

"I don't have time for horses."

"I do," Hank said quietly. "Not only that, I have time to make your life a living hell in ways you haven't thought of yet. You cause Sally Drexler trouble, I'll cause you trouble. I'll match you, and then I'll go you one worse. You've got friends? I've got friends. Plus I've got cause." He took a step back. "I don't know who killed my father, but you do. One way or another you'll take his death with you to your grave. *Sooner.* Or later. That's your problem."

"The hell you say." Tutan laughed. "I'm not superstitious."

"Neither am I." Hank's smile was cool and calculated. "You keep trying to kill Sally's sanctuary, you'll pay in *this* life, *Mr.* Tutan. And you'll pay dearly."

Hank watched the man and his little scooter shrink in his rearview mirror as he drove away. Regrets all around, he thought. He was already regretting his decision to leave.

But, hell, he had a job to do.

He jammed a CD into the slot in his dashboard and sang along with another Hank.

He was so lonesome he could cry.

Chapter Ten

Within a few months the new lease on tribal land would become the bridge between the Double D and the more isolated public land Sally hoped to add to the sanctuary. Tutan's leases were paid through October. After that, he was *outta there.*

Sally had it all now. Everything she and Hank had talked about—a place to be, people to see, a ton of work to do. Most of the work she had to do could be done on her place, and that was a good thing. She wasn't quite as limber as she had been when she'd last seen Hank about a month ago. *Exactly* a month ago if the month were February, which was what it felt like. Cold, barren, desolate—a feeling Sally kept bottled up while she served as a smiling Maypole for the newly-weds to chase around she couldn't have dampened Annie's and Zach's spirits even if she'd wanted to. And before Hank, she might have wanted to.

Before Hank, she might have retreated to her room and let them have the rest of the house, knowing full well that they would wonder and worry, at least a little. She always said she didn't want that. Now she meant it. She wanted what she had—a place to be, work to do and people to see. One in particular.

She glanced over Little Henry's rump and past the corral fence. The road was long and empty, but the place—*her* place—was shaping up the way she'd long dreamed. She was working on it. The round pen and the new bigger, better outdoor arena were already half finished. She worked on her people—volunteers were coming out of the woodwork since the training competition had been advertised.

She worked when she relaxed, if currying her new favorite mustang could be considered work. Little Henry loved attention, and she loved the way he smelled, the way he snuffled, the way his ears twitched, but mainly the way his hide felt against her palms. She liked the feel of feel. It made her feel alive.

She couldn't stand for hours on end anymore, and she'd stopped pushing it. Pretty much. Her cane stood ready to get her back to the house if a bout of no-feel threatened. Heat brought it on sometimes, but she loved the feel of the sun on her face. Stress could do it to her, but she hadn't heard from Damn Tootin' in more than a week.

Loneliness was a killer. Not literally, of course. She wasn't about to die from MS, and she could live without Hank Night Horse. He'd kept his promise, and he'd given her the best three weeks she'd had in years. She didn't blame him for taking off before she and Hoolie pulled in with the bride and groom. Who needed to ooh and aah over a thousand pictures of kangaroos and Australian ranches and horseback riding in the Outback? Hank, too, had places to be and people to see. Not to mention work to do. *Two* jobs. He was a busy man.

He'd called that night, said he'd just pulled into Denver.

"Hope I didn't wake you up," he said quietly. "I figured you'd all be up gabbing, but you sound…distant."

"I am distant. How far is it from here to Denver? I haven't been there in years."

"The Stock Show starts in a couple of days."

"A couple of days?"

"A guy called me—another PA—asked me to fill in for him. I owe him one."

"When did he call?" When he didn't answer, she felt foolish. She laughed a little. "I mean…I didn't know you'd be leaving so soon."

"It felt like the right time. You're back to a full house now."

"I wouldn't say that. It's a big house." *Say no more, Sally. You might look pathetic sometimes, but you never have to sound pathetic.* Jack up that voice. "But, hey, your work here is done."

"Yeah. Back to earning a paycheck."

"We didn't keep you from—"

"No. You didn't. I was…glad to help out."

She knew he was. Hank was an honest man. She loved that about him. Among other things. "If you ever feel like donating more time to a worthy cause…"

"You mean the horses?"

"All charity work here is tax deductible." She put on a happy face and gave a good ol' Sally laugh.

"Yeah." This was straight-shooter Hank she was talking to. No laughing matter. "I want to see you again."

"You know where to find me. The days of going down the road are pretty much over for me."

"You're in a good place, Sally. Doing good work."

"I know. I truly appreciate everything you did, Hank." She drew a deep breath. "Stop by whenever you can."

And that was that. She'd said she'd see him whenever. *See you when I see you.* And she meant it. She'd missed a lot of things in recent years. The rodeo was one of those things. Dancing, driving, getting from here to there without embarrassing herself were a few more things. Seeing clearly out of her right eye would have been nice. A man? Sure. Why not. Add Hank Night Horse to the list. When he came back through her corner of the world, maybe they could pick up where they left off for a day or two. If she felt like it.

If he came back.

Please come back.

She felt tired when she put the grooming bucket back in the tack room. She was glad she had her cane handy. She felt a few months of wheelchair rides coming on, but not, she hoped, before fall. Her right foot wanted to turn on her as she limped back to the corral with a feed pan full of oats for Little Henry. She should have used a bucket with a handle. It wouldn't be the first time she'd ended up face down in a pan of oats.

Nor the last. She called to the horse and laughed aloud when he came trotting toward her. She'd heard recently that several good belly laughs a day could make a huge improvement in a person's overall health, and her good ol' Sally laugh was always at the ready. She was all about improvement.

"Are you feeding my namesake?"

He startled her, but she kept her cool. No tripping over her own feet, no face in the oats. She turned, and her heart rate redoubled when she saw his handsome face.

"Can I help?" Hank asked.

"Thanks. I've got it." She hoped her smile wasn't

coming off all shaky. "You're sneaky, Hank Night Horse."

"I've got a reputation to protect."

"I'll spread the word."

He glanced at the horse inside the corral. "Doesn't look like he's been ridden."

"I've gotten lazy."

"Can't have that." He took the pan from her hand. "Little Henry should have to earn this."

"I'm really not up to—" She was nearly up to Hank's shoulders, swept off her feet by two strong arms. Like *that* would ever happen. "What are you doing, you crazy man?"

"We're going for a ride." He carried her to the fence. "Get the gate, will ya? I've got my arms full."

"I can't." But she did. She opened the gate. "I mean I shouldn't. Not—" He lifted her onto the horse's back like a sack of feed. "I'm gonna ride with a halter and lead rope?"

"Can you throw your leg over before you slide off and I have to lift you back up there?"

"You see, that's part of the prob—" He lifted her leg by the boot heel and gave her a leg over. She grabbed a handful of mane and scooted toward the withers while he made a rein from the lead. "Okay. But what's this *we* stuff?"

"Which is your good eye? Oh, yeah, the left. Watch over your left shoulder. You don't wanna miss this."

He took a step back and vaulted over Little Hank's rump almost faultlessly. There was one small *oomph*.

"Impressive performance," she allowed as he rested his chin on her left shoulder. "Of course, we named him *Little* Henry for a reason."

"And big Henry only does that trick once in a blue moon for a reason." He kissed her left cheek and whispered in her left ear. "There will be no second performance of any kind tonight."

She laughed. Hell, she was a woman. What did she know? Besides the fact that he had to be kidding.

"Just for that, I'm withholding the reach-around I was about to give you, too." But he did reach for the rein, and he pushed the open gate and nudged Little Henry with his boot heel. "I might as well tell you right up front—"

"I think you're riding what the drovers call drag."

"—that I'm crazy about you."

That shut her up. Briefly. "How do you know this?"

"I've been crazy before. Wasn't planning on goin' there again, but there it is." He slipped his free arm around her, sneaked his hand under the bottom of her T-shirt and spread his fingers over her bare skin. "Here's what I know. I truly appreciated everything *we* did. I appreciated falling asleep with you at night and sitting down to the table with you in the morning."

"Oh, come on. What about the part *before* the falling asleep?"

"That goes without saying." He chuckled. "I will say I appreciate your appreciation on that score."

"I did, didn't I?" She shivered as his little finger invaded her waistband. "You weren't easy, but I managed to score."

"I'm not easy with being crazy about somebody. Scares the hell out of me."

"So…how does this work, exactly?"

"Crazy doesn't really work. It just is." He tightened his arms around her as he guided Little Henry around the House that Zach built. "But if I work, and if you work, with any luck we can make crazy work. I can't just stop by. I want to be with you, Sally. All or nothing." She heard him swallow. Hard. "Of course, the feeling has to be mutual," he added softly.

"Oh, Hank." She let her head fall back and rest on his shoulder. "I have a disease—"

"I know."

"—that isn't going away."

"You're telling this to a halfways doctor?"

"You couldn't even tell."

"That's the half I'm missing."

"Sometimes…sometimes I look like a drunk staggering around because…"

"This is supposed to bother me?"

"Because I can't control what I can't feel, Hank!"

"What can't you feel, Sally?"

"My feet, my legs, my fingers sometimes. I told you, it's as unpredictable as…"

"You're unpredictable, with or without MS. And I'm as predictable as sunrise. I'm tellin' ya, it can work." He turned his lips to her temple. "I can't control what I *can* feel. And what I feel for you isn't going away. *Ever.*"

She closed her eyes. Her left one—the *good* one—leaked a damn tear.

And a pair of full, sweet lips kissed it away.

"Can you feel this?" he asked. And she turned her mouth to take the kiss she felt coming.

"You know what, Sally?"

"What?"

"Neither one of us is watching where we're going." She opened her eyes and drank the smile from his as he whispered, "This little mustang is one hell of a horse."

* * * * *

A COWBOY'S
REDEMPTION

BY
JEANNIE WATT

All the characters in this book have no existence outside the imagination of the author, and have no relation whatsoever to anyone bearing the same name or names. They are not even distantly inspired by any individual known or unknown to the author, and all the incidents are pure invention.

First published in Great Britain 2011
Harlequin Mills & Boon Limited,
Eton House, 18-24 Paradise Road, Richmond, Surrey TW9 1SR

A COWBOY'S REDEMPTION © Jeannie Steinman 2009

ISBN: 978 0 263 88864 5

23-0211

Harlequin Mills & Boon policy is to use papers that are natural, renewable and recyclable products and made from wood grown in sustainable forests. The logging and manufacturing processes conform to the legal environmental regulations of the country of origin.

Printed and bound in Spain
by Litografia Rosés S.A., Barcelona

Dear Reader,

I love writing about Nevada and the challenges people face in the high desert, especially those who make their living off the land. A person has to be hardy to survive and thrive in rural Nevada, and my hero, Jason Ross, thought he was as tough as any cowboy — until life walloped him a good one. Now he's reassessing and rebuilding, and he wants to be left alone while he comes to grips with what's happened.

Unfortunately, that's not to be. Enter Kira Jennings, the sister of an old nemesis, who wants something he has, something he is never going to give her, and Jason's life becomes even more complicated than it was before.

Jason and Kira were fun to write. I seemed to know both characters inside out from the moment they stepped onto the page — which made it all the easier to torture them. Not that I would … okay, I would, and did, but it was for their own good in the end.

Be sure to check out my website www.jeanniewatt.com, for information about my backlist and my coming attractions. I also blog with several excellent authors at www.loveisanexplodingcigar.com. Stop by and join the fun. I love hearing from readers. Please contact me at jeanniewrites@gmail.com.

Happy reading,

Jeannie Watt

Jeannie Watt lives in an empty nest in rural northern Nevada. Her kids—a son attending college and a daughter working as a structural engineer—live close enough to visit often. The fact that they left all their stuff at home helps the rest retain that full quality. Jeannie and her husband live off the grid in an historic ranching community, where she feeds many, many animals.

This book is dedicated to Sheryl Barlow
and Syd Moran.
Thanks for being my number one supporters!

This book is also dedicated to the wonderful parents
of Sheryl and Syd — Bill and Fern Watt and Walt
and Joy Eldred.
You're the best!

CHAPTER ONE

KIRA JENNINGS'S QUARRY sat near the back of the bar under the mounted elk head. Kira focused on the man, trying to ignore the poor beast on the wall above him. He was more careworn than in the photo she'd enlarged from an old Boise State yearbook, but it was definitely Jason Ross.

Now what?

Had he been alone, Kira would have crossed the room, asked if she could sit down, and made small talk while judging when to make her move, lay out her proposal. But he wasn't alone. Two other cowboy types and a striking woman with a mass of dark curls sat with him and Kira wasn't going to elbow her way into a private party. She would have to see him tomorrow, even though that was squeezing her for time. She only had two days to burn before her meeting with the Neary Farms people in Elko—in fact, her family, with the exception of her sister, Leila, thought she was there now. Her brother, Bryce, in particular, would not have been thrilled to know that she was in Otto, Nevada, a hundred and twenty miles to the southwest, trying to do what her aunt said was impossible: work out a business deal with Jason Ross.

Jason said something just then to the man next to him and everyone at the table laughed, cementing Kira's decision. She'd see him tomorrow.

She'd turned to leave, glad she'd ventured only a few feet into the crowded establishment, when an arm shot out, barring the door. Her heart lurched.

"Honey, you can't go." The big man in the black cowboy hat grinned sloppily down at her, his teeth showing white from behind a black beard, looking for all the world like Bluto of Popeye fame. "We need women here, and *you* fit the description."

"Is that a fact?" Kira asked, buying time as she stepped back, out of reach. No one in the bar seemed to notice that the Neanderthal in front of her was blocking her exit. She was on her own.

Wasn't the first time.

Kira kept her distance, but smiled pleasantly. When the big man began to beam back, she quickly ducked under his arm and shot out into the parking lot. He didn't follow—he was probably too drunk to follow—and if he had, Kira knew she could outrun him. She went directly to her low-slung car in the gravel parking lot and got inside, locking the door.

A couple came swaying out of the bar into the warm night and ambled past her, somehow holding each other up as they walked in tandem. Kira was glad to see that they didn't get into a vehicle, but instead headed down

the street toward the only other place that was open—
Harry's Café. Otto might be one of the smaller towns
in the state, but it had its share of nightlife. Kira had
enjoyed nightlife, once upon a time. Now…now she
concentrated on business. College was long over and she
had a career to build.

She turned the key and fired her Audi TT to life.
She'd driven the two blocks from the motel to the bar,
which bordered on embarrassing, but she hated to walk
alone in towns she didn't know, even small ones. One
never knew what might be lurking in the bushes.

"Was he there?" Dorrie, the skinny gray-haired lady
who ran the motel office, asked a few minutes later as
Kira unlocked the door to her room. Kira only knew her
name because of the plastic name tag that had been
pinned to her blouse when Kira had checked in.

Dorrie leaned against the carport post, dragging on
a cigarette. The smoke drifted off into the darkness,
past one of the many hanging baskets of petunias that
lined the edge of the carport. The woman had petunias
growing everywhere, adding a bit of cheer to the tired
exterior of the old motel.

"He was," Kira said.

"I thought I saw his truck." The lady blinked at Kira
over her glasses and gestured with her cigarette.
"What'd you want him for, anyway?"

Kira almost said, "Because our fathers used to be
friends." True enough, especially the "used to be" part,
but this was a small community, and it wouldn't take
long for the woman to connect surnames. So instead she

said, "Business," before stepping into the small room, ending the conversation. The last thing she wanted was to run into one of her father's childhood friends.

"Did you see that girl?" Menace asked as he sat in the vacant chair across the table from Jason. "I tried to get her to come back in, but—" he waved his almost empty glass "—she got away."

"It's a small town," Jason said, amazed, as always, that a woman hadn't fallen for Menace's subtle charm. "I'm sure you'll find her again."

Menace shook his head. "Probably won't do any good."

Dennis Mann, aka Menace, had been shut down by every woman in the community. He was mystified as to why and Jason wasn't going to spell it out to him. He could see that Libby Hale, their mutual friend, was tempted to explain where he'd gone wrong tonight, but was for once behaving herself.

"So what time tomorrow?" Jason asked. After a wildfire had nearly taken out his dad's barn the summer before, Menace had finally talked the old man into having a fire line put in before the lightning storms became a daily occurrence. He'd almost waited too long; they'd had a nasty storm the day before. The area was going on its fifth year of drought and the land was dry, ripe for wildfires. Libby had told him the Bureau of Land Management—BLM—fire crews were practically salivating at the prospect of weeks, or even months, of overtime pay.

"Dad didn't say what time," Menace said, reaching out

to pour the last of the pitcher of beer into his glass, "but I'm guessing he'll want you pretty early. Before the heat."

Which meant around dawn. Jason shoved his chair back, set his empty soda can on the table in front of him. "I think I'll be going then."

"I'll stop by tomorrow and see the baby," Libby said, idly twisting a curl. "Sometime in the afternoon? Or—" she smiled blandly "—will you be napping after your early morning?"

"No napping," Jason said. "I've got a foundation to rebuild." He nodded at his friends and then maneuvered through the crowd to the door. Though nearly ten o'clock, it was still hot and muggy outside. He'd parked a block away from the bar, knowing firsthand that parking in the lot often meant a new ding in his door. And his poor doors couldn't take many more.

"Hey, Jason," Dorrie Straum called before he could turn the key. He waited for her to saunter over from the motel parking lot, where she'd been having a smoke.

"So, did you talk to that girl who was looking for you?"

"What girl?" Sheet lightning glowed momentarily behind the mountains to the south of town, and thunder rumbled, making Jason wonder if Menace's father might have procrastinated too long. He hoped not. If the barn burned down tonight, he'd be out of a job in the morning.

Dorrie flicked her cigarette. "I don't know who she is. She's in room four, though."

"And she can stay there," Jason said, deciding this was not something he wanted to look into. "If she wants to say hello, she can stop by my place."

"Can I tell her that?" Dorrie asked, smirking.

"I don't think so." There was another flash of lightning, this time more distant, the thunder more muffled. The storm was moving fast, away from Otto. The barn would be safe after all. Jason would get a much needed paycheck.

Dorrie laughed. "You're never going to get laid if you don't ever hang around any women."

"Thanks for your concern about my sex life. Now stay out of it."

Jason eased his truck into gear, checking out room number 4 as he passed. A sweet silver sports car parked in the space in front of the door was the only vehicle he didn't recognize. It had to be hers.

So what was a woman who drove a high-priced sports car doing looking for him?

His gut tightened. Something about this just seemed… wrong.

THE MORNING IN OTTO WAS surprisingly crisp after the muggy evening, almost cold enough for a sweatshirt, but not quite. The tangy smell of sage hung heavily in the air, which had a dingy quality, like that of a smoggy city. Kira knew it came from a fire somewhere. It could be ten miles away or a hundred, depending on the air currents. After having several of their Idaho properties partially burned last year, her family had been hoping for a wetter summer, fewer lightning storms. It didn't appear as though they were going to get their wish.

Kira checked out of the motel on the off chance she wasn't coming back, dodged another prying question from the proprietress, then drove to Harry's Café for a surprisingly well-cooked breakfast.

And then, since Jason Ross didn't have a phone—or at least not one that was listed in the local directory— Kira left town to ambush him.

Most of the land between Otto and Jason Ross's property was federal, consisting of open desert and grassland that ended abruptly at the base of the smoky-blue mountains. Kira may have spent most of her life in Ohio before joining the family company in Boise, but she loved the desert. Something about the vastness, the stillness, got to her. As did the soft pastel colors, so unlike the vivid greens and earth tones of the farming area where she was raised.

A half hour after leaving Otto, Kira found Jason Ross's driveway—behind a big green stock gate, just as the waitress at Harry's had described. Kira fiddled with the stubborn latch for a moment before figuring it out. She opened the gate, drove through, closed it again. A person could get a lot of exercise in this county dealing with gates.

The driveway seemed to twist on forever, and the Audi was not happy with the washboards and deep dust. She pressed on, driving past stunted mountain mahogany trees and vigorous-looking sagebrush until she finally came to his place.

There wasn't much visible that wasn't related to animals or haying. Pole corrals with lean-tos and sheds, a barn and a hay roof. Big equipment… Surprisingly, she couldn't see a house, just a stone foundation.

Neat stacks of lumber stood near it, with a small cement mixer and generator next to a pile of native stones he seemed to be using to rebuild the crumbling rockwork.

Kira spotted Jason in a corral as she pulled to a stop beside his dusty blue pickup truck. He was crouched next to a chestnut foal, talking as he rubbed the animal's neck. He didn't look up when she got out of the car, though he had to have heard her drive up. His attention was centered on the baby, allowing Kira to appraise him as she walked toward the pen.

He was a striking man—even more so in the light of day. Very dark hair, lean build. Excellent bones. His ball cap lay upside down on the ground beside him, making Kira wonder if the foal had knocked it off.

"Hi," she said as she approached the corral.

The foal jerked its head up at the sound of the unexpected human voice and began to dance in Jason's arms. He tightened his grip and waited for the baby to settle before glancing over his shoulder.

"Lend me a hand here, will you?" He didn't seem surprised to see her, which struck her as odd. Drop-in visitors couldn't be that common out here.

"Uh, okay." She looked for the entrance.

"Just climb over the fence. The gate's tied shut."

"Right."

"Grab that first." He gestured with his head to a small cardboard box sitting near the gate.

"Sure."

Feeling awkward, Kira climbed the rails while carrying the box, which contained several loaded syringes and various ointment tubes. She swung her legs over the top of the fence and then dropped down on the other side, a small cloud of dust puffing up around her shoes as she landed. The foal jerked in Jason's grasp, half rearing. Again he waited for the animal to still, murmuring to it reassuringly.

It was then that Kira saw one of the baby's eyes was closed, stitched shut. Her stomach tightened.

"What happened?" she asked, fighting the impulse to look away. She'd never been good with injury, but she was damned good at hiding weakness. Sometimes it was a matter of survival in the professional world. Especially when her brother was involved.

"I don't know." He reached for a tube in the box. "His eye was injured when I got him. The vet stitched it up and now it's a wait-and-see game."

"Wait and see?"

"Whether he ends up blind in that eye. He's young, so he may not."

"And if he is?" Kira asked, fearing the foal would have to be put down.

"Then I'll have to take special care of him, won't I?" he said in a manner that made her feel ashamed for thinking he'd have the baby euthanized.

"How long do you have to wait?"

"The stitches come out in three days."

He squeezed ointment into the corner of the foal's injured eye, rubbing the area gently with his thumb before handing the tube back to Kira. "Give me the syringe with the blue top."

Kira took off the cap and handed it to him. He held the baby still as he squeezed a few drops out the tip of the needle before deftly inserting it into the foal's neck muscle. After depressing the plunger, he handed the syringe back, then took a few seconds to quiet the baby before releasing him. The foal cantered to the far side of the corral, then stopped to study the humans with his uninjured eye.

"How do you do this when you don't have help?" Kira asked as Jason picked up the box. The sun was rising ever higher in the sky and the breeze that wafted over them was growing hot. Kira pushed her hair behind one ear to get it off her face.

"Usually I have everything loaded in my pockets when it's doctoring time."

"This wasn't doctoring time?"

"Not till you showed up." His expression was closed now that he was no longer dealing with the foal and no longer needed her. "You've been asking about me."

"Someone told you?" she exclaimed, realizing now why he hadn't been in the least surprised to see her. The motel lady had ratted her out.

"You were seen driving out of town in my general direction."

She cocked her head. "Why would someone warn you about that?"

"Why not?"

"Well…" She gestured at the old stone foundation. "It isn't as if you need to tidy up."

He almost smiled. Came pretty close. But close didn't count, since it wasn't horseshoes or hand grenades.

"True," he acknowledged, the semi-smile still in place, giving Kira a glimmer of hope. "Why are you here?"

She held out a hand. "I'm Kira Jennings." She had the feeling he had to fight not to take back the hand he'd automatically extended to meet hers. The handshake was brief, firm. Done. At least he didn't wipe his palm down the side of his dusty jeans.

She pressed on, although she had a sinking sensation. Aunt Pat may have been right about this guy. "I have a proposal I'd like to discuss."

"What kind of proposal?" His expression was not encouraging. In fact, with the half smile gone, it was pretty damn distant and cold.

"I'm going to be doing some work on the parcel that runs along your northern property line."

Jason stilled. "What kind of work?"

"If we sit down together somewhere, I can explain in detail."

"Why don't you just explain now and save us both some time."

Because you'll say no if I do that. Kira hadn't expected to be welcomed freely, considering the history Jason Ross and her brother shared, but she hadn't guessed the man would shut down like this. He looked as if couldn't stand to be near her a moment longer than he had to be.

She'd played this wrong, but frankly, she didn't know of any other way to play it.

Jason picked up his hat, slapped it on his leg to get the dust off, then climbed the rails, still carrying the box. Kira stayed where she was in the corral, feeling contrary. She leaned on the fence, inside his domain, peering at him through the space between the top and middle rail.

"Will you at least hear what I have to say?"

He stared at her for a moment, then shook his head. "Sorry. I'm not interested."

"I'll make it worth your while." His chin lifted slightly and Kira assumed she'd caught his interest. He probably had a vet bill coming up, and from the looks of things, he wasn't swimming in money. She glanced over at the foal, which was still standing in the corner near the small barn, watching them warily.

"I said no."

"Why?" she asked, bringing her attention back to the man on the other side of the fence. "It wouldn't hurt you to at least listen."

"Honestly? I don't want to be with a Jennings for that long."

What the hell? Kira had to fight to keep from reacting. She hoped she succeeded.

"This isn't a personal matter," she said, faking a reasonable tone. "It's business."

And why, when he'd been the one to go to prison after the accident, was he blaming...

It came to her out of the blue. Bryce must have testified against him. Or made a statement. But if he had, he'd probably had no choice in the matter, whether Jason Ross saw it that way or not.

"It might be business to *you*." He shifted the brim of his worn ball cap so that she could see his eyes, green as moss. Incredible eyes—on anyone else. "Sorry you wasted a trip out here, but I appreciate the help with the foal."

And then he turned and walked back toward the small shed that stood near the stone foundation, leaving Kira alone in the dusty corral. She debated for a split second, then climbed the rails and followed him.

"You weren't that picky about me being a Jennings when you needed help a few minutes ago," she pointed out.

"I didn't know you were a Jennings then. I only knew some lady had asked about me." He cocked his head as he studied her face. "But now I see there is a resemblance between you and Bryce. And your father."

"I don't look anything like my brother." Or her father, for that matter, which had been commented on innumerable times since she'd joined the company. She had the high cheekbones, honey-colored hair and Nordic blue eyes of her mother. Bryce was a clone of their father, dark and handsomely chiseled.

"I wasn't talking about looks."

Okay, she'd just been insulted, but she wasn't quite sure how. "Would you mind explaining that?"

"You think you can make anyone do anything if you pay them enough."

Kira bit the inside of her cheek to keep from saying something she might regret, and waited for him to elaborate. There simply *had* to be more.

The silence stretched on until she felt compelled to break it. "Has my brother or father already tried to negotiate with you?" she asked, knowing as soon as she said the words that that hadn't happened. No one in the family would talk *about* Jason Ross, much less to him. No one ever mentioned the *incident,* which had occurred while Kira was in college on the other side of the country. No, she was certain she was the first Jennings to broach this matter, and if she'd had any doubts, Jason's incredulous expression instantly dispelled them.

It was time to retreat and rethink.

She forced a cool, professional smile. "I'll be at the Saddle Tramp Inn for another day, if you change your mind about talking."

"Don't hold your breath."

Kira kept smiling. Somehow. "I hope the foal recovers his sight," she said as if he hadn't slammed her again. Then she turned and walked toward her Audi, which seemed very out of place parked on a patch of bare ground next to a giant pickup. By the time she reached the car, her smile was gone, her teeth were clenched and she had to make an effort to relax her jaw.

Back to square one.

CHAPTER TWO

JASON'S HEAD HURT.

When Dorrie had told him that a woman was asking about him, he'd never dreamed it would be a member of the almighty Jennings family. He didn't seem to be able to escape them. And it pissed him off royally that they'd had the balls to want anything from him.

At one time Jason and Bryce Jennings had been friends. Until push came to shove. Then Jason had discovered just how much of a friend Bryce was. No *friend* at all, and now his sister was here to try to get the one thing he had that they wanted. His land, or access to it—of that he was certain. Well, he'd paid a hell of a price for that one thing and he was going to hang on to it.

Jason picked a lead rope off the fence, coiling it as he walked to the tack shed.

He hadn't realized Bryce had *two* sisters, which had to be the case, because this woman was not the sister Jason had met at Boise State parents' weekend almost a decade before.

Another Jennings out to finagle a deal. Money-hungry, self-important, privileged, untouched by consequences of actions…

About to upset his life again.

If they got access to the land bordering his property, they'd subdivide. They always did. He couldn't handle that. He liked his hermit existence, seeking out company only when he wanted it. Or when Menace and Libby decided he needed it.

There were reasons he was living here instead of in Montana, closer to his parents. Solitude was one of them. The refusal to answer to anyone unless he wanted to was another. After two years of having his every move monitored and directed, he was going to do what he damn well pleased. And he didn't want neighbors watching him while he did it.

Jason stood for a moment, regarding the stone foundation he was in the process of restoring—the only remnant of his great-great-grandfather's homestead house. It had burned in the 1950s and the family had moved headquarters to the main Bottle Neck Ranch property. Shortly after Jason had begun serving his sentence, the family had sold most of the ranch, with his blessing, and moved to Montana, leaving Jason the hay fields and the old homestead property. They'd ask him to come with them when he'd been released, to start a new life—as they were trying to do on a smaller, more manageable ranch—but Jason's dream had been to reclaim his old life, and part of it included rebuilding on this foundation. His place.

Jason had first discovered the stonework when he

was six years old, out on his old horse searching for a stray cow. The cow had been in the middle of the meadow and the stone chimney jutted out of thick sagebrush nearby. Jason had forgotten the stray and headed for the potential fort.

It had proved to be everything he'd hoped it would be, and he'd gone home covered with decades-old soot from having crawled under what was left of the floorboards, exploring. His mom had practically skinned him, talking about snakes and scorpions and black widows.

Those possibilities only added to the sense of adventure when he visited what he'd come to think of as "his place."

It had been so natural to come back here once he'd been released, and equally natural to start rebuilding. The house. His life. His self-respect.

The Jennings family was not going to ruin that. They'd bought him once. They were not going to buy him again.

INSTEAD OF RETURNING to town, Kira drove to the property her family owned, but had no legal access to. She wanted to see what she was fighting for, whether it was really *worth* fighting for, or whether she was going to have to come up with another brilliant plan to rectify the Bailey matter. *The Error.* The massive failure in due diligence that she was responsible for.

Bryce had been involved, too, but somehow the blame seemed to edge more into her court than his, until here she was, in Otto—secretly, no less—trying to finagle property access out of the ingrate who had almost killed her brother.

Talk about being out of her element, skulking around like this…. But desperation brought out the best and worst in people, and Kira was feeling just a wee bit desperate. Her grandfather was not in the best of health and if he stepped down, her father would take his place, which would open up the GM position. Kira wanted that job. Or at least a shot at it. Which wasn't going to happen unless she did something spectacular and pushed the Bailey Building out of everyone's mind.

Kira stopped her car on the shoulder where the faint dirt track leading to their land connected to the main road. She'd be walking from here. Her car was gutsy, but it had its limitations. And she didn't want sagebrush to scratch the silver finish.

She followed the road across federal ground to the fence line—Jason Ross's fence line—and then walked beside it to the property. She had a topo map with her, but had left her camera in the car. By the time she remembered it, she decided not to go back. The sky was looking stormy and all she needed was a general idea of what she was dealing with.

The parcel was a promising piece of land. Located in the foothills of the mountain, it had enough relief to make it interesting, while still being suitable for dividing into five- or ten-acre building lots. The area was so scenic, the view so spectacular, she could see selling some of the lots as getaway homes. The marshes at the other end of the valley offered excellent fishing, according to the woman who had served her breakfast that morning, besides the lure of trail riding, snowmobiling, biking.

And there was practically no other private land for sale in the area. No competition. Beautiful.

Kira stood for a moment with her hands on her hips, taking in the vast expanse of valley below, enjoying the feeling that she was the only human being for miles and miles. A person could move here for recreation, peace and quiet, or, for those who worked at the Lone Eagle Mine in the next valley over, proximity to work. Yes, this place was worth developing. But people needed to be able to get to it. And right now they couldn't.

Kira had already researched her only other option to gain access to the property—across the federal land that bordered two sides of the parcel. She'd had a long and depressing phone conversation and had been told by a *very* cranky woman that to make a road across federal land, Kira would have to put in an application, commission both an archeological study and a biological study, and even then, permission was iffy. It could easily take years. Kira didn't have years.

A rumble of thunder startled her. She turned to see dark clouds rolling over the mountain behind her, giving the desert below an odd yellowish cast.

The wind gusted, whipping her hair and whirling a small cyclone of debris past her. Time to head back… In fact, it was past time to head back. Storms moved fast in the desert.

She carefully climbed through the barbed wire fence, jumping as a horny toad scuttled out of the dirt when she stepped back onto the old road. Not a rattlesnake.

Good. She needed to get to her car ASAP, and a rattle-snake bite would probably slow her down.

The wind, which had been so pleasantly invigorating only a few minutes before, shoved against her back and blew dust past her. She hunched her shoulders and kept her head down. It had been a long time since she'd been caught in a storm. Possibly because she'd been spending too much time working and not enough time outdoors.

Lightning flashed behind her and she automatically counted until the thunder rumbled. *One-one-thousand, two-one-thousand.* Only two miles away. She started to jog, trying to remember the rules of thunderstorm safety.

Stay away from trees and tall objects.

Not a problem, since she was the tallest thing around…which wasn't exactly comforting. Another bolt of lightning speared the ground. *One-one-thousand…* The thunder almost deafened her, and Kira began to run.

By the time she got within sight of her car, rain was falling. Big fat drops that made indentations in the soft flour-like desert dust before disappearing. Moments later the real rain caught up with her.

Water ran down the back of her shirt and plastered her hair to her head by the time she unlocked the Audi and got inside, mindless of what her wet clothing might do to leather seats. She didn't have a whole lot of choice, other than drowning.

Rain beat heavily on the top of the car as Kira shut the door. She reached behind her seat to fish out the light jacket she'd worn when she'd left Boise, using it to mop off her face and arms. Shivering, she tossed the damp jacket onto the passenger seat, rubbing her upper arms for warmth as she watched the thunderstorm sweep over her at incredible speed. Ten minutes later it was gone, and the air was clear as the sun broke through. The smoky haze had been washed away, and the fire, wherever it had been, had quite possibly been put out by the rain. Kira finally turned her key in the ignition. The Audi TT purred to life and she managed a U-turn in a wide spot in the road.

She really needed to get outdoors more. She'd forgotten how much she loved the elements.

Now all she had to do was go back to Otto, reclaim her room and lay her clothes out to dry while she took a hot bath.

That and think of a way to get Jason Ross to listen to her.

"WHAT DO YOU MEAN, you don't have any rooms?" Kira asked forty minutes later, tucking her damp hair behind her ears. She had to have heard wrong.

Dorrie blinked. "I mean I don't have any rooms for rent right now."

"They're *all* rented?"

The woman stared at her. Blinked again.

Kira set her jaw, smiled tightly. "All right."

She stalked out of the motel into the post-thunderstorm mugginess. She stopped to count before getting in her car. Nine units. One car in front of unit number 5. If all those rooms were rented, she was the Queen of England.

She drove the few blocks to the end of town and

parked in front of the only other motel in Otto, the Pleasant View, which hadn't been painted in about fifty years from the looks of it. And just as she climbed out of her car and approached the office, the neon No in front of the Vacancy blazed to life. Kira stopped in her tracks. She remembered seeing a cell phone weighing down Jason Ross's shirt pocket.

She slammed the door shut behind her. Wesley was only sixty miles to the northeast. She'd be there in under an hour. Hopefully, Jason Ross didn't have pull in every single lodging place there, too. She did not want to sleep in her car. But she would.

And if she *did* have to do that, Mr. Jason Ross was going to wish he hadn't messed with one Kira Jennings. She might not be able to buy him, but given time, she could figure out how to make him miserable.

For a while.

Just long enough to justify his dislike of the Jennings family.

ON THE DRIVE TO WESLEY, Kira's anger cooled and she debated whether or not she should give up and drive on to Elko, where she was supposed to be, inspecting Neary Farms.

She was only ten miles from Wesley, and still undecided, when her cell phone rang. Her sister, Leila. Or rather, half sister.

Their father had married three times while expanding *his* father's land holdings into a multimillion dollar farming and real estate business, and he'd had three children, one from each marriage. Matthew had remained married to his third wife, Margo, which meant that—unlike her older siblings—Leila had grown up in a two-parent household. It was probably why she was the most secure of the three siblings. Kira and Bryce always seemed to be jockeying for position in the family business, whereas Leila seemed perfectly content working in the computer department.

"How's it going?" Leila asked.

"I'm working on things." Failing so far, but working.

"Grandpa's feeling better and there's talk of having a meeting and making a decision about the GM position while his health is improved."

Kira sat up straighter behind the wheel. "When?"

"I'll let you know as soon as I hear something definite. Suzanne is all in a tizzy because she and Bryce are supposed to go on vacation to Saint Croix and now she has to wait and see if this meeting materializes."

Kira blew out a breath that would have lifted the hair off her forehead if it hadn't still been stiff from the rain. "This might be another false alarm, right?"

Their grandfather, in spite of two small heart attacks in a row, was very reluctant to step down. He'd agreed more than once that he needed to do just that, but kept pushing his retirement date further and further into the future. But he couldn't keep pushing it forever.

"Quite possibly. It's happened before."

Kira hung up a few seconds later. She had to work fast. Just in case this one wasn't a false alarm.

The Bailey deal was still so fresh in everyone's mind

that if she didn't show up with a bona fide moneymaker to counteract it, she was sunk. She'd end up working for her brother—which wouldn't be bad if she wasn't positive he'd find a way to ease her out once he got control.

Bryce had made it clear early on that he might be her brother, but business was business. It was a dog-eat-dog world and he was going to do his part to see that it remained that way. He also assumed that Kira was of the same mind, working against him. He probably wouldn't do anything as blatant as firing her once he got control, but he'd certainly try to set her up to take a fall. And *then* he'd fire her.

Kira's decision was made. She had to put this day behind her and try one more time to finesse Jason Ross into listening to her deal. If she succeeded, then at least she could bring some tidbit of success to the family board meeting.

JASON WAS WORKING on the stone foundation when Kira parked beside his pickup the next day, and this time she noticed that the foundation was not his only house. He had a travel trailer parked out on the edge of the hay field, partially hidden by a haystack.

The injured foal was still in his pen, but now he had a buddy with him—a small burro. The animals moved off to the far corner as Kira got out of the car, the foal's nose bumping against the burro's back as they went.

Jason looked up from the masonry, his surprise clearly shifting to annoyance as he recognized his visitor. Kira spoke before he did, getting right to the point.

"It would be beneficial to both of us to discuss my proposal."

He straightened, his muscles flexing beneath his white T-shirt, which was stuck to his chest. "What part of *no*—"

"The part where you won't even listen to what you're saying no to. That's poor business."

He shook his head, then picked up a rock and went back to work. "I never claimed to be a businessman."

"I could make you one."

He glanced up, but Kira had the feeling he was trying to ignore her. She proceeded cautiously. "If you would give me twenty minutes to show you what I have—"

"I don't want neighbors. I'm not giving right of way. Apply to the BLM for access across the federal lands."

Kira tried to maintain a poker face, but she must have twitched, because comprehension suddenly lit Jason's green eyes.

"You already did that."

She debated for a moment, then decided she had nothing to lose by telling him the truth. "The mine will be out of production by the time the red tape gets taken care of."

Jason straightened again, the rock still in his hand. "Mine?"

"If you want to know more, you need to sit down with me."

"I don't need to do anything. What about the mine?"

Kira knew this was her only chance. "The people who work at the Lone Eagle Mine travel almost sixty miles a day from Wesley or forty miles from Otto, which has practically no available housing, so few miners live there. Because of the location of this parcel, people living there would only have to travel twenty miles. It would be a time-saver for them, and it would boost Otto's economy. And there are some people who would buy places just for access to the recreation the area has to offer. In fact, I assume that's what the homes would be used for after the mine goes out of production."

"What would it do to the Jennings family check-book?" he asked, shifting the smooth gray rock from hand to hand.

"We're in the land business. It would profit the company."

"Is there anything else you need to say before you leave?" he asked with studied politeness.

"I have maps, a tentative layout…" Which she'd worked on last night in her motel room, using the topo map as a guide.

"Is there anything you haven't told me that will in-fluence my decision?"

Kira swallowed. "The amount of money we'll pay."

"There's no amount you could pay that would tempt me, so I guess there's really no need to talk, is there?"

"Jason… Mr. Ross…" Even she heard the uncharac-teristic desperation in her voice.

He gave her a piercing look and she shut her mouth, instantly ashamed of having shown weakness.

"One last question." She hesitated.

"Shoot," he said wearily.

"What did you gain from seeing to it that I didn't have a place to stay last night?"

His dark eyebrows drew together. "I don't know what you're talking about." He set the rock he'd been holding in a space on top of the foundation. It fit perfectly. "Whatever it is, I didn't do it."

Kira raised her eyes to the sky. "Give me a break." But his expression didn't change. He was either an excellent actor or innocent. She was going with the former. "Every room in town was rented."

"They were?"

"Yes, *they were,*" she retorted.

"And you think I did that?"

She spread her hands. "Who else?"

A shadow crossed his face. It was gone in a heartbeat. "Yeah. Who else?" He went back to work, slapping some mortar into a crevice and settling the rock he had chosen into place.

"So you're saying you didn't—"

"Not saying. Said. And I meant it. I'm not going to work to convince you."

Kira walked a few paces away from him. She didn't get it.

"Not a lot of fun when someone screws with your life, is it?" he asked from behind her.

"What does that mean?"

"It means that it's not a lot of fun when someone screws with your life."

"Who screwed with your life? As I understand it, you screwed with someone else's."

She instantly regretted letting her temper get the better of her. It didn't appear that damage control was an option, either. The color left his face, but he didn't deny her statement. Instead he said, "I'd appreciate it if you'd close the big gate at the county road after you drive through. Otherwise the cattle will wander out. I had a rough time herding them back in after you left yesterday."

Kira stared at him. She'd forgotten all about the gate when she'd driven away in anger the day before. And it was obvious that today she wasn't going to get what she'd come here for, but she was not going to leave without an answer to her question.

"Why couldn't I get a room last night?"

"The hell if I know. Maybe the town isn't that keen on your family becoming part of the community again." He pulled the rock he'd placed a moment earlier back out of the foundation, then reached over to stir the mortar with the trowel.

"I'm going to pursue access across BLM land," she said quietly, laying out the only threat she had. "And I'm going to have lots hugging your fence line."

"No doubt. Please remember the gate." He slapped another trowelful of cement onto the foundation, then set the stone again. Conversation over.

Kira turned on her heel and stalked back to the car, grudgingly tallying the score.

Jason Ross, two. Kira Jennings, zero.

But the game wasn't over yet. Even if she had no clue as to what her next move might be.

AS LUCK WOULD HAVE IT, Libby drove up soon after Kira had left—so soon that Jason wondered if they had passed on his long driveway. She was on the road to Elko and had stopped to see the injured foal.

"Do you know anything about Kira Jennings not being able to get a room in town last night?" Jason asked before Libby had a chance to comment on the foal's condition.

Her eyebrows rose in mock disdain that should have looked out of place on a woman wearing worn jeans, dusty boots and an old cowboy shirt. And then her full lips curved slightly. "Maybe."

When Libby had called to say she wouldn't be able to stop by and see the foal the day before, he'd unloaded about the Jenningses wanting access across his land. But he hadn't expected Libby to rally the troops. He didn't need or want to be protected from the big, bad outside world. He merely wanted to be left alone, and the Jenningses to stay far away from him.

"Damn it, Lib."

"What?" Her eyes rounded.

He quit while he was ahead. It never did any good to argue with Libby. They'd been close friends since grade school, when her parents had moved to Otto, and he could count the times he'd won a debate on one hand.

"You don't want the rich chick hanging around."

"And I don't want to get her dander up. I just want her to leave me alone."

Libby's eyes were focused on the horizon in that faraway look she often got. Life had slapped her backward a few times, too. "I agree," she said. "But it was kind of fun shutting her down."

"I bet it was. Don't do it again."

He noticed that she didn't answer as she stepped away from the fence. "I've got to go do some head counts, and my plane is due to take off right after lunch if the wind doesn't pick up too badly. The drought's playing hell with the herd in Manning Valley and the fires aren't helping. A range tech found two dead horses. Old ones, but still…"

"When's the next gather?"

"That depends on the ladies in San Francisco," she said, referring to a group that protested every mustang gather, not understanding that drought conditions could lead to slow and painful death by starvation. Nature's way, they said, having never seen a walking equine skeleton searching for water and food where there was none. The gathers weren't the perfect solution by any means, but they helped ease the suffering. As the regional BLM horse specialist, Libby was very careful with her herds.

"Ready for more little guys if I have them?" she asked now.

"A few." He took as many leppies—orphan foals—as he could feed through the winter.

"How's the well?"

"It's doing fine." Which was a blessing, since he depended on irrigation to grow hay. Several people in the valley had lost wells, and he was grateful that his was still going strong.

"Good." Libby started moving along the path to her official government vehicle. "Give me a call when Junior gets his stitches out. Let me know the prognosis."

"Will do. And, Lib?"

"Yeah?"

"Leave the rich chick alone."

Libby sighed as she opened the truck door.

Jason walked back to the foundation as his friend drove off. He didn't have a lot of income, but he had enough. He owned his piece of land and his pickup, plus the haying equipment, old and worn-out as it was, and a backhoe and a used dump truck his dad had left behind. Every year Jason sold a few steers and picked up enough ranch work to feed himself and his animals and to build his place bit by bit. The corrals, outbuilding and hay cover had taken him three years to finish, but he owned them outright and was now buying materials for the house. He was content moving slowly, paying things off as he went. He even had a bit of a retirement program, putting away as much as he could into an IRA instead of a savings account. It made him feel more…normal, to do the things a guy his age should be doing.

Who was he trying to kid? A normal guy his age would have a regular job, probably a wife, a family.

Jason had no wife and family, no regular job. But he did have his ragtag bunch of leppie foals and burros, which made him feel like he was giving back. He had two hands and the equipment necessary to help him support his eating habit. And he had a few friends who still liked him in spite of everything.

Most importantly, though, unlike Bryce Jennings, he could look at himself in the mirror every morning.

CHAPTER THREE

"WHERE ARE YOU AT?"

Bryce. Kira felt instantly guilty, like the proverbial kid with the hand in the cookie jar. Up until fifteen minutes ago, she'd been walking their parcel of land, taking photos and thinking bad thoughts about Jason Ross. She'd spent almost two hours wandering, trying to come up with a different plan of attack. During that time the sky had taken on a yellowish cast, reminiscent of the desert the day before. Storm or smoke? She wasn't sure. She'd seen a thin plume of smoke on her drive down from Wesley, but surely someone would have taken care of it by now.

She maneuvered her car around a curve, keeping out of the thick gravel at the edge, and tried to sound nonchalant as she said, "I'm checking out the country south of Elko." She rarely lied, but instinct told her that the truth was not going to be well received. And Otto was south of Elko.

"What do you think?"

"I'm not that impressed."

"Don't let Dad hear you say that," Bryce said with condescending amusement. "His childhood home and all."

"I'll keep it to myself," Kira stated, glad that he'd bought her story. "Is something wrong?"

"As a matter of fact, Neary just called and they want to move the meeting up by a day. Can you meet with him this afternoon at the Holiday Inn?"

"I, uh—" Kira glanced down at her watch "—*should* be able to."

"Five o'clock? He's having some kind of emergency and has to leave town later this evening."

"Five would be fine," Kira said. She'd even be able to make the meeting without speeding.

"And I was wondering, are you still thinking of taking your vacation days soon?"

"Why?" Because it would make her look like a slacker?

"Well, I hate to say it, but I think you might need a break. I was just reviewing the last sale prior to closing— that mom-and-pop farm near Parma? Figures were off and some of the documentation was missing. I found the problem, but, you know...maybe you need a break."

Kira resisted the impulse to defend herself. "Maybe you can show me what was missing and what figures were wrong when I get back," she said calmly.

"You bet. Let us know how the meeting goes."

"Sure." Kira made a conscious effort to sound pleasant and upbeat. "I'll talk to you later."

"Take care."

Kira disconnected and then pressed the power button.

The musical tones cheerfully bid adieu to the satellite connection, and the face of the phone went black.

There had been nothing wrong with the documentation concerning that farm sale. At least nothing she was responsible for.

Never work for family. Her mother had told her that several times when she'd been growing up. Kira had eventually ignored the advice, because after her mother had died of breast cancer, Kira wanted to be near family. In fact, up until now, she'd liked working for family, and even kind of enjoyed the competition with her brother. She liked being a Jennings, being part of a dynamic family-owned company.

But if she wanted to keep working for that company in a dynamic capacity, she needed to get to Elko and do what she was supposed to have been doing in the first place—working on the Neary Farms property deal. She'd stop in Otto, fuel up, then hit the road. With any kind of luck she'd be in Elko in time to check into the Holiday Inn, shower and change before the meeting.

And she'd be driving through smoke to get there. The northern horizon was ominously dark when Kira topped the hill and started down the other side. The thin column of smoke she'd noticed earlier had spread. A lot.

Parts of Idaho had burned the previous summer, and because of that, Kira was familiar with wildfire. She just hoped the blaze was far enough away that her car wouldn't be dragging smoke in through the air intake on the way to Elko. She had enough headaches to deal with without adding a physical one.

Kira pulled into Harry's Café right after fueling up her car, and went inside to order a sandwich for the road. A small man with a full head of silver hair sat on the far side of the L-shaped counter. He winked at her and, in spite of her tension, Kira couldn't help smiling back. First friendly gesture she'd seen all day.

The old guy nodded, then took a sip of coffee. "Any luck with Jason Ross?"

Kira hid her surprise. "We're still negotiating," she said noncommittally.

"Well, when you're used to living alone, having a bunch of people moving in would be…unsettling. You know?"

"It isn't like they'd be right next to him," Kira said. How in the heck did this guy know so much already?

The man laughed. "You've never lived rural, have you?"

"Sure. I was raised in Ohio. Farm country." Where her mother had taken a job as a nurse after her divorce from Kira's father. After that, Kira has seen her father and siblings only briefly, on school holidays.

"Could you see your neighbor's porch light?"

"Probably." She seemed to remember seeing houses all around her.

"Then you're talking a different kind of rural."

"The houses would be over the hill from him. He wouldn't even see them." Or their porch lights.

"They'll be there. And the road will get lots more use, and people will wander. Water table could drop because of all the wells."

"Who are you?" Kira asked point-blank.

"Hal Monroe. Mayor of this burg."

"It's an honorary title," the waitress said dryly as she came over to take Kira's order.

"I see."

The man winked at her again.

"Can I get you something?" the woman asked, pulling the pencil out from behind her ear.

"Don't order the shrimp salad," Hal advised.

The waitress scowled at him, then fixed her attention back on Kira.

"Just the ham sandwich and a cola. To go."

Less than five minutes later, she was on her way out the door with a white paper bag in her hand.

Things were going to be okay. She had fuel, a meal and, traveling at seventy miles per hour, at least an hour to spare before the meeting. Or so she thought until she reached the city limits, where a sheriff's department vehicle was parked across the road, its yellow light flashing. Kira rolled down her window as the deputy approached.

"Road's closed," he said in a no-nonsense voice.

"What?" Her heart gave a big thump. *This wasn't happening.*

"The fire's too close to the road, so until I get a call from the BLM fire chief, no one is going north."

"How long?"

"No telling."

"But I have to get to Elko by five o'clock. If I don't…"

If she didn't, then she'd have to fess up to not being in Elko like she was supposed to be. And since she wasn't a liar by nature, she'd end up telling Bryce and her father where she was and why and… *Crap.*

The more she'd talked to Jason Ross, the more she'd come to suspect that there had to be something else between him and Bryce, and the more certain she'd become that her father and brother would not thank her for poking her nose where it didn't belong. Unless, of course, she got the access. Then it would be a different story. She'd be a hero.

"You okay, lady?"

"I'm fine. Thanks."

Kira reversed her car until she could turn around, then headed back to the gas station, around the corner and out of sight of the deputy.

She'd paid at the pump during her first visit, so it was something of a shock to enter the office and find the big bearded guy who'd tried to keep her from leaving the bar two nights ago manning the counter. But if he recognized her, he showed no sign, so Kira cautiously stepped through the door.

"Trapped by the fire?" he asked politely.

"Yes. I'm supposed to be traveling to Elko."

"Too bad."

"There's no other road out of here?" Kira asked.

"None that little sissy car of yours can handle."

"But there is a road?"

The man, whose name was Dennis, according to the patch over his shirt pocket, nodded.

"Do you have a map? Can you show me?"

She meant one that she could buy, but instead he pulled the office door open and pointed at a big one thumbtacked over his desk. Kira stepped forward to squint up at the tattered map. It didn't even show the interstate that crossed northern Nevada as being fully completed, but there definitely weren't many routes in and out of Otto, no matter how dated it was. She could see only two, one of which was now blocked. But the other ran directly past her land before continuing north to the interstate—or what would be the interstate on a more modern map.

"Sometimes they get these fires under control pretty fast," the big man said helpfully.

And she'd bet that sometimes they didn't. "Is that road passable?" she asked, pointing at the secondary route.

"It's rough in places."

"And the fire's over here, right?" She indicated at the road between Wesley and Otto.

"I guess. Now anyway. These things move fast, you know."

Not exactly comforting, but she had a strong feeling he was more concerned about her abusing her car than the fire catching up with her. "Thanks," she said.

"Hey, are you going to...?"

Kira didn't wait for him to finish his question. Two minutes later Otto, Nevada, was disappearing from view behind her.

JASON HADN'T JOINED the volunteer fire department when he'd had the chance. The organization had only the occasional opening, and filling positions was a nomination and voting process. Jason had been nominated once, but it had come along just after he'd gotten out of prison. He knew the firemen were trying to show support and acceptance, despite his crime, but he hadn't felt like socializing back then.

Now, as he watched the fire heading straight for his place, he wished he'd joined. Because then the fire-fighters might be here, at his place, instead of wher ever the hell they were—if they were even fully mo-bilized yet. This blaze had sprung up out of nowhere, which made him think it was caused by a careless smoker.

Without help, there wasn't a damn thing he could do except load his mares, the babies and the burros in the big gooseneck trailer, open the gates for the rest of his stock and abandon the ranch, hoping for the best. He'd loaded the backhoe on the trailer, which was hitched to the dump truck, but there was no one to drive it. His cell phone service was out, so he had to do what he could alone.

His haying equipment was insured. His buildings were insured. It was his animals and belongings that needed to be hauled out first.

He'd take them to Libby's place, which was close to town and better protected. Then he might have time to make another trip back for his cattle, maybe even find someone to drive the truck. If the wind didn't pick up.

A slurry bomber flew overhead as he drove out his driveway. The feds were on the fire. Now if they would just get the damn thing put out before it hit his home.

KIRA WAS HAVING one of those do or die moments. She'd misjudged the fire. It was closer than she'd expected and there wasn't a single firefighter to be seen. The smoke was getting thicker and she could see the orange line of flames in the distance—maybe ten miles away.

Her TT raced along the road, spraying gravel as she took the corners too fast.

How stupid was she being?

She'd be fine as long as she kept moving.

According to that map, the road turned to the east in a few miles and she'd be traveling directly away from the fire for quite a while before she turned north again.

It wasn't as if she hadn't dealt with something like this before. She'd been stopped on the road several times in Idaho when the fires had burned last summer. Half an hour or so, and she had always been allowed to drive on through the smoke.

The only difference between then and now was the absence of firefighters. But she saw an airplane in the distance, so they were fighting the flames somewhere.

Just not here. Where she needed them.

JASON SAW THE rooster tail first and recognized the car second. When he did, he purposely pulled to the center of the road. The Audi slowed to a stop, and a moment later Kira Jennings was out of it and striding toward him.

"I understand that the answer is *no,* and that you control all motel rooms in the vicinity. Are you claiming the roads now, too?" Her blue eyes were blazing.

"What are you doing?"

"I'm beating the fire and heading to the interstate."

"Don't."

"Excuse me?"

"The road gets bad farther along."

"I have an excellent suspension system."

He rolled his eyes. "It's not the suspension, it's your tires. Sharp rocks mean blown tires." He gestured over the top of her car to the dark horizon punctuated by the orange glow. "You don't want to be out there with two flat tires."

He wondered if any of this was sinking into her privileged Jennings brain. From her expression he thought not. "You need to go to Otto and wait this out."

"I have business in Elko."

"Must be pressing."

"It is."

"Worth your life?"

He could see that the logical part of her, the safe, sane part, knew he was speaking the truth.

"What are *you* doing?" she asked, nodding at the trailer.

"Taking my animals to a safer place."

"You still have cows in there."

"The gates are open."

Her lips parted. "So you just leave them?"

"I don't have a hell of a lot of choice here. I have one trailer, loaded with as many animals as I can carry."

And he was wasting time talking to her.

"Will you have time to come back?"

"Depends on if I ever leave," he said pointedly. "Why don't you turn that little plaything around and go back to Otto so I don't have to worry about you?"

"As if," she muttered, but she started back toward her car, having apparently come to the conclusion that he had no reason to lie to her. He hadn't made it a secret that he wanted her far away from him, so if he was sending her to Otto, it was a dire set of circumstances. And besides that, he wasn't going to move until she turned around.

He released the emergency brake and hoped the woman would make the right choice. Kira got into her fancy car—a car he'd love to test drive if it belonged to anyone else—did a tight three-point turn on the road in front of him and then headed back in the direction she'd come from. He followed her into Otto, where she pulled off at the motel. There was now a vehicle in front of every door.

Dammit, Lib.

He didn't want to feel responsible for this Jennings woman, but she was going to be stranded without a room because of him. And not only that—he glanced in his mirror—she was now following him.

Great. He had an emergency on his hands and he'd picked up a lost puppy with no home. Who tailed him all the way to Libby's fixer-upper ranch on the edge of town.

They got out of their vehicles at the same time.

"I have nowhere to go," she said before he could speak.

"I don't see how following me is going to change that."

"Whose place is this?"

"A friend's." Libby was hopefully still in Elko and not trying to do exactly what Kira had been doing, and driving the back road to Otto to take care of her place. He'd tried to call her a couple times before he'd lost service, but hadn't been able to get through. He hoped she merely had her phone off.

Jason opened a gate and chased the three horses in the pen out into a larger corral, closed that gate, then hefted a green fence panel and propped it against one side of his trailer. When he opened the trailer door, he'd made a perfect corridor to unload the animals through, directly into the pen. Marlene, a shaggy gray burro, stepped off first, followed by the injured foal, whose good eye rolled and showed white as he bunched up against the rear end of the burro.

"Come on, Ruben," Jason murmured with an edge of impatience as the next burro balked in the doorway. The animal shuffled its feet, then gingerly stepped down. There was a scuffle and then three more leppies popped out, followed by three large horses. A full load.

Jason swung the gate shut, then his trailer door. As soon as the fence panel was leaning back against the rails, he started back to his truck.

"Buster. Jiggs!" he called to Libby's dogs, since he'd probably need help with the cattle if any were left. The two blue-eyed, mottled gray Aussie shepherds—pups of his own dog, who'd passed away a few months before—darted from the corral to the truck, bounding over the sides and settling behind the cab.

"Where are you going?" Kira asked.

He would have counted to ten if he'd had the time. "My place."

"To get more animals? I'm coming with you."

He stopped, turned to face her. "Why in the hell...?" His mouth flattened as he got hold of himself. "Why?"

"Because I'm *not* going to sit in the bar or the café

in a town where they pretend they've sold out of motel rooms because they don't like my family, and wait for the fire to go out while making small talk with Hal, the honorary mayor." Her chin jutted out when she was done speaking. She appeared to mean what she said.

"I see." He wanted to argue, but the dark smoke in the distance was getting thicker. "I have to go."

Kira opened the passenger door and got in without further discussion. Jason started the truck, but once she had settled in her seat, he felt compelled to give her a reality check. "If you're doing this to get me to change my mind about access…"

"Wouldn't dream of it." She kept her profile to him as she spoke.

He didn't believe her.

"Then…thank you for coming," he said in Clint Eastwood tones, for lack of anything better to say and because he wanted to maintain the illusion that he was in control. He didn't like being strong-armed, and he didn't like that her perfume, a warm spicy scent, was already tickling his senses, making him feel oddly unsettled. He felt like rolling down the window and letting the smoke in.

"Bet you never thought you'd say that to a Jennings, did you?"

"Not in a thousand years."

CHAPTER FOUR

KIRA OPENED HER PHONE and hit the number for Neary Farms before she noticed the No Service icon.

Okay. This could be a problem. If she couldn't call out, she was going to miss the meeting. Mr. Neary would contact her family, who would in turn try to contact her to find out why she wasn't in Elko where she belonged…

She was sunk.

But at least everything she owned wasn't about to go up in flames. She glanced sideways at Jason's hard profile. His mouth was so tight that his lips were practically white. And even though she knew it had to be because of his place being in danger, she didn't think her presence was helping matters.

Tough. He could use her help. And at least she was wearing jeans and a tank top, which were more suited for wrangling cows, or whatever they were going to do, than the linen slacks and silk shell she'd almost worn for her meeting with Mr. Neary. At the last minute she'd decided that linen would wrinkle while she drove. Thank goodness.

The town was packed with people. The parking lots

of both motels were full and the BLM had already set up a firefighting camp on the edge of town. She was startled at how rapidly things had changed in the course of six or seven hours—from a beautiful day with a wisp of smoke in the air, to a full-fledged range fire that was, by all reports, burning out of control as the evening winds picked up.

And her car was too small to sleep in.

It was obvious that the road leading out of town was blocked at the end of the main street, so Jason turned down a side street. About a half mile on the other side of town, he turned off that onto a rutted dirt road.

He barely slowed down, even though the trailer sounded like it was about to come unhitched every time he hit a bump. Kira reached up to grasp the handle above the window when he encountered a larger pothole, but she kept her eyes straight ahead, refusing to show a reaction.

The smoke was getting thicker, and the distinctive smell of burning sage permeated the cab of the truck, making her throat hurt and her head ache. Kira wondered just what they were going to find when they got to his place—if they ever did.

She may have totally screwed herself with her family and the Neary Farms people, but she couldn't say she wasn't grateful Jason had stopped her when he did.

Flat tires were not her forte, and as far as outrunning a range fire on foot went—yes, she owed Jason Ross a debt of gratitude.

But she didn't think he wanted to hear about it.

DID IT GET ANY MORE *Twilight Zone* than this?

The empty aluminum trailer clattered and banged, but Jason didn't touch the brake. Kira Jennings sat next to him—and it was nearly impossible to believe that he was once again in a vehicle with a member of that family—hanging on for dear life, pretending everything was normal. But he noticed that she winced every time the trailer banged.

At least she wasn't making small talk.

Regardless of what she'd said before they'd left Libby's place, he knew she was there to get a toehold in his good graces. There was no other reason for a golden girl to abandon her sports car and ride with him through the smoke on what might well be a fool's mission.

"Can you drive a standard?" he asked, fully expecting her to say no. The TT was an automatic.

"Yes." Her quick answer surprised him. "Am I going to?"

"I don't know," he said as he negotiated a corner and the trailer once again attempted to go into orbit. It depended on the fire, but from the looks of things, it was possible. Since she'd insisted on coming, he assumed she wouldn't have a problem being useful.

"Won't your cattle be gone?" Kira asked.

Cattle did have a strong survival instinct, but Jason had to go back, just in case.

"If they are, we'll grab a few things, then leave."

The cattle were gone, smart critters that they were. When Jason drove into his place, it was deserted. The gates still hung open.

"Are we going to load the wood?" Kira asked.

Much as he'd love to save his lumber, and the cement mixer and generator, he had to get Kira out of here. He had to get both of them out of here.

"Not enough time." Not if he was going to drive his very slow dump truck. That had been his promise to himself. If he didn't have to spend precious time saving cattle, he'd save the dump truck instead of driving it to the middle of the field and hoping for the best.

And then he caught a flash of movement near the hay shed. Damn. Was one of his cows that dumb?

Just then a Hereford stepped out from behind the shed into the field, before pausing to look over her shoulder. Seconds later a new baby, the spitting image of its mother, with a copper coat and white face, followed.

Jason immediately recognized her as one of the escapees he hadn't located after Kira had left the gate open on her first visit. The cow, one of his best full-blooded Herefords, had come home because of the fire—with her late calf. The rest of the herd was long gone, but she was searching for them in the place she knew they were supposed to be.

"You're going to save her, aren't you?" Kira demanded.

"Yes," he said through clenched teeth. They'd try, anyway, and then he was going to get the hell out of here. "Buster. Jiggs. Put her in the pen."

The Aussies shot out the back of the truck. Jason didn't know how successful the dogs would be. The cow wanted to get her baby away from the fire, but she was confused.

Confusion worked in their favor. Since the corral was in the opposite direction of the fire and the cow wanted to go that way, the dogs were able to get her moving. And then, by some bovine miracle, the calf galloped ahead of its mom into the pen, and she followed.

Jason breathed a prayer of thanks as he closed the gate on a couple thousand dollars and ran back to the trailer. This cow was one of his friendlier animals, even in new-mother mode, so there was a chance he'd be able to save her, although there was no telling how the combination of fire, dogs and maternal instinct were going to combine.

JASON PICKED UP the calf and carried it into the trailer without the mama cow stomping him. She leaped in after him and he escaped out the side door, slamming it shut behind him. By the time he closed the back trailer door, the smoke was so thick Kira's throat felt raw.

"Can you drive this truck?"

"I've never pulled a trailer—"

"It follows the truck."

"But…" She pressed her lips together, then said, "I can drive the truck."

"Good. Now, if I get too far behind you, don't wait for me. Just go back through town to Libby's place."

She wanted to ask questions, but there wasn't time, so she nodded and went to the driver's side. Jason followed. His face was grimy from the smoke and dirt.

When she glanced in the rearview mirror, she saw that she didn't look much different.

The truck was pointed in the right direction, so Kira jumped in, put it in gear and started down the driveway. She would have preferred not to lead the way, but soon discovered why she was. The top speed of the dump truck appeared to be forty-five, as near as she could tell. She figured with the fire lapping ever closer to the road, Jason wasn't going slow for safety's sake.

With the trailer behind her, Kira felt as if she was driving something fifteen feet wide and at least a hundred feet long. She tried to ease closer to the edge of the road as she approached the corner. She was too far over the center and wanted to correct that, although she didn't think there'd be any oncoming traffic. Only a fool—or she and Jason, apparently—would venture this close to the front of the fire.

A slurry bomber flew low overhead, dropping a load of red material about a half mile from the road. She pressed the accelerator. She rounded the corner, then another, and then she stopped, the trailer swerving slightly behind her.

The fire was crossing the road.

She'd done lots of wild and crazy things in her younger years, but driving through fire wasn't one of them.

Jason's big truck lumbered around the corner then, rolling to a stop next to her.

He jumped out and ran up as she rolled down the window.

"Scoot over."

"What about your truck?"

"Scoot over!"

She scooted over. Jason got in, automatically adjust-
ing the seat, then reversed the trailer past the dump
truck until he came to a side road leading to a pasture.
Unerringly, he backed the trailer onto it. A few seconds
later he had turned around and they were headed in the
opposite direction.

"Where are we going?" Kira asked through gritted
teeth as she hung on to the edge of her seat. She hoped
the cows were all right. She hoped she and Jason would
be all right.

JASON WAS SWEATING. His hands were tight on the wheel.
He was going to lose his dump truck and backhoe—his
livelihood—but that was a very small consideration
right now. He had to get them out of here alive.

He shouldn't have returned for his cattle, or the
equipment. He was going to lose his truck and backhoe
anyway, and he was one dumb son of a bitch for letting
Kira Jennings come with him.

"How'd the fire get there?" she asked in a low voice.

"Wind change. These things make their own atmo-
spheric patterns. Vortexes."

"They can circle?"

"This one can."

"Where are we going?" She gave no sign of being
nervous, but she had to be. He was.

"To the flank of the fire and then in the opposite direction. I hope."

Kira didn't ask any more questions, letting Jason concentrate on his driving. He pulled off on a soft dirt track that stretched for miles, barely slowing as the truck and trailer bounced onto it. Kira looked back at the dogs who were glued to their usual spot behind the toolbox.

The soft dirt gave way to washboarded areas that punished both the truck and the trailer, then to deep, deep dust that swirled up around them, almost obliterating the view as it settled on the windshield.

"You are experiencing almost everything bad rural Nevada has to offer," Jason muttered. "Drought, fire, engine-choking dust…" The only thing missing was the tire-popping rocks, but those were probably coming.

And this woman was obviously a lot tougher than her asshole brother. So far she hadn't uttered one complaint, although she was probably mapping out a lawsuit in her head.

After they got farther into the valley, the road was actually in decent shape, since no one had driven on it while it was wet the past fall. Jason was able to put some distance between them and the fire. But not enough. He drove as fast as he dared, glancing in the rearview mirror every few seconds to make sure the blaze wasn't overtaking them, although he had no idea what the hell he'd do if it did.

"Look," Kira said. She was staring into the side mirror. Jason glanced into his and saw what she was talking about. The smoke was blowing in a different direction than it had been a few minutes before, perpendicular to the road they were traveling on. The wind had shifted again.

Jason didn't slow down.

IT WAS GETTING CLOSE to dark by the time the road Jason had been following connected to a broader, well-maintained gravel one. Kira could see the glow of the fire on the horizon behind them, but they'd outdistanced it. He pulled to a stop before turning onto the road. Kira drew in a breath, surprised at how shaky it was—they were safe now—and at how raw her throat felt.

"I want to check the cows." Jason got out of the truck and walked back to the trailer, where he jumped up on the sideboard and peered through the slits in the panels. Kira wasn't sure, but from the way the dogs were watching him, he appeared to be talking to the animals.

"Is she okay?" Kira asked when he returned.

"Yeah. I was half afraid she may have fallen at some point."

"The calf?"

"Fine. Wild-eyed, but doing all right."

He put the truck in gear and turned onto the gravel road. They hadn't traveled a mile when he glanced into the side mirror and then cursed and pulled to a stop.

Kira glanced at him.

"Flat tire on the trailer."

Her eyes rounded as the implication hit her. The trailer was one thing, but if they'd had a flat tire on the *truck* when they'd been trying to outrun the fire…

He squeezed her shoulder, then seemed to remember who he was touching, and pulled his hand back. "I'm sorry I put you in danger. I hadn't expected things to be that bad."

"I made my own decision," Kira replied evenly. She never liked to have people tell her what to do.

"But maybe you didn't know all the variables."

True. She'd been a little freaked out by the fire crossing the road. Make that a lot freaked out. And when Jason had abandoned his truck and equipment, well, that was when she'd realized just how much danger they were in.

"I'm not sorry I came." Now that she was miles from the flames and out of danger. "If the wind hadn't changed, you might have been able to save your dump truck and backhoe. It was worth a shot."

"Worth a shot? Damn, woman, we almost got killed. I should have tossed you out of the truck back at Libby's house." He reached for the door handle, and Kira did the same on her side, snorting as she left the truck.

"Good luck. I know karate. And don't call me *woman*."

He stopped and stared at her over the hood. And then he laughed, his teeth white against the soot on his face. Heart-stoppingly handsome.

"What?" she asked darkly.

"I just had a mental image of me trying to pull you out of the truck and you…karate-chopping me."

"You wouldn't have been laughing if it had really happened."

He laughed again, then shook his head and walked back to the trailer to assess the damage. Kira followed, wondering why guys who worked out in gyms never had quite the same quality of butts as guys who did physical labor for a living.

"Total loss," Jason muttered, resting his hands on his hips. There were two axels on the trailer and four tires. The rear tire on the driver's side was more than flat— it was practically gone—but the front tire had allowed the trailer to keep rolling along. The cow and calf would have had one bumpy ride if both tires had blown. Bumpier.

"I can't believe this happened on the maintained road. We must have punctured a ways back."

"Be glad it happened here and not…you know." Kira pushed her hair, now thick with dust, behind her ears to get it off her face. She grimaced at how stiff it felt. "Can you change the tire with the cows in the trailer?"

"Yeah."

"That's a plus," she said, since she had no idea what they would do if they *couldn't* change the tire with the cows in the trailer. But maybe Jason knew some rancher trick he used in those cases.

"Grab me the tire iron out of the toolbox, would you?"

"Sure…." Kira went to where it was mounted behind the cab of the truck, murmured to the dogs, who regarded her suspiciously, and reached in and pulled out the implement.

"That's a crowbar," Jason called.

Kira looked at it in disgust, then tossed the thing

back in the box. "I knew that." She dug deeper and finally came up with the tire iron. Meanwhile, Jason had unstrapped a double-wedged device from behind the wheel well and was positioning it in front of the undamaged tire.

One he'd loosened the lug nuts, he got into the driver's seat and carefully pulled the truck and trailer forward, letting the undamaged tire settle into the low spot, lifting the ruined tire off the ground.

"I wish I had invented that," Kira said, impressed with the clever item.

"You and me both," Jason replied as he put the head of the tire iron over the first lug and turned. "It might have eased the finances a bit." He removed the nut, placing it in the hubcap. "Although your financial situation probably doesn't need easing as much as mine does."

Kira had no answer for that.

Jason changed the tire in a matter of minutes and then slowly pulled the trailer off the wedge and back to the ground. He tossed the old tire into the bed of the truck. If it had taken much longer they would have had to use flashlights.

"Now, since I only have one more trailer tire, let's pray that we don't have another flat," he said.

"Do you ever get two flats?"

"A better question might be, on these roads, when haven't I had two flats? Tires seem to blow in a chain reaction."

Kira looked off in the direction they'd come from. The growing darkness accentuated the orange light warming the sky in the distance, and she didn't want to think about more flat tires.

"We'd better go," Jason said gently. "We still have some distance to cover."

THEY DROVE THE twenty miles back to Otto in silence. Kira was sitting so still that now and then Jason wondered if she had fallen asleep. But then she'd shift or let out a breath, in a way that made him think she was dealing with what had happened. Reaction was setting in. He'd almost killed her and she knew it.

It was only ten o'clock when they got to Libby's, but it seemed much, much later. Jason swung around in the wide gravel expanse between Libby's small run-down house and much larger well-kept barn. When she had bought the property, after her return to Otto six years ago, she'd chosen it more as a facility for her animals than as a home for herself. The weather-beaten house needed work. A lot of work. But it had a nice yard, and it wasn't on fire.

He unloaded the cow and calf, then praised the dogs for all their help before feeding them. Kira followed him into the house, and Jason wondered what she would think, since Libby sunk most of her paycheck into caring for her animals. Her furniture was secondhand, and looked it; the curtains and rugs were fresh from Wal-Mart. He knew because he'd gone with her to buy feed the day she'd bought them. And then, oddly inter-spersed through the secondhand stuff, were antiques—lamps, bowls, figurines that she scrounged from various antique stores and estate sales around the area. Most of the figurines were horses.

"There's probably some food in the kitchen," he said as he went to find the phone.

"Thanks," Kira answered, but she didn't go there. She watched as he dialed the Otto service station's number.

Menace answered immediately and Jason soon learned that while Menace's property was fine so far, things weren't looking as good for Jason's. No, Menace hadn't heard if it had actually burned. There was a chance the wind had changed, but Menace also warned him that no one was allowed to leave town except those helping with local evacuations—just in case Jason was thinking of trying to get to his place. Jason didn't bother revealing he'd already been, with near disastrous results. He hung up a few seconds later.

Kira gave him a questioning look from where she stood by Libby's desk, which was covered with BLM paperwork and horse magazines.

"Menace will call if anyone needs help, so we stay put." He sat on the blanket-covered sofa. He could tell by her expression that he hadn't answered her question.

"How soon until they let you go to your place?"

"Maybe by morning."

Silence settled between them. Kira watched him with those blue eyes so unlike her brother's beady rat eyes. She'd wiped the soot off her face in the truck on the drive to Libby's, but there were still remnants along her hairline, reminding him of what they'd just been through.

"Do you have insurance? Just in case?"

"On some of the stuff."

Another healthy silence followed and then Kira let out a sigh. "You're one taciturn guy at times, you know?"

"If you say so." And he was proud to admit he even knew what the word meant. College hadn't been a total waste.

"Can I make a call? My cell doesn't have service."

He gestured toward the wall-mounted phone. "Have at it," he added, in an attempt not to be taciturn. He watched her walk to the phone, trying not to notice that, in spite of the grime, she was one attractive woman with a very nice ass. He dropped his gaze to the floor.

There were other things he should be thinking about. Like what had happened at his place. Had the wind shifted in time? Where were his cattle? Had his lumber survived?

His stomach twisted.

After the prolonged drought, the desert was ripe with fuel—dried grasses, rabbitbrush and sage. There'd be no stopping a fire ripping through that stuff. And his corrals and outbuildings were close enough to the desert that if the blaze came that way, it would get ugly fast. He should have put in a bigger firebreak—more space between his living area and the native desert. The fields would provide a decent break if the fire came from the north, but his haying equipment was parked close to the shed, which was at the edge of the field. A couple sparks and that would be that. Then there were his feeding allotments—the federal ground he rented for his cattle to graze on. How much vegetation would be left?

And was he a total jerk for hoping the Jennings acreage had burned, too?

Yeah, under the circumstances, he probably was.

THE PHONE RANG AGAIN shortly after Kira completed her brief call. Jason, who'd been staring into space, still assessing possible damages, got to his feet and crossed the room to answer it on the second ring.

The conversation on his end was short and sweet, comprised of "Hello," and "Be there in fifteen minutes."

Kira looked alarmed when he hung up.

"I have to evacuate some goats." He paused only briefly before asking, "Want to come?"

"I have nothing better to do."

"I only asked because I don't want to get karate-chopped," he said as they headed for the door.

Kira nodded. "Good thing."

"Have you ever wrangled goats?"

"I've handled worse stuff, I'm sure."

"I'll remind you of that when we deal with the billy."

Jason waited for Kira to get in the truck, then pulled up in front of Libby's fuel tank, hoping it wasn't empty. Often Libby lived a more bare-bones existence than he did, putting all her extra money into caring for her horses.

He knocked, heard the reassuring thump of a full tank instead of the hollow clang of an empty one.

"Attagirl, Libby," he said under his breath. And once again he hoped she was doing the sane thing and staying in Elko. The land lines were still operational, so if she called Menace she'd know her place wasn't under threat.

Jason twisted the cap back onto the gas tank after fueling, told the dogs to load up, and got in the truck.

Kira smiled at him, a weary smile that seemed a touch ironic, too. He hated to admit that she'd surprised him tonight. Rich girls like her probably didn't often change trailer tires or flee range fires, but she'd been game and now she was ready to go again.

"Where are these goats?" she asked, turning toward him.

"East of town. The wind is shifting again, and they want to get the animals out."

"Let's do it."

CHAPTER FIVE

KIRA FASTENED HER seat belt, then checked her cell phone for the tenth or eleventh time to see if there was service. There wasn't.

"It could be a while before they get things straightened out with the tower," Jason said as he pulled onto the county road.

"Not much I can do even if I had service, other than call the office and explain what's happened."

"I thought you did that," Jason said.

"I left a voice mail for the guy I was supposed to meet today. I haven't let the family know what's happening yet."

"They should understand, given the circumstances."

"Yes," Kira said, sounding unconvinced.

"They won't understand?" Jason asked.

She looked at him across the darkened cab. The dash lights emphasized the angles of her face, the fullness of her lips. "It's complicated," she muttered.

So all was not well in Jennings land.

Jason told himself he didn't care. It wasn't his fault she was trapped here. He had a feeling she was glad she hadn't tried to make the trip in her souped-up car. On one level anyway. The sane one. But that Jennings monetary gene seemed to be strong, because he could see how much missing this meeting bothered her.

"Can you set up another meeting?"

"Yes."

He concentrated on the road, but his lips curved in a humorless half smile. Who was taciturn now? *Taciturn.* Helluva word.

KIRA WONDERED IF she would ever be able to smell wood smoke again and not think of Jason Ross.

As they pulled into the drive of a double-wide mobile home surrounded by myriad small pens and sheds, a short, stout woman of about sixty came out of the house. She shoved a cardboard box into the passenger seat of a compact car.

"Jason," she said, rushing over to the truck. "Thank goodness." The woman's unnaturally black hair was sticking out in all directions, as though she'd been pulling at it in frustration.

"Where's Mel?"

"Wesley. He went to Elko this morning, then couldn't get back. It's just me and the car."

Which was packed to the gills.

"How much more do you want to take?" Kira asked. The woman frowned, trying to place her. "I'm Kira Jennings. Jason and I were meeting on business when this happened."

The woman's brow cleared. "Oh. Well. I have a few

more boxes, not much room." Then she frowned again. "Jennings? As in—"

"Alice," Jason interrupted, "I'm going to start loading goats. You and Kira take care of the boxes."

"I have all the goats in one pen."

"Excellent." He headed off toward the back of the trailer to take stock.

"Show me what we need to pack," Kira said, ignoring the odd look the woman was giving her. Another old friend of her father's, no doubt.

She followed Alice into the mobile home and saw that the woman had been busy. At least ten boxes, of varying shapes and sizes, were lined up next to the door. And unlike her hair, Alice's home was tidy, with bright curtains and hand crocheted rugs. The woman appeared ready to start crying as she studied the many belongings she hadn't packed.

"The fire may not get here," she murmured, more to herself than to Kira.

From what Kira had seen, the fire was going to get there and soon. "Come on," she said, hefting a box. "We'll pack these on the back of Jason's truck around the hitch thing."

"Gooseneck."

Whatever.

By the time they'd returned outside, Jason had backed the trailer as close to the pen as he could get. "Panel?" he asked Alice.

The woman shook her head. "Don't have one. We use that chunk of fence."

The heavy wooden section looked as if it weighed

about two hundred pounds. Kira set her box over the side of the pickup bed and went to help.

It did weigh two hundred pounds. She struggled with her end, while Jason did the heavy moving. A minute later they had it propped against the side of the pickup.

"How in the hell does Mel move this?" Jason muttered, before opening the pen. The goats showed no desire to load, so he whistled for the dogs, who soon took care of the matter.

Jason closed the gate, and he and Kira shifted the fence back to its original resting place.

Alice had the truck all but loaded when Jason told her they needed to take off. "We've been cut off once today. I don't want it to happen again."

Alice dashed back into the house and came out with a cat under each arm, cramming them into her Toyota before getting in herself. Her big dog tried to jump into the pickup, but didn't launch himself high enough. Jason caught the animal and tossed him over the side. Buster and Jiggs stared suspiciously and the dog scrunched down between two boxes.

"Let's go," Jason said.

"Where are we taking these things?" Kira asked.

"The goats may be spending the night in the trailer."

Alice drove ahead of Kira and Jason. Otto was packed when they got there—with a few stranded motorists, like Kira, and a lot of neighbors supporting one another. A makeshift fire command post had been set up on the north end of town, easily visible from the south end ten whole blocks away.

Jason pulled the load of goats to a stop across from the café, and he and Kira got out.

"Do you want me to take them to Libby's?" he asked Alice.

She shook her head as a fluorescent green BLM fire truck rumbled past in the direction from which they'd just come. Alice watched it go by, swallowing hard. Kira touched her shoulder, but the woman's mouth tightened and her chin went up.

"Part of life, living here. Fires happen," she said.

"Where *do* you want me to take the goats, Alice?" Jason asked gently.

"Oh. Dorrie said I could use her place."

Jason unloaded the goats into Dorrie's backyard, behind the motel, while Kira helped Alice remove her boxes from the back of his truck. When they were done, they left the woman tending to her belongings, and then Jason stopped back at the café and went inside.

The place was crammed with people, but Kira could see Jason through the window, talking to Dennis, the big man from the service station, which was now closed for the night. A few minutes later, Jason came back, his face set in grim lines. It wasn't too difficult to figure why. Behind him, where his ranch was, where her property was, the horizon was bright orange and billowing with smoke.

He'd quite possibly lost everything he owned except for his animals, his pickup truck and horse trailer. He didn't seem to have any personal items except for a canvas bedroll and a duffel bag in the backseat of the pickup.

And from his closed-off expression, she concluded that he wasn't in the mood for sympathy. Kira simply pointed her eyes forward and waited for him to take them wherever they were going next.

JASON WOULDN'T KNOW until morning at the earliest whether the fire had burned through his place or if the wind had changed in time. He had to let it go for now. There was nothing he could do that hadn't already been done.

As he drove back to Libby's ranch, with Kira riding silently beside him, he didn't know if he was more physically or mentally exhausted. Kira had to be beat, too, but she hadn't complained. He'd been surprised at how willingly she'd helped, even though she was obviously stewing over the apparent bind she was in because of a missed meeting.

To his way of thinking, if the people she was supposed to meet with didn't understand being trapped by a range fire, then screw 'em. If her family didn't understand, double screw 'em.

He pulled into Libby's place. Thankfully, Menace had spoken with her, so she wasn't trying to get home to defend her property. Or she was pretending not to be trying to get home. With Libby, you never knew. Dennis had said he'd managed to convince her that her place was in no danger.

"I need a shower," Kira said as soon as he'd pulled to a stop.

"Shouldn't be a problem." Libby had all the necessary

equipment for a shower. And if Kira didn't use all the hot water, he'd be in line right behind her. It was going to be a long day tomorrow. He might as well start it clean.

Kira retrieved a suitcase from her car—some kind of green canvas-and-leather number that smacked of big bucks. Jason grimaced as he thought about the one duffel bag with his dirty laundry in the backseat of the truck. He hadn't had time to grab any of his good clothes out of the drawers.

"Where's the bathroom?" Kira asked when they got into the house.

"Down the hall, to the left."

"Thanks." She started in that direction, then stopped and glanced back. "Where should I sleep?"

"The sofa, just like me." Her eyes widened slightly and he added, "Different sofas." His was on the porch.

Kira mouthed a silent "okay," then continued down the hall.

"Hey," he called when she opened the bathroom door. She leaned back out into the hall. "Leave me some hot water."

She said something he couldn't hear, but it sounded a lot like, "Fat chance."

DESPITE WHAT SHE'D SAID, Kira honestly tried to leave some hot water for Jason. But it'd taken longer than she expected to get the greasy black grunge out of her hair, out from under her fingernails, and to just generally ease the weariness from her muscles.

She reluctantly turned off the faucet, combed her

hair straight back from her forehead and dressed in her pajamas and robe. Putting her hand on the doorknob, she drew in a fortifying breath and left the bathroom. She'd never been that comfortable staying anywhere she felt out of place, and here, in this run-down house with Jason, she felt that way.

Jason was sound asleep sitting up in an easy chair. He'd kicked his boots off, and his legs were stretched out in front of him. His fingers fell loosely over the ends of the armrests. His rather excellent mouth was relaxed, but a frown drew his eyebrows together.

Probably still fighting fires.

Kira stood for a moment, debating, then decided that the longer he slept, the more time the water had to warm up. The water heater was blasting furnace-like noises, so maybe he'd get his hot shower, after all.

She quietly sat on the overstuffed couch, wondering where the other sofa was he planned to sleep on. Kira suddenly realized that if circumstances had been different, she might not have minded sharing a small space with this man.

But circumstances would have to be different. He couldn't be holding her property hostage, for one thing. And he couldn't hate her family, even if it was justified in his own mind.

Surprisingly, though, she felt more empathy for him than she had in the beginning. Yes, he'd gotten behind the wheel when he'd been drunk, killed a friend. But he'd been young.

And he didn't strike her as a man who'd be able to

forgive himself easily, or at all, for taking the life of another.

But maybe this was the man he'd become after doing that. Maybe he'd been a different sort when he'd been in college with Bryce, and this was the scarred and repentant Jason Ross.

And maybe she needed to quit staring at him.

KIRA AWOKE WITH A START. She pushed herself up off the arm of the sofa, where she'd apparently passed out. Jason's boots were still lying where he'd taken them off, in typical male fashion, but the man himself was gone. The sound of the shower clued her in to where he might be.

Two-thirty.

Kira had no idea what time it'd been when she'd conked out. After midnight, but that was all she knew. She let her head roll back against the sofa cushions. It was chilly, but she wrapped her robe more tightly around herself. She really hoped she'd be able to get to Elko today. She had some serious damage control to instigate.

Though she doubted she would sleep, her eyes drifted shut again, only to snap back open at the sound of footsteps on the porch. A second later the front door swung open, and then the woman from the bar—the one with the dark curls—stepped into the room. She did a double take when she saw Kira on the sofa.

Kira immediately sat upright, self-consciously smoothing her untamed hair back.

"Uh, hi," she said.

"Hi," the woman said flatly, stepping into the room, one of the dogs following close behind her. She glanced down at him and said, "You need to sleep on the porch." The dog obediently turned and disappeared outside.

"I'm here with Jason Ross," Kira said, trying to sound normal, and wondering why she felt so utterly intimidated. Maybe it was because the woman had yet to smile. And she looked as if she never smiled.

But considering the woman was supposed to be in Elko, Kira imagined she had probably had a long and adventurous evening in her own right. *And…she was probably Jason's girlfriend.*

When he'd said they were at a friend's house, Kira had taken it literally, but now…this made more sense.

"I saw your car," the other woman said.

"All the motels were full."

"I noticed." The petite brunette nodded, then dropped her keys on the stand next to what might have been an honest to goodness antique Tiffany lamp with a crack in one of the glass segments. She glanced down the hall as the shower went off, making the pipes squeal.

"I'm Kira Jennings."

"Libby Hale."

Kira wasn't used to feeling at a loss. She thought on her feet, and didn't let other women intimidate her. But it had been a long day and night. Maybe just this once she'd allow herself to be intimidated, mainly because she was too tired to fight.

The bathroom door opened and Jason stepped out into the hall, a towel wrapped around his waist. He stopped when he saw the two women, the dim hall light accentuating the muscular contours of his torso. He grabbed the towel, hitched it an inch higher.

"You're supposed to be asleep," he said to Kira, holding the towel tightly, "and you're supposed to be in Elko," he said to Libby.

"Surprise," Libby replied blandly. "We're not."

NO ONE SLEPT MUCH that night. Jason borrowed a pair of sweats and a big T-shirt from Libby, then headed out onto the back porch, to the other sofa, apparently. Libby all but ignored Kira, disappearing into the bathroom and then, after a shower—quite possibly without hot water—going across the hall into her bedroom.

Kira lay on her back staring up at the ceiling. Just as dawn was turning the windows pale gray, she folded the worn quilt she'd been using as a cover, grabbed her suitcase and went out the front door to her car, still wearing her robe. She didn't want to spend breakfast with these two, feeling like an interloper. Nope. She was going to drive into Otto in her jammies and wait for the road to open.

"Please, *please* be open," she muttered more than once as she went.

And, indeed, the BLM camp was breaking up as she drove through town, giving her hope.

She slowed at the place where they were taking down the roadblock, and a state trooper waved her through. Kira nodded at the man, then headed north as fast as possible—before anything else could happen.

JASON'S LUMBER WAS TOAST. Literally. Well, more like cinders than toast. Whatever it was, it wasn't good.

It had been hard to drive by his burned-out dump truck and backhoe, but losing his trailer, his buildings and fences had more of an impact.

He'd called his folks early that morning, still wearing the sweats while Libby did him a favor and washed his clothes. His father had immediately offered both manpower and money, but Jason knew his parents' assets were tied up in their ranch, hard to liquidate. That was one of the reasons he downplayed the seriousness of the damages. The other was that he hated to upset his folks, again, and he hated taking money from them. So he wouldn't. It was a tenet he had followed since being released from prison. Jason couldn't say that his dad was happy when he hung up the phone, but he seemed to understand.

The fire had burned directly over the foundation. It had survived, but Jason's sheds were piles of rubble, as were his corrals and his outbuildings. The fields had been green enough, thanks to his remarkably dependable irrigation well, that they hadn't burned, except for the very edges. And the hay cover and equipment had been spared. He could make part of a living.

It could have been so much worse. He could have lost the animals, lost his haying equipment…. He was going to count his blessings. It was a habit he'd picked up since doing his time. When life seemed to be dumping on him, he took a moment to remember where he was *not*—prison work camp—and it helped put things into perspective.

He pushed his hat back, wondering where he was even going to begin.

Fences probably. The fire had destroyed big sections of his boundary fence, and if he was going to get the cattle back, he had to fix the fence.

And he still needed to find his cattle. After that, insurance claims, shed building, corral repair…replacing the lumber. That would just about wipe him out until he sold what was left of his hay.

And maybe most of his cows. It was going to be one tight winter. There wasn't even any guarantee that another fire wasn't going to sweep through the area and take out the rest of his assets.

He wasn't sure how he was going to get through this, but he was.

I've handled worse stuff. Kira Jennings's goat-wrangling words popped into his brain.

He'd handled worse, too. He'd bunked and worked side by side with thieves and drug dealers, a couple of white collar criminals, plus two who'd been convicted of manslaughter—although both those convictions had been pleaded down from murder charges. Amazing what a guy could get away with if he had the right lawyer.

Except for him. Jason hadn't gotten away with anything, and he'd even had a fine lawyer, thanks to generous Mr. Matthew Jennings. And all he'd had to do in return was sell his soul.

Helluva deal.

KIRA PULLED INTO ELKO exhausted, but at least she was clean. She'd driven through the burn in the early light, the road stretching like a gray ribbon through the smoking desert. At one point the wind came up, blowing so much soot and ash into the air she'd had to stop and wait for the blackout conditions to abate.

Once she was past the charred area, she stopped on a lonely stretch of road to change into her meeting clothes—the linen pants and silk shell she thankfully hadn't been wearing when Jason had intercepted her the day before. Kira combed her hair, put on some makeup while looking into the rearview mirror. A half hour later she found she needn't have bothered.

After finally reaching Robert Neary, she learned that the meeting would have to be rescheduled. He was apologetic, but he had business in Salt Lake, so it would be over a week before their schedules meshed again.

But at least he understood. In fact, he sounded quite relieved to find that she was all right. Apparently Leila had guessed what had happened, and even though she had to have been worried sick about it, wondering where Kira had been when the cell service died, she'd called and told Mr. Neary that her sister had been waylaid by the fire.

Kira phoned Leila, took about fifteen minutes to explain what had happened and assure her sister she was all right, then hung up and did what she was supposed to have been doing several days ago. She drove the peripheries of the Neary property, got a feeling for what kind of layout would best suit their needs, and then pointed her car in the direction of Boise.

"YOUR CAR SMELLS LIKE smoke." Leila wrinkled her nose. She'd been waiting in the guest parking spot when Kira had pulled up to her condo. In jeans and an olive-green T-shirt, her dark wavy hair twisted into a casual knot at the back of her head, she looked elegant in spite of her simple attire.

"It's not just the car," Kira stated, giving Leila a quick hug. Everything she owned smelled of smoke, but her car did have a strong eau de barbecue thing going. She pulled her suitcase out of the trunk, then let it drop to the ground with a dull thud. "That was some trip."

"I brought food," Leila said, giving Kira a critical once-over, as if to verify she was, indeed, in one piece. "Mac and cheese."

"Do you have anything to go with it?"

Leila's dark eyes crinkled at the corners and she held up a paper tote bag with a gourmet shop label on it. "Wine or chocolate?"

"We'll start with chocolate and move on."

"Grandpa thinks something is going on." Leila followed Kira up the three flagstone steps to the door of her ground-floor condo. Some people liked height and a view. Kira liked being able to step outside onto grass. "I don't think he believes you were on a pleasure drive south of Elko when you got cut off by the fire."

"I may as well have been for all the good it did me."

Kira unlocked the door and stepped into the living room, grimacing at the warm, still air inside. She should have left the cooler on, but hadn't, in an effort to be more earth friendly. Thankfully, the curtains were drawn. "Does Dad know what happened?" she asked, half-afraid of the answer.

"Only if he's been talking to Grandpa," Leila said, heading into the kitchen with its stainless-steel appliances and trendy concrete countertops, while Kira opened the curtains and turned on the air. "He and Bryce are still working on that ski lodge deal in north Idaho."

"That will be quite a flashy acquisition," Kira commented, reaching out to lift a limp philodendron leaf with one finger. All her plants were drooping pathetically.

"I don't know. The numbers actually aren't that impressive. Global warming and all, but I think they might be considering recreational housing. I'm not sure."

Leila, who avoided microwaves, saying that food tasted better when it wasn't cooked from the inside out, had started the oven to reheat the mac and cheese. Kira hoped she could wait for conventionally cooked food without passing out from hunger. She eyed the gourmet-shop bag as she passed by on her way to fill the copper watering pot at the sink.

"Any news while I was away?" she asked.

"None," Leila replied matter-of-factly. "Suzanne has been bugging me, though." Their sister-in-law took her role seriously, watching her husband's back and doing the good corporate wife act, even though, lately, their marriage didn't appear to be that strong. "Every-one seems to think I know something." Leila peeled the aluminum cover off the casserole dish and wadded it tightly.

"You do. Tell me about Suzanne."

"She asked me to coffee, which isn't that unusual, since we have that duty coffee klatch, what? Every two weeks?"

"Like clockwork." Kira was always included, even though she was Bryce's chief competition. She went in the name of family relations, and then Suzanne politely pumped her for information.

"But," Leila said, "we duty-klatched less than a week ago. And she kept probing, you know? 'What's Kira been up to lately?' and 'Where's Kira?' You would have been proud of me. I parried every thrust."

"Thank you."

Kira gave in to temptation and reached for the bag to pull out a slab of chocolate. Leila immediately took it from her and got out the cutting board to divide it properly. Her sister was as methodical as the rest of the family, and Kira knew she wouldn't be getting choco-late until after the main course. Leila was also strict.

"Tell me about the fire," Leila said after perfectly splitting the chocolate bar.

Kira got out glasses and plates as she told her again about the blaze, as well as about rescuing the cow and her calf, rescuing the goats, dealing with a flat tire after outrunning the flames.

"And then I spent the night with Jason Ross at his girlfriend's house."

"Was his girlfriend there?" Leila opened the oven door, wincing as the wave of heat hit her, and shoved the macaroni inside. She closed the door, then smoothed dark wisps of hair from her forehead with the back of her hand.

"She…showed up. A few hours later, I left." Kira's stomach rumbled. She wished her sister would use the microwave and let her eat.

"Yet, with all this cow rescue and such, he refuses to negotiate."

"So far, and frankly, I don't think I'm going to get another chance. There's a lot of bad blood there." Kira pressed her lips together thoughtfully.

"I don't know why. He committed the crime."

"Maybe it's guilt," Kira replied before changing the subject to one she liked even less. "I have to go talk to Grandpa tomorrow about missing the Neary Farms meeting. Fess up, you know?"

"Are you going to tell him where you really were?" Leila uncorked the wine and Kira nudged her glass closer, even though she knew Leila would insist on letting it breathe.

"I don't know. I don't want to upset him, but if he already suspects… I'll play it by ear." Kira leaned a hip against the counter, watching the oven timer tick down. Her stomach growled again. "So what's up with you?" she said, glancing at her sister.

"What do you mean?" Leila asked, blinking innocently.

"You said you had things to run by me. It sounded almost serious."

Leila glanced sideways. "I've been having a bit of a...fling?" She shrugged as she said the word.

"With who?"

"Tom Holcombe."

"The security guy?"

"Yep."

"But he's so shy." That was probably exactly why Leila had been attracted to him.

Her sister confirmed that a second later. "I practically had to seduce him. He was strong, but I was stronger."

"Does Dad know?" Kira asked curiously.

"Oh, yeah. Like Tom would still be working there if he did. Nope, he doesn't know. Which is why I have to stop seeing Tom. But Kira...he's like popcorn. Now that I've had some, I just can't stop myself."

Kira stared at her sister, then started to smile. "Between the two of us, we're going to give Dad high blood pressure."

"*Higher* blood pressure, Kira. Higher."

CHAPTER SIX

"JASON, I'M SO SORRY." Libby's dark eyes were filled with sympathy. She'd stopped by on her way to Elko to see the wreckage that had once been his place, and to pick up the list of the things he needed her to get at Wal-Mart—the only store he could afford to shop in at the moment.

"Yeah." Jason would have leaned on the corral fence—if he'd still had one. The cleanup was going to take a long time. But at least his cows had shown up five miles away, mixed in with the Benson herd. All he had to do was go get them. Soon. Right now he was paying Benson for feed. Menace had arranged to have his fire-damaged backhoe and dump truck hauled off at no charge. Parts of the backhoe might be salvageable. Overall, though, Jason was looking at a huge loss, both of property and income.

"Have you told your folks?"

"Kind of."

Libby smiled. She understood that he didn't like to worry his parents after putting them through hell a few years ago.

"I'm glad you were able to borrow the trailer."

"I owe Menace," Jason said. Or rather, Menace's father. "And I have learned one thing from this."

"What's that?" Libby asked as she started to move toward her pickup. Jason fell in step, small clouds of soot and ash mixing with dust as they walked. Buster and Jiggs were both in the front seat of her BLM vehicle, staring out the windshield, their eyes riveted on Libby.

"Don't waste time making a fire line for other people when you need one of your own."

"You had a fire line."

"Next year it'll be wider." Although in a strong wind, even a triple-wide one was no guarantee. But it wouldn't hurt.

"How'd the mustangs fare?" he asked.

Libby's expression grew serious. "They lost range. Again. But I don't think any got trapped. We're already planning an emergency gather to try to relocate some of these horses." Libby leaned a shoulder against her truck, staring out over Jason's burned property to where the green field stood out in stark relief.

"No adoptions?"

"Maybe a few. It'll depend on what shape the herd is in and how much range is left after fire season. For right now we may just hold them."

"Doesn't that take an act of Congress?"

"Almost," Libby said dryly as she pulled the door open, "but under emergency conditions, we may be able to hold them, feed them and rerelease."

"Good luck with that." Libby excelled at cutting through red tape for the sake of her horses. So far she'd come out on top every time. Jason wasn't looking forward to the day when she didn't.

"I take it you won't be in the market for any more leppies for a while," Libby said, studying his charred corrals. The dogs edged closer across the seat.

"No, but I'll be coming to get my own stock today or tomorrow. I'm borrowing some panels from Benny Benson to make temporary pens, and it won't take long to rebuild the boundary fence." Once he'd drained his savings to buy new materials. And then he had to rebuild the sheds before winter. Hopefully the insurance adjuster would be generous.

"Great."

Jiggs bumped his nose against Libby's arm and she idly started scratching him. Buster immediately crowded forward in turn. Libby glanced over the list Jason had given her, then shoved it into her front pocket. "Are you sure this is all you need?"

It was all he could afford. "For now," he said, so she wouldn't pad it out.

"What's with you and the Jennings woman?"

Jason was startled by the question. How could there be anything between them? "She needed a place to stay." Jason had thought that had been clear—especially when she'd left so early in the morning without speaking to either of them.

"People are talking."

Jason's jaw dropped. "Give me an effing break. About what?"

"Anything they can," Libby responded mildly. "But

in particular, they're wondering why you're so friendly with her. A Jennings and everything."

"Friendly? I gave her a place to sleep in an emergency. It was your place, for Pete's sake. And I let her come with me to rescue Alice."

"And that's where the talk is coming from." Libby smiled as if this was more than she could say with a straight face.

"Why?" Jason asked on a plaintive note. He hated having people talk about him, be concerned. Hell, he didn't even want them to notice him.

"I don't know. Ask Alice." Libby stopped scratching the dogs and told them to move over. Both immediately shifted to their side of the truck.

"Well, she's gone, so the gossip should die out," he muttered before blowing out a breath. "Eventually."

"You can hope."

He and Kira Jennings. Some of his neighbors were spending too much time isolated with their goats and chickens....

"She's gone for good?" Libby asked.

"I can promise you, she has no reason to come back."

KIRA'S GRANDFATHER WAS not an outwardly warm man, and his home reflected his personality. Cool, well-ordered, untouchable. It was a Spanish style house, built in the 1920s, with white stucco walls and a tile roof. Inside were broad expanses of tile and hardwood, polished teak cabinets, carved furniture. No expense had been spared in upkeep and maintenance.

David Jennings was approaching his eightieth year, and probably would have continued at the helm of the company he'd started when Kira's father was a teen, if his health had not finally begun to fail. He'd spent too many years with a cigar in one hand and a Scotch in the other. Not that Kira had ever seen him even approach inebriation. Sometimes she thought he carried the glass as a prop.

"Kira." Mrs. Middleton, the woman who cared for his house, hugged Kira as if she were her granddaughter. Her short curly hair seemed grayer every time Kira saw her, which she attributed to her grandfather's temperament. "So glad you came. David needs company, and over the past few days he's scared everyone else off."

Kira raised her eyebrows and Mrs. Middleton's plump hands fluttered, indicating the craziness of it all.

"He still hasn't adjusted to the idea of letting go of the reins?" Kira knew it was hard for him to accept passing control of the company over to his son. It wasn't that he didn't have confidence in her dad, but rather, didn't want to go out to pasture himself. But those two heart attacks had convinced him he *needed* to. Someday.

Mrs. Middleton snorted. "Come on. He's in here." She led Kira to the library.

"David. You have company. Don't eat her alive."

No one else would have spoken so candidly, but Mrs. Middleton had been with him for over a decade. She was highly competent, and had just the right wry humor and thick skin to handle a self-proclaimed curmudgeon.

Her grandfather looked up from the newspaper he'd

been reading when Kira walked into his lair. She knew he was comfortable with the sparse, masculine furnishings of the room—dark leather chairs, polished end tables, simple wool rugs—but she'd always found the space intimidating, off-putting. Quite likely the elderly man's intention. No doodads or bric-a-brac for her grandfather. Not even a collection of magazines next to his chair. He liked nice things, but hated clutter, and he didn't like people to linger in his space for long, either. Kira was certain Mrs. Middleton found his library very easy to dust.

"Kira."

She couldn't say that the way he spoke her name inspired confidence, but she smiled anyway.

"Grandpa." Kira crossed the room to where her grandfather sat in his leather wing chair that Leila called the throne. Heart attacks or not, he looked almost the same as he had when she'd first started working for the company. Thin, with fearsome angles to his face and a shock of white hair, expertly tamed.

He showed no outward sign of ill health, except for the slight tremor in his hands as he folded the newspaper on his lap. "Tell me what happened."

"What do you mean?" Kira wanted to tackle one issue at a time.

"I mean why was the Neary Farms meeting pushed back over a week?"

She took a high-backed leather chair opposite where he was sitting. She was careful as always to show deference, but no fear. Men like David Jennings fed on weakness—which was why every now and then she let herself be cheeky. It kept the old boy on his toes.

"I got cut off by a range fire."

"Yes. I heard." He leaned back, regarded her for a few seconds. "Did you inspect the Neary property?"

"I stopped on my way back to Boise."

"And before that?"

"I drove straight past it to Otto." Kira knew better than the lie to her grandfather. Trying to finesse him wasn't going to go over well, either.

"Would you explain your rationale to me?"

"I went down early, on a Friday afternoon—my comp time," she added, since he watched the bottom line. "I'd planned on looking over the country to the south, then driving back to Elko on Monday morning, when I was supposed to tour the property. The only rub was the fire."

"And the Nearys moving the meeting up."

"That didn't help," she agreed.

"You still haven't told me why you went *south,* thus screwing up our entire time line."

Kira pursed her lips. "I went south to check out the half section we own near Otto."

David said nothing.

"I wanted to see if anything could be done with it."

"What exactly did you have in mind?"

"Housing. For the Lone Eagle Mine employees."

The old man's expression shifted and his eyebrows lifted slightly. "Not a bad idea. Impossible as things stand now, though."

"So I discovered."

David leaned over to pick up an unlit cigar from the solitary crystal ashtray on the end table. Kira had never known him to actually light a cigar, although Bryce had assured her he'd once been a heavy smoker. "Did you talk to Jason Ross?"

"I did. I'd say he's ready to make a deal close to the time hell freezes. He hates us, Grandpa."

"It has to be hard to know you took a life. He was angry at Bryce for not stopping him from driving. And for making the statement against him."

"Yes. And he's still quite bitter."

Grandpa blinked and chewed on the cigar, his expression thoughtful. "His grandfather and I were friends, you know."

"How could you not have been? There must have been, what? Two families in the Otto area when you were a boy? The Rosses and the Jenningses?"

Her grandfather actually cracked a smile. "More like ten or twelve, although some were so remote we only saw them at community gatherings or sometimes at church."

"It's beautiful country," Kira said.

The old man's gaze sharpened. "You think so?"

"Yes." With her grandfather, simple answers were often the most convincing.

"Some people don't see it. They need trees and such. Did you see the family homestead when you were there?"

"I didn't really have time, what with the fire." Kira hated to admit that she hadn't once thought about a family homestead or its location.

"You should go visit sometime. See where your father was born. A person should know their background."

Kira had never considered Otto to be part of her background, but, oddly, it was.

And what a weird conversation. Kira had never known her grandfather to indulge in reminiscences before. But he'd never had two heart attacks in a row, either. It appeared he had emotional ties to his boyhood home she'd been unaware of. And he seemed to think she'd be going back there—to see the family homestead, if nothing else.

"Is Jason's grandfather still alive?"

David shook his head. "Actually, he was killed in the early days of the Korean conflict." He stared across the room for a moment, then fixed her with a laser gaze. "Why would you make a better GM than Bryce?"

When Kira had first joined the company, she'd been unnerved by her grandfather's sudden, aggressive shifts of conversation and rapid-fire, out-of-the-blue questions. Now she expected them. Some days she even enjoyed them.

"I don't know that I would say better, so much as different." She wasn't there to bad-mouth her brother. He was competent at what he did, and her grandfather knew it.

"How so?"

"I'm more of a team builder and I'm better with people than Bryce."

"All that touchy-feely bullshit?"

Kira smiled as she shook her head. "No. More like incentive than touchy-feely. Make the people who work for us feel valued and make the success of the company their success. Reward them for their contributions." Rather than hogging the glory and passing off the blame. She and her grandfather had had this conversation before. Sometimes she wondered if he forgot things, or if he just wanted her to state her position again, to see if it had changed.

"Bryce has more experience in the business."

"Maybe he's peaked," Kira said dryly, and her grandfather laughed at her audacity.

"I'm going to be blunt."

When had he been anything else? Kira nodded.

"I think you have people skills."

There was a big "but" coming here. Kira could feel it.

"But you need more than people skills to run a business. You need to pay attention to detail. You need to check and double-check surveys!"

Kira hoped she didn't wince. That damned Bailey project. She gritted her teeth and refrained from mentioning that Bryce had not checked the surveys, either. It had come as a shock to discover that the building they had just purchased extended more than a foot onto the adjoining property—the result of inaccurate land surveys a half century ago, and some good old boys turning a blind eye back in the day. Talk about a mad scramble to make things right.

Bryce had practically made a public announcement every time he moved to correct things, while Kira quietly worked behind the scenes with the owners of the adjoining property. She'd cleared the path, then her brother had ridden in like a knight in shining armor and clinched the deal.

Kira had never been comfortable tooting her own horn, but she was going to have to get better, with her brother on the scene.

"You need to be a master at due diligence," David said, "and frankly, I think you need more practice."

"Does Bryce need more practice?"

Her grandfather gave her another sharp look. "What does he have to do with it?" he demanded, and Kira realized he was not fully informed, didn't know the extent of Bryce's involvement. Probably because of his illness, and some nice manipulation of facts on Bryce's part.

But it was also no secret that David Jennings hated a tattletale. She needed to proceed cautiously here.

Kira toyed with the piping on the arm of her chair. "That incident was a fluke," she finally ventured. "An unfortunate one, but one I can guarantee you won't happen again."

"Why did you go to Otto in secret?"

"I think you know the answer to that."

The old man nodded. "You didn't want to make waves in the family. Hurt feelings."

"Not if I didn't need to. The experience was obviously painful to Bryce and to Dad. I figured, though, that if I succeeded, they'd learn to live with it. For the good of the business."

"And if you succeeded, it would put a feather in your cap. Make us all forget the Bailey?"

"Do you blame me for trying?" she asked.

"Nope. I don't. But you seem to have failed."

"I didn't have a lot of time."

"What if you had more?"

Kira met her grandfather's eyes. "What do you mean?"

"Do you think if you had a few more days, you could make some headway? Talk that Ross kid out of access?"

Her heart started beating faster.

Not very likely, but…she was willing to try.

David leaned back in his chair. "Granted, we have bigger irons in the fire, but there's not much private property available down there. And people like the fishing."

"So I've heard. And it's almost forty miles closer to the mine. People could initially buy for housing close to work, but I think the resale will be to folks wanting privacy and recreation. I figure we can have an area on the upper slope that will be entirely stick-built as opposed to mobile or manufactured. Manufactured housing on the lower lots would have to meet certain standards. A place people would want to come to to escape."

"What? No old trailers surrounded by wrecked cars?"

A joke. A very good sign.

Her grandfather stared off across the room, the cigar clenched tightly between his teeth. "I could almost see having a place there myself."

"Do you miss your old home?"

"I didn't for years, but now…I can see living in the area again." His mouth quirked. "Must be because I'm approaching middle age."

Kira laughed. Her grandfather's eyebrows drew

together then, in that expression that had terrified her the few times she'd met him as a child, and sometimes still had the same effect on her. "What's so funny?" he demanded.

"Nothing," Kira said, trying to look innocent.

"Have you spoken with the BLM?"

"Oh, yes." She rolled her eyes. "About ten different hoops to jump through and a multi-year time frame because of possible archaeological sites in the area."

"So it's a matter of getting Jason Ross to cooperate."

"Yes."

"See what you can do down there, Kira."

She leaned forward. "For real?"

"I wouldn't have said it if it wasn't *for real*." He was still frowning at her.

"And if I succeed…?"

"All I can say is it won't hurt."

"So it'll help?"

"Don't put words in my mouth." He pressed his lips together around the cigar and then said, "But if you can swing this deal, it *would* be impressive."

And that was what she wanted to do. Impress him.

"It's best that Bryce remains unaware," David said. "Knowing you're dealing with Ross will upset him on more than one level."

"I believe you're right." And since Bryce and her father were in northern Idaho, checking out property close to Coeur d'Alene, she should be able to keep them in the dark quite easily.

Her grandfather glanced at the carved wooden clock

on the bookshelf opposite his chair. "I have another appointment in a few minutes."

Kira got to her feet, then leaned down to kiss her grandfather's cheek.

"Let me know when you get back," the old man said.

"I'll do that."

WELL-GROOMED.

That was always the first thought that popped into Kira's head when she saw the company lawyer. Taylor Dixon was well-groomed. He was also pedantic, meticulous and a bit of a jerk when he chose to be—but more so with men than with women. Kira also suspected he was not a natural blonde.

Bryce called him Taylor Dickhead, which would have driven the lawyer crazy had he known.

Taylor knew he was a chick magnet with his cool sports car, triple-figure income and high-fashion wardrobe, and couldn't understand why Kira wasn't attracted to him. He also loved a challenge, so he kept on trying for her, conflict of interest be damned.

"Kira," he said when she entered his office, his decor shouting *if I wasn't a great lawyer, how could I possibly afford all this tasteful stuff?* "Finally come to your senses?"

Kira looked around, her eyes wide. "Why? Did you see a pig fly by?"

He grinned, unabashed, and then pulled a file off the corner of his sleek black desk, waiting for her to sit in an equally sleek black leather chair before getting down to business. "I have everything ready on the Parma deal, but I want to point out a few things…"

The meeting lasted twenty minutes and was the usual mix of competence and flirtation Kira had come to expect from Taylor.

"Is there anything else I can do for you?" he asked when he finally closed the file. She knew he was thinking lunch, but she had other plans.

"I was wondering if you'd discovered anything new concerning access laws in Nevada." She'd asked him to bill her for the call she'd made to him last week, but so far he hadn't.

"Well," he said with a tap of his pencil for emphasis, "the law hasn't changed since the last time we talked."

Kira repressed a deep sigh. "So there's nothing that can be done?"

"I can try to strong-arm the guy. Bluff a little."

"I don't know if this guy can be bluffed," Kira said, scooting to the edge of the chair, her skirt sliding smoothly over the leather. She picked her small blue clutch off the floor and settled it on her lap, gripping the top with both hands. Taylor's gaze strayed to her fingers. Her nails had suffered from the fire rescue efforts, but quite frankly, she didn't care.

"I'm pretty good."

"I'm sure you are," she agreed. He did personal injury work on the side.

"I ran a background on Ross."

"I know his background," Kira replied coolly.

Taylor set his pencil on his desk and leaned back in a thoughtful lawyerly fashion.

"Let me look into this some more, okay? I have a friend who practices law in Reno. I'll give him a call, see what he knows."

"I'd appreciate that." Kira stood. "And you will bill me this time?"

"Kira, this one is on the house."

"Taylor?"

"Hmm?"

"Have I ever given you any encouragement?"

"None in the least."

She shrugged before she started for the door. "Just checking. Bill me."

It was blisteringly hot as she walked the three blocks back to the building her father owned. Tom Holcombe was sitting at the security desk and, because of Leila's confession, Kira took a moment to check him out as she approached. An ex-Boise State football player, he was still solid muscle, and while Kira had her doubts about the authenticity of her lawyer's hair color, Tom's sun-streaked chestnut hair was undoubtedly a gift of nature. He met her eyes briefly, and Kira was surprised at how incredibly blue his were. She nodded casually, as if she had no idea this hunk was sleeping with her sister, and started down the hall.

Okay…she could see why Leila had gotten busy with him. He was both attractive and rather endearingly shy for being such a big man. Leila had taste, but she also had to be careful. Kira didn't think their father was going to want his daughter sleeping with the security man. It wasn't any of his business, as long as it was off-hours, but Matthew would make it his business. Over the years, their father had developed quite a sense of hierarchy, and Tom Holcombe was not high up enough to date his child. There were definite pluses to working for family, but the unwritten rules could be a killer.

"Kira!"

She turned back when she was hailed by her sister.

As she walked by, Tom glanced at Leila just long enough for Kira to see that, yes, there was indeed something there. Tom concentrated on the bank of small monitors in front of him, although there was probably next to no activity on any of them.

Her father liked to make sure all the exits were on camera at all times, along with the public waiting areas, the conference room and the parking lot. Twice his insistence on security had paid off—once during a hit-and-run in the parking lot, involving Bryce's new Jag, and another more serious incident when the disgruntled husband of one of Leila's coworkers had shown up. After the last episode, everyone agreed that perhaps Matthew hadn't been so much paranoid as farsighted.

"Come on. I want to talk in private," Leila said. When they were in her office, she shut the door. "Grandpa came to work this morning and spent a lot of time studying land sats of the Otto area."

"He did?"

"Not only that, he mentioned wanting to move back home," Leila said with a perplexed note in her voice. "Home meaning Otto. What did you two *talk* about?"

"Second chances. I'm going back down to Otto to see what I can do about getting that right of way."

"Really?" Leila smoothed wisps of dark hair from her temple. "Well, I think Grandpa's counting on you succeeding."

"That doesn't put any pressure on me." Kira was beginning to wish she'd never opened this can of worms, because she didn't know if she was going to be successful. She sincerely hoped her grandfather would wait to see if she managed to get access before conferring with architects. Professionally, this was not the time to disappoint him.

"One more thing." There was something in Leila's voice that told Kira she had a bomb to drop.

"Jason Ross lost just about everything he owned in the fire."

Kira's heart jumped. "How do you know that?"

"I called a friend at the BLM here in Boise this morning. After seeing what Grandpa was doing, and the way he was talking, I started thinking that if our property had burned it might put him off." Leila let out a breath. "My friend just called me back. As far as he knows, *our* property is fine."

But Jason had lost everything.... Kira's throat tightened as she thought about what he was going through right now.

"I hate saying this, Kira, but you might want to use that to your advantage when you talk to him..." Leila bit her lip. "For Grandpa's sake."

KIRA WAS PACKING FOR her trip to Otto and then Elko when Taylor called her that evening.

"Hi, Taylor, what can I do for you?" she asked, hoping against hope he'd found some Nevada access loophole.

"I just wanted to tell you that, honestly, you don't have a leg to stand on. No history of prior usage. The only thing you *can* do is start driving across his property regularly. If he doesn't stop you, then you could be granted access by means of—"

"Taylor, I think if I started driving across Jason Ross's property it would be the beginning of a range war. There's no way the man is going to stand by and let me do that."

"Like I said, that may be your only option...but I'm more than willing to talk to him. Unofficially."

"That wouldn't be wise."

"Are you doubting my abilities?"

"I'm saying I'll handle this. Thank you."

"Very well," the lawyer said, more coolly than he'd spoken a moment before.

She'd hurt his feelings, threatened his virility. Something. Kira pressed her fingertips against her forehead. Was it never going to end? Well, if his feelings were hurt, then maybe he'd simply bill her for the fifteen minutes she'd spent talking to him, and that would be that.

"Good night, Taylor," she said, resisting the impulse to make him feel better. All it would do was come back to haunt her later.

"Good night." The phone clicked dead.

Kira exhaled as she set the receiver back in the cradle. One less man to deal with.

CHAPTER SEVEN

THE DESERT WAS BLACK. Dark remnants of sagebrush twisted up out of the charred soil like skeletal hands reaching to the sky. The land had still been smoking the last time she'd driven through, on her way to Elko, but since it had barely been daylight, she hadn't absorbed the effect of the burn. Kira wondered how long it would take the devastated land to rejuvenate.

Otto appeared the same as it had been when she'd first arrived there several days before, except for the fire scar that extended up to the city limits on the east side of town. The fire crews were gone; the motel lots were empty.

Kira wondered if she'd be allowed to rent a room tonight. She was fully prepared not to be. She'd borrowed Leila's Jeep Grand Cherokee and had brought rudimentary camping equipment. Very rudimentary—sleeping bag, flashlight, gallon jugs of water, food in packets.

She'd camped out in the field with her friends when she was a kid. She was used to sleeping out—or had been almost fifteen years ago—but didn't think she'd be comfortable sleeping out in the desert. Too many creepy crawly things. Fortunately, with the seats laid flat, there was just enough room to stretch out in the Jeep.

But a motel room, with a shower, would be so much nicer…. Kira decided to get the bad news now, rather than after talking to Jason. If she had a chance to talk to him today.

She knew she was quite possibly on a fool's mission, but she had to give it a shot. Her grandfather expected it of her. *She* expected it of herself. And she wondered, now that Jason was hurting financially, if he would be more receptive to her plan. The money she would offer him was more generous than she'd originally intended, possibly because she was drawn to the man. She liked him. Jason Ross may have made a dreadful error years earlier, but he'd paid the price, and Kira believed he deserved a break. He didn't seem to be getting one.

Dorrie blinked from behind the counter, obviously surprised to see Kira again. Her salt-and-pepper hair was pulled back in barrettes on either side of her face and she was wearing a gardening apron.

"You're back?"

"Yes." Kira smiled. "Full up again?"

"Uh…"

Apparently Dorrie wasn't sure if she was full up. Kira kept smiling pleasantly. Waited. The woman cut a quick glance to the empty parking lot, visible through the window to her left.

"I understand if you are," Kira added sweetly. "Lots of people traveling this time of year." On the dead-end spur to Otto. "I should have called for a reservation."

"I have room," Dorrie said. "How many nights?"

"One." Kira hoped. "Maybe two?"

"Whatever. I'll hold a room."

"So, how's the economy here?" Kira asked as she finished filling in the old-fashioned registration card. She'd had to walk outside to get Leila's license plate number.

"Slow," Dorrie said.

Kira had gathered that from the number of closed storefronts on Main Street. "Has it always been slow?"

"Not when the copper mine was booming back in the sixties, but since then…yes."

"Many people come for recreation?" Kira pushed the card across the counter as Dorrie handed her a key.

"Fishing's popular. And hunting. We're usually booked up during hunting season."

"Do the people here want Otto to grow?"

"A little growth wouldn't hurt." The woman cocked her head. "Are you here to hammer on Jason again?"

Kira held up the key. "Want it back?"

"No." Dorrie came out from behind the desk and stared out the window. "*I* wouldn't mind seeing a few more people around here. But…I don't want anything to happen to us like happened to Elko, you know? Once it was a quiet little place and now it's hard to drive there for all the traffic. Very hectic."

"I like Elko," Kira said. Not that Otto had the resources Elko did. And it wasn't located on an interstate.

"It's a nice place to shop. But with people come problems."

"And money."

"True." The woman leaned back against her counter, pulled a cigarette out of the pack in her pocket, but only held it. "I knew your father, you know."

Kira paused before opening the door. "Did you?"

"We went to school together until your grandfather sold the ranch and moved. You're not much like your dad."

"I've heard."

Dorrie nodded, tapped the cigarette on her palm. "He's done all right for himself. He's much more of a promoter than his old man was."

Kira didn't know what to say, so she didn't say anything.

"Are you a promoter?"

"I'd like to develop the property east of town."

"How much development?"

"I don't know," Kira said truthfully.

"Not everyone would be in favor."

"Would some?"

"Yeah. Some would be in favor."

"Thanks for the information." Kira stepped out into the Nevada heat.

She knew at least one person who hadn't been in favor of development prior to the fire, and after a stop at the café for a take-out lunch, she was going to go see if the reality of his current situation had changed his mind.

STAN STEWART, the local vet, pulled his truck up next to Jason's in a swirling cloud of ashy dust, and Jason shut down his borrowed bulldozer before heading over to the makeshift panel corrals to meet him. Stan was already inside, inspecting the mustang foal.

"Tight schedule," the vet said, preparing a needle. "Sorry about your place."

"At least I didn't lose the fields."

"Small blessings," Stan agreed, tapping the foal's neck for a vein.

It was not a day brimming with good news, Jason thought twenty minutes later as the vet drove away again, after taking the foal's stitches out.

No doubt about it, the little guy was going to be blind in one eye. The opaque spot from the injury covered most of his pupil, so this mustang was probably going to be a lifelong member of the Ross equine family. It was difficult to sell a partially blind horse, unless someone wanted a pet.

"It's okay, Buck," Jason said as he rubbed the foal's forelock. "You'll just be part of the clan here, along with Ruben and Marlene." The jennet tilted her long ear at the sound of her name, and Jason went to scratch the wiry hair on the burro's neck. "Yep, Marlene, you've got yourself a baby."

She brushed her head against his shoulder.

Jason smiled in spite of his dark mood, then climbed the rails of the corral. It was quite possible that he was going to turn into one of those weird old guys who talked to animals and only went to town twice a year for groceries.

He had so much work ahead of him here that he might *not* be able to go to town more than twice a year for groceries. And he was trying desperately not to let it get to him, trying not to dwell on the fact that he was the only one around who'd lost property in the fire. Even Alice was now back in her trailer, surrounded by goats and coming up with gossip about him and Kira.

The fire had burned close to other places, had completely missed the Jennings acreage, but he hadn't been so lucky. He, who never seemed to catch a break, hadn't caught one this time, either. But feeling sorry for himself wasn't going to help matters. He'd done enough of that after he'd been sentenced.

It wasn't difficult to remember his emotions at the time, since there'd only been two seesawing back and forth: rage and self-pity.

Then...oddly, after a time, he'd experienced acceptance.

But he could see now that it hadn't really been acceptance. A gut-level self-defense mechanism had somehow kicked in to keep him from going crazy over what he couldn't control.

And he was still trying to hang on to that self-defense mechanism. Make it a part of his life. Part of his outlook. He tried to accept that people like the Jenningses would always have an advantage and never hesitate to use it.

But deep down...deep down he hated that family and people like them. He would never fully accept that they'd screwed him over so royally. That his life had ended up in shreds and Bryce had gotten away scot-free.

But Jason would continue to fake it as best he could.

He walked over to his future home, which would have one hell of a fire break around it once it was built.

The foundation had withstood the blaze well, as stone foundations tended to do. This was, at the very least, the second fire it had survived. If you're tough enough, you can withstand almost anything.

Jason surveyed the blackened remains of his sheds and his lumber, which he was about to bulldoze into a pile before he got on the tractor and started digging new fence post holes, and tried to steel himself against the wave of depression that hit him again. Hard.

Much as he'd like to be, he wasn't as tough as that foundation.

FOR ONCE THERE WERE NO storm clouds in the sky as Kira drove to Jason's place and turned in the drive. The paint on the metal gate was blistered and grayish, with only bits of green near the hinges, which were attached to a partially charred post. After opening and closing the gate, Kira wiped her hands on a towel Leila kept under the seat. A funky burned smell had attached itself to her palms, and she wrinkled her nose as she pulled down the driveway, past the skeletons of mountain mahogany.

Jason wasn't there. His truck was gone. Almost everything else was gone, too.

She stood for a moment, taking in the devastation. The place had been no great shakes when she had visited it the first few times, but now…well, the fields were okay. And the roof over the haystack was there, as was the haying equipment—the baler, swather and retriever—parked next to it. It was the area around the foundation that had suffered. New panel corrals were set up at the edge of the hay field, with animals in each one, but the sheds were missing, as were the pole corrals, which must have taken him a lot of time to build. The big stack of lumber near his house was gone. She could just imagine what it would cost to replace it. The land was scraped down to bare soil, with only a few scraggly, blackened sagebrush left behind. Everything else had been shoved into a pile. The bulldozer he'd used to do it was parked close by.

Kira let out a long breath as she realized the trailer that had sat at the edge of the field was part of the twisted heap of rubble. A different trailer, smaller, more beat up, was in its place. He'd lost his home, too, and whatever had been inside it.

Kira waited for him almost twenty minutes, staying near her vehicle because going to see the animals felt too much like overstepping her bounds. Finally she gave up and went to check her family's property. She found it hard to believe, regardless of what Leila's BLM friend in Boise had said, that the fire could cause so much damage to Jason's place and not have touched theirs.

But unlike at Jason's fences, hers were intact and the land unscathed. The wind must have shifted direction at just the right moment. Kira wanted to take a closer look, so she began to follow the property line, driving down what was essentially a trail. Fortunately, her Jeep was trail-rated—whatever that meant. When she came to Jason's western boundary, she stopped, got out and took in the view.

The long, low valley was golden, with the exception of the dark scar of the burn to the north. The distant mountains were that incredible mix of pastels that had seemed so otherworldly when she'd first moved west from the green farmland of Ohio. Violet, lavender, dusty blue.

The country was vast, peaceful.

Mine or no mine, people would love the area.

There had to be a middle ground. Something Jason could live with and her family could live with.

Kira started walking, the breeze ruffling her hair. She could practically feel her blood pressure dropping as she strolled along.

Maybe she'd been coming at this all wrong. Maybe she should be considering something more upscale than she had originally envisioned. Something more along the lines of the ranch conservancy she'd once visited in Texas. Amenities and privacy. Her grandpa would like that idea. Especially if he was honestly considering moving down here for part of the year.

Kira walked over to a smooth granite boulder, and after checking around the edges for creepy crawly things, took a seat. She spent a few minutes envisioning possibilities, then pulled the notebook out of her back pocket and started writing.

Fewer lots, higher prices, broad tracts left untouched for wildlife, a central lodge with amenities for the inhabitants. Surely Jason wouldn't have so much of a problem with fifteen or twenty lots instead of forty.

She was not going to dwell on the fact that her family had never done anything like this before, that the company motto was Squeeze in All the Houses You Can. She'd get access first, then worry about her family.

Maybe she could convince them it was time for a new direction, and maybe this could be their pilot program. Maybe this would be the project that would save her reputation and get her that promotion.

JASON RAMMED the posthole digger into the soil next to a burned off fence post that was too short to yank out of the ground with the handyman jack. In keeping with the rest of his luck, that morning the auger had gone on his tractor—which was too new to be an antique, but too old to be reliable—so he was working off his frustration the only way he could. Manual labor punctuated by aggravated thoughts of Kira Jennings.

And her freaking lawyer.

The man had called midmorning, just after Jason had returned from town, where he'd conducted a futile search for tractor parts. The caller had identified himself as Taylor someone, the Jenningses' lawyer, at which point Jason had almost hung up the phone. Almost.

But he knew he'd be better off knowing what he was up against, so instead he'd said, "What do you want?"

The guy had started pleasantly enough, and Jason had been about to tell him to get on with it, when the lawyer shifted his tone and began tossing around terms like "adverse possession" and "prescriptive easement."

Unfortunately for the lawyer, Jason happened to know enough property law to realize the guy was bluffing. It didn't slow the lawyer, though, even when Jason told him he had the facts wrong. It only seemed to wind him up more. Finally Jason told the man to blow it out his lawyer ass, and hung up.

As he should have done in the first place. And it pissed him off that the family had set the lawyer into action when Kira's efforts had failed.

Since the range fire, he'd actually come to think that maybe he liked Kira. That maybe since she hadn't been raised with Bryce, she didn't have the killer Jenningses-first-the-rest-be-damned attitude her brother and father did. And maybe that was why Jason felt drawn to her. She was different.

He could see now he'd probably been wrong in that assumption, and it bothered him more than it should have.

THE SUV PULLED UP at almost exactly eleven o'clock, while Jason was taking a water break. *Bingo.* He'd wondered if the lawyer's call would be followed by a personal visit, good cop, bad cop. He'd hoped not, hoped that maybe he wouldn't have to deal with Kira again, but obviously that was not going to be the case.

It was hot, and he'd taken off his shirt a while ago, but now he walked over to where he had tossed it over the panel fence, and shrugged back into it. He wasn't going to kick Kira Jennings off his property bare chested.

"Jason." Kira stopped, surveyed what was left of his place. "I don't know what to say."

"Not much you can say."

A dust devil swirled by, lifting ash and tousling Kira's straight, honey-colored hair. She put a hand up to hold it until the cyclone dissipated. "At least you got the animals out. Did you locate all your cattle?"

"Yeah," he said stiffly, seeing no reason to explain that he was still looking for two head, but the rest had ended up in a neighbor's herd. The word *taciturn* popped into his head again.

"That's good."

And then they just stood there. Jason's expression stony, Kira's compassionate, but not condescending. He could see himself buying into her concern, if Mr. Lawyer Man hadn't called earlier. She might actually *be* concerned, but that wasn't why she was here. She had a mission.

She cleared her throat. "You have a lot of work ahead of you."

He let out a frustrated breath. "Could we cut to the chase?"

"You know why I'm here." She didn't seem surprised.

"I'd say it's obvious."

"Then…" She hesitated for one brief second before saying, "let me show you what I have this time."

Fine. Show away. He nodded instead of answering. Somehow that seemed less a betrayal of his ethics.

Instead of producing a briefcase or a laptop, Kira pulled a notebook—the kind you bought at the grocery store—out of her jeans pocket. She opened it up.

"I've been making notes today. I have a proposal that will benefit us both, but before I lay it out, I want to assure you that the impact on you would be minimal. Regardless of what I said before when I was angry, the lots will not hug your fence line." One corner of her mouth tightened in acknowledgment of the threat she'd made. "There will be a buffer zone, and if you give me time to show you the plan and explain, I think you'll be pleasantly surprised."

He nodded again. He was already getting angry. Why the hell was she back here, doing this? Why couldn't she have disappeared from his life while he still thought kindly of her?

"I want to divide our property into twenty lots— most of them ten to fifteen acres. There would be restrictions on the kind of building that could be put up."

He felt the blood draining from his face as the reality of her proposal sunk home.

Twenty families. Oh, no, that wouldn't impact him. The water table alone was an issue, with twenty wells pumping out of it.

Twenty families over his fence line, with dogs and kids and who knew what else.

He wasn't antisocial, but his privacy, his solitude… He looked at Kira, knew there was no way she would understand. To her, solitude probably meant her neighbors went to bed early. She hadn't been to jail, so didn't understand having to share every privacy with whoever happened to be bunked with you or next to you.

"Go on." He'd hear her out once and for all, then be done with it. And he was going to be damn clear about the "done with it" part.

"I know this is hard for you, but the income from the access would help you rebuild. I have details worked out here, if you wanted to take a break." She held up a folder. "I, uh, brought lunch, thinking we could talk and eat at the same time. It's in the cooler in my Jeep."

That did it. A little sugar with the poison.

"You brought lunch," he said in a flat tone that belied his growing fury.

"Yes, I—"

"You're here to take advantage of my misfortune and you brought lunch."

Her cheeks flushed, telling him how close to the truth he was.

"Are you done with your proposal?"

She drew herself up. "No."

"Then you need to get done, because this is it. This is the last time we talk about it. And if it saves time, the answer is no. It'll never be anything but no."

"Don't you want to know how much we're offering?"

"I don't want your money." He wasn't selling out to these people again. "I want you to leave. And I don't want you to come back."

She stood there, her blue eyes fixed on his face, her lips pressed tightly together.

"Is there something you're not understanding?" he asked.

"Yes," she said coldly. "You."

KIRA WAS TRYING HARD to control her anger and bewilderment.

"What happened?" she asked as she shoved the

notebook back in her pocket. She missed, and the papers crumpled as she tried again.

He frowned. "What do you mean?"

"We weren't best friends when we last saw each other, but—" she held her hands wide "—you didn't hate me. In fact, I thought you might have even liked me, despite my being a Jennings."

"Kira, just back off, okay? I have some *stuff* I'm dealing with." He spoke sarcastically, indicating his burned property with a sweeping gesture. "And I'll handle it my way without any so called *help* from you. I don't care how much you offer, I'm not dealing with you guys. I'd rather lose the place."

"Then tell me one thing," she said. "Is the answer no because you don't want neighbors or because you hate my family?"

He just stared at her, coldly, with those green, green eyes. Answer enough. Hated the family.

Kira could not believe the depth of her frustration. If she'd had something handy to kick or punch—other than Jason, although he was looking good at the moment—she would have indulged.

She made an effort to compose herself before saying, "I cannot see where you gain anything by keeping us from using our property other than a misguided sense of revenge. And for what? I'm sorry Bryce didn't have the presence of mind to wrestle the wheel away from you when you made the choice to drive drunk! And I'm sorry he had to make a statement against you, but I don't think he had a hell of a lot of choice, did he?"

Jason showed no emotion when he said, "No. No choice at all." He continued to stare her down, cold and distant. Not at all like the last time she'd seen him—gripping a towel around his waist at Libby's house, embarrassed.

There was no sense staying here. She wasn't going to gain ground. Time to regroup.

She turned on her heel and headed for her car, a loser for the third time.

But even if she couldn't close the deal, she wasn't leaving. She had six more days to kill until her meeting in Elko with Mr. Neary, and she was going to spend it here…on her property if need be. If nothing else, she was going to make Jason Ross sweat, thinking she was going to come back and hound him again.

And come to think of it, she just might.

"HAD ENOUGH?" Dorrie asked from the petunia bed she was weeding in front of the motel office. Kira closed the Jeep door and pulled her room key out of her pocket, smiling as though she had no idea what the woman was talking about. *Never show weakness.*

She and Bryce might not look alike, and they operated under different philosophies, but they had that in common. They were survivors. Rather than say "uncle," both had a tendency to bluff when they had no idea what to do next. Bryce was a lot better at it than Kira, though. More practice.

"Don't feel bad," Dorrie said, plucking several small weeds as she spoke. "He's a tough nut to crack."

"Thanks," Kira said, hating that the woman had read her like a book. She went into her room and sat on the bed, loosely clasping her hands between her knees as she stared at the opposite wall.

She hadn't driven hundreds of miles down here to turn around and drive back. Besides, where would she go? She had almost a week until her meeting with Robert Neary, so that left three choices. Return to Boise and make the drive again—only this time in the TT. Go hang out in Elko for several days. Or stay here and see what she could dig up to give her an edge, an in, or simply inspiration on how to deal with this man.

She needed to think, and she didn't want to do it here, surrounded by limp curtains, depressing plastic laminate and dark wood paneling.

She went back outside. A small white truck drove by as she shut the door, and Dorrie turned to watch it, a slight frown on her face.

"Dorrie?" Kira said to get her attention. The woman looked up, trowel in hand. "Would you tell me how to find my family's old home ranch?"

"You don't know where it is?"

Kira shook her head.

"That was one of the first places your grandfather sold. And about the only one he didn't subdivide."

Knowing what she did of her grandfather's business, that was probably true.

"People need housing," Kira said, tired of being hassled about subdivision. The population was growing, and the Jenningses were providing something everyone needed—a place to call their own.

Dorrie's mouth tightened at the corner in a way that made Kira believe she wasn't fully in agreement.

"Go south out of town," the woman said, "and when you get over the big hill, there's a road going west at the bottom. Take that." She glanced at Leila's SUV. "You ought to be fine."

"The road isn't maintained?"

Dorrie shook her head. "Not much."

"Does…someone live there?"

"Not anymore. The place has been abandoned for years. The family that owns it just uses the land. The homestead house, well, you'll see if you go out there."

"I don't want to trespass."

"No one will care."

"Are you sure?"

"Positive."

Kira thought best while she drove, which was an expensive habit nowadays, especially in an SUV. But today she was going to indulge.

Dorrie sat back on her heels, lifted the brim of her straw hat with her wrist. "I take it you're not checking out?"

"I don't know when I'm checking out," Kira said truthfully. Because even though she didn't know what to do, she didn't want to give up so easily. "Is that a problem?"

Dorrie smiled, giving her the feeling that her uncertain checkout date was more entertaining than problematic. "No. Not at all."

CHAPTER EIGHT

KIRA TRAVELED DOWN the road at the bottom of the hill toward her roots—roots she'd barely been aware of until she'd taken up her father's offer and joined the family company three years ago. Until then, she'd known little about her paternal family. She'd wanted to know more, but hadn't investigated the matter because she knew her mother was insecure about it.

Kira hadn't realized until she was well into her teens that for most of her childhood her mom had been afraid Matthew would take her away. He had the resources to give Kira much more than her mother ever could, plus he was married, and could offer a two-parent home. Once she'd discovered that, Kira had stopped asking questions about him. And the few times she'd visited her father, she'd felt too shy to ask the questions.

Again the thunderheads were rolling in, only now, after the fire, Kira felt a twinge of trepidation. This storm appeared to be wet, though. The far horizon was solid gray, adding a melancholy ambience to her first visit to the place where her grandfather and father had been born.

There was a sorry wire gate across the road, and Kira got out to open it. She drove through, then closed it again, having learned her lesson from Jason. If a gate was shut, it was supposed to stay shut. Even if there wasn't a cow in sight.

She drove around a corner, over a small hill, and then slowly rolled to a stop when the dilapidated dwelling came into view.

Her grandfather's childhood home was small. Dorrie had said the current owners had bought the property only to use the land for their cattle, and now Kira could see why. The homestead appeared unsalvageable.

Next to what couldn't have been more than a three- or four-room house was a small wooden garage with a collapsed roof. In back of that, an outhouse. What must have once been a decent-size barn lay in a heap to the east, and the remnants of corrals poked up out of the waist-high weeds and grass.

How long had the place been abandoned? Had anyone lived there after her father's family had sold, before everything had fallen down?

She tried for a moment to imagine her grandfather and father there, on the property, but couldn't do it. The urbane men she knew seemed to have no connection with this land. Yet her grandfather now missed it.

Kira drove up to what was left of a picket fence around the front yard and got out. She stood still for a few minutes, drinking in the atmosphere.

She felt…nothing. No genetic memory here. Just an appreciation for the wild beauty of a lonely place.

Neglected and unkempt as it was, there was a peacefulness here, as if it were sleeping, waiting to be shaken awake. Would someone do that someday? Bring it back to life? Rebuild on the site? Or would everything slowly rot into the ground?

Kira felt no desire to go inside the sad little house where her grandfather had been raised—and her father, too, until he'd left for college at eighteen, and her grandfather had sold the ranch. She didn't want to see a place that had once been full of life empty and dirty, so instead, she walked toward the collapsed barn, jumping a mile when she nearly stepped on a snake.

The bull snake slithered harmlessly into the deep grass, but Kira reversed course to the SUV. The last thing she needed was to encounter a rattlesnake in the same way, and with her current run of luck, that seemed a very real possibility. She got in behind the wheel and started driving back toward town, no closer to figuring out Jason Ross than she'd been before, but with a slightly better sense of her grandfather and father's background.

She topped the low hill and could see the county road about a mile away, deserted except for a truck pulled off on the shoulder.

Amazing how the area was probably as isolated now as it had been back in the late 1920s, when her grandfather had been born. Automobiles may have changed slightly, she mused, as the truck pulled back on the road and moved south, but nothing else. It was only when she'd stopped at the wire gate that she realized for the first time in a long time she'd toured a piece of property without imagining a spanking new housing development on it.

HARRY'S CAFÉ WAS FILLED with people when Kira got back to town. Way more people than normal. Something was up, and since she was both hungry and curious, she parked at the motel and walked the two blocks back to the restaurant.

When she entered, there was a brief lull in the noise level before the meeting—and it was indeed a meeting— resumed. Kira felt wildly out of place.

"He won't take charity, so it has to be in the form of goods and services he can't return or refuse." Hal, the unofficial mayor, was talking. He paused to smile at Kira. "We're organizing donations for those affected by the fire," he explained.

Kira nodded in silent acknowledgment, wishing now she hadn't been so curious. One look at Libby and she knew for certain she was an interloper in a place she did not belong. Jason wouldn't appreciate her presence at a meeting concerning him. In fact, Kira had a strong feeling he would not appreciate being the subject of a charity gathering.

"I'm donating a hundred gallons of fuel," Dennis said in his deep voice. "And I'm filling his tank when he's not at home."

Several people laughed.

"Well, we can't go overboard or it'll piss him off. Just

a few essentials. Fuel, fencing materials… He doesn't need hay, since he only lost the one old stack…."

"He wouldn't let me comp the vet work," a tall, lanky blond man complained.

"I thought I paid for the vet work," Libby said.

"Yeah." The blond man glanced at her over his shoulder. "I owe you."

Kira quietly backed out the door, no longer hungry or curious. No one seemed to notice.

JASON SAW KIRA'S JEEP parked at the motel as he rounded the corner close to sunset. She was still here. Why? For round two? Tomorrow?

Damn, he hoped not. But if she came back, he'd send her sweet ass hustling off the property again. Pronto. No more talking.

That had ended when she so blatantly tried to take advantage of his situation.

When he was young, his mom has taught him to forgive and forget. The lesson hadn't taken, though. At one point he'd thought he'd been close to the forget part, but after Kira showed up, he'd discovered it had been more a case of tamping resentment down deep and never thinking about it. As to forgiving? He'd never found the charity in his soul to forgive Bryce and Matthew Jennings, and he doubted he ever would.

He pulled into Libby's drive with his ton of hay and backed up beside her own stack. She had plenty of hay now, but he knew she figured her finances to the penny, added a certain percentage for the occasional unexpected animal she needed to feed through the winter—like last year, when she'd adopted the floppy eared mustang no one wanted—and that a spare ton as a thank-you for keeping his animals would not go unappreciated. It was more than his stock had eaten while they were there, but it seemed a proper token of appreciation.

The trick was to get in and unload it before she found out, because Libby was worse at receiving thank-you gifts than he was. Neither of them liked to be beholden to others. He knew that, ultimately, she'd accept, for the good of her animals, but he didn't feel like wasting energy arguing, so he unloaded as fast as he could. His shoulders were sore from another day on the posthole digger, but the ache was worth it. He was done digging and had worked off some Jennings-induced frustration at the same time. Now all he had to do was buy new posts.

The insurance adjustor had cheerfully assured him that morning that the check would take some time to process, but it would be coming. However, in the meanwhile, his cattle had no pasture.

By the time Jason got home, the storm clouds had started to drop rain—without lightning for a change. Not that it would matter; he didn't have a whole lot left to burn.

This may not have been the best summer of his life, he thought as he pulled a tarp over the hay he kept stacked near the portable corrals, but it still beat the ones in his midtwenties, out on a work crew, in a blue chambray shirt with a bandanna over his hair as he hoed weeds, or painted buildings, or raked gravel. Having people walk by and study him like a bug, passing judgment. He didn't blame them, but he'd hated it. Yeah, he'd rather lose most everything he owned a few times over rather than do that again. At least when you lost material things, you still had your self-respect.

KIRA SPENT THE DAY talking to people in town, asking how they felt about economic growth, more families, a larger tax base. She occasionally asked a question about her family or Jason's. Everyone in town seemed to know why she was there. They answered the general questions happily enough, but clammed up when she mentioned Jason's name.

No in, no edge, no insight.

No better off than when she'd started. Kira headed back to the motel to shower before going over to the bar for the barbecue dinner more than one person had recommended that day.

Dorrie was working in her petunias again, this time fertilizing the flowers in the wooden half barrels beside the carport supports. She looked up to see her only tenant.

"Do you know some little Hispanic guy?"

"Well…probably," Kira replied, surprised at the question. She knew several Hispanic guys. "Why?"

"He was asking about you in the bar."

"Asking about *me?*" she repeated, mystified.

"This morning when you went out to see your grandfather's place? He drove past here right after you left. And then he drove by again later today, when you came back."

"You think he's following me?" Kira asked incredulously.

"I don't know. I just know he showed up around the same time you did, and I heard him ask about you when I went to lunch at the bar."

Ridiculous. Except… "Does he drive a white truck?" Like the one she'd seen parked on the shoulder when she'd returned from the homestead.

"You've noticed him, too?"

"Probably a coincidence."

"Probably." Dorrie let out a little snort.

Kira went into her room and turned on the air-conditioning unit that protruded out the window. Then she kicked off her shoes and collapsed back into the molded plastic chair.

Was someone following her?

It was a crazy idea.

Who would have her followed?

Bryce? That seemed pretty desperate, even for someone with his competitive nature—and besides that, he wasn't even supposed to know she was down here. No one knew, except for her grandfather and Leila, and she trusted both of them. That left one very big possibility.

Could it be that Jason Ross was trying to intimidate her by having one of his buddies tail her?

If so, it wasn't working, because she hadn't even been aware she'd been followed. *Until someone made certain she knew.*

Asking a question in front of Dorrie, who Kira was beginning to recognize as gossip central, was not exactly the act of someone trying to remain unobtrusive. Whoever it was had to know that Dorrie would ask Kira about it. Tip her off, make her think twice about staying in Otto.

Kira wondered if Jason was aware that tactics like that only made her consider taking up permanent residence.

But then, as she thought about it, she realized the theory had a problem. Dorrie would know Jason's buddies. And frankly, this didn't seem to fit Jason's style. He appeared more forthright than sneaky.

Back to Bryce, although she wondered how the heck he knew she was down here and what he expected to gain by having her tailed. His minion could have asked anyone in town what she was up to, and she was quite certain they would have told him. In detail.

And then there was the very real possibility that no one was following her. The guy had asked about her in the bar for reasons that had nothing to do with any kind of nefarious activities, and Dorrie was just in the market for something to gossip about.

Kira decided she liked that theory best.

SOMETHING WAS UP. People were looking at him oddly since he'd walked into the bar.

"What's happening?" he asked Menace, who had his soda waiting for him.

"Nothing," the big man said, shaking his head.

Yeah right. Well, he'd let it ride for now. It had been a long day and tomorrow he actually had a paying job, digging out a ditch with a borrowed backhoe. One good thing; he'd heard from the insurance adjustor, and even though he wasn't getting replacement value for the backhoe, he'd be sent a big enough check that he'd probably be able to buy another used one. But as far as his dump truck went, he'd be drawing a pittance.

It wasn't easy getting a loan with a felony on record, even from the local bank that lent to ranchers. Menace's father had helped him bankroll a few items, such as the trailer. But Jason couldn't ask to borrow enough to pay for a dump truck, and he didn't particularly want the new bank manager to turn him down, either.

"That girl's back in town," Menace said, as if Jason didn't already know it.

"She tried to negotiate for access again. After the family lawyer chewed on me for a while."

"When?" Menace asked.

"Yesterday morning."

"What are you going to do?"

"I may sic Libby on her."

Menace laughed and then pulled out his wallet. "Before I forget, Dad wanted me to pay you for the fire line." The big man's color went up a little. "It, uh, worked great."

"I'm not taking your money, Menace," Jason said.

"But the job—"

"Your dad already paid me."

"You sure?"

Jason tapped the table with his forefinger. "I notice things like getting paid. Yes, I'm sure."

The problem with Dennis Mann was that he was a stubborn SOB—especially when he had his heart set on doing good—even if the victim, or rather the object of his philanthropic intentions, wasn't interested. Jason might take some help around the place, but he wouldn't take money, and he said so.

Menace seemed mildly uncomfortable, and that was when an awful thought hit Jason. Were people eyeing him funny because they were cooking up some kind of a rescue effort? He looked his lifelong friend in the eye. "What's going on?"

"I can't tell you," Menace answered, in the same serious tone.

"Is it going to piss me off?"

"Probably. But it's for your own good."

Jason was about to reply when Wes Caruthers, a big man with distinctive red hair, graying at the temples, walked into the bar. The place stilled momentarily. Jason jerked his head toward door. "I think maybe we should move along. I saw his brother in town today."

"Oh, yeah," Menace said, automatically pulling a tip out of his still-open wallet and dropping it on the table. "The last time I dealt with the Caruthers boys…not good."

"Stitches never are," Jason agreed as he led the way out the back.

They'd barely exited when Randall Caruthers, just as large, redheaded and mean as his brother, pulled his pickup to a stop in the alley.

"It's the smell of barbecue," Menace said, as he and Jason started around the building toward the street, toward their respective vehicles and away from trouble. "Attracts them every time."

"Probably just as well they showed up," Jason said when they reached Menace's open-topped Jeep, which he'd put together from salvaged parts. "I got a lot of work ahead of me tomorrow."

"Me, too. Dad wants me at his place early to move hay." Menace made a face before climbing into his rig. The Jeep chugged to life.

After Menace drove away, Jason headed down the street to where his truck was parked, relieved to have an early evening. But then he saw Kira Jennings crossing the street to the bar. The woman might drive him crazy, but she was walking into danger—in a pair of jeans that fit her like a glove.

He felt as if he was back in ethics class.

Did he help her or didn't he?

He did.

"Don't go in there, Kira."

She stopped in her tracks, obviously startled, but recovered rapidly, her expression cold. "Why not?"

"It's going to get rowdy tonight." And Kira, all five foot four of her, was probably not going to hold her own too well in a bar fight.

"Is it?" She didn't appear to believe him.

"Yes."

"How do you know?"

"I have a feeling for these kinds of things."

"How?" she asked, settling a hand on one hip.

"Prison," he answered mildly, wanting to see her reaction. "We learn to read the crowd." Color rose in her cheeks. "Not the answer you were expecting?"

"I never get the answer I'm expecting from you," she said in a low voice.

"Don't you mean the answer you want?"

"That, too." She shifted her weight, dropped her hand. "So what happens if I go in there? I mean…" She shrugged carelessly. "What? I've been in the bar several times, alone, and nothing happened."

"That's because the Caruthers brothers haven't both been in there at the same time. They aren't supposed to frequent the same establishment." She raised her eyebrows. "Court order," Jason said.

"So…"

"When they both show up at the same place, they fight over which of them has to leave."

"Shouldn't it be the second one to arrive?"

"You'd think so, but it never seems to work out like that. The one who leaves is usually the one on the stretcher."

Her eyes widened. He could see she was torn between doing what she wanted and what she was told—and probably wondering if he was spinning a yarn, which he was not.

The brothers lived on different ranches, at opposite ends of the valley, appearing in town on the same day only once or twice a year, possibly due to some alignment of the planets. And when it happened, a fight invariably broke out—somewhere—and some innocent bystander would get roughed up, if not actually injured.

"Do what you want, Kira," Jason said. He'd done his duty. He nodded and continued on toward his truck.

"Are you having me followed?"

This time he stopped. Turned back. "What?"

Kira tilted her chin up and repeated, slowly, "Are you having me followed?"

He shook his head, wondering what on earth she was talking about. "What makes you think you're being followed?"

"I look behind me and see the same white Ford Ranger all the time. Some guy I don't know is asking about me in the bar."

"He probably wants to ask you out." Jason imagined most of the men in town would like to ask her out.

"Then maybe he should talk to *me*."

"Why do you think *I* would have you followed? I want you to leave me alone, and I don't think I've been all that secretive about it."

"To intimidate me into leaving."

"Oh?" He lifted his eyebrows in an innocent expression. "Just like you're trying to intimidate me into granting access?"

"Oh, yeah," she said, propping the hand back on her hip. "I'm so intimidating. I noticed that I had you shaking in your boots when you kicked me off your property."

"I'm talking about your lawyer."

Kira's eyes rounded. "What lawyer?" she demanded.

"The lawyer you had threaten me…?"

Her jaw dropped. "The lawyer I had *threaten* you? I don't *think* so." But her cheeks were red again. Kira was a very bad liar for being a Jennings. "Jason, I did not tell anyone to threaten you." She cocked her head, narrowing her eyes as if daring him not to believe her.

"Then there's a man who says he's a lawyer throwing your name around without your permission." And lawyers rarely worked without direction and payment.

"What's *his* name?"

"Taylor something. Dickens, maybe. I wasn't taking notes."

This time her face lost a lot of blood.

"Is that your lawyer's name?" Jason asked.

She focused on the ground for a moment, only looking up when they heard shouting in the bar, followed by a crash.

"Let's get out of here," Jason said.

"I didn't have my lawyer call you," Kira said stubbornly, staying right where she was. "He did it on his own."

"Yeah. Lawyers do that a lot."

"Jason—" She stopped abruptly, shooting a look over her shoulder as they heard another crash in the bar. He didn't think he was going to have to worry about her going in there.

"Maybe you'd better go back to your room until this blows over," he suggested. "And if you're being followed tomorrow, call the sheriff."

Her mouth tightened briefly. "Fine," she said, before turning on her heel and stalking off to the motel. Jason waited until she was inside with the door closed before he got into his truck and started the engine.

He drove through town looking for Cal Johnson, the deputy sheriff on duty that night. He expected to find him close to the bar, where the Carutherses were tuning up, but instead he was near the café, writing a ticket.

Once Cal was done writing and the teenage kid drove away at a snail's pace, his illegal straight pipes rumbling, Jason strolled over to apprise the deputy of the situation with Kira—just in case she wasn't crazy. *And* just in case she was trying to set Jason up somehow. He did not have a deep abiding trust in her family's tactics.

"I'll keep an eye out," Cal said. "I've just got back from vacation." He shook his head. "Missed the fire. Sorry to hear about your place."

"Insurance covers a lot," Jason said stiffly, uncomfortable with Cal's sympathy. "And if you do happen to spot a white Ford Ranger that doesn't belong in town, would you run the tags, see who it's registered to?"

"Sure." Cal glanced over Jason's shoulder at the bar and clenched his teeth. "Here comes Mike," he said, indicating the other deputy on duty, who came driving in from out of town. "I guess it's time to referee the Carutherses. I was kind of hoping they might go their separate ways, but…"

"Yeah," Jason agreed. "Good luck."

"Leila. Finally." Kira lay on her bed fully clothed, staring up at the ceiling, the phone at her ear.

"I was swimming laps," her sister said. "Is something wrong? I have what, nine missed calls from you?"

"I'll probably go to Elko tomorrow. I'm having no luck down here and, this is so weird…the motel owner thinks someone is tailing me."

"What?"

"Yes. This little white truck. I mean, I could be wrong, but the motel lady was the one who mentioned it to me. She's noticed it hanging around more than I have. Apparently it shows up after I drive away."

"Have you contacted the police?"

"No," Kira said in a small voice.

"Do it."

"I accused Jason Ross. He denied it."

"Call the police, Kira," Leila snapped.

"I will. And I'm going to tear a strip off Taylor when I get back. He called Jason and tried to strong-arm him into giving access. Probably fired off some legal mumbo jumbo."

"Can he do that?"

Yes, because she hadn't talked to him about the situation on the clock. No lawyer-client privilege here. "He was trying to help. And I don't think he'll bill us for the time," Kira added dryly.

"Is he ever going to stop trying to jump you?"

"I hope so." Kira pressed a hand against her forehead. "Anyway, it's clear I'm not going to get access. Taylor pretty much took care of that. Believe it or not, Jason Ross, ex-felon, didn't appreciate being threatened by a lawyer."

"I'm sorry, Kira."

Kira paused for a moment, then asked the big question. The one she'd actually called to ask. "Is there any chance at all that Bryce knows I'm down here? I mean… if I am being followed—" and she had to admit that she felt foolish saying it out loud "—could he be the one behind this?"

"Wow, Kira. I don't know…. He's still out of town with Dad. Dad called just before I went swimming, to touch base, and I haven't heard from Bryce at all."

"Grandpa?"

"Grandpa isn't going to have you tailed."

"No, but do you think Grandpa told Bryce?"

"He asked you not to, so I don't know why he would."

The whirr of a siren brought her off her bed and she went to part the curtains. She couldn't see anything, so she stepped outside. Not seeing a white truck or any place where someone could hide and suddenly attack her, she crossed the parking lot to where she could view what was happening, the phone held to her ear. Apparently Jason had not been kidding about things getting rough in the bar that night.

"Kira, you still there?"

"Yes, I'm just watching the locals celebrate Saturday night. And as far as the other thing goes, I don't know…maybe the motel lady and I are imagining this. Maybe it's just a coincidence."

"Contact the police."

"I will," Kira said, although she had a feeling she was going to look like a nut. "I'll talk to you later."

Two deputies went into the bar and a few minutes later came out with a big redheaded man in handcuffs. He was bleeding from a scalp wound.

As she walked back to the room, she caught sight of Dorrie peeking out the curtain, and gave a silent sigh.

The white truck guy wasn't the only one who was keeping an eye on her.

CHAPTER NINE

KIRA DIDN'T FOLLOW THROUGH with her plan to go to Elko the next day. It felt too much like running, and why run?

If Bryce was having her tailed, he'd probably continue, because he didn't know she was onto him. Although Kira still believed it was a very un-Brycelike tactic. If it was Jason, the tail would stop. And if it was her imagination, she'd be foolish to leave when she wasn't ready to.

But she also knew she'd keep an eye in the rearview mirror—just in case it was none of the above.

"Who owns my grandfather's homestead?" Kira asked Dorrie when she stopped by to pick up her complimentary cup of very weak coffee. Or maybe it was tea. It was hard to tell.

"That would be Hal Monroe."

"The unofficial mayor?"

"Biggest landowner in the area."

"But he seems to be at the café night and day."

"He owns the café. His boys run the ranch. He prefers to just hang out in town, and the boys like him being there, out of their hair. Drives the waitresses crazy, though."

Kira processed the information, then asked, "Where is the public library?"

"In the basement of the city hall."

"Thanks."

The city hall was one of the larger buildings in town, a remnant of the Victorian age mining boom that had stretched on into the early 1970s. Kira climbed the steps to the entrance. As she was opening the door, she caught the reflection of something white in the glass. She quickly whirled around, only to realize she'd been spooked by an older model Cadillac with a tiny woman at the wheel.

Kira blew out a breath, told herself to get a grip, and then went inside to see if she could dig up anything about her heritage. If nothing else, maybe she could find some photos. After growing up with virtually no family, since her mother had only a few scattered relatives, she wanted to know about her pioneer roots, which up until recently she hadn't even realized she had.

KIRA SPENT THE ENTIRE morning in the library, perusing local history, viewing photos of her grandfather's family in the archives, along with Jason's family and Dennis's. She found several photos of the homestead before it had deteriorated, and although it was windblown and forlorn in the early ones, it took on a much homier appearance in the later pictures. And now it was rotting into the ground.

After leaving the library, Kira did what was for her a very unusual thing. She stopped by the café and casually asked Hal if he'd consider selling the home-stead—just the house and a few acres.

Kira had never in her life approached a deal like this, showing interest in a manner that almost begged a person to start jacking up the price.

Hal scratched his head. "Are you going to subdivide?"

"That hadn't been my intention," Kira replied, inwardly wincing. Jenningses…subdivision. Apparently the two were inexorably linked in these people's minds. "No. I was just curious." And she was. She had no ties to the land, or so she thought. But she kept thinking about that sorry house, and wondering what could be done with it.

"More of a personal interest than business?"

"You might say that."

"Still no luck with Jason?"

Kira shook her head. No sense trying to hide anything around here. People knew when you were bluffing.

"Well, I'd have to think about the homestead. Run it by my boys."

"It wouldn't be a Jennings Inc. deal," Kira said. And she didn't even know if she was that interested. Again a matter of testing the waters. "By the way…have you seen a white truck driven by a small Hispanic man?"

"You mean the one following you?"

Kira's mouth popped open. "You've seen it fol-lowing me?"

"No. I talked to Alice, who'd talked to Dorrie. But yeah, I have seen the truck a few times. Not today."

"Do you know who owns it?"

Hal shook his head. "No idea."

Kira ordered a salad to go, then went back to her motel room and holed up for the night. Tomorrow she'd go out to the property, ink some possible development layouts on the aerial photos and then give Jason one last desperate shot.

THINGS KEPT SHOWING UP at Jason's spread whenever he went to town—fuel, lumber, fence posts, rolls of wire— to the point that he was beginning to think he'd have to stay home and guard the place. He knew his neighbors would do the same for anyone in similar circumstances, and that he'd be in there helping them, but it was much harder being on the receiving end.

And even more difficult admitting he needed the help.

He could do contract work on borrowed equipment, but not that many places had the equipment in the first place. Or if they did, it was broken-down, which was why they called him. He was losing money turning down work from steady customers as far away as Wesley. He would be selling his hay shortly, but he was still going to fall short.

His belt was practically on the last notch and he was going to have to tighten it again. He'd already told Libby no more leppies for a while. And he was going to have to sell cattle at a loss, since the fire had consumed so much of his grazing land.

By the time he'd finished adding up columns of figures, factoring in best case and worst case scenarios, he was flat-out depressed. But no more ready to deal with Kira than he'd been before.

At least he had a paying job scheduled for the Benson Ranch that afternoon. And he wondered if more stuff was going to show up while he was gone. If so, he hoped it was food. He was tired of trying to cook in the tiny trailer kitchen.

It was going on noon when he drove to his fire-blistered gate, planning to sand it smooth prior to painting it the next morning when the wind was supposed to have died down. He'd barely started working when Kira's Jeep drove by.

No white truck followed her.

Who the hell knew what she was up to now?

He couldn't shake the feeling that she was setting him up, backing him into a corner where he'd have to give her what she wanted in order to get out again. Somehow the imaginary white truck fit into it.

The imaginary truck Dorrie had seen. Scratch imaginary.

Jason finished sanding and was returning to the trailer when his cell phone rang. He didn't recognize the number, but answered anyway, hoping it was a job and not a political announcement. And clenched his teeth when a voice very much like that of the lawyer said, "Do yourself a favor and cooperate with the Jenningses."

The line clicked dead and it was all Jason could do not to throw the cell phone across the truck.

Cooperate with the Jenningses? And Kira complained that he was following her?

Someone was screwing with him, and he wasn't going to put up with it.

KIRA LOVED the development she'd laid out. After marking it out on the aerial photo, indicating the areas she would leave wild, the places where homes would be tucked into the landscape, she felt as if she had a winner.

And she also felt as if she was touching a sore tooth with her tongue repeatedly to see if it still hurt. The chances of getting access from Jason were nonexistent in her estimation. Her grandfather was going to have to live with the fact that she'd failed.

She was going to have to live with the fact that she'd failed. But for some reason, she couldn't let it go. Maybe it was Jennings tenaciousness, or maybe she just didn't like to hear the word *no*. Or maybe she was beginning to like the little town—when she wasn't being paranoid about people following her.

Although seconds later, as she drove around a corner, she didn't feel paranoid at all. She felt vindicated.

There, coming out of Jason's driveway, was the white truck.

Kira instantly slowed down, let the guy get so far ahead of her that all she could see was settling dust.

Bastard.

She was seething by the time she pulled into Dennis Mann's service station. No white truck.

"I need Jason's phone number," Kira said in a surprisingly even voice.

Dennis didn't even ask why. He pulled a pen out of the metal sprocket on the counter, wrote a number on the back of a credit application brochure and handed it to her.

"Thank you," she said.

"Need fuel?"

"Tomorrow. Thanks."

Kira stepped back out of the building, glancing around for the white Ranger—just in case the guy was stupid—then dialed the number Dennis had given her. Jason answered on the fourth ring.

"Your friend in the white truck just left your place," she said point-blank.

"What?"

Kira didn't need to see his face to know that she'd startled the hell out of him.

"Did you have a nice talk?"

"I wouldn't know, because I'm not there."

JASON DIDN'T THINK TWICE about abandoning the ditching job at the Benson Ranch and jumping into his truck. Benson would understand. Besides, Jason would finish it tomorrow. Ten minutes later he stopped at his drive.

Yes, he could see tracks heading in and out that were a narrower gage than his tires, but they stopped at the gate. Somebody had turned around there. Big deal.

He'd been through enough hell with Kira's family that he wasn't going to avoid potential embarrassment and handle this alone. He put a call in to Dispatch as he drove. He wanted everything as out in the open as possible. It was the only way he could think of to defend himself against whatever was going on.

Once in town, Jason headed straight for the motel,

ready to have a chat with Miss Jennings about her accusation, when he spotted her Jeep at Menace's station. He flipped a U and pulled into the gas station parking lot. A moment later he was out of his truck and walking toward Kira's Jeep.

"Have you called the sheriff?" he demanded after she rolled the window down.

Her jaw was tight, but her gaze didn't falter as she said, "No."

"I did."

And then, as if on cue, the sheriff's department cruiser rolled into the lot from the side street. Kira's eyes widened and then she shot Jason a killer look. "Gee, thanks."

The cruiser parked two spaces away and the deputy got out. Cal Johnson was sporting the remnants of a black eye—probably a souvenir of the Caruthers brothers' night on the town—but Kira didn't seem to notice. She got out of the Jeep and shut the door, turning her back to Jason as Cal crossed the short distance between the vehicles.

"I hear you're having some trouble," the officer said.

"Yes, sir," Kira replied. "I am."

And Jason didn't doubt for a minute she was referring to him as well as the alleged white truck that was following her.

JASON HAD CALLED the sheriff. The jerk.

Kira hadn't because she had nothing concrete to report other than a white truck leaving Jason's place.

Not exactly earth-shattering, and she didn't want to come off as being loony tunes or a troublemaker. Being a Jennings in this town was detrimental enough.

"I've been noticing a white truck following me," Kira said in as calm a tone as possible, focusing on the deputy and ignoring Jason, although she would have loved to have wiped that self-satisfied expression off his face. "Dorrie at the motel has noticed it, too."

"You know," Cal said slowly, shifting his attention from Kira to Jason and then back again, "I'm pretty sure I know what vehicle you're talking about. Did you get a plate number?"

"No," Kira said, but she was beginning to feel a surge of optimism. It was some harmless guy. Someone local. And the deputy didn't appear to think she was paranoid or crazy.

"Was it a blue plate?" the officer asked, referring to the old-style Nevada plates.

"Yes."

"Little guy? Hispanic?"

"That's the man Dorrie described," Kira said.

"He's here doing some installation work for an irrigation company."

Kira should have felt a rush of relief. She didn't. "Which irrigation company?" she asked faintly, already certain of the answer.

"WaterPro. It all checked out."

Kira felt the blood draining from her cheeks, but her voice was steady when she said, "Well, I guess this was much ado about nothing."

"Better safe than sorry," Cal replied with a smile. "And if you have any more issues, just give us a call, all right?"

Kira smiled back, knowing it didn't come off as sincere, but it was the best she could do. "All right."

She turned on Jason as soon as the deputy reached his SUV. "Why did *you* call the sheriff? Were you *worried* about me?"

"A bit," he allowed. "And there's the off chance you're setting me up."

"Setting you up…?" Kira's mouth dropped open. "Now who's paranoid?"

"Me," he said simply, resting his hands loosely on his hips. "You going to tell me about WaterPro?"

Damn the man and the things he picked up on.

"No."

He waited, his head cocked at a stubborn angle. She wished he didn't look so flipping sexy when he stood like that, and she wished she didn't notice those things about him. She turned and got back in the Jeep. "I'm going to my room."

Where I'm safe. From men driving white trucks, and you.

Jason followed Kira to the motel, parking beside her in the spot reserved for the neighboring unit. She got out of the Jeep and started for the room without looking at him, key in hand, then suddenly stopped and turned. Jason nearly ran into her.

"Why do you think I'm setting you up?" she asked.

At the same time, he demanded, "What's up with WaterPro?"

Kira fully expected to have her question answered first.

Jason was apparently of the same mind, so she gave him a nudge. "What would I gain from setting you up?"

"Access."

"I don't follow."

"I'm a convicted felon. How hard would it be to put me in a position where I might feel compelled to negotiate?"

"You're kidding," she said, outraged.

"The lawyer threat didn't work and this may be the next step in your plan."

"Do you honestly think I would do that?"

A car turned onto the street that ran past the motel, so Kira turned the key in the lock and pushed the door open, glancing darkly up at Jason, waiting for an answer so she could blast him out of the water.

"You're a hell of a housekeeper, Kira," he said. Not the answer she'd been expecting.

She looked into the room to see what he was talking about, and then took a step backward, into his solid chest. He grasped her shoulders.

"Not the way you left the place?" he asked quietly, his grip tightening.

Kira shook her head. The place was trashed, her clothing and toiletries thrown everywhere, and something dark and thick had been poured over them. All she could think of was blood.

"Stay here."

Kira stepped aside and Jason went into the room,

quickly checking the bathroom before he knelt and experimentally dabbed the tip of his finger in the dark substance. He rubbed his thumb and forefinger together, then sniffed.

"Motor oil. Used."

"Like the stuff you have sitting in the back of your truck?"

He looked up. "I didn't do this, Kira, and I didn't hire someone to do it. Hell, I couldn't afford to hire someone."

"You have friends. Lots of friends. They organize fire relief drives for you. They'd probably do this, too."

"Kira…" He stood up.

She didn't move away from the door, her escape route.

"I'm not the bad guy," Jason reiterated.

"We'd better get Dorrie," Kira said, as if he hadn't spoken.

"I'll call Dispatch."

Dorrie wasn't in the office. The cardboard clock on the motel office door had its Will Be Back hand pointed at 1:30 p.m., and Kira remembered her mentioning a hair appointment at noon. One of the local girls was back in town, fresh out of beauty school, and Dorrie had promised the girl's mother to be one of her first appointments.

Deputy Cal showed up a few minutes later. He whistled under his breath when he saw the mess, then set about investigating the scene. It didn't take long for him to point out where the bathroom window had been jimmied open, then shut again. He took down the information, had Jason and Kira both write statements.

"Are you going to stay here tonight?" Cal asked.

Kira immediately shook her head. Nope. She'd be

going elsewhere, even though she hated to think of how spooked and vulnerable she was going to feel driving the lonely highway to Wesley.

"I have your contact information, and will let you know if anything comes up." He smiled at her with more than professional concern, then looked over her head at Jason. "Call me if anything else happens," he said. Kira couldn't tell which one of them he was talking to. Maybe both. "And, uh, I'll stop by later to talk to Dorrie."

Once he was gone, Kira slowly shook her head as she perused the scene, feeling numb. Someone had come into her room and done this. What if she had been there?

"Kira!"

She lifted her gaze from the mess on the floor. "I think I know what's going on," Jason continued in a gentler voice.

"Oh, do tell."

"Why don't you sit down?"

Kira sat in the molded plastic chair and Jason settled on the edge of the bed. After a few silent seconds, he reached out, lightly took her hand in his and squeezed her fingers reassuringly. She squeezed back, almost involuntarily, knowing her fingers had to be icy, since her entire body felt chilled.

Bryce wouldn't do this.

And her gut instinct was telling her that Jason wouldn't have done it, either. So that left…?

She hadn't a clue.

EVEN THOUGH HE WAS ONLY touching her hand, Jason could feel the tension in Kira's body. She stared at the trashed room, then swallowed, her chin jerking slightly as she did so.

"Tell me about WaterPro," he said. He released her, and Kira clasped her hands together on her lap.

"WaterPro is a company we contract with almost exclusively. We're their biggest contractor."

"'We' meaning…your family."

Kira nodded. She studied her clasped hands for a moment, then tapped the tips of her fingers together nervously. "Why would my family be watching me? I mean, even if my brother and I are in competition, how is this helping him?" She spoke more to herself than to Jason.

"You and Bryce are in competition?"

"Big promotion coming up. Only one of us can get it. He's been on the job longer, but I have more education. If I get this job finished satisfactorily, it'll help my chances."

"Then my idea makes even more sense."

She frowned at him. "How so?"

"I think your brother is trying to pit us against each other."

"And what does he gain?"

"He makes you nervous enough to leave town before you get what you've come for."

Or he makes certain you never wring the truth out of me and use it against him. To Jason, that was the more reasonable answer.

And up until that moment, he had assumed Kira

knew what had happened between him and her brother. He'd assumed the entire family knew. If poor Seth Craig hadn't died in the accident, he could almost envision them chuckling about it at family gatherings.

But if Kira *didn't* know, and if she was in a position to find out and use it against her brother professionally…it made perfect sense to Jason.

"Bryce doesn't know I'm here. He and my dad are working in northern Idaho."

"The lawyer knew."

"I told him. Taylor and Bryce hate each other, because Bryce doesn't treat Taylor with the proper respect and vice versa. Also, Taylor is…interested in me. He's not going to run to Bryce with my secrets."

And are you interested in him?

Jason didn't like the question that came into his mind any more than he liked the thought of Kira attached to some skanky lawyer.

"Is there any possible way Bryce could have found out? By accident, even?"

"Well, of course that's possible."

"I think Bryce did find out and he's trying to piss me off with the threatening phone calls from the so-called lawyer, so I won't deal with you. I think he's trying to scare you so you'll leave." Jason paused a moment, then said, "Has it struck you that these…events, I guess…have been kind of heavy-handed? The guy following you out of the blue. Me getting 'cooperate with the Jenningses' phone calls, knowing I'd do the exact opposite?"

"You got phone calls telling you to cooperate?" Kira asked, stunned.

"One call," he amended.

She stood and took a couple paces, then pushed her hair back from her forehead with both hands. "Okay, what you're saying makes sense in a sick way. But—" she gestured at the ruined clothing "—this just isn't that important a deal. I mean, Grandpa said it would help my chances if I succeeded, but it wouldn't have made the promotion a slam dunk by any means."

She frowned as she made another slow circuit of the room, stepping around the clothing. "Why would Bryce take a chance like this? If he did get caught, he'd never get the job."

"Maybe he never planned on getting caught."

"This doesn't make sense. I mean, he has no reason to behave this desperately."

Jason simply nodded. He was not going to tell her just how desperate her brother might be, because he still wasn't exactly sure what was going on.

KIRA BENT DOWN and picked up a shirt, watching as a bead of oil formed at the hem. She dropped it again and pressed her lips together.

"I don't think it's Bryce," she said stubbornly. "The motivation isn't there." Although she wished it was, because Bryce was less frightening than an unknown alternative. Even when he hogged the glory or side-stepped the blame, he always made certain he was in a position to justify his actions if questioned. She didn't see how he could justify this if their grandfather found out.

"So the WaterPro connection is a coincidence?"

"It has to be." Maybe.

"You want to find out if your brother is behind this?" Kira jerked her gaze up to his. "How?"

It took him several seconds to answer. "How soon do you have to be in Elko?"

"I have four more days before the meeting."

"If we're seen together a lot, look like we're cooking up some kind of plan for the development, I think you'll be hearing from him."

Kira considered his proposal in stunned silence. "What do you mean by *seen together?*"

"I don't know. Lunch. Time at the bar."

"Don't you have work to do? Isn't that going to seem suspicious if you suddenly start spending all your time in town? Maybe I should go sleep on my property. I brought camping gear."

It took him a moment to say, "Your property won't do."

"Fine, then I'll camp on *your* property for a couple days." Because she sure didn't want to stay here. Part of her said go to Elko, but another part—a stronger part—wanted to know if his theory was correct. Because if it wasn't, she had a different problem. And if it was, well, that was a problem, too. She needed to be aware of what she was up against.

"That would work," he conceded.

"And then I'll be hearing from Bryce?"

"I think he'll mention it. It may not be until you go

home, but I guarantee he'll be nervous if you're hanging out with me. He'll want to know what's going on."

"Why, Jason?" It seemed a reasonable question, but not one he seemed to want to answer, so she shifted gears. "How can I be certain I can trust you? Maybe he's nervous because you're dangerous."

His eyes met hers, and she found herself staring into the green depths. "Then why hasn't he called to warn you?"

Good point, Kira thought. She drew in a steadying breath.

"Do *you* believe I'm dangerous?" he asked softly, and she found herself focusing on his lips.

Maybe, but probably not in the sense he meant.

"We'll tell Cal you're coming with me. If you want, you can stay in the trailer, lock the door. I'll sleep in the truck bed."

"What if it rains?"

He smiled unexpectedly. "I'll get wet."

Kira smiled back, but it was more of an automatic response than reaction to his comment. She didn't know what she hoped for. If Bryce was behind this, it meant serious trouble in both the family and the family company. And if it wasn't Bryce…then that meant she had an honest-to-goodness stalker.

She didn't want to consider either possibility, but it had to be one or the other.

"There's Dorrie," Jason said. "I'll go get her."

Dorrie's satisfaction with her new do, a short wispy style that complemented her gaunt features and salt-and-pepper hair, faded the second she walked into Kira's room. She let out a loud cry and then demanded an explanation.

Kira told her what they knew. Jason pointed out the window frame, and then they both explained that Deputy Cal would be in touch.

Dorrie shook her head in outrage, her new do quivering. For the next several minutes she rambled on about insurance and deductibles, punctuating her soliloquy with sharp accusing glances at both Kira and Jason. Finally Kira told the woman she would pay for new carpeting and a new window frame, plus she'd have the room professionally cleaned. Dorrie perked up at that, and then Kira further brightened her day by telling the woman she was checking out.

"That might be best for everyone," Dorrie agreed. Then she took down all the information she possibly could, including Kira's driver's license number, to assure herself she could indeed contact her about the carpet and cleaning.

"Will you be going back home now?" she asked with a sniff.

"Uh…" Kira glanced over at Jason, who settled a hand on her shoulder. "Not yet."

Amazement crossed the little woman's face as she processed the meaning of Jason's possessive touch, and then she practically vibrated as the gossip possibilities became apparent. What a story she had to tell!

Jason squeezed Kira's shoulder and said, "We'd better get your clothes down to the Laundromat and see what can be salvaged."

"Yes," Kira agreed. "Let's do that."

They were barely out of the parking lot when Dorrie went scurrying over to the bar.

SITTING IN A LAUNDROMAT with Kira Jennings was almost as surreal as outrunning a fire with her. They'd stopped at the hardware store and bought a container of industrial-strength grease remover, then spent a good twenty minutes rubbing it into her clothing.

Jason had expected her to run to the mercantile and pick up some new clothes, but she'd told him she'd wait and see if they could get the oil out.

They'd stuffed the clothing into two washers, shoved in quarters and a ton of soap, and then sat in silence as the machines churned away.

Every now and then Kira would pull in a deep breath, then release it, but she didn't look at him, didn't speak. Jason felt like taking her hand again, just to let her know she wasn't alone—because he knew what it was like to be alone—but he didn't. He was going to proceed cautiously. Consider consequences before acting on impulse.

Because impulse was telling him to comfort this woman.

The washers stopped spinning within seconds of each other, and he and Kira stood in unison. She opened one lid, he opened the other.

"Didn't work real well, did it?" he asked, pulling out a light blue shirt with a dark streak across it.

"It mostly came out of the jeans," Kira said. "I'm going to put these in the dryer."

When all was said and done, she had her underwear, which no one would see, her jeans and two shirts. The rest she stuffed into the Laundromat garbage can. And although she felt a pang as she tossed her favorite red T-shirt, she wasn't exactly unhappy to see the ever-wrinkly linen pants go.

"I guess I'll be shopping before my meeting," she said as she folded and stacked the scanty pile of warm clothes.

Jason paused before pushing the glass doors open, scanning the street outside.

"See him?"

"Nope." He looked over his shoulder at her. "Let's go grab something for lunch at the café, and then hit the road. If Dorrie hasn't alerted half the town by now, I'll be surprised. Lunch at the café will ensure the other half is aware. Even a stranger."

Kira shrugged. "I'm game."

And if there was one thing he'd discovered about her, she was indeed game.

CHAPTER TEN

"COME HERE, BUCK," Jason said as they walked up to the panel corral. The foal ambled out of the plywood lean-to Jason had built only a few days before, with lumber that had mysteriously appeared on his place, along with a full tank of diesel, while he'd been off working on the Benson Ranch ditches.

"Oh," Kira said when she saw the opaque bluish-white spot on the little horse's pupil. "Can he see anything at all?"

"I don't think so."

"So, you just keep him?"

"Until I can find him a home." Kira glanced over at Jason and he explained. "I'm really a halfway house for these guys. I take them, feed them mare milk replacer, get them healthy and then Libby finds homes for them. I have to keep them for a year to get title, but usually they're put up for adoption."

"But you could keep them if you wanted?"

He nodded. "In return for saving them, yeah. Libby comes out and freeze brands them so that they're identified as mustangs, then they're mine."

"How many have you kept?"

"Just the burros. And now little Buck."

"If I had a place, I'd like to have Buck."

"What kind of place do you live in?"

"A condo. Owned by the company."

"What happens if you leave the company?"

"I have no idea about the condo," Kira said. "I'm pretty sure I'd have to give back the Audi."

"The TT's not yours?"

"It's in the company name for tax purposes."

"Of course." Jason tried to imagine perks like that, instead of being thrilled when he was asked in for lunch wherever he happened to be working.

Oh, and he did get free fuel every now and again.

"I'm not going to quit, though," she said.

"Well, if you move to a place where you can have a blind horse, Buck will probably be here waiting for you."

"Someday I may give up the condo. It was fine when I first went to work, but I've been thinking about getting a dog." Kira smiled, reached through the fence. "And maybe a blind horse." The baby hesitated, then stretched his nose out to take a sniff.

"His muzzle is tickly with all those whiskers."

Jason couldn't help smiling at her obvious delight. She had a lot on her mind, and a lot of unknowns floating around. He was glad she was able to forget them for a moment.

"Libby was supposed to bring one or two more leppies—orphans," he elaborated, when he noticed her perplexed look. "But I can't take them on right now.

They're working on an emergency gather to shift some horses around."

"Why are there so many orphans?"

"There usually aren't that many, but things happen to horses in the wild—especially in drought conditions. Lack of food and water. Nursing can be more than mares are able to handle."

"So after the moms die, the babies die."

"Sometimes the leppies can steal milk off another mare and survive, but lots of times they can't and…"

Kira got the picture. "You don't get anything out of this but satisfaction, do you?"

He shrugged. "It's all I want."

FOR DINNER THAT NIGHT they made macaroni and cheese out of a box. It was quick and easy after a rather traumatic day.

"What do you do in the evenings?" Kira asked when she'd thrown away the paper plates. He had a satellite dish attached to the trailer and a small television, so she assumed he'd say "watch television."

"I sit outside and watch the place, then I go inside and read."

"What do you read?"

"Everything. I lost some of my books in the fire, but I have stuff stored at Libby's, so I didn't lose all of them."

He started out the door into the cooler evening air. "Come on."

He had a lawn chair near the front of the trailer, and he waved her to it while he sat on the stoop.

"By the way, I'm serious about sleeping in the truck. I do it a lot when I'm out on a distant job. Feel free to take the trailer."

"Are you sure?"

"It's only for a night or two." He suddenly pointed to the edge of the field, where two coyotes were trotting. "Hunting for mice."

Kira watched as one pounced and snapped at something in the grass, then moved on before pouncing again.

"Back when I could own guns, while I was living on the folks' ranch, I would fire warning shots to scare them away from the place. But now that I can't do that, well, we've developed a relationship. Live and let live. I've changed my attitude toward coyotes."

Although he'd brought it up casually, Kira believed Jason had an ulterior motive for mentioning his past. And she pretty much knew what it was. He was trying to put up more of a wall, because the one he'd had was starting to crumble.

She decided not to be put off. "How hard is it, being an ex-convict?"

He didn't take his eyes off the coyotes as he said, "I can't shoot varmints on the property. I can't vote. I have a hell of a time getting loans. Employment, well, I like being self-employed. Then I don't have to deal with it."

"How will you replace your dump truck and backhoe?"

"Backhoe will be with insurance. Truck…I'm still working on that one."

Kira hesitated for only a moment before she said something she knew he'd probably hate. "Maybe I could help."

"You have enough money to finance a dump truck?"

"The company does."

His expression instantly shuttered.

"Never mind," Kira said. "Tainted Jennings money. I understand."

"No. You don't."

Kira turned back. "Then explain."

He reached out and touched her face, just…touched it. "I don't know if I can."

And Kira left it at that.

TRUE TO HIS WORD, after showering in the tiny trailer bathroom, Jason laid out a bedroll in the back of his pickup truck. Kira was surprised to see that a bedroll was indeed a bed—a foam pad with sheets and a blanket—wrapped in canvas.

"My home away from home," Jason said. "I'm glad I had it in the truck during the fire."

"It's about all you rescued, isn't it?"

"A few clothes in a duffel." He smiled wryly. "Laundry day. I wish I hadn't been so lazy, though. I only brought my work clothes. Figured I could do the rest later."

"And now you don't own the rest." Kira was becoming familiar with that feeling, the difference being that she did have tons more clothes at home.

"Pretty much."

"So the dishes and everything in the trailer…"

"Loans. It's Menace's dad's trailer. My folks sent me a check to help tide me over, so I had Libby make a Wally World run for me in Elko. Towels, dishes."

"You and Libby are close?"

"We have been for years." He left it at that, left Kira wondering. And she *was* wondering. She did not want to step on toes, but there was something about this man. She felt a strong connection to him on a very basic level. One that surprised her.

He boosted himself up onto the tailgate and pulled off his boots. "It's going to be totally dark soon. You'd better get situated."

"Right." But she didn't move immediately. "Do you really think Bryce is behind this?"

"Yes." He offered no explanation, and Kira decided not to push for one. Yet.

Heading for the trailer, she realized it was going to be a while before she fell asleep, if she slept at all. Because if thoughts of Bryce and the white truck guy didn't keep her awake, she had no doubt that lying in sheets with Jason Ross's masculine scent attached to them would.

A DISTANT METALLIC CRASH brought Kira rearing up out of Jason's bed, heart pounding. She heard a shout, then another crash. Kira pulled her pants on, shoved her feet into her shoes, and then, before opening the trailer door, moved the curtain aside to try to see what was causing the noise.

She couldn't make out a thing except for a beam of light waving wildly through the darkness as Jason ran for the corrals. Kira grabbed the flashlight he had left near the door for her earlier that evening, and stepped out into the night without turning it on.

Jason had reached the corral, but the light was still waving erratically. A second later the beam stilled and Kira started walking toward it. She could hear Jason talking to the animals, trying to sooth them.

No one else seemed to be around, so she took a chance and clicked on her light. Jason's face was set in hard lines when he glanced up at her. "There's a first aid kit in the toolbox of the truck. Go get it."

Kira didn't ask what had happened. She turned and ran for the truck, found the kit and jogged back. By that time, Jason was in the pen, his arm wrapped around the foal's neck.

"Shine the light on his face, but not so that it goes into his eye."

Kira did as she was told, swallowing a gasp. The baby's face was bloody on the side with the bad eye.

"What happened?" she asked quietly, wondering if the coyotes had attacked.

"He was spooked," Jason said. "And bolted. Hit the fence on his blind side."

"Coyotes?"

"Maybe, but they don't usually go near burros."

Jason slipped a rope around the young horse's neck. "I'll need some water. And a clean rag. Check under the sink."

Kira was back in less than a minute with a bowl of water and a cloth.

"I'm going to hold him, while you dab the blood off. I want to see what's what, okay?"

"Okay." Kira's voice shook a little. Here she was yet

again: not good around blood, but excellent at faking it. She swallowed hard and started gently dabbing.

Her breathing became steadier as she concentrated, working closer and closer to the wound, dipping the cloth into the now bloody water and then wringing it out with one hand. Jason held the foal steady as she worked, and the two burros, Marlene and Ruben, moved closer to see what Kira was doing to their foal.

"It's a puncture," she said. A V-shaped laceration over the eye.

"I don't think I need to stitch it."

Kira's gaze shot up. "You stitch things?"

"When I have to. Just about anyone who works on a ranch can stitch up an animal in an emergency," he explained as he studied the wound.

"Yuck!" Kira didn't even try to hide the shudder that went through her at the thought of putting a needle into flesh.

"You do what you gotta do. And besides that, I planned to be a vet at one time, so it doesn't bother me."

Kira almost said, "What happened?" Almost. But she was glad she caught herself, because the answer was obvious. Prison had happened.

"Do you think you can hold him?" Jason asked.

"I can try." Kira shifted positions, reaching for the rope with one hand, looped her other arm around Buck's neck and held the light while Jason dressed the wound. He placed a gauze pad over it, then wrapped tape under the foal's throat and over the top of his head to try to keep it in place.

"I hope it's still there by morning."

"Yeah," Kira said.

"And I think I may borrow Libby's dogs for a while."

"Why don't you have a dog?"

"I had one. An old one. She died last year and I haven't found one yet to replace her."

Kira's heart squeezed. Was there anything in life this guy hadn't lost?

Jason walked Kira back to the trailer.

"Do you want to sleep inside for the rest of the night?" She had to offer. Part of her wanted to offer for reasons other than safety. This guy was sexy and he made her feel safe.

"I don't think so."

She could barely see his features in the glow of the flashlight he had pointed toward the ground. Maybe that was good.

"Be careful out here," she said.

He smiled slightly, then reached up with his free hand to cup the back of her head before leaning forward to lightly kiss her lips. It was over before she was even aware of what he'd been about to do. She pressed her fingertips to her mouth.

"Thanks for the help, Kira. I'll see you in the morning."

He had no idea how lucky he was that she let him walk away.

KIRA STEPPED OUT of the trailer the next morning to find Jason's bed neatly rolled up and no sign of him.

She walked along the edge of the field to the corrals.

The foal was still wearing his bandage, although it had a big green smear across it from where he'd lain down.

"Hey, Buck," Kira crooned. She would like to have this little guy, give him a home. Maybe she could get a place farther out of town…. But in Boise that would mean a long drive to work. The condo was only ten minutes away.

She went back inside the trailer to try to figure how Jason made coffee, which she was in desperate need of, and shortly after heard him outside the trailer. He tapped on the door.

"Where's your coffee making stuff?" Kira asked as soon as she opened the screen.

"I don't have any."

"You don't…oh, this is bad." And then she noticed how serious his expression was. "What?"

"I have something to show you."

Kira did not like the sound of this. She slipped into her shoes and followed him out the door and up his drive to the first corner. And there, in the fire-darkened road dust, were footprints.

"Tire tracks lead to my gate. Whoever it was parked there and walked. They stopped here, where they could see your Jeep, then went back."

A chill ran through her. "This is what spooked the foal?"

"I would imagine, although the guy probably didn't mean to. Look at the size of these boot prints. Not a big man. I think you'll be hearing from Bryce soon."

She shook her head. "This is not Bryce's style."

"I hope you're wrong, because if it's not Bryce trying to scare you, then…"

"Thanks. I really needed that."

"Hey!" Jason spread his palms.

"I know. Better to know what I'm up against. It's just that the whole thing sucks. What did I do to deserve this?"

He gave her a long look and for a moment she thought he was going to say something, but instead he clamped his mouth shut.

"Let's go get some breakfast. And I think Menace's dad may have left some of those single coffee packets under the bench seat."

But Kira didn't move. Instead she stared at the tracks.

A moment later, Jason's arm came around her, pulling her to his side. "This is going to sound harsh, but if the guy meant you harm, he could have done you harm. He was probably just checking to see if your car was here."

"But we don't know that for sure."

"No," Jason allowed. "We don't."

"Should I call someone?"

"I called Cal already, let him know."

"Thanks."

"And if you want to go to Elko right now, I'll go with you. Hell, I'll even stay with you until you finish your business."

She sucked in a breath, touched by his offer when he had so much he was dealing with himself. She also wondered whether, if she went to Elko or Boise, she would lose whoever was tracking her.

"Maybe we should get Libby's dogs and give it another night." Kira met his eyes. "You can't have a firearm, but I can."

"Maybe we'll talk to Libby," he said. "But I don't think we'll be needing firearms."

"You still believe it's Bryce?"

"I still do."

AFTER A HEARTY BREAKFAST of cereal and milk in plastic bowls, Kira went with Jason to feed, following the trail to the pens and the small stack of hay nearby. He pulled out his jackknife and quickly cut the three strings holding a bale together. The hay accordioned out as he folded the blade and shoved the knife back in his front pocket, where it fit perfectly along a pale wear line in his jeans. "Do you know what a flake is?"

"Only the human kind."

He smiled slightly. "See how the bale separates into these layers? Each small animal gets one, big animals two. The burros count as small. Just toss it over the fence into the feeders. There's a wheelbarrow there for the far pens. If you'll do this, I can get started on the posts."

"I think I'm their favorite person," Kira said as the animals all starting pressing up against the edge of the pens.

"No doubt," he said. She looked up at him, thinking how odd it was to be here, basically being watched over the same way he was watching over these animals. Was she a project to him? A method of revenge against her family?

Or was he what he seemed to be—a decent guy? A caring man who kept getting slapped backward in life?

A loner by choice, and here she was, trying to bring people into his solitary environment.

"I'll be working in the field. Come on down if you get bored."

After feeding, and then picking the blown-back hay out of her hair and bra, Kira returned the wheelbarrow to its spot near the small haystack.

Was she being watched right now?

Probably not. But she was creeped all the same. Maybe she should just get into the Jeep and drive to Elko, or call her father and tell him what was happening.

Or maybe she should give it one more day.

Prove to herself it wasn't Bryce.

WHEN HER PHONE RANG later that morning, Kira's heart jumped. But it was her sister, not her brother.

"Where are you?" Leila asked.

"Otto." Or close to it. She and Jason had agreed that she wouldn't tell anyone exactly where she was. If Bryce did indicate he knew, he could only have found out through a spy.

"I hope that means you're making headway."

"I'm working on it." Although, truthfully, the only progress she was making was in her relationship with Jason…and she was discovering that the connection she'd felt the night of the range fire was not a figment of her imagination.

"Any more signs you're being followed?"

"None," Kira said, wincing inwardly at the lie. She never lied to Leila. She'd confess later, but right now she felt it was best to go with Jason's plan.

"But there's something else," Kira said. "About Jason and Bryce." She glanced out to the far edge of the field, where Jason was wrestling a post out of the ground. He was too far away for her to see his expression, but he radiated a sense of purpose. The guy didn't have much, but what he had he took care of. And when he got knocked down, he got up again. Without whining or shifting blame.

"What?" Leila asked curiously

How did Kira explain without explaining?

"I don't quite know how to put this, but there's a missing piece to this situation between them."

"How so?"

Yes, how so? She bit her lip, chose her words with care. "I just believe that the bitterness between these guys is over the top, and there's something here I'm not understanding." There had to be. "I was wondering if you could quietly check with Aunt Pat and see if you can shake loose some more data."

"I don't know if I have enough money for that. Do you have any idea what Roselli's 2004 Pinot Noir costs these days?" That particular wine was Aunt Pat's weakness. Kira wasn't certain if it was the wine or gratitude, but their aunt was usually freer with information after a few glasses of the stuff.

"I'll pay you back. I just, I don't know, feel as if I'm operating without all the information. And it's putting me at a disadvantage."

"I'll see what I can do," Leila said resignedly. "Although without you to help, she'll probably drink me under the table before I get anything out of her."

"And please—this is really important—don't give her any clue why you're asking. You're just curious for your own reasons."

"Which I am. You've got me wondering."

"Thank you. I'll make it up to you."

"I'll hold you to that. When you're in charge, you can nix the no in-house dating rule."

"How are things with your secret beau?" Kira asked, making a stab at sisterly conversation.

"The guy is such a rule follower. If he didn't have the hots for me, I'd be in big trouble."

Kira laughed. "You won't jeopardize his job?"

"Of course not. We never acknowledge one another during working hours."

"Must be hard."

"You have no idea."

Jason carried the butt end of the burned post over to a pile he'd made, wiped his gloved hands down his pants, then started for the trailer.

"Hey, I've got to go," Kira said. "If you do manage to discover something in the next day or two, before I head back to Elko, call."

The front of Jason's shirt was nearly black from charcoal and he had a long smudge of the stuff across his left cheek and forehead. Kira wrinkled her nose when he got close.

"I won't touch you," he said dryly, pulling off his gloves and reaching for the sandwich she handed him.

Jason ate standing up, as if he couldn't wait to get back out to the field.

"Do you need some help?"

His gaze traveled over her. "I don't think you need to get filthy."

She checked out her shirt—her only one without some remnant of motor oil on it. "Good point. I can put on some something else, like, say, something from your extensive wardrobe."

"Ever set fence posts?"

"I think you know the answer to that. Ever ramrodded a business deal?"

"We felons don't do a lot of that." His expression was mildly challenging, but she didn't look away and she didn't apologize, either. Facts were facts. He was a felon.

"What I was getting at is that our life experiences are different, but that doesn't make them less valuable."

He smiled at her schoolteacher tone. "And what *I* was getting at was do you think you can be of any help setting posts?"

She smiled back at him. "I'll try."

He finished his sandwich and then jerked his head toward the field. "I have extra gloves in the truck. Let me grab them and we'll go set a post."

Setting posts was monotonous and strenuous work. Kira was in charge of monotonous, while Jason handled strenuous. And there was no arguing with him. He said he got to use the bar and shovel because he knew what he was doing, but Kira thought it was because he knew his head would explode from boredom if he was the one checking the leveling device and holding the post vertical while she shoveled soil in the hole, then tamped it down with the bar.

But no matter how boring it was holding the level, she preferred being out here with him rather than alone with her thoughts at the trailer. She was still fixated on figuring out what the hell was going on, and what her next move was going to be, but at least being with Jason was comforting. And distracting.

His shirt was open in a deep V because of a missing button, and the sheen of perspiration made the flex of his muscles as he worked even more evident. Though she rather welcomed the view, Kira tried not to stare. Much.

She distracted herself by thinking about that quick, gentle kiss last night.

He finished tamping the last of the dirt by stamping it with his foot, then tested the stability by putting his hand on top of the post and shaking. It didn't budge, so on to the next one. He plopped the eight-foot post into the hole, then Kira held it up as he began to shovel in the dirt.

He even smelled good. No, he smelled sexy, in a way that made her consider possibilities, no matter how improbable they seemed.

He smelled of possibility.

Kira pressed her lips together to keep from smiling as the adage zinged into her brain. She wasn't exactly thinking of business possibilities at the moment. No, not at all.

"Is it level?" Jason asked, and she jerked her attention back to the job. No. It wasn't. She pulled on the post until the bubble on the level centered.

When she looked up, Jason was studying her, his shovelful of dirt poised in the air. Their gazes locked for one electric moment and then he dumped the dirt into the hole.

Kira concentrated on keeping the post perfectly vertical, but her nerves were humming. Too much tension. Too much sun. She glanced sideways at Jason. Too much guy.

He was keeping his head down now as he worked.

Damn, she was losing it.

But then she decided to cut herself some slack. She needed something positive to focus on and hot guy was positive.

Hot guy who'd almost killed her brother. Not so positive.

But he'd done his time, paid for the crime, which she knew still haunted him. How could it not?

After they'd finished five posts, Jason suggested a water break. Kira drank a little, he drank a lot.

"Shall we do another?" she asked, nodding at the three posts left in his rapidly dwindling pile.

"I've had enough for one day."

"Let's go check the baby."

"Sure." He shoved his gloves in his back pocket, while Kira carried hers. His man-size gloves had hung on her hands and were too big to shove into the pockets of her jeans.

Together they walked across the toasted grass at the

edge of the field to where Jason had the panel corrals set up. And once again Kira noticed that Jason Ross smelled sexy.

She needed to tread lightly here or she might be getting in over her head.

CHAPTER ELEVEN

JASON SPENT MOST OF the day servicing his haying equipment, more because he needed to think than because it needed servicing again.

Was he doing the right thing having Kira stay there? Because he was beginning to suspect that it was for reasons other than just proving to her that her brother was the bad guy.

He was attracted to her…and he had the feeling it was mutual. He also knew he was not going to get involved with the woman unless she learned the truth.

So how did you tell a woman that what she believed true about her family was really a lie? Without ripping her world apart?

But if Bryce tipped his hand, then Jason would tell her.

Kira came down to talk to him midafternoon. The incidents of the past two days hadn't been easy on her, and he didn't blame her for hanging close to the only other person within miles—he hoped—even if it messed up his concentration.

"I did some research in the library," she said as she perched on the fender of the tractor. "Your family owned a bigger ranch down the road from here."

"Yes, they sold out to the Bensons," Jason said as he tightened the oil plug.

"Where are they now?" she asked conversationally.

"They bought a smaller place in Montana while I was doing my time," he answered, ratcheting a bolt.

"Do you see them very often?"

"Couple times a year, yeah. They wanted to drive down and help me out after the fire, but I told them there was nothing they could do. They're in the middle of haying."

"Are you close?"

"Yeah."

Kira looped her arms over one raised knee. "I didn't see my dad or brother and sister much until I was in college. Just a week or two during summer vacations. It wasn't until my mom died that I really got to know them."

That explained a lot, and it made him feel a whole lot better about finding her attractive. "Your mom was his second wife?"

"Yes. And my sister is his child by his third wife. That marriage took."

Jason dropped the ratchet and reached for a rag. "Did your mom ever remarry?"

Kira shook her head. "She told me she never saw the need, but I have to admit, I would have liked to have had a stepdad and maybe younger siblings. There's good and bad to being an only. She died four years ago of breast cancer."

"I'm sorry."

"So am I. We were close."

"That's when you joined the family business?"

"I wanted to get to know the other side of the family better, so I flew out for a vacation. I liked them." She smiled. "Especially Leila, my sister, and her mom and—" Kira shrugged "—what can I say? There was a lot of energy. A lot of…family…and I liked it. It was very different from the way I grew up, and when my dad suggested I join the company, I jumped at it."

Jason frowned as he mentally put the pieces together. Kira and Bryce were competitive, Bryce was a jealous asshole and Kira enjoyed being part of a bigger family. She also liked working for the family, being a Jennings. A lot.

"Why is getting access to this property so important to you? The place hasn't been looked at in years and now, suddenly, access is of utmost importance."

He started wiping his hands on the rag as he waited for her to respond. She fiddled with a stalk of hay she'd pulled out of a crack in the fender of the baler.

"I messed up on a business deal a few months ago. I didn't perform due diligence to the extent I should have, and bought a building that extended over the property line by a couple of feet. The original construction surveys weren't done accurately and no one double-checked them before building."

"I can see where that would be a problem."

"You have no idea." She bit the end of the stalk, twisting it as she stared off into the distance. "I ended up with a professional black eye."

"Hey. It's a family company. You're family."

"So's Bryce. My grandfather's stepping down. My father will, of course, move into his position. Bryce and I are both equally qualified for Dad's position—or we were until the Bailey building fiasco."

"Was Bryce involved in the…fiasco?"

She glanced up. "Yes."

"Yet you ended up with the brunt of the blame."

"Yes."

He didn't say anything else, although he would have liked to. Kira twirled the piece of alfalfa. "To redeem myself, I did some research, hoping to find some brilliant way to regain my position as a contender, and that's why I came down here. It was obvious from what Aunt Pat told me that Bryce would never come to you. I can see him sending an envoy, but *he* wouldn't do it. So…it was a long shot, but I tried."

"What happens if Bryce gets the GM position?" Jason asked. "Do you just continue in the job you're in?"

"Yes, but honestly? I think he'll figure out a way to get rid of me."

Jason was surprised. "Why?"

"Because he assumes I'll work behind the scenes to try and get rid of *him*. It's the way he operates, and he believes I'm the same." Her mouth flattened. "He believes *everyone* is the same. We're okay now because we're equal."

Jason frowned. "Yet you don't believe he'd have you followed. Trash your motel room."

"And risk getting implicated if things went wrong?

Accomplices talk, you know, and Bryce is not the trusting kind." She gave Jason a sharp look. "There's no reason for Bryce to take a risk like that…unless there's something here I don't know." She waited a heartbeat, then asked, "*Is* there something?"

Jason got to his feet and started picking up tools. "Your brother and I were friends once. I know Bryce rather well. Maybe even better than you do. Which is why I'm pretty sure he's behind this."

"That's not an answer, Jason."

"It's all I can give you."

Kira stared up at him, and then, just when he'd thought the Jennings family had done everything to him they could possibly do, she took his face in her hands, rose up on her toes and surprised the hell out of him by kissing him. It was not a gentle kiss, either, but a passionate one, deep and long.

He forced himself not to respond. Much. It almost killed him. He bunched his into fists by his sides, and she lowered her heels back to the ground.

"What was that for?" he asked, his voice ridiculously uneven.

Kira cocked an eyebrow. "I guess it was because I wanted to. Because I'm frustrated and worried. And I guess because I want to break that awesome self-control you have. But I don't seem to have succeeded."

She gave him one last appraising look, then turned and walked back to the trailer, leaving him with a raging hard-on and not a lot he could do about it.

Awesome self-control. Yeah. Right.

KIRA HAD SOME THINKING to do. She felt as if she understood Jason, the man, even if she did not understand
the past.

Neither of them mentioned the kiss, but Kira found that
she was glad she'd done it. It represented a shift in power.
She might not know the secrets, but she had the power to
move him—even if he had fought it like a champ.

She helped Jason change the foal's bandage later
that day, doing her best to ignore the awareness that shot
through her whenever they touched. And she was
unable to forget why the foal had a wound in the first
place—because someone had come creeping in on foot
to spy on her.

"Thanks," Jason said after the job was done, and then
she went to the trailer to make sandwiches while he
moved hay. She had only been inside for a few minutes
when her phone rang, startling her.

She picked it up, and then for or a long moment just
stared at the display.

Bryce.

Bryce was calling. Contacting her. Just as Jason had
said he would.

But there were many legitimate reasons for him to
call. It didn't have to be because of where she was, who
she was staying with… That theory got blown out of the
water immediately after she said hello.

"Are you in Otto, Nevada?" her brother demanded.

"Bryce…what does it matter where I am?" she
replied in a surprisingly normal voice. "I'm on vacation."

He let out a sigh. "I know you're down there and I know what you're trying to do. It won't work."

"How do you know?"

"I talked to Margo." Leila's mother.

All right, that was possible. Leila could have let something slip. She was very close to her mom. And Bryce, under the guise of concern, could have probed an answer out of her. It *could* have happened like that....

"He's unbalanced, you know."

"Excuse me," Kira said, surprised that her normally cautious brother would cut to the chase without knowing exactly what was going on first. Everything Jason had told her would happen was happening.

"Jason Ross. He's unbalanced. I'm…just warning you. I don't want to see you hurt."

"Hurt?"

"In any way." The words sounded sinister, as she was certain Bryce intended them to.

"How do you know I've been anywhere near Jason Ross?" Kira asked quietly, matter-of-factly. "You aren't having me followed, are you?"

"Of course not."

"Then why *am* I being followed? By a guy from WaterPro?" Her voice took on a sarcastic edge. "Is it for my own safety and well-being?"

The brief hesitation on the other end of the line was damning. Kira waited, letting the moment grow in magnitude.

"What has he been telling you, Kira?"

"Bryce…" She bit her lip, not sure what to say. She didn't need to say anything because Bryce took over.

"He lies, Kira. I know. Firsthand. If Dad hadn't stepped in and saved the day after the accident, well, I don't like to think about it. Jason tried to set me up. Tried to set *me* up." There was an intense note in his voice, one Kira had never heard before. It was unsettling.

"Bryce, please tell me what you're talking about."

"I can't. So much of it is a blur."

"The night?"

"I don't want to think about that night," he reiterated. "I never want to think about it again. It was bloody, Kira. Really bloody. And then the fire…"

Kira shut her eyes.

"I'm sorry," she murmured.

"Kira, for the good of the family, just back off."

"All right. I'll leave soon."

"How soon?"

"Immediately," she said, hoping to placate him. "Is there anything else?"

"No." He still sounded shaken, as if he'd faced something he hadn't wanted to face, exactly as he'd told her. Something he'd shoved to the back of his mind. "I'll see you when you get back from Elko. Maybe…well… maybe we can talk then."

"Yes," Kira agreed. "See you then." He hung up the phone and she slowly disconnected.

So who did she believe here? Her brother or Jason?

Heaven help her, she believed Jason. Bryce was the one who'd had her followed. And even more frightening, he'd had her belongings trashed. The implications were shattering. Did their father know? Did she even know her own family? Or was Bryce working alone, jockeying for position?

And what was all this about being set up? Exactly the claim Jason had made about her.

A shaft of sun shone down in the hay field as Kira left the trailer, casting it ultrayellow against the blue-gray backdrop of an approaching storm. Jason had his truck backed up to the haystack and was shifting bales onto the bed.

He was so intent on his work that she had to clear her throat to get his attention when she approached.

"I didn't hear you," he said, jumping to the ground and pulling his gloves off, tossing them onto the tailgate of the truck. He wiped the back of his hand over his forehead.

"What am I missing?" Kira asked.

His expression shifted none too subtly. "I don't understand." The thunder rumbled distantly as a light rain began to patter on the hayshed roof.

"Neither do I," Kira said. "And I want you to tell me what it is I'm not understanding. Bryce called. Just like you said he would."

"Kira…"

"Bryce said you tried to set him up. You accused me of setting *you* up. What's happening here?"

He started to speak, drowned out by another deep rumble. The storm was moving in fast. Lightning forked to the ground in the distance, and Kira suppressed a shudder.

No more fires. There'd been enough fires.

She turned back to Jason. He was no more unbalanced than she was, but he had scars. More scars than her, though she had her share.

And then, instead of demanding answers, as she had intended to do, she put her arms around his waist and leaned against his chest.

"Damn it, Jason. This is all too weird."

He returned her embrace, one arm wrapping around her back while his hand came up to lightly stroke her hair. The whisper touch sent her senses into overdrive.

Another rumble of thunder sounded, louder this time.

The hay smelled sweet; the air was damp, heavy. A huge blast of thunder shook the ground and then rain began to drum on the metal roof. Kira lifted her head and asked *the* question. The one she was afraid she didn't want the answer to. But she had to know.

"What happened that night, Jason?"

He stepped back, releasing her, then looked away as he shoved his hands into his back pockets.

"Jason?" It was a plea for truth, answered again with silence.

She dropped her chin to her chest for a moment, frustrated. What had her family done to this man?

She was going to walk away, go back to the trailer and give them both some space as she thought this out, but she only made it a few steps when he took hold of her shoulders and turned her around to face him. "I don't want you to be hurt."

"You don't want *me* to be hurt," she said incredulously, knowing he'd just answered the question. "Damn it, Jason, how can I not be hurt if my family hurt you? And how can you…" She lost the words. "How can you do this? Sit on this secret?"

"What else can I do?" he asked. "It's over. Done. I'm trying to get on with my life."

"Or you were until I came along."

"Or I was until you came along. Then things changed."

"For better or worse?" she asked with a note of bitterness.

"Both." His expression was shuttered, giving her the feeling that there'd been more bad than good.

She started to respond, to ask for an explanation, but the words stopped when he reached out to caress her face, cupping it in both hands, and then his mouth came down on hers and she was immersed in a wild, almost desperate kiss. Kira caught hold of his shirt, and then his shoulders, hanging on as they clung together, their tongues meeting, then parting, meeting again.

They sank down on the hay without breaking contact, their bodies molding together. And still Kira tried to get closer. She kissed him, nipped his lower lip, pushed her hands up into his hair.

She had no idea where this was going, but every part of her was telling her to let it play out.

Jason finally lifted his head, his lips leaving hers. The rainfall diminished as they stared at each other.

And then Kira shivered.

"Come on," he said. "Let's go to the trailer."

THEY MADE A DASH through the rain as the skies opened up again. Jason halfway hoped that getting drenched would bring them to their senses. No such luck.

As soon as he pulled the trailer door shut and turned around, Kira was back on him, taking his face in her hands, kissing him hard, as though she could make up for what her family had done.

He didn't protest. There were lots of points he could have brought up to stop them—past history, current history, ten thousand reasons it wouldn't be anything but a one-time occurrence—but he had no reason that Kira didn't know or hadn't guessed at. And what was wrong with a one-time thing?

Only one thing could be wrong with it. He raised his head, looked down into her blue eyes.

"This isn't to make up for what's happened to me? This isn't a mercy—"

She touched her fingertips to his lips, silencing him.

"I'm not going to have any mercy on you, Jason," she stated matter-of-factly.

And she didn't.

From the moment she peeled off her wet shirt, tossing it carelessly over the built-in table, and started unbuttoning his, she had no mercy. Her bra was thin, shimmery, almost see-through.

She smelled of sage and rain, and when Jason brought his lips down to taste her skin where her breasts welled up, she shuddered, grasping his hair. And then she pulled back to finish disposing of his shirt, running her hands over his rain-damp skin, tense muscles. She hooked her fingers into the waistband of his Levi's, tugged him forward again, kissing him as her fingers started popping buttons.

"Kira…"

She ignored him and slipped her hand down into his boxers, grasping him. He felt as if he was going to explode.

"It's been a while…."

She trailed the tip of her tongue over his lips as she squeezed him, then slowly released the excruciatingly pleasurable pressure before too much damage was done.

"I thought I could do this without a why. I can't." He looked down at her again. "Why?"

She met his gaze. "I need to."

He swallowed. Okay. That was clear. And damned heady stuff because she was one beautiful woman. But he also knew this was a way for her to avoid thinking about what she was soon going to be facing when she went home. The truth about her brother.

"Now I have a question," she said, once again bringing her fingers up to the waistband of his jeans.

"Yeah?"

"Do you have condoms? Lots and lots of condoms?"

He couldn't help smiling. "Yes," he said solemnly. "I do. In that drawer there." She stepped away to open the drawer and pull out the package, holding it lightly between her thumb and forefinger as she came back to him, a remarkably predatory smile on her lips.

He reached behind her to release her bra. She shrugged her shoulders forward, letting it fall to the floor between them, and then he brought his hands up to caress her breasts, pressing his lips to the cleavage he formed before going on to circle first one nipple, then the other with his tongue.

Her breath caught for a moment, and then she said huskily, "The jeans?"

He answered by unsnapping them, then pulling down the zipper. The denim was molded to her from the rain.

"You'll never get them off," she said.

"Wanna bet?"

"Let me, so I have some skin left." She put a hand on either side of the waistband, seesawing them down to her knees, then stepping out of them. Her panties had traveled the same route, and Jason realized he was staring. Quite possibly drooling. This really was one beautiful woman. He wanted her to feel good.

He undid the remaining buttons on his own jeans. He was barely out of them when she pushed him back onto the bed, then straddled him, her thighs smooth and strong as she took his erection in her hand. In a matter of seconds, she'd rolled the condom into place.

"The merciless get the top," she declared.

"Okay," Jason said weakly as she eased him into her, slowly, oh so slowly, until finally he couldn't take it anymore. He grasped her hips and firmly pulled her down, burying himself to the hilt. Kira dropped her head back, eyes closed, exposing her throat. She sucked in a breath through her teeth and had Jason doing the same as they started moving. Slowly. Matching the staccato rhythm of the rain.

How long could he last? How long could he hold

back from coming, with her riding him, squeezing him, controlling him?

Long enough, it seemed. Kira suddenly tensed, then bit back a small cry, and he felt her contracting around him, pulsing rhythmically until she collapsed forward. With a quick series of final thrusts, he, too, came.

And damned if there weren't dots still dancing before his eyes when he refocused on the beautiful woman lying on top of him. He'd never had that happen before.

"Do you always take control?" he asked, for something to say.

"I knew if I didn't, you'd find a reason to stop."

"Did you want me that badly?" He tried for an ironic tone.

"Yes." And for the first time since they'd started to make love, she smiled. Then she rolled off him. He missed her weight, her warmth.

"I'm going to leave tomorrow morning," she said, but she kissed him after she said it, tracing her tongue over his lips.

Not much he could say to that. He'd proved his theory. Her brother had called, warned her off. There was no reason for her to stay…except for maybe one. And he knew they were both going to skirt the issue of attraction. Future meetings. Realistically, this couldn't be anything but a one-time thing, but he knew, one time or not, he'd be playing this over in his mind for some time to come.

"Before I leave, I want the truth," she said, propping herself up on one elbow.

"You're not going to let this lie, are you?"

"Someone died that night. I can't go back, be part of my family, without knowing who's responsible."

And she probably couldn't go back and be part of it in the same way if she did know. But who was Jason to protect her from the truth?

"Who was driving that night?" she asked. "My brother?"

When he rolled his head on the pillow to look into her eyes, it was all the confirmation she needed.

"Why?" she asked. "Why did you plead no contest?"

"So many reasons."

"Ah, Jason."

He turned his gaze back up at the ceiling. "We barely knew Seth, you know? He'd just wanted a ride back to the frat house. I was too drunk to drive, but Bryce swore he wasn't. That's the last thing I remember about the night."

Kira closed her eyes.

"We were all ejected, but Seth was crushed under the truck. I had head injuries, no memory of the accident. As your father pointed out while I was still in the hospital, there was no evidence that I wasn't driving, and it *was* my truck. There weren't even any fingerprints because of the heat of the fire. They tried, but got nothing. I couldn't afford a civil suit or restitution if I lost a jury trial. I knew my parents would sell the ranch to make restitution."

"So you pleaded no contest?"

"In exchange for your father paying the restitution to Seth's family." Jason gave her an ironic look. "He, uh, bought a piece of property that once connected to the ranch in order to give me the money for restitution in an aboveboard kind of way."

"The piece of property you cut off access to?"

"The same." He rolled over, propped himself up. "I thought you were incredibly ballsy, coming down to ask for access."

Kira blew out a breath. "No doubt." And no wonder it had been animosity at first sight.

"I thought you knew." He touched her forehead with one callused fingertip, smoothing away her frown. "But when we were outrunning the fire, it dawned on me that you probably didn't."

"And then the lawyer called."

"And then the lawyer called," he agreed. "Which didn't help." He pulled her lips down to his. "Let's make the most of this night. Because I don't think we'll have another."

"How come?"

"Because you can't be involved with both me and your family."

She sucked in a breath, and he knew she was acknowledging the truth in his statement. She exhaled and reached for him, silently agreeing to lose herself in the moment, in him, once again.

CHAPTER TWELVE

JASON COULD NOT BELIEVE how difficult it was to walk Kira to the Jeep the next morning.

"Don't worry about me," she said, touching his cheek with her palm. "You can't follow me everywhere. I have to deal with this on my own."

"I can follow you to Elko." He couldn't help the need he felt to protect her. It was the way he was wired. Protect those you care about, and he cared about Kira.

She shook her head. "I'll call you when I get there." She tilted her head, touched his lips with one finger, tracing them. "My brother won't hurt me."

"You didn't think he'd have you followed, either."

Jason hated that he had no business watching her back. Hated that Bryce Jennings was her brother. Bryce probably would back off now that he'd won, but...Jason hated taking the chance.

He opened the back of the Jeep, stowed Kira's bag, then closed it again. There was an air of finality to the thump of the hatch latching. He tipped her chin, lightly kissed her lips. "Don't go trying to right wrongs on my behalf, okay?"

"Jason," she started, but he kissed her again, cutting her off.

"It won't help me." And she'd never be able to prove anything. All she'd get was heartache.

She looked as if she wanted to argue, but changed her mind. "I'll call when I get to Elko," she repeated. Then she rose up on her toes and kissed him one last time. Hungrily. He hugged her to him, not wanting to let go, but knowing he had to. It was inevitable. Back to their separate lives. It was astounding they had managed to connect at all.

After the Jeep had disappeared around the corner, Jason turned and headed for the field, where he tamped dirt around new fence posts until he finally had to give up the battle.

Jason Ross, who needed no one, needed company.

KIRA HAD THOUGHT THAT, in her twenty-eight years, she'd experienced the entire spectrum of emotion, from the joy of first love to the pain of losing her mother.

It appeared she was wrong. She hadn't experienced deep betrayal before, which was what she felt when she thought about Bryce. And shame, for being associated with the family that had done this to Jason.

She was amazed Jason cared enough about her not to include her in his justifiable bitterness toward Bryce and her father.

Her father.

How could he have done something like this? To protect Bryce, yes, but…was it possible he didn't know the truth? That Bryce and Jason were the only ones who knew exactly what had happened?

And what about her grandfather? Had he known?

If he wasn't aware of the situation, Bryce's reaction to her and Jason being together made sense. Perfect sense.

He wouldn't want Kira taking tales to their grandfather.

But it was all speculation.

Speculation that was going to be sorted into truths and untruths because, regardless of what she'd told Jason, she was not letting the matter lie. Jason deserved vindication.

She might have to choose between her family and him, but she knew that regardless which she chose, the truth was going to come out.

Kira leaned her elbow on the window and rested her head on her hand as she drove. With the exception of the time surrounding her mother's death, these had undoubtedly been the longest, strangest, most life-altering days of her life.

THE PHONE RANG while Jason was stripping off to take his minishower in the minibathroom. He fully expected it to be Kira when he didn't recognize the number, fully expected to feel a surge of regret at the sound of her voice.

"I'm going to say this one time. Stay away from my sister or you will regret it."

"Gee, Bryce," Jason said, trying to regain his equilibrium, "good to hear from you."

"She doesn't need to hear your lies, and I will sue you for slander if you persist."

"Yeah? What'll you get if you do that? I don't have a hell of a lot."

"I'll take that pathetic hay property of yours and then we'll see who has access."

Jason refrained from pointing out that his land was homesteaded and couldn't be taken from him by legal action. "Are you sure you want to play this game, Bryce? Are you sure *you* won't get damaged in the fallout?"

"I won't get damaged, because I have the truth on my side."

"You're delusional. There's nothing you can do to me."

"Don't mess with me, Jason. Leave my sister alone."

Too late.

Bryce hung up abruptly, leaving Jason holding his phone, trying to remember the conversation. The little rat hadn't said one thing that could be viewed as a malicious threat—just in case someone had been listening in, like say, Dorrie, who had an antique and illegal scanner that picked up cell phone calls.

Bryce had threatened legal action. Big deal.

But Jason was not going to get pushed around by this twerp again, and he wasn't going to let him push Kira around, either.

He showered and changed into his one suitable traveling outfit—jeans with no holes, and a white shirt with no barbed wire rips.

He called Libby as he drove north toward Elko, and when she answered, he asked if she would feed his animals and change the foal's bandage.

"No problem," she said. "Just stop leaving hay at my house."

"Stop leaving lumber at mine. And if you see some SOB in a white Ford Ranger, steer clear. Call Cal."

"Will do. Are you going to explain why?

"Just as soon as I get back."

THE NEARY FARMS PROPERTY tour and subsequent meeting moved along at a nice clip. Neary was anxious to make a deal, he liked the price Kira was offering, even though he pretended not to, and they both left satisfied. In a business sense, anyway.

Kira had called Jason, as she'd promised when she'd gotten to Elko, only to receive the message that the person she was trying to call was out of service range. Apparently there was trouble with the transmission towers again, and she couldn't even leave a message.

Kira checked into her room and then called the office to update her father about the meeting. He was happy with her progress, and in turn reported that things had gone well with the Coeur d'Alene acquisition. By the time they said goodbye, Kira knew Bryce couldn't have mentioned her whereabouts to their father. If Bryce had, her dad would have asked about it—maybe even reprimanded her for opening a can of worms.

Bryce was keeping his secrets.

Bryce had good reason.

A SOFT RAP AT THE DOOR startled Kira as she was checking over some figures before going to dinner, and when she peered through the peephole, she almost fell over. Jason was on the other side.

She knew from his expression when she opened the door he hadn't come to pick up where they'd left off. Something was wrong. He stepped inside, taking off his hat.

"Your brother called me," he said without a hello. "Warned me off."

"From me?" she asked incredulously.

"From you. It worries me."

"It gives *me* a headache," Kira said truthfully. Her brother was going off the deep end. She rubbed her forehead. "I'm going to kill him."

But she could see that Jason was indeed worried.

"I can deal with this," she said. "You didn't need to drive all this way to warn me."

"I have other things to do, but I wanted to talk to you in person. Be careful around Bryce."

He was making it a whole lot harder for her to put what happened between them the night before out of her mind.

She gave a small snort. "Bryce doesn't scare me."

"Yes. But he's scared you know something." He paused for a moment, then repeated what he'd said the day before, "Don't try to fix this, okay?"

"How can I not try, Jason?"

"Because I'm asking you not to."

She swallowed. Paced over to the window to look out at the parking lot, the shopping mall across the street, the hills behind town. Jason came up behind her, hesitating for only a moment before sliding his hands around her waist, pulling her back against him. She leaned into his warmth, and then shivered as his lips moved down to her neck. She reached up to hold his head, her fingers tightening as he nuzzled her.

"*Please.* I'm asking you," he murmured.

"I don't know if I can do what you want."

"Kira…"

"I'll try."

He seemed to know that was as much assurance as she could give him. He turned her in his arms. "Did your deal go okay?"

"Very well, thank you."

"Are you going to Boise tomorrow?"

"First thing. But I won't be seeing Bryce until the next day, and our father will be there when I do."

She couldn't take the polite conversation anymore. She leaned her head against his chest. "Can you stay?" Kira asked softly. "Until morning?"

"As I drove, I told myself I'd come, talk some sense into you, and then leave because it would be easier on both of us."

"What are you telling yourself now?" she asked, hoping for the correct answer.

Jason proved to be an excellent student. "I'm telling myself that it's my turn to have no mercy on you."

Kira pushed her hands into his hair, tipping his head forward until their foreheads touched. "Go ahead, then. Torture me. I'm ready."

"I HAVE A QUESTION."

"Hmm?" Kira rolled toward Jason, propping herself up on one elbow, studying his profile as he in turn studied the ceiling, a slight frown drawing his eyebrows together.

"Would it be possible, if I allowed access, to limit the amount of traffic on the road?"

"What?" Kira sat up straight, letting the sheet fall down around her waist.

Jason rolled his head on the pillow to look at her. "I trust you, but, no offense, I don't trust other members of your family. So is there any way to guarantee there won't be more than fifteen lots?"

Kira was shaking her head. "Don't give access."

"Why?" He frowned.

"I don't want you to."

He pulled her back down next to him, then rolled her over onto her back. "Let's see if I have this straight. You hound me for access, I offer it and you turn me down."

"That's right."

"Why?" he asked seriously.

"My family has already screwed you over once. I'm not going to open the door for them to do it again."

"Kira, there's something you have to understand here. I don't need you to run interference for me. I made a choice a long time ago, and now I'm living with it. I'm doing okay."

"It's not right."

"No. But like I said, I can live with it. And if giving

access will help tip the scales in your favor, well, I'd rather see you in the GM spot than Bryce."

Kira swallowed. "Big sacrifice, Jason."

"Hey. It's only fifteen families. There'll be a buffer. It'll allow me some satisfaction not seeing your brother advance within the company."

"So the lie continues. Bryce gets off scot-free."

"He will no matter what, Kira. There's no proof. My word against his. I pleaded no contest." Jason smiled wearily. "He's not likely to make a confession."

Kira closed her eyes. If she wanted to stay with the company, she couldn't pursue a relationship with Jason. If she wanted to be part of her family, she couldn't pursue a relationship with Jason. No matter how she looked at it, it wouldn't work.

She didn't even know how she could spend enough time with him to see if it would work. She'd already used half of her vacation.

But she wasn't ready to let him go. She'd never felt a connection like this one.

He got out of bed. "I should leave soon," he said. "You'll be okay?"

"I'll be fine. And trust me, Bryce won't threaten you anymore."

That stopped him cold. "Don't do anything, Kira."

But she couldn't make herself open her mouth and promise she wouldn't. She wasn't ready to close off her options.

"Maybe we could get together. Sometime?"

He smiled gently. "You mean sneak around and meet?"

"For now. Until I figure things out."

"I did a lot of thinking while you slept. Kira, I shouldn't have come this time. It's just making the inevitable more difficult."

"The inevitable?"

He put his hands on her shoulders. "You're going to manage Jennings Inc., Bryce is going to lick his wounds and I'm going to disappear back down south where I belong, never to be heard from again."

"That's not funny, Jason."

"No," he said softly. "But it's true."

Kira wanted to argue, but her case wasn't strong.

It was anything but strong. And hanging around her would only make things harder on him. The Jenningses had done enough damage to this man.

She was just lucky to have had the short amount of time with him she did have.

IT WAS NOT AN EASY phone call to make. Jason dialed the number he'd looked up on the Internet in a coffee shop in Elko. He wanted Kira to have the advantage. And stunningly, he wanted that for her, not to get revenge on Bryce.

"David Jennings, please."

"Who may I say is calling?"

"Tell him it's Ben Crandall's grandson," he said. That way he didn't have to announce to the world that Jason Ross was calling Jennings Inc.

The old man's voice came on the line a few seconds later.

"Jason? Jason Ross?"

"Yes, sir."

"What can I do for you?"

"I have a few questions. After talking to Kira, I'm considering allowing limited access across my property."

"Limited," Jennings said flatly.

"Quality of life, sir."

"I can see that."

"Considering the circumstances…"

"What circumstances?"

From the mystified tone in the old man's voice, Jason suddenly realized that David Jennings might not know what circumstances he was referring to.

"The accident," Jason said, letting the man draw his own conclusions.

"Oh. Of course. Forgive me."

David Jennings sounded tired, and slightly ashamed of himself for not instantly putting two and two together.

"If I give access, it's entirely because of Kira. I said no to begin with, but she kept talking and eventually made some sense." Jason hesitated. The old man didn't say anything, so he went on. "If I could be guaranteed no more than fifteen lots, I'd consider granting that access."

"Fifteen isn't many."

"I think you'll sell them for a healthy price. Kira has a plan. Check it out. If you're interested, call me."

"Very well."

"Oh, and one more thing."

"What's that?"

"You might want to take a deeper look into who's responsible for that Bailey building situation. Sounds like a fifty-fifty deal to me."

"What the hell would *you* know about it?"

"Look into it," Jason said, ignoring the other man's outraged tone, and then he hung up, hoping he hadn't done more harm than good.

Kira was not going to be happy when she discovered that he'd tried to intervene on her behalf. In fact, she was probably going to be miffed. But he was not going to let that slimeball, Bryce Jennings, ooze away.

There wasn't much Jason could do for Kira, but he could do this.

"WHERE ARE YOU?" There was a note in Leila's voice that Kira didn't like. She shifted the phone to her other ear.

"Actually, I'm driving home. I met with Mr. Neary again, and we'll be faxing him paperwork. I'd say the deal's all but done."

"That's great," Leila said absently. "Did you say anything to Granddad about Bryce?"

"No. I was careful not to. I didn't want to seem petty."

"Well, something happened. He went to meet Granddad, all cocky, and came out of the conference room mad enough to choke someone."

"How could you tell?"

"That's the scary thing. I *could* tell. He was…furious. I was there when he left."

"I promise I didn't say anything."

"Well, when he came out he was muttering something about the Bailey building."

Kira's heart stopped. "The Bailey?"

"Yeah." There was a pause and then Leila said, "You *did* say something to Granddad?"

"No. Honest. Granddad told me I stunk at due diligence and I asked him if Bryce was any better, but that was before I went back down to Otto. Days and days ago."

"He has been under the weather."

"I didn't say enough to set Grandpa off. I was careful of his health."

"Well, all I can say is that the family dynamic is getting kind of strange. I'm glad I'm a computer girl."

"You may have been smart to go that route," Kira agreed. "I'll see you this afternoon."

"Stop by," Leila demanded. "I'll feed you and let you know if anything else happens."

"I'll do that."

Kira hung up feeling decidedly uneasy. If Bryce was showing emotion, there was sure to be hell to pay somewhere.

IT WAS ALMOST 11:00 p.m. by the time Jason stopped at his gate after shopping for supplies and worrying about Kira more than he cared to think about. He was surprised to find it open and two sets of fresh tire tracks in the deep dust. Someone had recently come and gone. Then he noticed the glow of light over the top of the sage.

Fire.

And there was no lightning tonight. The sky was clear.

Shit. He couldn't remember the number for Dispatch, so he dialed Menace.

"What?" the big man growled into the phone.

"I think my place is on fire," Jason said.

"Again?"

"Send help." He tossed the cell onto the seat so that he could steer with both hands as he negotiated the corners leading to his property.

An inferno blazed at the edge of the hay field. The trailer he'd borrowed from Menace's dad was a goner, and if he didn't act fast, what with the evening wind picking up, he was going to lose the hay roof, too.

There must not have been much going on in Otto that night because he'd barely gotten hoses strung together and the water on before the first volunteer firefighter pulled in. Seconds later two more pickups and a fire truck arrived.

Hal jumped out of the truck, his hat almost falling off in his hurry to start directing.

"Stand back, Jason."

Gritting his teeth, Jason stood back.

"Damn it, Jason." Libby came striding up, Menace at her side.

"How'd this happen?" Menace asked.

"I think it's been torched."

Libby nodded and Jason went to his truck to get his phone. He found it deep in the crack between the seats and dialed Cal Johnson.

"I'm on my way," Cal said once Jason had identified himself.

"You might want to keep an eye out for that white Ranger. I think my place has been torched."

"Shit."

"What?"

"I just saw a Ranger heading out of town toward Elko."

"Well, I'd chase him down if I were you," Jason said from between clenched teeth.

He snapped the phone shut and went back for his truck.

Libby caught up with him, grabbed his sleeve. "Where are you going?" she demanded.

"Boise."

"Don't be stupid."

"No. There are things that need to be settled and I'm settling them."

"Wait and see if they catch the Ranger guy."

"Don't have time."

"Jason…rebel that I am, I can't believe I'm saying this, but you'll never win with these people. Look what happens when you try. They hire someone to torch your house."

"Lib, what can they do that they haven't already done to me? What do I have left?"

"Your acreage, your freedom and your animals."

"I'll risk it."

Libby's expression clouded, but she didn't argue. How could she when she didn't have a leg to stand on?

CHAPTER THIRTEEN

AS WAS HER CUSTOM, Leila showed up at Kira's place about a half hour after Kira got home, bearing a pan of store-bought lasagna and a bottle of Chianti.

"No salad?" Kira asked as they walked to the kitchen. Leila, she noted, was glowing, and for once her dark hair was down, waving around her shoulders. Apparently her sister's star-crossed love affair was going better than her own.

"Not unless you have something lettucelike in your fridge."

Kira shook her head. "I'm afraid to open the fridge. I didn't clear it out before I left."

"You haven't been gone that long." Leila turned on the oven while Kira settled onto an upholstered bar stool next to the counter and rested her chin on her hands.

"It *seems* long," she said wearily.

Leila came over to massage Kira's tense neck muscles. "Tell me."

"I don't know what I can tell, can't tell...." She turned her head to look up at her sister.

"Let's start with the easy stuff. Where the hell were you for the past three days?" Leila's hands dropped away.

Kira raised her eyebrows.

"I couldn't get hold of you on your cell a couple times, so I called the motel, but you'd checked out. Then when I did reach you, you said you were in Otto. I was worried sick."

"Why didn't you just come out and ask me?" Kira asked.

"Because after Bryce got back, he started acting so flipping secretive and weird, I had no idea what to think. So I just played along. Like a good sister."

Kira put an arm around her shoulders and gave her a quick hug. "You are a good sister, and I was staying with Jason Ross."

Leila's mouth dropped open. "Again?"

"Again. And, well, it was interesting."

"*Real* interesting?"

"Couldn't have got much more interesting," Kira said, splashing a healthy amount of Chianti into her glass just as the oven sensor dinged, indicating it was preheated and ready to go.

"Wow," Leila said as she opened the door and slid the aluminum tray of lasagna inside.

"That's just the tip of the iceberg."

"I think I'm afraid to hear the rest."

Kira nodded, sipping her wine. Her sister stayed near the stove, gripping the concrete counter on either side of her.

"It, uh, wouldn't be wise to fall for this guy." Leila jutted her jaw sideways. "*Have* you fallen for this guy?"

"I think I could," she hedged.

"Could?"

"I'm on my way."

Leila exhaled loudly. "Your situation is worse than mine."

Kira cast her a baleful glance. Leila didn't know the half of it. Kira didn't know if it would help matters to tell, other than to give her a sounding board, which she sorely needed.

She'd been so blissfully satisfied with her life before she'd gone to Otto and now…not so proud of being a Jennings anymore. And she didn't know if she wanted to stir Leila up the same way.

"Tell me about Tom," she said, settling back on the stool.

"Well, I like him," Leila said tentatively. "He's a rule guy, but I help him bend the rules every now and then." She smiled cheekily, but it faded too soon. Clearly her heart wasn't into cheeky. She must be worried about her big sister.

"What are you going to do if it gets serious?" Kira asked, trying to keep Leila deflected from the subject of Jason.

"Gets?"

Oh, dear.

"Either Tom gets employed elsewhere or I quit the business, I guess."

Kira was becoming quite familiar with both of those

options; she'd thought about them long and hard on the drive up from Elko. Did she quit, lose her security, risk losing her family, because of what Bryce had done? If she did stubbornly pursue her feelings for Jason, would she have to give up her family? Would it hurt Jason?

Did the truth have to come out?

Could she live with herself if it didn't?

And…if she stayed away from Jason, would she ever stop thinking about him?

"What's wrong?" Leila asked.

Kira had met her eyes, debating whether to tell her, when her phone rang. The land line. Aunt Pat and a few of her older relatives—relatives who worshiped Bryce and would probably hate her for knocking him off his pedestal—were the only people who used the land line. Kira almost pulled the plug out, but thought better of it and picked up the heavy receiver of the old-fashioned phone.

"Kira?" a vaguely familiar female voice said.

"Yes?"

"This is Libby Hale. I had a hell of a time getting your number."

Kira grabbed the phone cord with her free hand. "Is Jason all right?"

There was a brief pause. "He's driving to Boise. Someone burned down his trailer tonight."

"What?" Kira shot a glance at her sister, whose dark eyes were now round with alarm from Kira's reaction.

"Yeah. They're looking for that guy in the white truck. I thought you should know. Cal agreed, which is how I got your unlisted number. Watch your back, and—" she hesitated "—maybe watch out for Jason. Try to talk some sense into him."

"Do you know why he's coming to Boise?" Kira asked. She twisted the phone cord around her hand as she waited for the answer.

"He said he'd had enough."

"I need to call him."

"Don't bother," Libby said, obviously pissed off. "I've been trying. He's turned his phone off."

Kira promised to call if she needed long distance backup.

"Okay, spill," Leila said as soon as Kira had hung up.

Kira met her sister's eyes. This was getting too serious to *not* spill.

"I think Bryce was driving the night of the accident. I think he's the one who should have gone to prison."

"You think Bryce was…why? Did Jason Ross tell you that?"

"No. Actually, he refused to tell me. I had to work it out for myself."

Leila tilted her head, her eyes narrowing. "Maybe he's just very clever and made you *think* you worked it out. Maybe that was his objective."

Kira pulled in a shaky breath, knowing how Jason must have felt arguing with her. "You know how I told you I was being followed?"

"Yes."

"There's more to it, and I think Bryce is behind it. He pretty much tipped his hand and now…"

"I need a drink."

By the time Kira finished her story, the Chianti was half-gone, and Leila was nodding sadly in agreement.

"All right. I don't know Jason, but I have to admit, what you're saying, well, it sounds plausible." She set her glass aside. "But there's no proof."

"Bryce called Jason and threatened him, and then his trailer was burned. They're searching for the guy who was following me."

"Jeez, Kira." Leila brushed her hair back from her forehead. The timer started dinging, but she ignored it. "What the hell is going on? I mean, do we even know our own family?"

"Apparently not," Kira said as she got up to turn off the timer and pull the lasagna out of the oven.

"Is Grandpa aware of all this?"

Kira slowly shook her head. "My gut feeling is that he's not."

"Dad?"

"I'm not sure. Jason says he and Bryce are the only ones who truly know what happened. There were no other witnesses."

"Except Suzanne."

Kira's eyes shot up. "What do you mean?"

Leila set her glass aside. "Once, when she and Bryce were going through that rough spot a few years ago, she had too much to drink at dinner, and said something about Bryce never being able to divorce her until she was ready to get divorced. I asked her why and she'd just smiled and said it was good to know things." Leila poked at the top of the lasagna with a knife she'd pulled out of the butcher block, then turned back toward Kira. "That could have been what she was talking about. Bryce had nightmares for a long time. Maybe he talks in his sleep. Maybe he confessed."

"Suzanne will never rat him out. She likes her security too much." Kira spoke the unfortunate truth aloud.

"So what do we do?"

"Honestly? We're going to try to get some sleep. It's almost one o'clock and tomorrow may be a long day."

"Do you expect Jason to come here?"

"No. The office. And I'm expecting Tom to control him when he does. I'm not going to have him going to prison for a crime he *did* commit—no matter how justified."

BY THE TIME he hit Elko and started up the two-lane highway to Boise, Jason was exhausted. But he pushed on. The night was lit at intervals by dry lightning.

The guy at the service station had told him there were small fires to the north, and that he was worried because his parents had a ranch up there and had suffered badly the year before. Jason could commiserate.

He wanted to call Kira, but his phone was dead and the charger had burned in the trailer fire. He'd never bothered to get a car charger and now he was cursing himself. There hadn't even been any place open to buy one when he'd driven through Wesley and Elko. He was out of communication.

Perhaps it was for the best. He could think rather than react. What was he doing? Why was he doing it?

Easy. He was going to teach that son of a bitch that

he couldn't get away with torching Jason's trailer. He and Bryce were about to have a meeting the likes of which Bryce had never seen before. Jason wasn't quite sure how that would happen yet, but it would.

And he was going to make sure Kira was safe as her much protected big brother was being backed further and further into a corner. Bryce wasn't feeling so protected now, and he'd be desperate to maintain his secret.

Jason was just over the Idaho border when he realized he needed to sleep before he confronted Bryce Jennings. His wallet was nearly empty, so he pulled off into a roadside picnic site with a few tables, and a stream running nearby.

He balled up his jacket, shoved it against the window, leaned his head on it and closed his eyes, thinking he'd sleep maybe an hour before hitting the road again. He awoke with a start when someone tapped on his window.

A highway patrolman stood there looking serious in the early morning light. Jason rolled down the window.

"Are you all right, sir?"

"Fine," Jason said. Except that he was cramped and had to pee. "I drove too long, needed to pull off."

"That's wise." The trooper craned his neck and Jason knew he was checking for bottles.

"I haven't been drinking." It was the last thing he'd be doing. "I was headed to Boise and got tired."

"Can I see your license?"

"Sure." Jason pulled it out of his wallet.

"You know you need a front license plate in Idaho?"

Jason nodded.

"Registration and proof of insurance?"

"I'll need to get those out of the glove compartment."

"Fine."

Don't call it in, Jason thought numbly. He didn't want the guy to see the conviction, give him a field sobriety or whatever he had in mind. Waste his time when he needed to be traveling. He shouldn't have slept so frigging long.

For once the Fates were with him.

"All right," the trooper said, handing back the paperwork and driver's license. "Have a safe trip."

"Thank you," Jason mumbled. He waited for the trooper to pull back onto the road, then got out of the truck to take care of business. He washed up in the small stream, knowing his chances of getting into Jennings Inc. would be a whole lot better if he didn't look like a homeless man, which he was once again, thanks to Bryce. He got back into the truck and started to drive.

KIRA ARRIVED AT WORK at her usual time. There was no sign of Jason or his truck. His phone was still off, so she had no idea where he was, what he was doing. She just knew he wasn't at the office, and she hoped he didn't show up here. She didn't want the added distraction of a security alert while she did what she had to do.

She and Leila had talked long into the night, hatching their plan for a surprise attack—the only kind that was going to work. They couldn't give Bryce time to build a defense.

And so while Kira got ready for work, Leila had

called Suzanne for an impromptu breakfast. Kira hoped Bryce was aware that his wife was going out with Leila that morning, because it would give her an edge when she confronted him.

He would be meeting with their father one on one late that morning in the small conference room, where they had room to spread the plats while hammering out the details of the north Idaho deal. Kira was intending to take advantage of them being alone in that room. She just hoped her idea wouldn't backfire on her.

Or Leila.

She was doing her best to keep her sister out of the line of fire, and her sister was doing her best to throw herself into the middle of the fracas.

"*I'm* turning on the cameras tomorrow," Leila had insisted the night before.

"Don't," Kira said. "All it'll do is get you in trouble." If she was successful. Big "if." Make that huge "if."

"I have as much right to be outraged and get in trouble as you do. And so does Grandpa. This is our *family.* It affects every one of us." Kira had to agree that her sister had a point. "Besides, I don't want Tom to get into trouble. I'll…have to distract him." Leila laughed. "Who would have thought he and I would solve our problem by *me* getting fired?"

"You're not getting fired," Kira muttered. But she, on the other hand…she was quite possibly about to write finis to her career with Jennings Inc. She didn't see any way around it.

She just didn't know what she was going to do about the family. Go looking for a new one of those? She'd always have a sister, but what about everyone else? Would she still be a niece, daughter, grandchild?

But even if she never saw Jason again she couldn't let Bryce get away with this. If he wasn't guilty of the trailer fire, he was at the very least guilty of vehicular homicide while under the influence. And if she couldn't get justice, at least she'd have the satisfaction of showing him that she knew the truth. That Grandpa knew the truth.

LEILA POKED HER HEAD through Kira's door. "They're in the conference room and the camera's running. Grandpa's on the phone with someone, but I promise I'll get him down there at the right time."

Kira's heart had been beating fast all morning, but now it shifted into double time. "Thanks." She got up from her desk, nervously smoothing the skirt of her suit. She'd worn navy blue and twisted her hair up into a knot, which was already giving her trouble, since her stick-straight hair resented restraint. But she wanted to appear professional. Reliable. Believable.

There was no telling what the repercussions of the next few minutes would be. She still didn't know if her grandfather was in on things, in which case her goose was cooked, or if he would even do what Leila was asking of him this morning if he wasn't.

Kira walked to the double doors of the conference room, took a breath and pushed them open.

Both men looked up with matching frowns, not used to being interrupted when they'd asked to be left alone.

"Oh, Kira, I'm glad you're here," her father said. His face relaxed and the frown disappeared, making Kira's gut twist with apprehension and guilt for what she was about to do. "I wanted to talk to you this afternoon about Neary."

She nodded. "I'm here on another matter right now. It's important." She stepped inside and pulled the door shut behind her. "It's a question for Bryce, actually."

Her brother smiled tolerantly. "What is it?"

"Who was driving the night of the accident?"

Bryce didn't blink. He'd obviously expected something along these lines. "You know who was driving."

"Yes, I believe I do. What I want to know is how you manipulated Jason into doing the time."

Her father's face turned to stone, and Kira forced herself to stand up straighter, give no sign that she'd asked a bone-jarring question.

"Kira, Kira, Kira." Bryce shook his head. "I can't believe you've actually fallen for this guy's line of rubbish." He confidently glanced over at their father for backup, but Matthew's expression was unreadable. He remained silent as Bryce turned back to Kira, appearing completely unconcerned. "Why would Jason Ross have pleaded no contest if he wasn't culpable?"

"Because he was afraid he'd lose in front of a jury and have to pay restitution?" Kira said.

"There is absolutely no evidence he wasn't driving," her father interjected, and Kira's heart sank. No doubt whose side he was on.

"There's no evidence he was," she replied.

"It was his truck," Bryce argued. "He never let anyone drive his truck."

"Unless he was too out of it to stop them?"

"Kira." Their father stood, gripped the back of the chair with both hands. "Nothing positive will come of this. Nothing. Jason did his time."

"I can't believe it," Kira said, rolling her eyes up toward the carved ceiling tiles.

"Believe what?" Bryce asked. "There's nothing to believe other than the truth."

"Funny how the truth varies person to person," she retorted.

"What did Ross tell you?" her father asked.

"About the deal you made with him."

"There was no deal," Bryce stated adamantly.

"Suzanne says there was."

The color seemed to drain from Bryce's face. "She never said that."

Kira simply raised her eyebrows and held up Leila's miniature tape recorder. "She and Leila had breakfast, remember? You should be careful not to treat your wife so poorly. Especially when she has secrets."

CHAPTER FOURTEEN

JASON HAD LUCKED OUT. He remembered how to get to Jennings Inc. despite the huge changes Boise had gone through since his college days.

The offices were in the same building as they'd been ten years ago when he'd visited the place, only now, according to the sign, Jennings Inc. had all three floors to itself. Buying and selling land, owning a farm implements dealership and have a fertilizing sideline must be lucrative.

So lucrative there was a reception desk just inside manned by a guy in a security guard uniform.

"Name?" the big man said pleasantly.

Jason's name was probably on some list that would get him instantly ejected. He launched into his best bet to get into the building. "I'm here to see Kira Jennings. Is she available?" *Oh, that didn't sound psycho at all.* "We've been discussing a land deal."

Mr. Security did not appear to be impressed.

"Name?"

Jason glanced around, hoping that by some miracle Kira would stroll through. She didn't. He looked back at the security guy. "Jason," he said quietly.

The guy's eyes lit with recognition and Jason believed he would be on his way out the door in about a nanosecond.

"Ross?"

Jason nodded grimly. "It's important that I see her."

"Just a sec." He swung around in his chair and picked up the phone. After a few clipped sentences, he said, "Mr. David Jennings will be out in a moment."

Mr. *David* Jennings?

Jason's heart rate bumped up. Why would David Jennings meet him? Maybe to watch the security guy toss him out on his ear? Or wanted to tell him something about Kira?

Jennings appeared from around the wall at the corner of the security desk, accompanied by a young dark-haired woman who Jason recognized as Bryce's other sister.

"Leila," she said, extending her hand. "It's been a while."

"Yes." From her expression, he knew something was definitely up. "Is Kira here?"

"In a meeting," David told him. His face was pale, his expression pinched as though he was in pain.

"Is she all right?"

He nodded. "We were going to join the meeting. Would you mind waiting here with Tom?"

"I think he should come with us, Grandpa."

The old man looked at his granddaughter, startled. "Leila, we don't know…"

Leila gave Jason a candid once-over. "Would you do Bryce bodily harm?"

"Probably."

"Then we'll have Tom come to restrain you. Tom?" She gestured and he came out from around the desk.

David's eyes met Jason's. "If you come along, you have to keep your mouth shut and your hands to yourself."

The old man started down the hall, Leila beside him. Jason hesitated, then followed, muscular Tom by his side.

"Mr. Jennings is dealing with some deep shit and you're involved," Tom murmured out the side of his mouth. "So do him a favor and do as he asked." The *or else I'll have to hurt you* went unsaid, but Jason understood.

They continued down a carpeted hall with art in small alcoves, and Jason realized he was on an entirely different planet than his own. And he was also going to come face-to-face with the men who'd sent him to prison.

This had happened many times in his fantasies, and after some deceptively civilized chitchat, Jason had always beaten the crap out of Bryce. He glanced over at Tom, eyeing the security man's eighteen-inch biceps.

So much for fantasies.

For now, anyway.

"I DON'T BELIEVE YOU," Bryce repeated, nodding at the tape recorder. "Suzanne wouldn't say anything so blatantly untrue."

"Want me to play it?" Kira asked, her stomach twisting as she waited for him to call her bluff. Where were Leila and her grandfather? "Oh, and just so you know, the cameras are running. I thought Grandpa should be aware of what's going on—whether you deny it or not."

"Kira!" Her father had obviously had enough, but whatever he'd been about to say was cut short. The doors behind Kira opened and David and Leila walked in.

Bryce's demeanor cracked slightly at the sight of his grandfather, but then he managed a dismissive smile. "Grandpa, this is all crazy." His arrogant expression faltered again when he saw that his grandfather's hard gaze was trained on Matthew, not him. Then David stepped aside to let Tom enter, and Kira's heart all but stopped when Jason followed, looking exhausted and grim. Well, now she knew where he was.

"What the hell—?" Matthew began, half rising from his seat when he saw Jason, but his father raised a hand and he slowly sat back down.

"I got a phone call from the Nevada authorities, Matthew, just before Jason arrived. Bryce apparently hired a man to commit arson." David glanced at his grandson, who'd gone white. "They've arrested the arsonist—one of our contract employees from Water-Pro. He implicated Bryce."

Jason was obviously as surprised as Kira was, but it was her father's reaction that caught Kira's attention. First his eyes had widened at the mention of the arsonist, and then he'd closed them briefly, pressing his lips together. He hadn't known about the fire. That was something.

"Grandpa," Bryce said, doing his best to retain his wronged facade, "you don't understand. I'm being framed here. I never hired an arsonist. Don't you see what's happening? Kira's been sleeping with this guy. They planned all this to get me out of the picture."

David's expression remained icy.

"No!" Bryce continued. "This is crazy. You can't believe this guy! All he wants is revenge and you're falling for it!"

Bryce stood up so fast, he sent his chair skidding backward. He started around the table.

"Bryce!" Kira grabbed at him, but he shoved her sideways, knocking her off her feet.

Jason lunged, getting in one hell of a punch before Tom, moving with surprising swiftness for a guy so large, jumped between the two of them, shoving Bryce up against the wall with one hand and knocking Jason backward with the other. "Cool it, Ross," he said. "I'll take care of this."

Reluctantly, Jason stepped back. Bryce's face was smashed up against the wall and Jason saw a satisfying smear of blood. He'd broken Bryce's nose.

"Kira, Leila, wait for me in my office. Mr. Ross? You, too." There was an edge of steel in David Jennings's voice.

Jason waited until Leila and Kira had walked past him into the hall before he followed. He caught a glimpse of Tom depositing Bryce in a chair before the door closed.

"Come on," Leila said to no one in particular. "I have the key to Grandpa's brandy case."

IT WAS ONLY AFTER they'd dealt with the police, which took hours, that Kira and Jason were finally alone in her office. He touched the door with one hand and it swung shut with an elegantly muffled click.

He looked out of place surrounded by the modern furnishings, standing next to the sleek Danish desk while wearing the clothes he'd probably slept in the night before. Kira didn't give a damn. She stared at him from across the few feet of tasteful Berber carpet that separated them, memorizing his face. And if she closed her eyes, she could remember the feel of his body.

She didn't want him to go, had no idea how she could make him stay. Then he opened his arms and she walked into his embrace, hugging him tightly. His jacket smelled faintly of sage and smoke. Kira squeezed her eyes shut. It was possible that wood smoke and sage would always be her favorite scents.

"I can't stay up here, Kira."

She lifted her head to look into his eyes, searching for some sign that everything might work out. Eventually. Somehow. It wasn't there.

"I need to go back home, where I belong."

She tried to imagine him living in Boise, but couldn't. Tried to imagine family functions, company picnics with him by her side. Couldn't picture it.

Jason's discomfort aside, Bryce was part of the family, and she'd known within an hour of the blowup that the aunts and many of her cousins firmly believed perfect Bryce couldn't have done what Kira said he'd done. Even the arsonist had to be lying.

According to them, poor Kira had been duped and it was all a setup by Jason to get revenge on Bryce.

"We could see still each other," she said tentatively. "On neutral territory?"

"Why?" he asked gently. "To come to the conclusion that our lifestyles don't mesh? That I'll never fit into your family? Too many hard feelings, Kira."

"I could quit."

"You can't quit a family."

She pressed her lips together, conceding his point. And then she rose up on her toes to kiss him, tasting him one last time.

Knowing when she did that it couldn't possibly be the last time. She had some things to figure out here.

"It'll get easier once you start the new job," he was saying. "You won't even remember the guy who tried to drive you into a fire."

"Fat chance, Jason." And damn it, she began to feel tears forming. She lifted her chin.

He touched her lips with a work-roughened finger.

"I need to go home, Kira."

CHAPTER FIFTEEN

JASON DISCOVERED THAT he was indeed as strong as the old stone foundation he was once again rebuilding.

If he hadn't been, he wouldn't have been able to walk away from Kira Jennings.

He knew through contact with David Jennings that the story almost had a happy ending. Kira got the promotion she deserved and Bryce was probably going to plead guilty to a lesser charge in a plea bargain, thanks to the lawyer Matthew had hired for him.

Things had ended fairly well, except for that part where Jason had torn a family apart.

At one point in his life, Jason had truly wanted retribution against the Jenningses, and he'd wanted to be vindicated for the crime he did not commit.

That wasn't going to happen. The old man had made it clear, speaking without actually saying anything that could come back to haunt him later, that Bryce would pay the price for hiring the arsonist, but as far as the other offense went, there wasn't much he could do. It was still Bryce's word against his, and Bryce wasn't backing down. Suzanne wasn't going to help, either, although it was clear from her hostility when she'd arrived at the office that she knew the truth.

Jason could live with having to wait ten more years to have his record expunged without Bryce admitting guilt. He could even live with his life being exactly the way it was now—lonely.

He could live with just about anything except for screwing up Kira's life. He could tell himself Bryce was a loose cannon, but he honestly believed that he, Jason, was the one person who could have sent the man over the edge, because of what he knew. And he had.

Now Kira had to deal with the aftermath in the family that meant so much to her.

He missed her.

They hadn't been together long enough to know if things would have worked between them, but he believed that when it's right, you know.

He'd known Libby would be his friend for life within days of their first meeting. He'd known the same about Menace. He'd had reservations about Bryce, but their fathers had once been friends…. And that was how he'd learned the important lesson: Ignore Instincts, Invite Trouble.

With Kira those instincts were mixed. He cared for her, knew they definitely had something between them. But then he'd think about her having to walk a line between him and her family, and he came to his senses.

The past four weeks had passed quickly in some senses, slowly in others. He had a new trailer, as did Menace's dad, thanks to David Jennings. It was the one charity he'd allowed himself to accept, waving off the offer of recompensing him for "other" damages. It still felt too much like being bought. His "new" used backhoe was due to be delivered any day, and he'd found a dump truck to lease for the time being. If he decided to buy, the lease would go to payments.

Yes, everything was falling into place. Still, he felt a strange emptiness as he sat in his chair every night. Watching the place. Alone.

He needed to get out more.

The wind picked up and he went to secure the tarp over the extra hay he'd just baled and stacked. Yet another thunderstorm was brewing, and Jason hoped that the guy who'd called about adopting a leppie foal would hurry and get here before the rain started. The man had actually sounded interested in Buck, which had surprised Jason, but apparently, the horse was to be a pet, not a riding animal. And little Buck was already a pet, bumming attention whenever Jason went out into the pasture to work, following him around like a dog, with Marlene the burro tagging along. The other burro, Ruben, watched from a distance, disgusted with the lot of them.

They were probably quite a spectacle, but there was no one around to see.

The storm blew through with no lightning and no rain, and still Jason waited for the potential adopter. When the vehicle finally came into view on his driveway, Jason was stunned to see that it was familiar.

Very familiar. As was the driver.

Jason's heart did an honest-to-goodness flip in his chest.

Kira parked her sister's Jeep Grand Cherokee beside his truck and walked over to where he was standing next to the corrals. She looked so good it made his throat tighten.

"You aren't the person who called."

She shook her hair back, smiled. "Tom called. He wants to adopt a horse. I told him about these little guys and he thought it was an excellent idea."

"Are you his agent?"

"I wanted an excuse to see you, so, yes, I'm his agent."

Okay. "They can't leave the state for a year."

Her eyebrows lifted. "I didn't know that."

"Sorry you wasted a trip."

Her chin tilted up sharply. "Oh, it's not wasted."

She took a step closer to the corral. Buck moved over to nuzzle her hand. "Do you think he remembers me?"

"How could he forget?" Kira smiled, letting Jason know that she'd received his double meaning, and he warned himself to be more careful. "How's your grandfather?"

"He's doing all right now. What happened was kind of a shock to him. Some of it was a big shock to Dad, too, but they're working things out. Revamping, so to speak. Grandpa and Dad are both staying in their former positions for a while." She glanced at him sideways. "They're thinking of hiring an outsider as GM and then Dad can move up to the top spot."

"I thought you were in that position," Jason said quietly.

She shook her head. "I'm still part of the family. But I'm not an employee."

"You quit."

"Soon. I've given notice. With Bryce in trouble, it's really shaken things up, so I offered to stay on for as long as they need me. But I made it clear I'm leaving."

"Why?"

"Because working there keeps me from pursuing some matters that are important to me," she said, reaching out to scratch jealous Marlene's long ears and fuzzy topknot. "And I realized that it was healthier for me to take a job where I wasn't so reliant on the family name. It was kind of heady in the beginning, going from being a nobody to a somebody, but…I want my own identity, not a corporate one."

"I think you always had your own identity."

"Maybe so, but I like being on my own."

"The condo, the Audi?"

"Keep the condo for now, lose the wheels."

"What will you do?"

"Leila and I are going into business."

"Espionage?"

Kira laughed, but she sounded nervous. He was feeling the same. Nervous. Edgy.

"We're going into real estate. Houses. Small farms." She smiled slightly. "No subdivisions, though. We have the expertise and we like working together. I think it'll be fun." She ran her hand along the top of the fence. "It solves more than one problem."

"Like what?"

"Like Leila is free to date Tom now, and he can continue running security for the company."

"Sounds like things are working out well," Jason said.

"Yes," Kira agreed, leaning on the sun-warmed rail and smiling at Jason in a way that suddenly made him think he was about to be eaten for dinner. And in spite of everything, he didn't believe he'd mind.

"Well," Kira said briskly, suddenly pushing herself off the fence, dusting her hands. "I should be going."

"Okay," he said slowly. Talk about misreading things. His gut felt as if it had just hit his boots.

Damned if he wasn't in love with this woman.

Apparently oblivious that she was stomping on his heart, Kira walked to the Jeep, opened the door, then paused to look at him over the top of it.

"If you see a glow on the horizon—" she pointed in the direction of her property "—it's just me roasting marshmallows. I brought an extinguisher, though, so you shouldn't be in any danger of range fires."

And then, with a Mona Lisa smile, Kira Jennings got into her vehicle, put it in gear and drove away.

IF HE DOESN'T SHOW UP...

Kira paced around the tent again, trying to burn off excess energy. She'd actually set up a pretty nice camp. It was level. She'd gotten the tent up, no sweat, just like she used to in the backyard in Ohio. Actually, it was the same tent.

But meeting with Jason, acting cool and casual, had been the hardest thing she'd done in a long while, and she'd been through hell these past few weeks. All she'd wanted to do was jump him, but that wouldn't solve anything. He was the one with justifiable reservations about her family. Her job. It had to be *his* choice to come to her.

She'd paved the way. There wasn't much else she could do.

Except accept reality.

So, if he didn't come—

Kira suddenly stopped pacing as headlights shone through the twilight on the county road below. She held her breath until they slowly turned up the dusty fence line road.

He'd come.

It was a step. If it went all right, then they'd take another. Go slow. See what happened. She had hopes for the relationship because she'd never felt this kind of connection to a man before.

And here was the man.

He parked the truck and took his time climbing through the fence before walking over to where she stood by the tent, her hands behind her back. He moved with loose-limbed, unconscious grace, her long, tall cowboy.

"I thought you said there'd be marshmallows."

She held up the bag. "I was beginning to think you didn't like marshmallows."

"I like marshmallows just fine," he said gruffly.

Their eyes met and less than a second later the marshmallow bag was on the ground, forgotten, and Kira was in Jason's arms, her face pressed into his neck.

She inhaled deeply, breathing in his scent. "I didn't think you would come."

"I drove to Boise to see you while everything I owned went up in flames. Why wouldn't I drive over the hill?"

"Because of all those things you said in Boise."

"I was being noble."

"And now?"

"Not feeling so noble." He leaned back so he could look down into her face. "I missed you."

"Enough to try to work through a few things?"

He touched his forehead to hers. "Enough to try to work through a lot of things. And damn, Kira, there will be a lot."

She linked her hands behind his neck and smiled softly. "I'm game."

EPILOGUE

LITTLE BUCK WORE A wreath of daisies around his neck. Leila had insisted, and since it was her wedding, in her backyard, no one, including Tom, said a word.

The kids loved him.

Matthew walked by after the ceremony, nodded civilly at Jason, who, for the sake of his wife and good family relations, nodded back. It wasn't always easy going to family functions, but since Bryce had taken a job on the other side of the country, after pleading guilty to a lesser charge, it was getting better. No one spoke of the past when the family got together, following the Jennings code of not discussing the unpleasant, and everyone focused on Leila and Tom, allowing Kira and Jason to fly under the radar, which they did quite happily.

The odd thing was that Kira seemed content with the way things were. She and Leila and her grandfather were close, and Matthew was making a real effort for her sake. He'd even talked to Jason about some of the things he and Jason's dad had done as boys. It had been a stilted conversation, but Jason had appreciated the effort. Especially in light of—

"I think I'm going to throw up," Kira suddenly said.

"I'll get you a Popsicle." Jason knew the routine. He started for the kitchen, but she grabbed his arm.

"No. I'm better. But maybe we can wait awhile before we drive home?"

"We can spend the night."

"You can stay with me," Matthew said gruffly from behind them.

"No, Dad, I don't—"

Jason gave her shoulder a light squeeze and Kira glanced up at him before turning back to her father and saying, "I am feeling kind of queasy. If you're sure Margo won't mind."

"Margo won't mind, and neither will I."

Jason had a sneaking suspicion Margo was behind the invitation. Margo was eager to be a grandmother and she wasn't going to let a family feud stand in her way.

"This should make for an interesting evening," Kira said as her father went to join his wife.

"Are you up to it?" Jason murmured in her ear.

She smiled. "If you're there, then yes, I'm totally up to it."

And somehow, when they were together, they seemed able to face anything.

"Count me in," Jason said, pressing a kiss to the top of her head.

* * * * *

EXPECTING ROYAL TWINS! by *Melissa McClone*

Mechanic Izzy was shocked when a tall handsome prince strode into her workshop and declared he was her husband! Now she's about to face an even bigger surprise...

TO DANCE WITH A PRINCE by *Cara Colter*

Royal playboy Kiernan's been nicknamed Prince Heartbreaker. Meredith knows, in her head, that he's the last man she needs, yet her heart thinks otherwise!

HONEYMOON WITH THE RANCHER by *Donna Alward*

After Tomas' fiancée's death, he sought peace on his Argentine ranch. Until socialite Sophia arrived for her honeymoon...*alone*. Can they heal each other's hearts?

NANNY NEXT DOOR by *Michelle Celmer*

Sydney's ex left her with nothing, but she needs to provide for her daughter. Sheriff Daniel's her new neighbour who could give Sydney the perfect opportunity.

A BRIDE FOR JERICHO BRAVO by *Christine Rimmer*

After being jilted by her long-time boyfriend, Marnie's given up on love. Until meeting sexy rebel Jericho has her believing in second chances...

Cherish

THE DOCTOR'S PREGNANT BRIDE?
by Susan Crosby

From the moment Ted asked Sara to be his date for a Valentine's Day dinner, the head-in-the-clouds scientist was hooked; even if she seemed to be hiding something.

BABY BY SURPRISE
by Karen Rose Smith

Francesca relied on no one but herself. Until an accident meant the mother-to-be was forced to turn to fiercely protective rancher Grady, her baby's secret father.

THE BABY SWAP MIRACLE
by Caroline Anderson

Sam only intended to help his brother fulfil his dream of having children, but now, through an IVF mix-up, enchanting stranger Emelia's pregnant with his child!

Her Not-So-Secret Diary
by Anne Oliver

Sophie's fantasies stayed secret—until her saucy dream was accidentally e-mailed to her sexy boss! But as their steamy nights reach boiling point, Sophie knows she's in a whole heap of trouble...

The Wedding Date
by Ally Blake

Under no circumstances should Hannah's gorgeous boss, Bradley, be considered her wedding date! Now, if only her disobedient legs would do the *sensible* thing and walk away...

Molly Cooper's Dream Date
by Barbara Hannay

House-swapping with London-based Patrick has given Molly the chance to find a perfect English gentleman! Yet she's increasingly curious about Patrick himself—is the Englishman she wants on the other side of the world?

If the Red Slipper Fits...
by Shirley Jump

It's not *unknown* for Caleb Lewis to find a sexy stiletto in his convertible, but Caleb usually has some recollection of how it got there! He's intrigued to meet the woman it belongs to...

On sale from 4th March 2011
Don't miss out!

Available at WHSmith, Tesco, ASDA, Eason and all good bookshops

www.millsandboon.co.uk

2 FREE BOOKS
AND A SURPRISE GIFT

We would like to take this opportunity to thank you for reading this Mills & Boon® book by offering you the chance to take TWO more specially selected books from the Cherish™ series absolutely FREE! We're also making this offer to introduce you to the benefits of the Mills & Boon® Book Club™—

- **FREE home delivery**
- **FREE gifts and competitions**
- **FREE monthly Newsletter**
- **Exclusive Mills & Boon Book Club offers**
- **Books available before they're in the shops**

Accepting these FREE books and gift places you under no obligation to buy, you may cancel at any time, even after receiving your free books. Simply complete your details below and return the entire page to the address below. You don't even need a stamp!

YES Please send me 2 free Cherish books and a surprise gift. I understand that unless you hear from me, I will receive 5 superb new stories every month, including two 2-in-1 books priced at £5.30 each, and a single book priced at £3.30, postage and packing free. I am under no obligation to purchase any books and may cancel my subscription at any time. The free books and gift will be mine to keep in any case.

Ms/Mrs/Miss/Mr _____ Initials _____

Surname _____

Address _____

_____

_____ Postcode _____

E-mail _____

Send this whole page to: Mills & Boon Book Club, Free Book Offer, FREEPOST NAT 10298, Richmond, TW9 1BR